WHISKEY ROSE

BOOK 1

Jocelynne Jones

© Jocelynne Jones
2016

2nd Edition
ISBN 978-0-473-35041-3 (paperback)
ISBN 978-0-473-35042-0 (kindle)

Published by Little Red Hen Community Press,
Tauranga, New Zealand.
Printing: Createspace.com
Retail: Amazon.com
Cover picture: Public domain

ABOUT THE AUTHOR

Jocelynne Jones is the pen-name of a writer living in New Zealand. Retired, with two grownup offspring and a granddaughter, she is a quiet-living family person whose writing has, up until the age of eBooks, been little more than a hobby. With the establishment of 'indie publishers' Jocelynne has found an outlet for a passion that was hitherto stifled by previous publishing systems.

Other titles by the same author are:

'*Whiskey Rose: Book 2*' – The second part of this story about an average family faced with the constraints of caring for their elderly relative.
'*Lucifer's Story*' – a fantasy tale of good-over-evil, which envisions the end of evil forever. It is set in a parallel universe called Eternity. Presented in two volumes.
'*Freedom: Ours for the* asking' – A work of non-fiction under the genre of 'mind, body, spirit,' which explains how people have become separated from their intrinsic identity, and what to do about it.
'*Guarding My Angel*' – A drama based on the author's autobiography.

To Jenny.

With grateful thanks, as always!

WHISKEY ROSE

BOOK 1

PART ONE

CHAPTER ONE

The funeral was almost at an end. While Father Patrick blessed the people assembled at the graveside, Emily Thompson relaxed. It had been quite an ordeal for her, burying her beloved husband Arthur.

Kristine slipped her arm through her grandmother's.

"I thought Grandpa looked at peace, after all those awful weeks in pain," she said thoughtfully. "It's such a shame he couldn't see in the new millennium, though. I know he was looking forward to it."

Emily squeezed the teenager's arm affectionately. How astute of Kristine to be aware of little things like that; unlike her mother. Emily's twin daughters demonstrated concern in quite a different way.

Nevertheless, Emily could not fault how both Fiona and Ruth had looked after her these last few days.

They had certainly done all the right things when Arthur died, to the point of suffocating her; as though they were afraid to leave her on her own. Didn't they want her to grieve for him?

...Or was it because they couldn't cope with her grief as well as their own?

As if reading her thoughts Fiona, the twin who was Kristine's mother, slipped through the mingling group to talk to Emily.

"Mother, I think you had better stay with us tonight. You should not be by yourself just yet. Kristine can collect an overnight bag from your house later on."

1

Emily scowled. Interfering busybody, she wanted to say to her daughter. Why doesn't she allow me to make my own decisions? I'm not senile! The last place I want to be, Fiona, is in your noisy household.

Then she added privately: present company excepted of course, and squeezed Kristine's arm again.

The gravel crunched beneath their feet as the family group in silence trudged back to the waiting cars. It was a large cemetery; the biggest in the city.

At Fiona's instigation the twins had reserved a plot for their dear father in the centre, on a raised site overlooking the suburb where he had lived and worked all his life. Fiona's logic had suggested that it would be good for the family image. He had been well known in that part of the city. The sisters both wanted him to be remembered.

Yet Emily thought only of the long trek to visit him each day. Far better it would have been to lay him to rest in a secluded area around the perimeter of the cemetery, where she could visit with him quietly and in private. She did not want to feel that the whole city, past inhabitants as well as present, was witnessing what, to Emily, would be a very intimate moment. However, the deed had been done. There was nothing she could do about it now.

"I suppose I should be grateful for their generosity," she had reluctantly conceded.

At last the solemn group reached the road. It had started to rain – only lightly, though; not yet enough to send them scurrying to the waiting cars. Just sufficient to dampen Emily's spirits still further. Oh well, she thought, at least it didn't rain while we were at the graveside. So many times she had seen films on television where the mourners were gathered around the grave in pouring rain; their big black

2

umbrellas bumping against each other, vying for positions where their owners could see what was going on, and dwarfing the spiritual significance to the proceedings. For Arthur's funeral she had wanted the sun to shine. He deserved it. After a life of service to the community – even if it was not appreciated by some people – and after the cruel and undignified end that lung cancer brought, she had at least wanted the sun to shine for him on the day of his final departure.

Be thankful for small mercies, she chided herself as she waited to get into the car.

Fiona, Kristine and Emily climbed into their limousine.

While Emily and Kristine slid along the wide back seat, Fiona and her husband Royston sat in the front.

It was a rental car; Royston's momentary pride and joy: big and black and shiny. He pulled away from the kerb, the powerful Daimler engine purring quietly.

Fiona had insisted on a big car, so much more fitting for the solemn occasion than her own humble Toyota. Ruth, less pretentious than her twin sibling, declined the offer of riding with the others in favour of her own vehicle. She and Wilbur followed along behind.

Wilbur was Ruth's husband. Tall, graceful Ruth could dwarf diminutive Wilbur at times, especially if she ventured into high heels or when he slouched. In height she was no taller than him – exactly the same, in fact – but her posture was such that she carried her head high upon her neck; not out of aloofness but with a natural love of life.

Ruth met everything square on; calmly and precisely. Fiona, on the other hand, though fractionally smaller than her twin, exhibited an air of superiority over her which, when Ruth found herself in Fiona's presence, affected her sensitivity and left her feeling drained. Consequently, the two sisters, conveniently living the greatest distance apart while still within the city limits, rarely communicated and lived their separate lives in very different ways. Their husbands preferred to stay in the background; the twins being the decision-makers: Fiona, brashly and without thought for others; Ruth, quietly but with a confident authority which could not be contradicted, as though the decisions she made came from a higher source and should not be questioned; the only exception to this being Fiona, who contradicted just about everything Ruth said.

Throughout their lives an intense rivalry had developed between the twins. Fate in its wisdom had chosen not to bless Ruth and Wilbur with offspring. Despite years of hoping, the pair finally gave up on ever having a child of their own, and yet chose not to adopt; or rather Ruth chose not to adopt. Without family ties, she insisted, they were free to travel and pursue their respective careers; which they did wholeheartedly. But Fiona could not wait for the status of motherhood, and in the fullness of time delivered a beautiful healthy girl, now fourteen years old; a triumph which she regularly flaunted in her sister's face. And although the reason for the marriage had more to do with an unplanned pregnancy than romantic inclinations, Fiona revelled in the fact that she had one over Ruth which could not be equalled.

Whilst Ruth would never admit to it, the real reason she decided not to adopt was because Fiona would interpret it as admitting defeat, and she refused to give her that kind of satisfaction; it would hurt too much. To justify her decision was more dignified if less truthful.

In order to compensate for being denied motherhood, Ruth concentrated her energies into her position of school secretary at the local primary school where Wilbur was headmaster. At least, she conceded, she enjoyed regular contact with children, even if they were not her own.

...And naturally, she relished the company of her niece Kristine when she managed to steal her away from her domineering mother.

Kristine witnessed the rivalry between her mother and her aunt distantly, not allowing it to unduly affect her. She loved her Mum and Dad, but she cared for her aunt and uncle as well. They were a different type from her parents, and provided welcome relief whenever the situation at home became a little tense.

Kristine also loved her Nana – the tiny tower of strength who had guided her throughout her childhood; who now sat beside her in the limousine a shadow of her old self.

In her grief Emily, a proud, prematurely white-haired seventy-year-old, had become suddenly frail; the spark now gone from her life. Kristine worried about her. How would she cope, now that Grandpa had gone? He and Nana had been the perfect married couple; two people acting as one, as though each was an extension of the other. Never a quarrel had passed between them – that Kristine knew of, anyway; never a cross word to either of their feuding twins, but just a quiet contemplation of the world around them and the instinct to do the right thing.

Perhaps, Kristine once reflected, that was why Grandpa got into trouble with the local council in the way that he did; because he witnessed the corruption within a system that had been established and maintained by a group of men too long in their official positions, and whose ideas had become stale. His letters to the council and to the local paper; his involvement in community work, had all demonstrated to Kristine just how concerned he had been

5

for the state of affairs in his part of the city, and how sincere had been his motives in attempting to make a few changes to their civic laws.

Yet Grandpa had always been a man alone; a sole voice crying out into the commercial wilderness.

Despite many private confessions by equally concerned citizens that they were in agreement with him; despite well-wishers who would shake his hand and commend him on his courage to speak out, not one person ever openly stood by him in support – except for Nana.

Kristine slipped a hand through her Nana's arm again.

Emily liked that. It said more to her than the superficial words of comfort Fiona was showering on her. Kristine, she maintained, possessed more sincerity in her little finger than Fiona had in her whole being, and right now she appreciated the girl's company and closeness.

Suddenly Kristine had an idea.

"Nana," she whispered, scarcely audible above the purr of the car's engine. "Instead of your staying here with us, how would you like it if I were to stay with you for a while? It's still the school holidays. We're not due back there until next week."

In spite of her years, Emily's hearing was excellent. She caught enough of her granddaughter's hushed tones to get the gist of what she was asking.

Encouraged by what she heard, she whispered back, "I would like that very much."

Emily smiled into the youthful brown eyes of the girl beside her. What love and worldly concern she saw there. Kristine deserved the best in life. Emily hoped that she would receive it.

Kristine leant forward to speak to her mother in the front seat. Both Fiona and Royston had sat in silence, concentrating on manoeuvring the expensive car through lunchtime city traffic. A bump could prove costly.

"Mum, can I bunk down at Nana's house for a couple of days, instead of her coming to us?" Kristine asked. "She doesn't really want to stay here."

Emily stirred uneasily in her seat, suddenly wary of Fiona's reaction. She had not expected Kristine to speak quite so bluntly, even though there was indeed an element of truth in what she said.

Fiona strained round to look at her mother.

"Is that what you really want?" she asked curtly; then, without waiting for an answer she went on, "I presumed you would still prefer to have people around you for a while. You shouldn't be alone just yet – you might brood."

Emily looked from one to the other, feeling somehow excluded from her own fate.

"She wouldn't be alone, Mum," argued Kristine. "She will have me with her."

"I suppose so. But be sure you don't make a nuisance of yourself, Kristine," retorted Fiona; quickly adding, "...And give me a ring if you need help at all."

"I won't need your help! Nana is perfectly capable, and so am I, for that matter."

"I know. It's just that... I don't want you in a depressing atmosphere any more than can be helped. It's not good for you, what with school starting up again in a few days. Nana is likely to get upset occasionally, you know."

She stared at Kristine; trying to encourage the girl to read her thoughts.

Fiona's respect for her mother's abilities had dwindled in the face of encroaching old age. Now Arthur was no longer around, Emily would be alone; something she had not experienced before – not like this, anyway.

For sure, Emily had been by herself plenty of times: when Arthur went off on business trips in his younger days, and more latterly, on fishing trips. But never had she known the sense of isolation that accompanies living by yourself; of knowing that no matter how many visitors you have, sooner or later you will always be left to spend the nights alone. This was Fiona's concern. What would go through the old lady's head? Would she brood, as already intimated to Kristine? Would she, heaven forbid, talk to her deceased husband as though he was still around? Or would the memory of the time they spent together be too painful to bear and compel her to shut him out of her heart altogether? This, if she were to live alone, the rest of the family would never know; for Emily, whose private thoughts had always remained private, would not divulge or let slip to her daughters just what was going through her mind; of that Fiona was certain.

The Daimler pulled up outside Fiona's home. Royston leapt out of the driver's seat and rushed round to the footpath to open Kristine's door. Chauffeur-style he held the door open while the two passengers got out.

"Mum, Royston will drive you back to your house after you've had some refreshments," said Fiona when she had also emerged.

The car door under Fiona's hand closed effortlessly with only a slight push, rather than the slam required shutting her own car doors. Bemused, Fiona opened and shut the door again. How marvellous it would be to own a car like this, she fantasized. Reluctantly she turned away, and took hold of her mother's elbow to escort her up to the house.

As they walked Fiona went on, "Come to think of it, Mum, you may have to stay here a bit longer than that, as Royston has to drive the limo back to town and pick up our car. And, of course, Kristine will need to pack an overnight bag. So you might as well make the most of the short time you will be spending with your family;" her last remark said with a hint of sarcasm.

Anxious to get home, Emily muttered under her breath, "We could always walk."

Emily was forever disturbed by the atmosphere in Fiona's pretentious household.

The negative air her pseudo-wealthy daughter carried around with her affected Emily as much as it did Ruth, and as often as not she would go home with a headache. Why Fiona had to make out to her family and acquaintances that she was well-off, Emily did not know. Anyone who cared was aware of their financial situation: quietly comfortable. So why the ostentatious show of wealth?

Slowly Fiona was undermining their financial stability with her needless excesses. It was about time Royston said something to her...

Inside the house, Emily gasped with the sudden onrush of stale air. Outside, the air was fresh and cool, but inside, with the windows perpetually closed for security reasons, the atmosphere became unbearable. The lingering smell of old cigarette smoke was usually present in Fiona's house, and for a moment Emily felt quite nauseous. She longed to get the next hour over with so that she could go home.

"I'll put the kettle on," she offered to take her mind off it, and moved in the direction of the kitchen.

"No, you sit down and rest. I'll make the tea."

Fiona motioned her towards the lounge. Emily was too tired to argue. Maybe she really was ready for a rest. For a while she would just let the world revolve around her. That way she wouldn't feel so claustrophobic in Fiona's house, and maybe the time would pass more quickly.

Even Ruth and Wilbur, when they turned up, paid little more than a courtesy visit, and Fiona, as pleased to have them leave as they were to go, waved them off at the door as though to confirm their departure.

Emily momentarily took advantage of Fiona's absence from the room. "Kristine, dear," she said secretively to her granddaughter. "You'll pack your bag quickly, won't you? I'd like to get out of here as soon as possible."

Kristine smiled. She understood Emily's reluctance to remain under their roof any longer than was necessary. Far from taking it personally, she was just as anxious as her grandmother to be away from the place for a few days. A spell with Nana – just the two of them – would make a welcome change.

Later on, Royston drove Emily and Kristine home.

After responding to his goodbye toot with a cheery wave, Emily stood outside her own front door; the key poised ready to enter the lock. But before doing so, she turned to Kristine waiting behind her and said anxiously, "Kristine, what do you think the future will hold for me, now that Grandpa has gone?"

"I don't know, Nana. But one thing's for sure. You won't be alone. I will always be here for you."

The next few days went by smoothly for Emily and her granddaughter.

The two shared an empathy that had somehow skipped a generation and bypassed Fiona altogether. Both knew and understood this; never trying to remedy the situation but merely enjoying and making the most of opportunities to develop their relationship. So that, at a mature fourteen years of age, Kristine was more like a close friend to Emily than a grandchild.

To pass the time the two lovingly sorted through all of Arthur's effects, parcelling up articles of clothing for the Salvation Army's opportunity shop in town, along with sundry items no longer of any use to Emily.

Yet some items she could not bear to part with: Arthur's pipe, so much a part of him throughout the years; his fishing rod, symbolic of the relaxed days of their retirement; and his wedding ring.

As she fingered the plain band of gold a lump formed in her throat, and she wept silently. Emily had not had time to grieve properly since Arthur died; her daughters had seen to that, never leaving her alone for a minute. Now, with the formalities of death over with, she was free to let her true feelings surface, which they did now: naturally and without restraint.

Kristine appeared at the bedroom door to find Emily bent over the bed in deep sorrow. She rushed up to her and took her in her arms.

"It's alright, Nana," she stammered, her own tears not far away. "Have a good cry. You don't need to be gallant anymore; not around me, anyway."

"What will I do without him?" sobbed Emily. "He was my whole life; the breath that I breathe. There's nothing left for me now."

Kristine looked around the big room with its enormous bed; then at Emily. The tiny form of her Nana seemed misplaced in its vastness, as though something of immense proportion was now missing – the love Emily and Arthur had shared together for so long.

Kristine felt for her.

For a moment it was not only Emily who had suffered the loss, but also Kristine. Her powers of perception were such that she found herself in the same position, knowing exactly how it felt to lose a loved-one.

11

She shuddered. Would Nana really have to experience the extreme loneliness she had so keenly sensed just now? Not if I can help it, she thought, and resolved on the spot to check in on her every day; to say hello on the phone, pick a bunch of roses for her table, run an errand... With Emily's home only a couple of minutes' deviation from her route to school, and with a reliable 10-speed bicycle to help make up the lost time, there was no reason why she couldn't call in regularly; without her mother knowing, if she could get away with it.

The next morning, Emily waved goodbye to Kristine, with great reluctance to see her go. But their break together was over, and school summoned the student who needed time to mentally prepare for her new term.

She sighed as she faced the empty house; alone now for the first time since Arthur died. Slowly she surveyed each room in turn.

On the mantelpiece in the lounge, propped up carefully against the chimney breast, was her wedding photograph: hers and Arthurs; taken so very long ago and yet still fresh in her memory.

"My, how fashions have changed through the years," she chuckled as she studied it closely. The lace-trimmed dress, the height of elegance in her time, looked drab in the old photo, but the memories that the sight of it revived were bright and alive.

The youthful Arthur at her side looked so different from the husband she had known in recent years. This young man had none of the wisdom and maturity of his older persona, but he sure had charm.

Oh, yes, she reflected, Arthur had plenty of charm. ...That was why she married him.

A tear slid down Emily's cheek.

"I must learn not to wallow," she told herself sternly, and brushed her face with the back of her hand.

To occupy her time she spent an hour or so cleaning the house. Strangely, there seemed so much more of it now. Maybe it was because she would have to do it all on her own...without Arthur to share the load.

"I'll be doing everything by myself, now," she realised.

With the vacuum cleaner put away, she went into the kitchen for a drink of water.

Standing before the window, she looked reflectively out over the rose bed in the back garden. Arthur's domain, which he had tended lovingly each week, would be like a jungle soon. Just now it was reasonably well manicured. Ruth and Wilbur had kept the gardening up to date while Arthur was ill, but she couldn't expect them to help out indefinitely. They had their own lives to lead, too. Perhaps the young lad up the road could help her out. She would ask him some time.

Later on, Emily saw the postman arrive.

He briefly stopped his bicycle to deposit something in the letterbox by the front gate.

Emily at once livened up, and hurried to retrieve the mail: three white envelopes, which she presumed were bereavement cards or messages.

Only one had an address on the back. It was from an old friend who had maintained regular contact over the years. Emily opened it up before re-entering the house.

A brief letter accompanied the card. It read, 'Dearest Emily. Peace at last. The ordeal is over for you both. Just remember, my friend that Arthur is never far away, and although you can't see him he will be with you for all eternity. Hold that thought in your heart, and you will never be lonely. God Bless. All my love, Ada Simcock.'

13

Emily read the letter through twice, her hand grasping the door handle for support. For some reason her knees felt weak. Was Arthur really close at hand?

Stepping through the doorway she looked about, as though gazing into the ethers for a sign that he might be present. But she saw and felt nothing. Around her was only emptiness...familiar emptiness.

If he was with her, surely she would know.

Her moment of contemplation over, Emily turned her attention to the unopened envelopes still in her hand.

The first was a polite printed card from the secretary of the local bowling club where she and Arthur had been members. At first it seemed rather impersonal, but then Emily remembered they sent messages of condolence for all bereavements in the club.

Even so, it was nice of them to think of her, and Emily was touched.

The last envelope she glanced at, turned it over ready to open the flap, and then took a second look at the name on the front. It was addressed to 'Mr A Thompson.'

They must have made a mistake, she thought, and left off the 's' of Mrs.

But there was no mistake. The envelope contained not a bereavement card, but a 'Get Well' greeting from a Jack somebody: a name she could not read. An almost illegible note was scribbled inside the card, but she managed to decipher, 'Heard through the grapevine you've been ill old man, but hope to see you up and about again soon.'

Suddenly Emily burst into tears.

"Arthur... Oh, Arthur, my darling. Why did you have to leave me? I am nothing without you."

The message in the card was like a heartless though unintentional joke, and it hurt Emily deeply. Instead of standing it up on the dresser along with all the other cards, she tore this one up into little pieces and threw them angrily into the kitchen waste-bin. A few fragments missed and fluttered onto the floor around the bin, but Emily did not even notice.

The mind of the normally fastidious lady was gripped by torment; unable to grasp that her beloved partner in life was no longer there.

Throughout the night, her first completely alone, Emily kept having some bizarre dreams. All the activities and emotions of the last few days blended together in a series of unreal images.

She awoke exhausted as the first grey light of day crept through the blinds; unable to remember anything of detail after her night's ordeal.

Yet, had she remembered; had her tormented mind extracted from its deeper recesses other impressions of her imagining, she would have recalled another dream: a brief flight of fancy; a respite to soothe her troubled heart, when Arthur, in spirit, sat at her bedside and spoke words of reassurance to her. Yet, nothing had broken through the barriers, and the dream slipped away; leaving the weary widow still grieving and alone.

On rising, Emily showered and dressed, ate a piece of toast for breakfast with coffee to wash it down, and mechanically set about the morning's chores. Nothing else came to mind to offer her encouragement and raise her flagging spirits. ...Not until Kristine arrived, that is.

The sight of the girl's curly chestnut hair and warm, smiling face as she dropped in on her way to school eased the burden for Emily. She threw her arms around Kristine and shed silent tears of relief that the night's isolation was broken, if only for a few minutes.

15

When school had finished for the day, Kristine arrived home to find Ruth sitting with her mother at the table.

"Hi Mum. Hello Auntie Ruth. ...This is a surprise," she remarked, for the twins rarely socialised.

"I was just on my way round to see Mum," said Ruth cheerily. "I rang her before I left the school and told her to expect me right away, so I'd better not dawdle. But I just wanted to go over something with your mother, Kristine."

The accounts, so it seemed, had arrived for the funeral expenses. Though outrageous after Fiona's extravagance in ordering the best of everything, Ruth had agreed to pay half the cost. She signed the cheque she was writing out, slipped her ballpoint pen into her shoulder bag, and stood up ready to leave.

"Oh, Auntie Ruth, please don't rush off. I've only just got home!"

Kristine put out her hand to stop her but Fiona, anxious to see the back of her unwelcome sister, insistently cut in with, "Your aunt has to leave now. Nana is expecting her, and we don't want to keep her waiting."

Ruth smiled to herself, catching Fiona's motive behind her comment. She, too, was glad to be leaving the house, although a few moments in the company of her niece would have been nice.

"I thought you were very rude to Auntie Ruth," Kristine told her mother when Ruth's car pulled away. "It was really quite obvious you were trying to get rid of her."

"Ruth and I have a quiet understanding," came Fiona's discerned response. "Don't worry, Kristine, your aunt will not have been offended by what I said."

In fact, Ruth gave the remark no further thought, for her attention had moved on to her mother. Emily had seemed distant when she phoned: a cause for concern to Ruth.

16

When she saw her, she immediately noticed the strain on her face.

"Oh, Mum," she said, hugging her warmly. "What am I going to do with you? You seem so unhappy..."

The sadness in Emily's eyes cut Ruth to the quick, and she wondered what was to be done to alleviate it. Perhaps it would help if she could get her to open up and talk about Arthur; release some of the emotion, which she felt sure lay just beneath the surface.

Receiving no response, she went on, "...You look weary, as well, Mum. Are you sleeping alright?"

"Not too bad," was the mechanical reply.

Emily had never been one to complain, and although still suffering from a disturbed night, she did not want to confess this to Ruth; for to be honest about her wellbeing would not have occurred to her. But Ruth instinctively sensed the falsity; she knew her mother only too well. And whereas Fiona would have taken the words of reassurance at face value, Ruth knew better. Deeper probing would be necessary if Emily was ever to divulge how she really felt.

"Mum, you don't need to be brave for my benefit," she said gently. "I know you're tired and hurting still. I can see it in your eyes."

Emily sighed; too weary to resist Ruth's probing. "As a matter of fact, I didn't have a very good night's sleep. I had some strange dreams. They upset me quite a lot."

"Were they about Dad?"

"I don't know. They were all jumbled."

Emily distractedly walked through to the kitchen, saying on the way, "Come and have a cup of tea. I was just going to put the kettle on."

"I won't have a drink just now," Ruth replied, following her. "I've not long had one, but I'll sit and talk while you have yours."

17

Emily busied herself at the sink bench. She filled the kettle, and fetched out cups and saucers, the sugar bowl and a milk jug. Without realising what she was doing she laid out two sets of cups and saucers, forgetting already what Ruth had just told her.

For the moment this went unnoticed by Ruth, who was reporting on some of the kind remarks about Arthur made by members of the school board. It was not until Emily inadvertently poured milk into the sugar bowl as though into a third cup that Ruth's attention was arrested.

"Mum, what are you doing?" she cried; causing Emily to jump and spill milk on the bench.

All at once Emily, too, realised the mistake. She raised her hands to her face in dismay.

"Oh dear," she said apologetically. "Whatever has come over me? I'm such a scatterbrain."

"Never mind, it's not a big issue; however, you haven't done anything like that before...have you, Mum?"

"No... No, of course not!"

Ruth got up from the kitchen table and walked over to where Emily was now leaning against the bench, a dazed expression on her face.

"You sit down, Mum; I'll make your tea," she said with compassion, and pulled out a chair for her.

Confused by what she had done, Emily automatically complied with Ruth's request.

How could she have been so bumble headed as to pour milk into a sugar bowl? she reflected. This was most unlike her. Normally she was in full control of her faculties...

While Ruth made tea for them both she told herself sternly, "Pull yourself together, Emily!"

The hot drink soothed Emily, the slight sweetness of half a teaspoon of sugar supplying much needed energy. Soon she felt like her old self once more.

18

"Mum, would you like me to stay here tonight?" asked Ruth. "I can if you want me to. I have to admit, I'm not very happy about leaving you on your own."

Emily looked at her oddly; unsure about the implication in Ruth's suggestion. It sounded as though her favourite twin didn't trust her any more.

"I'm quite capable of looking after myself, thank you Ruth; I'm not senile yet," Emily replied; more tersely than intended. "You don't need to go to that much trouble."

Ruth was taken aback. "If I sounded bossy I'm sorry. I didn't mean it that way. I'm concerned, that's all. You've already missed one decent night's sleep by the sound of it. Another could make you unwell. I'd just like to be on hand in case you need me."

Emily softened her stance. "No; really," she said. "I'll be alright. You get on home. Wilbur will be wondering where you've got to. Ring me in the morning if you want to check up on me."

Yet Ruth felt uneasy as she left to go home, and for two good reasons:

Emily still wasn't quite herself, but also because she was beginning to suspect a seed of resentment may have developed in her mother's heart. If she wasn't careful in the future, her concern for Emily might be interpreted as interference; something to be avoided if the harmonious relationship they had always enjoyed was to survive.

The following day, instead of phoning Emily directly, Ruth contacted Kristine. To her relief, the girl was able to report that Emily seemed a lot brighter.

In fact, Emily had enjoyed a much better sleep; for her dreams, less disturbing than during the previous night, had remained in her memory until well into the morning.

In one dream Emily, Ruth and Fiona were standing over Arthur's hospital bed; Fiona urging him to get up and mow the lawns. In another, Emily was trying to catch a giant fly for him to take fishing, using an enormous fly swat which could have been a tennis racquet.

And then, in the corner of her mind came the memory of a reverie, which seemed more realistic than dreamlike, where she and Arthur were strolling in their rose garden, deep in conversation.

If only she could remember what he said...

That evening, Emily's thoughts strayed back to the card from Ada, and she reached up to the mantelpiece for it.

'Arthur is never far away,' she read again. 'Although you can't see him he will be with you for all eternity.'

Emily smiled to herself, a glow of unexpected pleasure swelling her heart.

Maybe he really had come to her. The bonds of love nurtured throughout their wonderful years together could not be severed by death alone.

Arthur, she was sure, would make every effort to cross the barrier and make contact with her. She could imagine him sitting on the other side of consciousness waiting for her to relax; then occasionally, when the time was right, reaching across to touch her and make her fully aware of his presence – as he appeared to do last night.

"Dear Arthur," she whispered into the void. "I love you so much."

And then she shed a tear.

CHAPTER TWO

The weeks passed quickly. For Emily, life now took on new meaning. The emptiness of Arthur's passing was replaced by the joy of expectation; a satisfying knowledge of what she knew to be taking place:

Arthur had not abandoned her.

Yet the family were worried. Mother, as all had noticed, was behaving quite oddly for one supposed to be grieving.

Fiona called in one day with an armful of flowers: the prize dahlias Royston had saved for her before taking his choice blooms to the horticultural show. The front door was open when Fiona arrived, and she walked straight in; calling as she entered. Receiving no response she went into the kitchen. Through an open window she saw Emily sitting on a bench seat near the rose garden, apparently talking to someone, but nobody was there; not that Fiona could see.

She called out cheerily to her mother, who looked up at the house in alarm.

Emily shouted back, "Oh, it's you. I'll be right up."

"No; stay there!" Fiona insisted. "I'm coming down."

Fiona was driven by curiosity to see who Emily was talking to. Maybe her neighbour was just over the fence; or perhaps one of Emily's friends stood in a place not visible from the kitchen; though once outside it became obvious that nobody was around. "Who were you chatting to just now?" she asked when she stepped out into a garden empty but for her mother's solitary form.

21

"I was just talking to Ar…um…to myself."

Embarrassed, Emily pulled herself up with a jolt. She was back in this world now, the world of reality, the world of Fiona; a world which, to Emily, was fast becoming one of appearance only. Her true reality, the one with Arthur as a focal point, was too precious to share, especially with her overbearing offspring.

To validate her actions she must demean herself.

"I was speaking my thoughts out loud…"

"…You mean, you were away with the fairies! Just be careful, Mother, or people will think you are becoming senile. We don't want any of that in the family, do we? …By the way," Fiona added quickly, thrusting the flowers towards her. "Royston pulled these out for you. They're the best of the bunch. …Well, actually they're his second best. The best have gone to the show."

Emily took them while uttering heartfelt thanks for his generosity. She cradled the firm, colourful blooms in her arms, savouring an imaginary perfume.

"That husband of yours certainly has green fingers. He can grow anything. …Unlike me. I don't seem to be having any luck at all. Arthur is… er, was….the gardener, not me."

Emily looked around her.

The lawns had been cut; Royston still came in every other weekend to do them. But her vegetable patch, flower borders and circular rose bed at the centre of the lawn were now crying out for attention.

A thick growth of weeds covered the soil, surrounding the now overgrown plants. Arthur's favourite 'whiskey' rose bush in the middle of the patch had long-since gone over and needed pruning.

It was a task too great for an elderly lady.

Fiona realised it at once.

"I can see you're going to need help with your garden, Mother," she said. "There's far too much for an old lady like you to tackle all by yourself. Why don't I put an ad in the paper for somebody to come in part time?"

"Perhaps you're right," Emily conceded, surveying the unkempt grounds. "The garden does appear to be running away from me."

Emily pulled herself awkwardly to her feet; her back stiff from sitting for a long time.

She slowly walked up to the rose bed. A picture came into her mind of the plot as it was beforehand. She could see Arthur bent lovingly over the whiskey rose, secateurs in hand, pruning away the old stalks to promote vibrant new growth. She remembered how, as if responding to his gentle touch, the rich yellow roses always bloomed afresh, charged with her husband's vital energies.

At least, that was how Emily liked to think of it, such was the esteem in which she held her husband and his gardening skills

But now the life seemed to have gone out of the plants. The whiskey rose bore only one pale flower, and its scruffy foliage reached upwards without purpose, revealing only sharp thorns and disease ravaged leaves. Arthur's pride and joy, as with the rest of the garden, was overrun with weeds. She needed help with the garden, of that there was no doubt, but the thought of some stranger replacing him was unthinkable. Perhaps that young man up the road might like to earn a little extra cash...

"I don't really want a total stranger coming in here," she decided privately.

She turned back to Fiona who was jotting her idea down in a notebook she kept in her bag, as though the notion of placing an advertisement had already been agreed upon.

23

"Don't bother with that," Emily said, pointing at the jotter. "I'll find someone myself."

But the garden, once out of sight, also slipped out of Emily's mind. It was another week and abundant growth in the weeds, before the subject of its maintenance was once more brought to her attention; this time by Wilbur when he came to do the mowing.

"...Oh, that's right," she reminded herself. "I was going to speak to someone about it."

...And this time she did. Three doors up the road lived Michael, a student at the local university. His mother had once remarked to Emily that Michael was constantly short of money – and how expensive he was becoming now that he was growing up.

Once Wilbur had left the house, Emily looked up their number on her phone pad and rang Michael. He was out, she was told, but after Emily explained the problem, his mother assured her that he was bound to be interested in earning some extra cash at the weekends, and that he'd come round to see her the minute he returned home.

Emily felt self-conscious when the tall, good-looking youth came to the door. Michael dwarfed her, standing in the narrow hallway; but once they had moved out into the garden she felt more at ease.

The young man swore under his breath when he saw her overgrown wilderness.

Emily, though failing to hear his exact words, caught the tenor of his comment and said, "Oh dear, will it be too much for you? I could pay you extra until it's tidy again; then perhaps a basic rate of pay. What do you say?"

Michael grunted, dubious about the enormity of the task. ...But, he reminded himself, he did need the money, and it wouldn't take long to get the garden shipshape

24

again. Yes, he told Emily, he would like to take the job. ...And he would start the following Saturday, if that was alright with her.

That night Emily shed a tear, yet not out of sorrow but from relief that the responsibility for the garden was at last off her shoulders. And glad, too, that Arthur's domain would once more be a source of pride.

In her dreams, Arthur voiced approval of the selection of Michael to look after it. But he also chastised her. Unknown to Emily, he had been trying to plant the idea in her head ever since Fiona suggested placing an ad in the local paper.

"I practically wore myself out trying to get through to you," he told her one night not long afterwards, and insisted she adopt a more listening ear in the future. "I won't only be talking to you in your dreams, you know, so just watch out for me. ...And by the way, Emily," he added as an afterthought. "You would love it up here. There seems to be an ever-present scent of roses."

Emily settled down contentedly after that. The pressure was off her now, and she could cope. No longer alone, no longer with the worry of maintaining a property hanging over her, she began to enjoy her life again – for the first time since Arthur's passing. And that was how she now regarded his death. Her husband had not died as such; he had merely crossed into another realm. The knowledge of it gave her great comfort.

Even some of her family noticed the difference in her state of mind:

She was more like her old self again – the mother and grandmother who, as Arthur's wife, had a zest for life. But rather than considering the real reason for her happiness, they attributed it to better sleep and the relinquished burden of looking after the garden.

Fiona and her family, living much closer to Emily than Ruth, felt a greater obligation towards her than did Ruth and Wilbur. Ruth went out to work, Fiona did not; thus Ruth considered her mother only when time permitted.

On the other hand Fiona, with plenty of spare time and only a few regular commitments during the week, could not relieve her mind of concerns where Emily's unusual mental condition was concerned.

"Is mother really going senile?" she often wondered; the eccentric behaviour still a mystery.

The episode in the garden where Emily was talking to herself made her realise she should pay more attention to a widowed mother who now lived alone.

To Fiona, Emily was little more than that: a widow who should be cosseted and supervised, lest the senility she feared and had already witnessed should go unchecked, and even set in prematurely.

Fiona knew nothing of the companionship her father posthumously brought to her mother, and neither would she. Emily kept it to herself; sacred and secluded from outside comprehension. ...Especially from her daughters; for they would never understand, but rather consider her to be unbalanced.

Over the ensuing weeks Fiona took Emily out shopping, to the garden centre and on a tour of the art gallery. She chauffeured her to see friends who could not be easily reached by bus, and to doctor's appointments.

After a while Emily, not needing to be mollycoddled in such a fashion, became wary of the motives behind her daughter's kindness.

"I don't want you to be on your own too much; you know that," Fiona answered when Emily questioned her about it. "Solitude is not good for you. I've already caught you talking to yourself once. Lots of old ladies go to pot when they're left to cope after the husband dies, and I don't want it happening to you."

"You've no need to worry on my account. I quite enjoy my own company – and I'm not really alone; I have…"

Emily stopped abruptly, remembering the necessity to keep Arthur's presence a secret.

"You have what, Mother?"

"I… I was going to say…I have you twins for company, and of course, there's Kristine. So I'm never alone enough to become lonely."

Emily squirmed inwardly, hoping Fiona saw nothing suspicious in her obvious hedging.

Fiona remained unconvinced about her mother's self-sufficient declarations; or, for that matter, her sanity. But she said nothing, her opinion on the subject unchanged. However, the next time she phoned to take Emily out she was much surprised to hear Emily state, "I won't go out with you today, love. Our feverish activity is becoming too much for me…besides, I'm having company this morning."

"Oh, and who might that be?"

"A couple of members from Arthur's bowling club are coming for morning tea."

So Fiona, though taken aback, had little choice but to accept her mother's polite refusal.

The couple of bowling club members materialised as four: three ladies and a gentleman; all dressed to the nines in their white bowling outfits in readiness for a special club luncheon and tournament that afternoon. The three ladies Emily knew of old. She and Arthur had once been regular members of their bowling club, and in their heyday the

27

ladies, two of whom were also now widowed, had once been part of a regular playing team in the company of their enthusiastic spouses.

Emily greeted and embraced each of them in turn; then asked after the third lady's husband: an old and close friend of Arthur's.

After making her reply the lady said, "We thought it best to allow you some time to yourself before descending on you. A rush of visitors at a time like this can be so upsetting. Bert sends his love and condolences, and so do all the other members. A special mention was made at our last meeting of you and Arthur. I believe the club secretary has sent you a bereavement card."

Emily nodded as she recalled the condolences card. She voiced her appreciation of the kind gesture.

"By the way," the same lady went on, turning to the fourth member of the visiting group. "I almost forgot my manners. This is James Forsythe, a widower who recently joined the bowling club. I believe he was an acquaintance of Arthur's, too."

At the mention of Arthur's name again, Emily looked with interest at the man who had apparently once known her husband. She saw before her an immaculately dressed gent standing apart from the ladies. He was a well-built man of average height, with a mass of white hair brushed severely back, and a serious expression on his face. At first his demeanour, though neat and tidy, seemed unnatural to Emily when she stepped forward to shake his hand.

But as the static first impression altered slightly on introduction, she witnessed a transformation in him as though ice was melting, and he beamed towards her a warm smile through laughing grey eyes.

James Forsythe, it appeared, had charm: a charisma such as Emily had only ever known in one other man:

Arthur. As their hands touched she felt a tingle of exhilaration shoot through her which thrilled and then shocked her, and she withdrew her hand more abruptly than seemed polite; at the same time lowering her eyes to escape his captivating glance, and causing her to withdraw from him.

What would Arthur think of me? she wailed inwardly.

Surprised by her reaction on meeting James Forsythe, Emily sought refuge in order to regain her composure, and retreated to the kitchen to make the tea. As she lifted the kettle to fill it she discovered that her hands were shaking. Meeting this man had for some reason unnerved her. It was with real difficulty that Emily readied the tray to take in to her guests.

Yet, once back in the lounge her composure returned, covering all trace of anxiety, and nobody present in the room would have guessed that Emily was anything other than completely at ease.

All throughout the get-together James Forsythe fidgeted awkwardly.

Encouraged to meet Emily by ladies of the bowling club who missed no opportunity to introduce members to one another, he had agreed to the visit more to silence them than out of a desire to meet somebody new; especially not a recently widowed woman. Yet, much to his surprise, he appreciated what he saw in Emily: a gentle, vivaciousness lacking in most of the other female members of the bowling club, many of whom were too brash and officious for his liking. However, Emily's embarrassed and hasty withdrawal from their introduction had left him feeling uncomfortable, and he waited edgily for the morning tea to be over.

Emily joined in mechanically with the conversations of her lady guests, which consisted mostly of gossip about people in the bowling club, about her dear Arthur and, 'Did she know about Mrs Smith's mastectomy'; adding still more to James Forsythe's embarrassment at being there.

Their hostess heard little of their chatter. Instead, she was constantly aware of her quiet male guest; watching out of the corner of her eye for every move he made: every twitch, every change of expression; unwittingly checking to see whether or not he was looking at her; half hoping he was, half hoping he would make his apologies and go away. She felt secure with only the affections of her phantom husband to contend with. This flesh-and-blood male was stirring up her emotions in a way she resented, and just at the moment she did not want to even think about another friendship; especially with an unknown man.

Just before noon, James Forsythe could stand the tension no longer. He rose to his feet, bowed army style to Emily and the ladies, at the same time thanking them for the delightful morning and for the opportunity to meet Emily.

Insisting: "Please don't get up," when Emily began to do so, he retired hurriedly into the sunshine.

Through the window Emily watched him go up the path to the gate. The expression on his face as he turned to shut it revealed the strain he had really been under.

She felt deeply sorry for him. Even though it was the presence of the other ladies that had been the cause of his disquiet rather than Emily, just then she was unaware of it. At that moment she, too, was self-conscious about the awkward meeting, and held herself wholly responsible for James Forsythe's discomfiture.

The rest of the day went badly for Emily. The aftermath of their morning tea remained with her long into the evening. She could not get James and the troubled look on his face out of her mind.

That night she slept fitfully and did not even try to bring Arthur into her consciousness. She felt sure he somehow was aware of their unfortunate meeting and assumed his disapproval; a disapproval which in fact did not exist.

For Arthur, who had indeed witnessed the morning's trials, was pleased his wife recognised in James the same qualities she once saw in him, and was flattered. So, too, did he realise that the annoyance in his former friend's features was not brought about by Emily herself, and he wanted to tell her so...

...But that night, Emily was not listening. She felt too ashamed to confront him.

The following evening, Ruth called in to see her carrying a box of expensive liqueur chocolates. These she presented to a startled Emily who, though grateful, was curious as to the reason for the extravagant gift, and said so.

Apologetically Ruth replied, "Well, actually, they were given to me at the school for some work I did for one of the teachers. But Wilbur and I don't eat chocolates, so I thought I'd bring them over to you. And..." she added, head bowed sheepishly, "...they are by way of an apology for not being in touch recently."

Emily thanked her. "You've no need to worry that you're neglecting me," she insisted. "I know how busy you are, and that you're thinking about me. I've got plenty to keep me occupied, what with Fiona's outings and Kristine's visits." She decided not to tell Ruth about James.

"To be honest, Mum, I'm finding full-time work too much these days. I don't seem to have the stamina I had

31

when I was younger...I guess it must be the change of life. How working mothers manage, I don't know. I really take my hat off to them."

Ruth slumped into a chair in the lounge without waiting to be invited; an action completely out of character for the usually restrained twin. Normally she was meticulous about the way she conducted herself.

Suddenly Emily felt concern for her younger daughter. Her own problems now seemed unimportant next to the difficulties Ruth was apparently experiencing, and Emily suspected there was more to her visit than had so far been revealed in conversation.

It looked like the box of chocolates was a cover for something else.

"Ruth, is anything amiss?" Emily asked cautiously. Arthur had complained of reduced stamina before it came to light that he had cancer...and now one of his daughters was complaining of the same thing. "It's so unlike you to be under the weather," she went on. "You're not sickening for something, are you?"

"No, I don't think so. ...I mean; I'm not ill or anything. But I am definitely under the weather.

"Why, dear...what's the matter?"

Ruth paused, as though reluctant to divulge something confidential.

Then she said almost secretively, "Actually...I'm worried more about Wilbur."

"Oh! Is Wilbur unwell?"

"He's been off-colour for a few weeks now, complaining of breathlessness. I almost have to nurse him when we get home from school. Before now he always pottered quietly in the garden as a means of unwinding, but just lately he's been going straight to bed and sleeps until his tea is ready; hardly mustering up enough energy to eat it at times."

"No wonder you're worried; and no wonder you look as peaky as you do."

Emily squatted on a footstool next to Ruth's chair. She patted her hand affectionately.

"Is there anything I can do?" she asked. "...Shopping, housework or anything like that. I'm always available."

"No, I don't think so Mum, but thanks all the same."

Suddenly Ruth sat up; jolted out of her musings.

"Heavens above!" she exclaimed. "I can't expect you to come over to the other side of town to housemaid for me! You've got enough on your plate without worrying about us as well!"

She sprang to her feet, shaking off the seeds of self-pity that had threatened to take root.

"Don't take any notice of me," she said. "I was just tired and feeling sorry for myself. I don't know what came over me. I apologise."

And Ruth, it seemed, was once more in control.

Emily struggled up off the footstool and gave her a hug.

"I'm not so busy that I can't give some time to my own daughter," she said.

"...But it should be the other way round! I should be giving help and attention to you, at your age and stage of life. You've done your bit for your girls. Now it's your turn to be waited on and be set free from family woes. I had no right to burden you with my worries." And then, as if to return everything into its proper perspective, she quickly added, "What I came to tell you was that I've decided to reduce my workdays at school to three so I can catch up on everything at home that I've been neglecting. It also means I've got more time to spend with you, and I wondered if you would like to do that on a regular basis; say, once a fortnight for lunch in town. What do you say, Mum? Is that a good idea?"

"It's a lovely thought, and I appreciate your offer…but we'll just play it by ear, shall we?"

Emily was touched by Ruth's invitation, but her concern for her daughter's situation had been aroused, making her unwilling to commit to anything that might impose on her. What's more, the thought of a pre-arranged catch-up did not really appeal.

Emily always liked the family to drop in unannounced. The surprise of seeing them unexpectedly was refreshing, and infinitely more pleasing to her than the regimented outings Fiona liked to arrange.

However, after Ruth left, Emily became remorseful that she may have seemed a bit off-hand in her reaction to the suggestion, and determined to make amends. If Ruth felt a need to give her mother time on a regular basis – out of love, out of duty, whatever her reason – then she should accommodate her.

The younger woman obviously needed peace of mind just at the moment, and if accepting Ruth's proposition helped to achieve it for her, then it would be Emily's pleasure as the mother she still was, despite the maturity of her daughters, to do what she could to help. A mother, she declared, does not cease to be a mother just because her children have grown up and flown the coop!

So it was with surprise and a degree of relief that Ruth later accepted Emily's change of heart. A day was set aside for the following week.

"…And I would like to come over to your house instead of meeting up in town," Emily insisted. "It will be more of a day out for me."

As it turned out, a visit to Ruth on every other Thursday suited Emily down to the ground, for as yet she had no commitments of her own; her day to day activities running along no ordered lines. Even so, Emily had always been a creature of routine. Visiting Ruth once a fortnight meant shifting her Thursday chores to another day; a move she envisaged should cause very few problems.

In order for Emily to reach her daughter's home on the far side of town necessitated a double bus ride: the first into the central terminus and another out to the suburb where Ruth lived. As luck would have it, both Emily's and Ruth's homes each lay within easy walking distance of a bus stop, and although the trip took Emily over an hour to complete, there was actually very little walking involved. ...And, Ruth had insisted, she only needed to take the bus one way. Her return journey would be made by car.

So Emily started visiting her younger twin on a regular basis; the arrangement working well for both women.

Ruth was happier now, because she did not have to carry the burden of Wilbur's infirmity alone and saw enough of Emily to alleviate her guilt for not keeping in touch with her.

Emily, for her part, enjoyed taking an active role in the day-to-day life of a daughter to whom she had previously been something of an outsider.

Furthermore, Emily discovered, it gave her an outing she could regularly look forward to. ...So much so, that as a result of the stimulation her visits to Ruth provided, she decided to again take up her old pastime of bowling.

Emily had to admit, though, that there was an ulterior motive behind her decision to re-join the bowling club:

The thought of James Forsythe had begun to infiltrate her emotions. She felt herself drawn to the man she briefly met all those weeks ago. ..And although she did not fully understand why, it was the possibility of seeing him again that prompted her to arrange to call in at the bowling club one day when a match was in progress; not with the intention of playing, as she explained to the club secretary, but merely to get the feel of the place again.

She found sitting in the clubroom with the other ladies a very pleasant experience. Some of them were strangers now, having joined during Emily's long absence. But many of her old or familiar friends were still there, and they welcomed her warmly.

Yet, no men were present in the club that day. Emily had happened along on Ladies' Day. She had been away from the bowling club scene for so long that she had forgotten about the two days in every month allocated to ladies only.

Oh, how easily one forgets! she declared afterwards.

Emily felt a twinge of disappointment that she did not see James that day.

Still a little ashamed of her attraction to him the day they met, she had not mentioned the encounter to Arthur during their nightly encounters.

But Emily had no need to tell Arthur, for he already knew of her infatuation, and was quietly bemused.

As her soul-mate, he recognised her need for the kind of companionship James Forsythe could bring in order to live a fulfilling life again.

So it was by no coincidence, the following Thursday, that Emily came across him again while making her regular bus journey into town.

When she saw James sitting halfway down the aisle, Emily felt her knees turn to jelly. Her heart pounded so violently she was sure her face must be scarlet from its increased blood flow – and this so embarrassingly obvious that she felt every occupant of the bus must surely have noticed it;

yet nobody did. As always, each passenger was intent on their own business: gazing out of the window, reading the daily newspaper or chatting with the person sitting closest to them.

Even James did not see her at first. He was on the way into town for an appointment with his solicitor who had reminded him that, since the loss of his wife, he should alter his Will. Having no family except for a son on the other side of the world, deciding on his beneficiaries was becoming a matter of some urgency.

"You're not getting any younger, and you never know when the Lord will take you," he had unwaveringly stated.

James thought about it again as he struggled to make his difficult decision.

It was this problem that held his attention when Emily staggered down the aisle of the lurching bus as it slowly pulled away from the kerb.

Emily thankfully sat down in the first available space, which happened to be opposite the seat on which James Forsythe sat; his head leaning against the window.

Yet, still he did not see her.

At some point during the journey James ceased his train of thought, stretched his stiffening neck, and for the first time since taking his seat focused his attention within the confines of the bus. As he strained his head sideways he caught sight of a familiar figure.

The dainty lady, whose face was partly obscured by the man sitting next to him, looked very familiar to James. But the morning tea at Emily's house some weeks previously was now almost a distant memory; and he couldn't quite place her.

When, two stops later, the passenger next to him stood up to get off the bus, James left his seat and, much to Emily's surprise, slipped into the one directly opposite her.

He apologised profusely for taking her by surprise and invading her privacy. "...But," he insisted, "I just had to find out who you are. You see, I know I've met you before, only I can't quite remember where..."

Her heart thumping, and not wanting to appear forward, Emily responded with, "You're James Forsythe, aren't you?"

"...Yes, I am," he replied without hesitation. "Then I am right. We have met somewhere before."

"...At my house," Emily put in; still holding back. "It was a few weeks ago. You came round with some ladies from the bowling club for morning tea."

"...Yes...of course! How could I possibly have forgotten? I do apologise!"

He slapped his hand on his forehead in a recriminating gesture, and then laughed.

"The old memory's not quite what it used to be!"

Emily enjoyed the warmth in his tone of voice.

She found, as their conversation progressed, that the nervousness she experienced, both at the time of their initial meeting and just now when she got on the bus, slowly abated and was gradually replaced by a sense of ease; almost one of contentment, to be sitting beside him and talking to him.

When eventually the bus reached the city terminus, the two of them, having exchanged basic information about one another other, parted company. ...But not before James insisted he be allowed to see her again; to which Emily happily agreed. Thus, they arranged to have lunch the following Monday at tearooms in their local shopping mall, and Emily continued on her journey to Ruth's; eagerly looking forward to it.

Such was Emily's frame of mind when she arrived at her daughter's home. The second leg of the bus journey had passed quickly, with Emily blissfully lost in thought.

Ruth noticed the faraway look in her eyes, and laughed.

"Mother, you're not quite with us, are you?" she said in appreciation of Emily's mood. "What have you been up to this morning?"

Emily attempted to hang her coat on the hook behind the kitchen door, but without looking at what she was doing allowed it to fall to the floor instead.

"I'm sorry dear," chuckled Emily, while Ruth picked up the coat. "I met a friend on the bus into town and we had a lovely, stimulating conversation. I'm afraid I still have my mind on that."

"She must have had something very interesting to tell you, that you should be affected this way!"

Ruth laughed as she hung the coat up properly.

"Not she...he," said Emily, correcting her.

"Oh! ...I see!"

Ruth was suddenly taken aback. She could not imagine her mother choosing to have a light-hearted conversation with any member of the opposite sex just yet; it seemed disloyal to the memory of her father's name.

"Have you known this man long?" she asked.

"No not really. He was introduced to me shortly after Dad passed away, by some ladies from our bowling club. He's a widower. ...And very charming," Emily added coyly.

Ruth noticed the bashful look on Emily's face, and felt distinctly uneasy. She had a slight but niggling suspicion about this new acquaintance of her mother's.

Just then her train of thought was interrupted by the sound of her telephone ringing.

She hurried to answer it before the call clicked over to the answer phone.

It was the school where both she and Wilbur worked. An anxious voice – that of the school nurse – hurriedly told her, "I'm sorry Ruth, but your husband has collapsed...just a few minutes ago... It looks like a heart attack... An ambulance is on its way... You'd better come quickly!"

"Ruth dear, what's the matter? You've gone as white as a sheet."

Without a word to her mother, Ruth gathered up her bag and three-quarter coat, and locked the back door. Then, handing Emily her own coat, briefly explained the need of their hasty exit.

All thoughts of James Forsythe suddenly dissipated as Emily followed her out of the kitchen with the belongings she had only moments before set down.

"I knew something was brewing," was all Ruth said on the way to the school; just a short distance away.

Normally both she and Wilbur walked, but now urgency dictated speed, and Ruth's little car arrived at the main gate just seconds after the ambulance, its siren wailing, sped up the driveway to the administration block.

Ruth was shocked when she saw her husband. The effect of the attack had distorted his fine features, and he looked strange; alien even. ...Nothing like the man she knew and loved. However, not being the type to give in to emotion, she calmly answered all the paramedic's questions while Wilbur was prepared for the ambulance.

Moments later she spoke to Emily.

"Mum, will you travel in the ambulance with Wilbur?" she asked. "I need to bring the car or we'll have nothing to get us back home."

"Yes, of course," came the immediate reply, with not an ounce of uncertainty affecting Emily's strong response.

Yet Emily was actually beginning to feel the effects of the urgent situation. The shock and unexpectedness had rocked her stamina, and she suddenly felt weary.

Nevertheless, out of necessity her feelings had to be put to one side in the face of a need for self-control.

So, with little hesitation she carefully climbed into the ambulance behind a stretcher bearing the cosseted form of her son-in-law.

A ride in a speeding ambulance to a child would be an exciting experience, but to an apprehensive old lady who was starting to feel some of the symptoms of shock, it was an unnerving ordeal.

Even though the journey was soon over, Emily arrived at the hospital feeling flustered, but still revealing little of her distress; for had she given in to the feelings, far from being of help to her family, she would have become an additional burden to them; something, in Emily's opinion, to be avoided at all costs.

She stepped down again and waited to one side of the ambulance, leaning against the barrier of the Accident and Emergency entrance for support, while the paramedics deftly whisked Wilbur into the hospital.

At this time, Ruth was nowhere to be seen. Emily had watched the car following along behind the ambulance as they journeyed to the hospital, but now there was no sign of either her or the car.

She guessed Ruth was trying to find a parking space in the hospital's vast car park, and sighed that she should be plagued by this perennial problem even in an emergency.

Her quandary then was: should she follow the orderlies wheeling Wilbur quickly down the corridor, or just stay put and wait for Ruth to turn up. She decided to compromise, and caught the arm of the ambulance driver as he was about to leave.

"Excuse me," she said with a sense of urgency. "Could you please tell me where they are taking my son-in-law: the man you brought in just now?"

"Probably up to Ward Sixteen on the third floor. That's where the cardiac arrests usually go. Use the elevator."

He pointed to a pair of shiny steel doors on the far side of the foyer and, politely touching his hat to excuse himself, rushed on.

"Ward Sixteen...third floor." Emily repeated the words to imprint them in her mind before the state of shock caused her to forget them.

Then she settled herself onto a seat by the reception desk to wait for Ruth.

The panic of the last half hour was subsiding now. Looking at her outstretched hand, Emily realised the trembling was not so pronounced. She was, thankfully, recovering from shock and could therefore be of assistance to Ruth.

It seemed like an eternity before Ruth finally appeared in the doorway, yet it was just a few minutes.

During that time she took in the unfamiliar scene that confronted her.

The only experience she'd had of hospitals recently was from the daytime soap operas on television.

Yet, the hustle and bustle of this real life hospital was coldly and clinically efficient; where nobody has the time to stop and chat as they do on the soaps.

Emily was briefly reflecting on this comparison, when Ruth walked in.

Straightaway she hurried over.

"Sorry, Mum," she said breathlessly. "It took me ages to find a park. Someone blocked me just as I spotted a place close by, and I lost it to someone else. I finished up parked

42

on a grass verge down the road. No doubt I'll get a ticket for it, but just at the moment I don't care."

Though visibly annoyed, the unflappable Ruth quickly seized control of their situation again.

Looking around she calmly asked, "Did you happen to notice where they took Wilbur?"

"Ward Sixteen, third floor," echoed Emily as she stood up to join Ruth. "...And we take the lift over there," she added, pointing to it.

Some time had passed before a doctor approached them in the third floor waiting room with welcome news of Wilbur's condition.

After a cup of coffee each and several old magazines mindlessly thumbed through, the women were becoming impatient for some information, and leapt to their feet when he came in.

They were told he had suffered a severe heart attack, but that his condition had stabilised and he was now resting comfortably.

In a twin-bedded room, divided only by a draw-round curtain, Ruth was allowed to see her husband; briefly so as not to wake him from his much needed rest.

Close to his bed, an electrocardiogram machine beeped rhythmically, and the oxygen cylinder providing him with life-giving air breathed it out in silence.

Suddenly the reality of the situation sunk in.

At the sight of Wilbur lying alone and helpless in the uncomfortable hospital bed, Ruth showed her first signs of weariness and emotion.

As she turned to leave the room again, Emily noticed tears glistening in her lower eyelashes and she slipped her arm around her concerned daughter's waist for support and comfort.

"Come on, love," she said. "There's nothing we can do here for the moment. Let's go and have a bite to eat. I saw a sign in the foyer for a cafeteria. We both need something to keep up our strength. We can come back later."

When, later on, they did go back, they discovered there had been no change in Wilbur's condition.

In fact, the nurse told them, there was unlikely to be any real change in his condition overnight, and they might as well go home rather than wait there endlessly.

Reluctantly, Ruth agreed it was pointless staying on; so with assurance from the nurse that she would be notified immediately of any change, she gathered up Emily and left the hospital.

No ticket adorned the windscreen when the tired women at last walked back to the car.

Ruth breathed a sigh of relief. To be booked for illegal parking would have been the last straw on such a trying day as this.

On the way home, they debated a plan of action with regard to visiting the hospital. Naturally, Ruth realised, she would have to give up work completely for an indefinite period. Wilbur's stay in hospital may not be lengthy, but he would need to recuperate at home for a sizeable interval before there could be any suggestion of picking up where he left off at the school.

"Please let me know how I can be of help," Emily said when Ruth dropped her off at home.

"I will. Thanks, Mum," replied Ruth. "...And I'll let you know when I hear from the hospital."

Inside the house, a strange silence enveloped Emily with the door closed.

Compared to the harsh echo in the hospital corridors or the noisy engine of Ruth's little car, the sudden quietness gripped her like a vice, and she opened the door again to let in comforting outside sound. Silence as well as solitude she could do without at present.

Emily desperately needed to do some reflecting; though not the contemplative thought of meditation, but rather the abstract wandering of a mind too long held in abeyance by the needs of others.

Over a cup of tea, Emily took stock of the day's events. She realised, looking around her, that when she left home that morning she had no idea of what lay in store. The meeting with James Forsythe had come as a complete surprise, and now the incident with Wilbur...

Whatever, she wondered, was going to happen next?

Later, after a meal she did not really feel like eating, Emily telephoned Fiona.

She suspected Ruth would not think to ring her twin. There had never been sufficient interest in each other's affairs to prompt Ruth to notify her of Wilbur's misfortune.

Emily was aware of this as she waited patiently for her call to be answered.

It was Kristine who picked up the phone.

"Hello, Nana," she said cheerfully. "It's so nice to hear your voice – we haven't seen you for ages! You weren't in when I called on the way home the other day."

Curious, Emily cast her mind back.

Now that Kristine's daily visits were less frequent, she had stopped making a point of being home during the afternoon.

Yet, she had not been out lately; except for her visit to the bowling club.

Perhaps Kristine had called in then...

"Sorry love, I didn't realise you were going to pop in. By the way, is your Mum home? I have something important to tell her."

Fiona received the news about Wilbur dispassionately; unaffected by her sister's troubles. She was interested to the point that Wilbur's rushed admission to hospital was something out of the ordinary, but indifferent beyond that. As far as Fiona was concerned, her sister had no children to think about, so as the change in circumstances would only cause a ripple in Ruth's life; there was no need for her to get involved.

Besides, Fiona thought to justify her disinterest; Mum seems to be helping out. So with a clear conscience and a courteous enquiry as to Emily's own health, Fiona bade her a snippy goodbye.

Emily sighed as she hung up the phone.

Fiona was so self-centred...and so very different from her sister, Ruth.

Why did her twins turn out to be complete opposites in personality: Ruth, gracious and caring; Fiona, cold and flamboyant?

Admittedly, Fiona had been there for her after Arthur's death – Emily was only too aware of Fiona's self-righteous sense of responsibility. In that respect her generosity could not be faulted. But it was performed by way of duty, not out of concern; which, to Emily, somewhat negated all the good contained within the act.

Now Ruth, on the other hand, was equally generous, but generous in spirit – out of love; never from a sense of obligation. The invitation to spend Thursdays with her had been issued with a genuine desire to see more of her mother, not to perform a duty as with Fiona. For that, Emily was grateful.

Even Kristine, though Fiona's daughter, was more like her aunt in temperament.

Emily's thoughts monopolised her mind as she quietly went about the chores that her extra time away from home had brought into neglect.

The emotional pressures of the day were beginning to build up, and occasionally she needed to stop what she was doing to take a deep breath.

Emily had never been very good at coping with her own emotional problems.

Throughout her life, Emily had experienced very little of an adverse nature, with few happenings to cause her much grief or suffering.

Arthur's disappearance on a fishing trip when the girls were still infants, frightened her and shook her badly; but he had returned none the worse for wear. The death of her mother also rocked her emotionally. To lose her when Emily was still a teenager had devastated the girl, and she took a long time to recover. But in retrospect little else had torn her apart.

...Except for Arthur's passing.

Now, that was something completely different.

Arthur had been a part of her; an integral, vital part of her whole being. When he died, in many respects Emily died too. Only through his returning in spirit did she once more find the strength and vitality to live a normal life.

However, this business with Wilbur for some reason was sapping that strength. Had Arthur been there in the flesh he would have comforted her and lent her his stout shoulder. She would not have carried this burden alone. In a way, she felt quite abandoned...

Suddenly Emily broke out of her reverie.

Of course!

The reason she felt alone just now was evident. Arthur had not abandoned her; she had shut him out.

Ever since the meeting with James she had excluded Arthur from her thoughts.

Whether this was out of guilt or the fact that she now had another interest, she did not know. But of one thing she was certain: Arthur's presence had been missing from her life over the past few weeks.

The realisation was startling.

"I must make amends immediately," she announced when the last of the washing had been folded and put away. "No matter what he might say about my friendship with another man, I have got to bring Arthur back into my life!"

CHAPTER THREE

That night, Emily went to bed early. Usually she would play the evening's television programmes through till after the late news; that way, by waking later in the morning, the day would not seem so long. But this night she was in bed by nine. The warm bath she took before retiring had been soothing after the rigours of her long day, and Emily soon fell asleep.

The dream, when it came, almost woke her up with its suddenness; for Emily had slipped into a flight of fancy that was far too vivid to merely be a dream.

Arthur appeared as he had in the past at the side of her bed. On seeing him Emily sat bolt upright, and was amazed to notice that her body still lay peacefully in its sleeping position on the bed.

While Emily adjusted to the phenomenon, Arthur gently took her by the hand. Then the two ethereal forms glided effortlessly through to the lounge.

...Yet, its appearance was not the same as in the waking experience.

Emily gazed at all her familiar, but somehow unfamiliar surroundings. The lounge suite was in its usual place; the television also: still in the far corner. The ornamental light fitting looked the same. And yet something about the room was strangely different.

There seemed to be a glow to each object; an aura, such as the light from a prism. Iridescence enveloped each piece of furniture, causing individual features to become crisp and clear; and Emily's perception of what lay in front of her took on a new dimension.

She turned to look at Arthur. He was dressed in his favourite sports jacket and trousers, but their colours, too, were sharper and brighter than she remembered of them; and they, also, were enveloped by the same ethereal glow. His face, while expressive beyond anything she had seen in him before, was at the same time somehow otherworldly; though not frighteningly so. Nothing about Arthur could frighten her. It was just that this new appearance of both Arthur and the room was so strange it momentarily took her by surprise.

As their eyes met, the light of recognition between them lit up each face, casting radiance about both Emily and Arthur.

All the fears and doubts Emily had harboured dissolved away, and without a sound passing between them, she sensed in an instant that there was nothing to worry about; that Arthur bore her no resentment for her recent conduct, and that Wilbur and Ruth would be alright.

Arthur took both of her hands in his. He looked deeply into her eyes, a gaze that penetrated her soul; for as spirit there was nothing to inhibit total communion.

"Emily... My dear Emily..."

Arthur's voice came over distorted from his treasured physical voice, but nevertheless Emily thrilled once more to hear it. Her eyes shone as she returned his gaze.

"I'm here, Arthur," she responded, also in a strangely distorted voice.

"Why have you shut me out?" he asked. "Have I done something that offends you – or perhaps frightened you in any way?"

"Arthur my love; you could never offend or frighten me. Rather, I may have offended you. I was ashamed to face you over something I have done. But now I realise I was foolish to shut you out."

"Was it because of this man who has become attracted to you?"

Emily's eyes widened. She looked at him; startled.

"How did you know?"

"As spirit I don't need to receive an invitation to witness what transpires in the physical realm; only to enter your consciousness. I saw the introduction between the two of you, and sensed both of your reactions when you first met. I went with you to our bowling club, and shared your disappointment that he was not there at the time. And then, earlier today I prompted you to catch a particular bus because I knew he would also be catching it. Emily, I want you to be happy. I know that what you see in James you once saw in me, and I'm flattered to think this drew you to him. If you wish to continue seeing him you may do so with my blessing. For you to lead a fulfilling life is important to me. All who reside in the presence of the Infinite care greatly for those still on the earth. As for me, I am content to wait. I know that one-day you and I will be together again. In the meantime, be happy my love."

Emily felt tears well up in her eyes; so overcome was she by Arthur's tenderness and compassion. But when she lifted her hand to brush them away she found her cheeks to be perfectly dry.

No moisture was present; for only in her emotions had she wept with tears.

As Emily and Arthur embraced, it seemed as though for a moment their phantom bodies united and became one.

"If this is what it's like to be dead, then I can't wait," said Emily contentedly.

But then she abruptly pulled back from him, a look of concern now stemming the glow of happiness.

51

"Arthur," she said, "I am being so selfish. How could I have forgotten?"

"...About Wilbur?"

"Yes...Ruth and Wilbur."

Once again Emily was startled by Arthur's insight.

"You've no need to worry. The heart attack was merely a warning. He'll recover quickly. If he heeds the advice of the doctors he will continue to lead a full life. But Wilbur is headstrong and will need plenty of encouragement to slow down. He must be made to understand that his recovery was a gift, not a God-given right, and he must not abuse it. Just now he needs to rest and recuperate. Not until he is strong enough will he be allowed to resume his work. You and Ruth must persuade him over this."

Emily sighed as one relieved of worry. "Thank you for your reassurance. It's of great comfort to me, as I'm sure it will be to Ruth and Wilbur."

"...One more thing," Arthur continued. "You must not make mention of our conversation to Ruth. She would not understand. Neither must you quote anything I have said. Only through love and service to her can you convey my message. She will grasp the meaning inwardly, and it will register with her far more deeply than if you spoke the words to her. And now I must go and you must return to your physical rest. It will soon be daylight, and time for you to wake up."

Emily glanced at the window. In the distance, beyond the houses across the road, a slight brightening of the sky was evident. Arthur was right: daybreak was approaching. How could the night have gone by so quickly?

Arthur noticed her puzzled look and told her, "Only in the physical world is there a perception of time and space. The consciousness in which you and I are now suspended knows none of that. When it is time for you to enter the realm beyond yours it will be my pleasure to escort you around its eternal present. But for the time being I must see you safely back into your sleeping body, ready for whatever your new day may hold for you."

Emily and Arthur returned to the bedroom. As their hands separated, what seemed like a spark shot between them; creating a slight tingle in Emily's fingertips.

In an instant she was back in her resting body.

Moments later, Emily awoke from sleep. She lay quietly in the twilight, reflecting on what had taken place.

Just as the conscious mind cannot remember all the details of a dream, so Emily fought hard to bring through and relive the time she had just spent in the company of her beloved husband.

But then a smile gradually crossed her face, and a glow of contentment warmed her heart; for not only did she know with every fibre of her being that she had actually been with him, but that Arthur had given her much needed reassurance as well: a strength which would guide her through the developing relationship with James, and which would enable her to be of help to Ruth.

As she got up, dressed and made herself a cup of tea, Emily felt good. She was no longer a lonely old widow but a complete person again: loved, wanted, and needed.

Just after breakfast the telephone rang. With euphoria still warming her heart, Emily took the call.

Immediately, her bubble burst.

The phone call was from Kristine, and she sounded deeply troubled.

"Nana, can I come round and see you this afternoon?

There was a pronounced sense of urgency in Kristine's hurried request.

53

"It's very important. I've just got to talk to somebody about this..."

"...Yes dear...of course you can come round."

Emily's confidence wavered slightly as she caught the concern in Kristine's voice.

"Is anything wrong? You sound terribly worried."

"I am, but I can't talk now; not on the phone." Kristine suddenly dropped her voice almost to a whisper. "...It's about Mum. I've got to go now... I'll see you later." Then she hung up the phone.

"I wonder what that was all about," Emily said into thin air, the receiver still clutched, shoulder high, in her hand. Slowly she lowered it. All kinds of strange thoughts raced through her mind as she tried in vain to sense what was bothering Kristine.

It's about Mum, she had said. ...Surely Fiona's not ill as well? That would be just too much at present!

But then, Emily thought in retrospect, Fiona sounded alright when she spoke to her the previous night. ...Or maybe it's her behaviour. Fiona had always been prone to emotional outbursts. And poor Kristine; dear, sensitive Kristine, had always endured them gallantly.

Has she now reached the end of her tether and can no longer tolerate her mother's sporadic tantrums?

Over and over during the morning Emily reviewed these possibilities but kept them in perspective.

They were only possibilities, not known facts, and she resolutely kept herself in complete control over them. How easy it would be to allow them to get out of hand. The still-grieving Emily would have given in to her uncertainties, but this revitalised Emily was much stronger now. With Arthur's love and support behind her she was sure she could handle any developing situation objectively.

The problem with Fiona should be no different.

To boost her morale Emily busied herself – in the house, around the garden, and later at the shops. She picked an armful of brightly coloured flowers from her front borders. Her young gardener had worked wonders and she was well pleased with the results. Out of a wilderness Michael had restored Arthur's Garden of Eden, a real Elysium of which Arthur would have been proud ...And indeed no doubt he was already; for Emily was certain now that he could see everything clearly.

Lovingly she arranged the cut stems to brighten up the house for Kristine. And, just in case Fiona needed cheering up too, she set aside a posy of the blooms, kept fresh in a bucket of water, with a sheet of cellophane paper set aside in which to wrap them later. Kristine could take them home with her in the basket on her bicycle.

After a cup of coffee and a quick snack, Emily jotted down a grocery list for the local supermarket, including a reminder to herself to stop off at the little bakery which sold novelty pastries; Kristine would no doubt enjoy a treat with her afternoon tea.

And then she set off.

Emily's neighbourhood shopping centre was within walking distance from her home.

With a trundle shopping bag in tow, Emily was always able to take care of her grocery needs without bothering the family for a lift or taking a taxi. A couple of trips per week kept her cupboards full and herself well exercised. Out on this particular day – a warm, sunny day with only a hint of a breeze – she realised how lucky she was; how fortunate, considering her circumstances and stage in life, to still have her health, her independence, and most importantly, the continuing love of her husband.

So many widows she knew had alienated themselves from their surroundings once their emotional roots were cut and their securities removed. Their husbands had died, their families perhaps had relocated to other parts of the country or were too busy to keep in touch; friends of their own age had been taken either in death or established in rest homes closer to relatives. And these poor old souls had not the courage and incentive to move ahead: to begin life afresh on their own.

But here she was: Emily Thompson – going on seventy-one; still as spritely, as self-sufficient and well-loved as she was in her youth. In the short stroll to the shops Emily counted her blessings a hundredfold, wishing fervently that she had the power to shine her light on other less fortunate women; to bring a little joy into their lonely lives...

"...Hello, Mrs Thompson!"

A voice to one side startled Emily. She turned to see the vicar of St Aiden's Anglican Church approaching from out of a shop doorway.

"It's good to see you again," he said, "...And looking so well! How do you do it?"

Emily laughed. She had always liked this vicar. Though much younger than her, he carried himself with the dignity of one many years his senior, and was well loved as a man who treated all souls with equal respect.

The Reverend Bill Marriott had chosen not to marry, but instead devoted himself to his God, his parish and the local community. Emily herself was a Catholic although, as she shamefully admitted, these days a non-practising Catholic. She had on many occasions been involved with St Aiden's alongside Arthur through his community work. In his time Arthur had commandeered many fund-raising efforts for community projects, and St Aiden's not only provided a venue for his functions but also supplied manpower and money.

So, even though Arthur and Emily had been in his debt, it was Reverend Bill Marriott who felt indebted – to a couple who had done so much for so many.

"Reverend Marriott; how nice to see you, too. I hope life is treating you well?"

Emily shook his hand heartily.

"I'm afraid life is treating me too well at present," the vicar said, patting his belly: a little more portly than when Emily last spoke with him. "My parishioners are very kind in offering refreshments when I visit them, and it's impolite to refuse. But the old body can't handle it quite as well as in days gone by." He laughed cheerfully, and then went on, "Talking of refreshments, I've had a heavy morning which robbed me of my usual elevenses, and now I'm parched. Will you join me for a cuppa, if you're not busy? I would love to hear how you're getting on since Arthur passed away; especially as I see a bit of a twinkle in your eye."

Emily smiled, knowingly. "Thank you for the invitation, but I've already had morning tea."

"Oh, couldn't you squeeze in another cup, just a half a one; just for me? The café's right here, and I may not see you again for a while."

Emily light-heartedly looked into his eyes.

Here was yet another utterly charming man, who had such powers of persuasion he could soften the hardest of temperaments. How could she refuse!

"Alright...I'll join you," she replied in submission. "...Just for a few minutes."

The Copper Urn café was empty when they walked in. It was late in the morning by now; the in-between time, when most patrons had already consumed their morning tea but were not ready for lunch.

Once the assistant at the counter had served them and handed Reverend Marriott his change, Emily and her host had the place to themselves.

"Ah, that's better!" said the vicar after his first sip of tea. "I always have two cups. As the saying goes, 'the first to refresh, the second to revive.' Does that sound terrible: that a member of the clergy should place a dependency upon stimulants?"

"No, I wouldn't think so," said Emily, enjoying both his company and the comparative privacy of an almost empty café. "After all," she added. "Who am I to judge? Surely it's a case of each to his own."

"Maybe you're right. To be quite honest it doesn't worry me anymore. What other people think about my lifestyle doesn't really bother me now. As long as I don't do anything outrageous, I see no reason why I shouldn't exercise my God-given freedom of choice – like any other human being. I am still one, you know!"

"One what?"

"A human being!"

"Oh! Was that ever in any doubt?" chuckled Emily.

"You wouldn't believe what people expect of me. Just because I wear this dog collar they think I must be some kind of saint; that is saint with a small 's', of course. ...But nevertheless a person who's supposed to remain detached from normal human behaviour. Once in a while it's nice to be with somebody with whom I can feel more at ease; like your good self, for instance."

Emily blushed at the sudden outspokenness, while the Reverend Marriott continued.

"Sorry Emily. I can see I'm embarrassing you; I didn't mean to. But seriously my dear; you and Arthur were such down to earth people – a pleasure to do business with. It is a privilege to have known you both. Seeing you again after the difficult times you have been through – and looking so well – has given me a real lift. Oh, hark at me, chattering on about myself when I invited you here to tell me all your news. What has put that sparkle back into your eyes?"

Though unaware of it, the walk, the warm beverage and the vicar's kindly remarks had brought a glow to Emily's already enlivened face; which had the effect of making her eyes twinkle brightly in the reflected light from outside.

Unknown to her, she looked beautiful; not like an elderly lady at all, but more like a young girl out on a date.

Yet this man was nobody special to her to make her blush; for if there was a sparkle in her eye it had not been stimulated by the Reverend Marriott's company, but was due to the continued presence of her departed husband; something she had discussed with nobody.

So how then could she explain away her good spirits?

...Though on reflection, Emily realised, if anybody was likely to understand, it would be Reverend Marriott.

She had been embarrassed when he implied he felt at ease with her, but was that not equally true in reverse? Didn't she also feel completely at ease with him?

There sat before her a person who was not just the local vicar; he was also an old friend who had just, if only briefly, opened up his heart and spoken frankly with her. Could she not do likewise with him, and reveal what was in her own heart; especially as he apparently wanted her to share it with him?

Dare she, in fact, tell the Reverend about Arthur's visits; his perpetual presence in her life which alone gave her the will to go on living?

...Or would it be an appalling betrayal of a very special relationship between two souls who were in essence still man and wife?

And then, as if in answer to an unasked question, Emily had her answer.

"Reverend Marriott..." she began.

"...Emily, please call me Bill. My friends do, and I'd like to think of you as a friend."

"Alright...thank you, Bill. If indeed there is a sparkle in my eye or in my soul, it is there for a reason. And I would very much like to tell you why. ...Only, there's a condition."

"Oh, what is it?"

"I would have to insist that you treat what I am about to tell you in strict confidence..."

"...Naturally; you have my word."

"Thank you. It...it has to do with Arthur."

Emily paused to gather her thoughts. This was going to be tricky, putting what she had to tell him into the right words. Should she just come out with it – that her dead husband visits her; or go back to the beginning – to the message from Ada Simcock which offered hope, and which spurred her on to becoming aware of Arthur's presence?

"Bill, do you believe in ghosts?" she asked timidly, after a long silence during which Reverend Marriott witnessed deep sighs and much soul searching in his companion.

"In ghosts?" he replied quizzically. "I don't really know. I've never seen one for sure, but I can see the possibility of a departed soul returning to the scene of his former life. Is this what has happened with Arthur?"

"Yes."

Emily was taken aback by Bill Marriott's perception, yet chose to show nothing of it in her response to his question. Instead, she gathered her thoughts in order to continue.

60

"Arthur visits me in my dreams, and at times I'm aware of him during the day as well. He told me he is constantly at hand in case I need him. It is a wonderful source of comfort to me, I can tell you."

"I imagine it would be. But are you sure it is a genuine appearance and not just the outcome of your longings – a product of your own imagination?"

"Do you mean, 'Wishful thinking'?"

"Yes. It is a possibility, as you are no doubt aware."

"I understand what you are saying, and I'm as sure as I can be that it's not wishful thinking. What happened last night was too real to be mere fantasy."

"Would you like to tell me about it?"

"I think so... I think it would do me good to discuss it with you. The actual details of the dream have faded now, but I remember quite clearly Arthur's coming into my..."

Suddenly Emily tailed off in her narrative as a looming figure appeared in the doorway of the tearooms; abruptly breaking into the developing rapport between Emily and the Reverend.

A large, buxom woman carrying a heavy shopping bag of groceries fleetingly occupied the doorway.

Before either could comment, she headed straight for their table.

"Rev'rund Marriott! How nice to see you," she called out in a broad English accent, before lurching up to them. "Do you mind if I join you for a minute? I must take the weight off my poor old feet..."

Emily looked helplessly across the table at her willing but compromised confidante.

A feeling of despair crept through her. The tale had been left untold; she had not even begun to explain herself. What thoughts must be crossing his mind? For sure he would think unfavourably of her now: that perhaps she was turning into a delusional old woman.

Emily watched his face for any clues, but could not decipher, from his impassive expression, just what his response might have been.

As always, Reverend Marriott was polite; even in the face of this intrusion. He stood up to pull out a chair into which the woman then squeezed her generous frame.

"Mrs Anderson... Um... How are you? Can I get you a cup of tea?"

"Ooh, Rev'rund; that would be luv'ly. I haven't had one for ages. Thanks ever so much."

Reverend Marriott went back to the counter to order a fresh pot for his unexpected guest, while she apologised to Emily for interrupting their conversation.

"I'm Rosalie Anderson," she informed her. "We're in the vicar's parish. And you are...? I don't recall seeing you at Church... Are you new around here?"

"Oh no! I've lived here all my married life. My name is Emily Thompson. In fact, I don't even belong to your parish. I'm Catholic. Reverend Marriott and I know each other from his past associations with my husband..."

"...What does he do then?" Rosalie Anderson asked.

She sat back as the Reverend placed a small round tray on the table in front of her. With a nod of thanks she poured herself a cup of tea.

Still in a state of shock, Emily watched on as the activity took place. Then she remembered Mrs Anderson had asked her a question.

"Um... What does who do?" she said hesitantly.

"...Your husband. You said he has associations with our vicar here. I wondered why a Catholic would be associating with an Anglican vicar."

Emily fidgeted awkwardly. The woman was beginning to irritate her.

Reverend Marriott sensed Emily's uneasiness, and saw the need to rescue her.

"Mrs Thompson's husband isn't with us anymore," he slipped in quietly. Then by way of an explanation he added, "I knew Mr Thompson through business dealings; so Mrs Thompson and I are old friends."

He leant over and squeezed Emily's hand in a gesture of reassurance.

Emily smiled in response; appreciating his support.

There was no possibility of further discussion between Emily and Bill Marriott from then on; Rosalie Anderson had seen to that. Emily, who was only completely at ease with other people on a one to one basis – especially when she had something critical to discuss – sat back and allowed the interloper to dominate further conversation with a stream of meaningless chatter.

The previously quiet sanctuary of the tearooms had become more like a noisy roadside café; an unbearable situation, Emily determined; and one which she needed to escape at the earliest opportunity.

After only a few minutes she could stand the cackle no longer. Making a trumped up excuse, she rose from the table to leave.

Reverend Marriott stood up, too. He sympathised with Emily for wanting to get away and, wishing to have a private word with her before she left, he escorted her to the café door.

"I'm sorry," he said, taking her hand in his. They stood outside, out of earshot of Mrs Anderson. "We'll continue our discussion some other time. Give me a ring when you have a few minutes. Here's my number..."

He reached into his breast pocket and pulled out a business card on which was printed in bold lettering his name, address and telephone number.

Emily took it silently and slipped it into the side flap of her shopping bag.

With a brief, "Thank you, I will," she bade him goodbye and hurried away; feeling completely deflated.

The rude woman had destroyed what could have been a beautiful moment; when she would have shared with a kindred spirit a very precious secret.

Yet as things stood, all that emerged from it was a half confession, which told Reverend Marriott nothing except that Emily Thompson was seeing things. And on top it was a growing suspicion in her mind that in divulging even that basic piece of information, she had also betrayed her husband's confidence.

In a daze, Emily mechanically bought her groceries and trudged back home.

With a heavy heart she put her purchases away and sought the comfort of Arthur's favourite chair. She had no sooner sunk back into its soft upholstery when a thought popped clearly into her head.

"Don't worry, Emily; it really doesn't matter."

Startled, Emily came to attention and listened.

It was Arthur...not visible this time; just in her thoughts.

"Arthur," she blurted out, "I'm afraid I've made a fool of myself with Bill Marriott."

"No, my dear," came the reply within her soul. "You have not made a fool of yourself – not to me, anyway. It just seems that way at the moment. There will be another time to tell Bill about me. And he is the right person to tell. Nobody else, mind you – only him. So don't give it another thought. There is no harm done."

Suddenly Emily put her hands to her head, and wept. The strain of the last couple of hours had taken its toll.

After a shower and a bite of lunch Emily felt better. Her spirits had lifted and her strength returned; a strength she knew she would need for Kristine's visit after school; for the activities of late morning had masked her concerns over possible reasons why the girl wanted to see her.

Thinking about her again caused some of the previous fears to resurface.

To take her mind off it Emily watched her lunchtime soap operas on television. After that, she washed up her lunch dishes and settled back down in the chair; this time with a library book for company.

For an hour or so Emily read, but her mind was not on the words in front of her.

The book was interesting enough; a novel about a man persecuted for his political beliefs. When she first glanced down the synopsis of the book while in the library, it reminded her of Arthur's experiences with the local council, and this prompted her to take the book home for further scrutiny. But now the words she read seemed meaningless, for nothing was registering in her mind.

Instead, her thoughts kept drifting back to the tearooms; back to the confidence she had been so close to divulging. If only that rude woman hadn't come in when she did, and interrupted their conversation...

Other people's opinions did not normally bother Emily. However, Reverend Marriott's opinion of her just now was another matter entirely.

Her husband's afterlife presence was an experience so unusual, so precious to her, that the person with whom she shared the knowledge of it must be a soul of discretion; a spirit whose empathy should lighten the burden of confession, not complicate it.

He must, therefore, accept her explanation without need of question.

Did the Reverend Bill Marriott meet those criteria? Arthur, in her thoughts just now, had intimated Bill would understand, but Emily needed confirmation that he did not consider her to be just a foolish old woman.

This, if nothing else, was important to her; for she knew it to be completely untrue.

Before Kristine was due to arrive, Emily decided she could wait no longer; the tension too much to bear. With trembling hands she took out the Reverend's business card and dialled his number.

Shakily, she asked his housekeeper if he was there and could she speak to him.

Yet, when he eventually came to the phone, Emily found her nerve had given way to such an extent that she stumbled through her questioning; her words incoherent and strange.

"Dear Emily," was his kindly response when she paused on completion. "I could never think you foolish; neither do I suspect you are hallucinating. If you are sure of Arthur's presence, then I have no reason to doubt your judgement. In fact, of all the people I know I would say you are one of the few whose judgement I trust. But look, Emily... I'm sorry; I'm not actually at liberty to discuss this any further at the moment; I have an overseas visitor. However, at the first opportunity I will give you a ring and perhaps call round to continue our chat. Meanwhile, please rest assured I don't think you're cracking up; quite the opposite in fact!"

"Thank you, Bill. You have set my mind at ease."

"And now I really must go. Be at peace, Emily. Enjoy your relationship with Arthur...and," Reverend Marriott added cheekily, "please give him my best regards!"

"I will. Goodbye."

Emily put the phone down with immense relief. As she prepared for Kristine's visit she chuckled inwardly that she should have been worried at all. After all, Arthur had promised her it would be alright to share their secret with Bill Marriott. Did she not trust his word? If there was a lack of confidence it was not in Arthur's promise, but in her self-esteem.

She had always been a tower of strength with Arthur standing beside her; but it is much more difficult, she maintained, to depend on someone you cannot see!

Since his death her faith in him had been put to the test, and the fragility of her trust was now painfully and embarrassingly evident.

"I must acquire more self-assurance," she told herself sternly. "I'm not alone now, and my interests are still being protected. Therefore I must not fret over concerns which have no substance!"

Emily resolved there and then not to allow an old lady's weaknesses prevent her from heeding Arthur's subliminal advice. Though an unusual experience, in time his ethereal presence would surely become as natural to her as having him by her side...

Satisfied at last that the episode was over, and having seen Kristine's bright red ten-speed bike sparkling in the sun as she wheeled it up the front path, Emily hurried to the door to let her in.

Kristine looked haggard; as though she had the weight of the world on her shoulders.

Emily patiently stood back to give her some space; then embraced her warmly. Kristine, she felt sure, would tell her what was wrong when she was ready.

"It's good to see you again, Nana," said Kristine, holding on to the hug longer than usual. "I've missed your cheerful face recently."

"It hasn't been all that long since we last saw each other, has it?"

"No, but I can be myself when I'm with you, and that's important to me. I miss it when you're not here."

"Thank you, Kristine," Emily countered; freeing herself from the embrace. "Now, come into the kitchen. I've a nice afternoon tea ready for you. Can you stay long?"

"Oh no; I go straight home from school these days. If I don't, Mum gets inquisitive – and I sure don't want her to know I've come here. So this had better be a quick visit."

"Of course," Emily said with compassion. "Whatever you want to do is fine by me."

Emily dropped two tea bags into the pot and poured over boiling water. Kristine, she remembered, preferred her tea with lemon rather than milk and sugar, so took a lemon out of the fruit bowl and cut off a slice.

"You sounded troubled on the phone this morning," she went on after placing the thin slice of lemon in Kristine's saucer. "As you are short of time, would you like to tell me what's worrying you straight away?"

Kristine acknowledged the drink offered to her and sat thoughtfully, dunking the lemon. Then she eyed up Emily's plate of pastries, and selected one.

At last she said, "Nana, I feel awful snitching on my family like this, but I'm so worried, I've just got to talk to somebody about it!"

"You're not snitching, Kristine. If something is bothering you, then to share the problem is seeking help, and I'm

68

gathering at the moment you're in need of my help. It's about your mother, isn't it?"

"How did you know?"

"You told me on the phone."

"Oh... That's right, I forgot. It's just that..."

Kristine sighed dejectedly, reluctant to begin her sorry story. "Nana, please help me, I've never done this before!"

"Done what, my love?" asked Emily, a sense of concern creeping in.

"I've never told tales on anyone."

"Oh Kristine; you're not telling tales, either! Just take it slowly and start at the beginning."

"I'm not even sure where the beginning is!" Kristine searched her mind, and then said more decisively, "Oh, I know; it was the lounge suite..." Then, still concentrating on what she wanted to say, she took a sip of tea followed by a bite of cream puff. When she had swallowed, she went on. "Do you remember our lounge suite? There were two dark green chairs and a three-seater settee."

"Yes, of course. Grandpa and I gave it to your parents as a wedding present. How has that caused a problem?"

"Wait, I'll tell you," said Kristine; a further swallow of tea providing the stimulus to continue. "Mum was getting fed up with it. She said it looked old and shabby, although I don't know why; there was nothing wrong with it. Anyway, Mum decided to have it recovered. Dad was really cross. He said we couldn't afford it. He and I both reckoned it just needed dry-cleaning. Eventually Mum backed down and agreed to have it professionally cleaned. She called in one day at the local furniture store to enquire about getting it cleaned, and instead of following through on it, she used the old suite as a trade-in on a brand new one, which was delivered and installed the next day without her telling anyone. Dad and I couldn't believe she had done it! He hit the roof and said some awful things to her. I've never heard him talk like that. It quite frightened me, Nana..."

"...I imagine it would. ...Go on."

"From my room I could hear them arguing. Dad was obviously worried they would not be able to afford the payments on the new suite. Mum was trying to justify getting it by insisting they needed to keep up appearances. It was awful, Nana. The whole street must have heard them shouting at each other."

"But is this all that's bothering you – the business over the three-piece-suite?"

"No. That was just the beginning. Since then Mum has gone from one new thing to another, insisting we need them – paying with Dad's credit card, would you believe! She came home one day with one of those home gyms, supposedly to get the exercise she misses out on by not walking to the shops, but hasn't even assembled it. Last month she smuggled in an imported leather bag, which would have cost the earth, and when it came to light she'd bought it, she insisted she needed to replace the old one because it was no longer fashionable. ...Nothing wrong with it, mind you – just out of date. Honestly, Nana, Mum is running up credit like there's no tomorrow. Dad should take the card off her, but I think he's a bit scared of her, too. Mum can make a terrible scene when she wants to..."

"...Have you said anything to her about it?"

"I've tried to tell her she's being too extravagant, but she just fobs me off. She says things like, what do I know about their finances or, it's none of my business. If Dad can't get through to her, how can I?"

"I'm sorry, love. I had no idea this was brewing. Is there any way I can help?"

Kristine hung her head. "Nana," she said sorrowfully. "You haven't heard the worst of it yet."

"What do you mean?" asked Emily, a look of dread on her face. "Whatever has your mother done now?"

"Well, she bought the lounge suite on hire purchase, and assured Dad the monthly payments were being kept up to date out of her own money..."

"..How do you know about that?"

"Mum told him during an argument. They argue around me these days, as though I'm a rag doll that can't hear what's going on, with no brain and no feelings. Once upon a time they would go out of the room to quarrel if I was around. At least then they had a bit of consideration for me, but not now. Their rows last a few minutes and end up with one of them storming off; usually Dad. I think he goes off to the pub to escape. I feel so sorry for him. I'm sure he can't take much more of it..."

Kristine started to cry, groping in her blouse sleeves for a handkerchief, without success.

Emily reached for a box of tissues and pulled out two, which she handed to Kristine.

"I'm sorry, Nana," she said, taking them. "I didn't mean to bawl like this."

"That's alright, love. Now...you were telling me about the repayments – that your Mum assured Royston she had been making them."

"Oh, yes, that's right. Well, one day last week I fetched in the letters from the post-box, and there was a window envelope from the furniture store where Mum bought the suite. It hadn't been sealed properly. I don't know why I did it, and I feel terrible for having done it, but I opened the envelope to see what was inside."

"...And?"

"It was a final demand threatening legal action if she didn't clear the arrears on the suite within fourteen days. Nana, she hasn't paid anything on it for over four months;

which means she can only have made one payment since the day she bought it, because it hasn't been in the house much longer than that!"

Emily pursed her lips in thought.

"I wonder if Royston knows about this," she said; more to herself than to Kristine.

"I haven't told him," answered Kristine. "I haven't heard them arguing about it, either. But I bet you any money she hasn't paid it. To be quite frank, Nana, I think Dad will leave her if this thing blows up in their faces... And I don't want them to split up..."

Kristine tailed off, sniffing dejectedly; the already damp tissues at the ready.

"You should have come to me sooner, Kristine. If this has been going on for months, you should certainly have told me when you saw the final demand. I don't know how, but I'm sure I could have helped."

"I guess I was hoping it would resolve itself. ...Or maybe I was burying my head in the sand; I'm not sure which. I felt so guilty for opening the letter that I didn't dare mention it to Dad. After all, their finances are nothing to do with me. They'd have my guts for garters if they knew I've been looking in their mail; Mum especially."

Kristine paused again, lost in thought. And then, as if suddenly remembering something, she went on.

"Oh, that's right; I never got round to finishing what I was telling you..."

"Yes, you said I hadn't heard the worst of it... What did you mean by that?"

"Have you not heard about Mum's new car?"

"Good grief!" exclaimed Emily, sitting up abruptly. "Oh, Kristine! What now?"

Out of the blue, Kristine suddenly burst out laughing.

"What's so funny?" Emily asked in surprise.

72

"Well, it's not really funny; more like completely potty. It's unbelievable that after everything she has done, that my mother – your daughter – who we would both have credited with having more sense, is seriously thinking of buying a new car. Honestly, it's all so out of character for her. It's like she's gone off her head, or something."

Emily frowned deeply, trying hard to apply some reason for Fiona's actions. Then she said, "And why would she go so far as to think of getting a new car on top of all the other things she has bought?"

"They've had their little Toyota for years. Dad has on occasions talked about changing it for a newer model, but that has only been because he gets frustrated with it when something goes wrong. As soon as it's fixed again he's fine. This is different, though. It's Mum who wants to replace it. ...And not just with a newer one. She wants to move up. She wants to get a flashier car – a brand new one at that, with all the latest gadgets. I was out with her the other day and she dragged me into a showroom. I thought she was looking out of curiosity, but she was serious. It seems she was so taken with the fancy limousine they used for Grandpa's funeral that she couldn't be satisfied with the Toyota any more. It's just like the suite, Nana. She's aiming higher than we can afford, and right now we can't afford anything! At the rate Mum's going, we'll soon be broke!"

"Oh, heaven's above, Kristine! I hope it never comes to that! But she does seem to being going through some kind of obsessive phase: champagne tastes on a beer budget; that sort of thing."

"What can I do, Nana? Money-wise, it doesn't affect me. Dad still gives me my allowance, and I'm never without clothes or money for school stuff. He's good that way. It's just tearing me apart, what she's doing to our family. ...Dad in particular. I love my parents and I don't

73

want to lose either of them. Why does she have to be so irresponsible?"

Kristine thumped her fist on the table, causing crockery to rattle. Abruptly she came to her senses and glanced at her watch.

"Good grief!" she said, jumping up. "Look at the time! I didn't mean to stay this long."

Kristine grabbed her schoolbag and dashed to the front door, with Emily close behind.

"I'll mull over what you have told me, and let you know tomorrow if anything comes to mind. Can you call in on the way home like you did today?"

"Tomorrow's Saturday. It'll have to be next week."

"Alright, love...whatever suits you."

Emily opened the door for her.

As Kristine strapped her bag onto the bicycle rack, Emily quickly added, "...And try not to worry about it. We'll work something out."

"Thanks, Nana. I feel better from talking to you."

Afterwards, Emily thought through their conversation.

To her dismay she realised there was in fact little she could do to help. If Fiona would not even listen to her immediate family she was not likely to heed the advice of an interfering mother. And if she did listen, she would no doubt insist there had been no transgression, no error committed; that she was merely exercising her right in the modern world to make purchases.

But it takes money to pay for her purchases; money that cannot be endlessly accessed through the use of a plastic card. Kristine and Royston, Emily concluded, are going to have their work cut out if they ever hope to convince Fiona of this fact.

A feeling of helplessness gradually crept over Emily. Was there really nothing she could do to help; short of paying any arrears herself?

Furthermore, when Ruth phoned to give her report on Wilbur, stating she no longer needed Emily's help, the old lady's sense of uselessness increased.

Suddenly Emily was filled with an overwhelming need to help her family. She knew she could be of help to one or other of her daughters, if they would let her.

It appeared to Emily that even with the loss of her husband, she was leading a life more settled than the other members of her family, and yet she could do nothing to even out the distribution of fortune.

Where support for her family was concerned, just now Emily felt completely superfluous.

That night, Emily could not reach the blessed state of consciousness into which Arthur might enter, and awoke in the morning feeling drained.

As always, she sought distraction from her thoughts in activity. The fine morning drew her out into the garden: to pick some roses for her vase, and to do some work by way of therapy.

Emily was tidying out the shed when Michael arrived. Even after he had finished his gardening, earlier than usual she noticed, the disturbed state still haunted her.

She could not get Fiona out of her mind. That was the trouble with living alone: it was too easy to linger within one's own thoughts. Reluctantly, she decided the only way to achieve some relief was to go and see Fiona, and find out for herself what was going on in her daughter's head.

Normally, Emily would never turn up at somebody else's home without first checking it was alright to do so. But this time when she used the phone, it was not to call Fiona but to order a taxi, and she arrived at her daughter's house soon afterwards; still unsure what excuse she should give for the unscheduled visit.

With trepidation Emily knocked on the door. A moment later it was opened by Kristine's hand.

Immediately the girl looked perplexed on seeing her grandmother only a matter of hours after their clandestine conversation.

But before she could say anything, Emily shushed her by touching a finger to her lips.

"Don't worry, love; I won't give away your secret," she whispered. "I just wanted to find out for myself what the trouble is. I'll make some excuse for being here..."

"...Who is it?"

Fiona's voice was heard coming from the kitchen; then moments later her head appeared around the door.

"Mum! What on earth are you doing here?"

"That's a fine greeting for your mother!" said Emily, feigning offence at Fiona's attitude.

She affectionately brushed past Kristine.

A look of insistence in the girl's eyes urged her to halt, but Fiona's sudden appearance prevented any further communication between them, and Emily had no choice but to ignore her.

"Sorry, Mum. I didn't mean it to sound that way," said Fiona, drying her hands. "I was just surprised to see you; that's all. Usually I come over and fetch you for one of our outings. How did you get here, anyway?"

"...By taxi."

"...By taxi?" Fiona echoed. "Why did you waste money on a taxi just to come over here? Is something wrong?"

She ushered Emily through to the lounge and invited her to sit down on the new suite that had been the cause of all the trouble.

Kristine stood back uneasily; at that moment wishing she could be somewhere else.

"Nothing is wrong," began Emily, still searching for an excuse; a plausible reason why she should visit Fiona.

...And then it came to her.

"Surely I don't need to wait till something's gone wrong to call on my own family! I haven't paid much attention to you all of late, and I must admit I've been feeling just a little bit isolated myself. So, as it is the weekend, on the spur of the moment I decided to come over. And here I am! I'm very sorry if it isn't convenient. I can always ring for another tax and go back home!"

"No, that won't be necessary," said Fiona, irritated. "And it's not inconvenient. ...Not really, anyway. It's just that... Things are a bit awkward here at present."

Now it was Fiona's turn to be uneasy. She and Kristine exchanged knowing glances; the action noticed by Emily.

Annoyed, Kristine turned away to avoid further contact with either her mother or her grandmother.

Emily saw a chance to probe deeper.

With deliberate bluntness she asked, "What do you mean by 'awkward', Fiona? Should I be the one asking if anything is wrong?"

Fiona scowled, as though she was being interrogated.

With marked reluctance she replied, "Not that it's anybody else's business, but there's just a little bit of trouble in paradise at the moment. ...And it's nothing we can't handle by ourselves, so you don't need to concern yourself." Then, to change the subject she said, "Do you want a cup of tea or something?"

Fiona made towards the kitchen, anticipating a reply in the affirmative.

"Yes...thank you. That would be nice."

Emily quickly realised that Fiona's absence from the room gave her a few seconds alone with Kristine.

Instantly, she mouthed, "What's going on?"

Kristine moved furtively over to Emily and slid onto the settee next to her. She whispered back, "Dad has moved out. I was trying to warn you."

"Oh, no!" gasped Emily. "How did it happen?"

"Mum and Dad had a flaming row last night – right here in the lounge, in front of me and my friend Kylie. ...Nana, it was so embarrassing." She paused briefly to check her mother was out of earshot; then continued. "Dad found out about the car. He overheard Mum on the phone. She was telling someone that she wanted to surprise him with it next week. Surprise! Wow! It was a surprise all right. He blew a fuse! Kylie was supposed to be staying the night, but she was so shocked that she left, and some time later so did Dad; bag packed 'n all. Mum asked when he'd be back and he said, not at all if he could help it. I tried to stop him but he wouldn't listen..."

Kristine sighed miserably.

"...Nana, what am I going to do?"

Any response from Emily was halted by Fiona's sudden reappearance.

Immediately she recognised that the two had been in close conversation, prompting her to suspect a breach of confidence by her daughter.

"What have you been telling Nana?" she barked angrily at Kristine.

"I told her about you and Dad fighting, and that he has walked out on you."

"You had no right to do that! It's none of her business!"

"Now just a minute, Fiona," cut in Emily. She was taken aback this time by Fiona's violent outburst and began to see why Royston saw fit to leave. "I'll thank you to keep a civil tongue in your head! ...And as for it being none of my business, you're wrong there. Anything that concerns our family's welfare concerns me."

Fiona backed off sheepishly; shocked by the telling-off.

"I'm sorry. It won't happen again."

"Now... I can see something is eating at you, Fiona. I suggest you allow me to finish getting the tea while you sit here and try to relax. Then we can discuss this whole issue a little more rationally."

Emily went into the kitchen and flicked the kettle back on. In the background she could hear Fiona and Kristine arguing in a harsh whisper, and wondered what they were saying. Fiona, she assumed, did not know about Kristine's confession the day before; she hoped it wasn't about that.

While she waited for the kettle to boil, Emily reflected on the aggressive manner in which the older of her twins greeted her; for she had never done that before.

Fiona had always come across as being hot-tempered but aggressiveness was out of character. For the first time a real sense of worry descended on her. Getting through to an obstinate person is often one of life's most difficult tasks. She would have to tread very carefully if she wanted to succeed with Fiona...

With a full tray balanced on her arms, Emily returned to the lounge. The room went quiet when she entered, an indication that they had been talking about her.

"Don't let me interrupt your discussion," said Emily with an element of sarcasm. "I'm quite sure the topic of your secretive conversation was something I should really know about."

Emily placed the tray on Fiona's mahogany coffee table; then carefully pulled it closer to the settee. She sat down beside Kristine and began to pour the tea.

Fiona remained in silence; for the moment at a loss for anything to say.

But Kristine, it appeared, still had plenty to say. While she watched her grandmother's passive activity, she said to her mother, "I went to see Nana yesterday, and told her everything that's been going on here."

"Kristine! How dare you!" exclaimed Fiona angrily. "Are there no secrets in this family? My affairs are no concern of anyone but me!"

"Mum, it's gone too far for that, now!" Kristine snapped back at her.

Emily attempted to pour the tea in a nonchalant manner, while at the same time feeling as though she was going to faint.

She put the teapot back down on the tray, her hands shaking so badly the crockery clattered. Then she took a deep breath.

She had anticipated a scene and was more or less prepared for it; but not like this.

"Don't you think we should discuss this rationally," she said during a pause in shouting, while each threw a glance at the rattling crockery.

"...We? What do you mean, 'we'!" barked Fiona, her eyes still blazing. "What makes you think you're involved in any of this? It's none of your business!"

"Fiona, you said you'd keep a civil tongue. The whole street will know your business if you don't stop shouting."

"Let them! I don't care. I resent the fact that my own daughter has been tittle-tattling behind my back to an old woman who is nothing but a busy-body!"

"Mum! That will do! Don't speak to Nana like that. She's still your Mother!"

Kristine's anger at that moment had risen as though she was rebuking the devil itself.

She cared about Fiona and desperately wanted to see the problem solved, but she was not going to allow her to insult her grandmother.

Fiona's demeanour suddenly changed.

Her fury, fierce though it still was, now wore the colour of bitterness, and she turned spitefully as she confronted her only daughter.

"Yes, Kristine, she may 'still be my mother' – but she never was in my childhood!"

"Whatever are you saying?" cried Kristine in despair.

"You needn't sit there, miss high-and-mighty, defending your so-called innocent grandmother. It's alright for you. As a child you had everything you wanted. I've always given you the best. But dearest darling Nana here; she and your Grandpa... When I was a youngster it was always, 'We can't afford this thing you want so badly;' and 'this other thing you would like is just an unnecessary extravagance'. They never let me have anything I really wanted. You, mother..." she hissed, pointing accusingly at Emily, "...were mean and stingy, and I've never forgiven you for it!"

Emily gaped in disbelief at her first-born twin.

It was inconceivable that Fiona had just made such vile accusations; yet the shocking impact of them rang loudly in both her ears and her heart.

Kristine slipped her arm through Emily's, buried her head in her shoulder and burst into tears.

"How can you be so rotten to her, Mum?" she sobbed. "Nana doesn't have a mean streak in her body. She's the sweetest person I know!"

Emily kissed the top of Kristine's head in thanks for her supportive comments.

She frantically thought back to the twins' youth. Times were indeed hard back then. She and Arthur had to be careful in those lean years, and thrift became their watch-cry until they were materially established; which took them well into middle age, when the twins were all but grown-up and living their own lives. Maybe a child who was basically self-centred, as Fiona had turned out to be, would interpret their thrift as being tight-fisted, and resent it deeply; even into adulthood.

Emily was no psychologist, but was this resentment, she wondered, now manifesting as excessive spending when Fiona herself should be exercising thrift?

With her arm still through Kristine's, Emily made to stand up.

"Come on, love," she said to the tearful girl. "I could do with some fresh air. The atmosphere in here has suddenly become overpowering."

Still sobbing, Kristine meekly followed as Emily led her out through the front door. With a groan the older woman lowered herself onto a wrought iron seat in the porch: another of Fiona's recent purchases.

The sunshine was soothing. As Kristine sat down beside her, Emily breathed deeply to rid her lungs, and her whole being, of stale air.

After a few moments of quietness Kristine's weeping ceased. She blew her nose gently from the handkerchief habitually kept up her sleeve.

Then, tucking the handkerchief away again she looked at Emily.

A tear glistened in Emily's eye: a tell-tale sign of how she had really reacted to Fiona's accusation. But of need, her emotions were kept under control.

Inside, Fiona's rage was now recklessly being taken out on her own home.

Heavy footsteps pounded the kitchen's wooden floor; then the cutlery drawer, wrenched open, fell noisily onto it, scattering the contents far and wide. Fiona's ensuing string of expletives resounded throughout the house and out through the front door, where the two quickly put two and two together.

"I think I'd better go," said Emily, getting up. "I came here to help, but I only seem to have made things worse."

"Oh Nana, please don't go yet," begged Kristine. "I don't want to be left on my own with her."

Responding to Kristine's heartfelt plea, Emily paused in her intentions.

"Perhaps that's what your mother needs – to be left alone for a while in order to gain some perspective on all of this nonsense."

"Do you think that's wise?"

"I don't really know. But I do think she's the only person who can rectify this situation. ...And I believe she can only do it if she is free of family pressures; namely, just at the moment, you and me."

Emily sat back down to give the matter more thought; then she stood up again, pulling Kristine with her.

"I know what we'll do," she said, as an idea came to her. "Go and pop a few things into a bag. You can come and stay with me for the rest of the weekend. It'll give your mother a chance to simmer down. Maybe by then she'll have come to her senses."

But Kristine was unsure.

"I'd like to come with you, of course, but I don't know how Mum would take to the suggestion."

"Darling," Emily said seriously, "I'm not suggesting it. I'm not going to ask your mother if you can come and stay with me, I will just tell her you're coming. ...Now," she asserted, patting the girl's arm. "Run on in and do as I ask while I call for another taxi."

When Emily entered the kitchen, Fiona was still on her knees replacing the last of the spilt cutlery in the drawer, and muttering under her breath as she did so.

Promptly, she stopped her grumbling and leant back on her heels.

One look at her face told Emily that Fiona, too, had been crying...but whether out of anger or remorse, she could not immediately tell.

"Now look...what you made me do!" Fiona stammered reproachfully. "Why did you...have to come here?"

"Fiona dear, you have brought all of this on yourself. You alone are responsible for your actions, and though it suits you blame me for your troubles you must look to yourself for the solution. I can't help you. However..." Emily went on before Fiona could get a contradictory word in; "...I didn't come in here to continue the argument, I came to tell you that Kristine is coming to stay with me for the rest of the weekend. She needs a break from your tantrums, and you need time to sort yourself out. She's gone upstairs to pack. I've already ordered a taxi."

"Well, good riddance to the both of you, I say."

Fiona was on her feet now. Any remorse she may have felt was stifled by a stubborn last show of defiance.

"You and Kristine – and Royston, for that matter – can all clear off. I don't need any of you. In fact, I'll quite enjoy being by myself. I'll be able to do what I like without any of you interfering. So go away; both of you. ...And don't bother coming back!"

By the time Kristine returned home on Sunday evening, Fiona had had plenty of opportunity to think.

Yet, far from sorting herself out as Emily and Kristine had hoped, she was feeling even more alienated towards her mother and the family in general.

84

Emily, on the other hand, was full of remorse. Quarrels between family members always left a bitter taste in her mouth. In Emily's opinion they should be patched up as quickly as possible. But this one seemed to be different. She doubted it would be mended just yet.

Even Arthur gave her little by way of encouragement. He, too, thought Fiona needed time to decide what was for the best. "...And by the way," he added before slipping out of her consciousness, "I'm sensing an unsettled spirit around you just now. Please be vigilant."

Yet no sooner had the advice been given than it was forgotten. At that moment, Emily's mind was preoccupied with existing concerns.

CHAPTER FOUR

Emily readied herself with less than enthusiasm for her date with James Forsythe.

The sourness of the weekend's events had used up all her energy, and although she looked forward to seeing him again with a slight flutter of her heart, her spirits were generally depleted.

James noticed this straight away.

"What happened to that vivacious smile?" he asked as they drove into the village. "Has something happened to upset you?"

"...Just family trouble; nothing we can't handle," Emily replied hopefully, and realised that she must buck herself up if she was not to wreck their get-together.

On the whole, Emily enjoyed her morning: James was such pleasant company.

He had the knack of touching her heartstrings, with the same charisma Arthur exuded; which initially caused her to feel guilty but without the sense of betrayal.

Yet, Arthur had set her mind at ease about that now. With a clear conscience she could allow herself to enjoy the company of James Forsythe to the full.

Emily discovered a lot about James, and he about her. He had, it turned out, been in the police force, rising to the rank of Chief Constable for the region before a car accident a couple of decades earlier forced him to retire sooner than he had hoped.

Further conversation revealed his acquaintance with Arthur; that he had come into contact with him through the police force on various occasions. Now a widower, a fact that Emily already knew, he had but one child – a son by the name of David – who had settled overseas with a family of his own. And so James, since the death of his wife not long after Arthur died, was completely alone; save for the odd greetings card from his son. He told Emily he had visited them several years ago, and was hoping to pull in a second visit. But that was before his wife died...

As they chatted on, oblivious of what was going on around them, Emily felt completely at ease; so much so that she divulged a great deal about herself and Arthur, but very little about her current family circumstances.

James had already heard she was the mother of twins, and she told him about Kristine, but Emily felt she did not know him well enough to discuss her latest family crisis. Besides, she conceded, it hurt too much to resurrect it just now. The mood between them was too convivial to think about family problems.

...Anyway, she reflected with hope in her heart, they might be resolved soon; then it won't be necessary.

Emily met James regularly after that; opening up a new way of life for her.

James took her to play bowls, which drew Emily back into the social circle she once enjoyed with Arthur.

It was strange, she noticed, how readily the ladies in the club accepted her when she had her escort, but not quite so much when she went there unaccompanied; which lead her to the conclusion it must be something to do with social etiquette...or maybe they had a soft spot for James...

87

All the same, Emily was pleased to have friends of her own again. The family had been time consuming of late. Either they flooded her with tea and sympathy, as in the weeks after Arthur's death, or they bombarded her with their problems.

Whilst she felt deeply for them and wished she could be of more help, she was pleased to have some distractions that enabled her to live her own life once again.

And this she did: she and James. Without living in each other's pockets, they provided for one another the perfect recipe for companionship.

In the meantime, Kristine reported often to Emily on her mother's behaviour.

"She's all over me like a rash these days," she told Emily a couple of weeks after their quarrel. "She can't seem to do enough for me. It's almost as though she's trying to buy back my affections."

"At least she's being civil to you."

"Yes, I'm grateful for that; but it's becoming stifling. I do wish Dad would come home; then she might settle down again and be a proper wife and mother."

"Have you heard from your father?"

"No, and I miss him terribly. He hasn't been in touch with us at all; although one of my friends at school said she saw him in the village, so he must be living locally."

Emotion started to show in Kristine's voice, but she shrugged it off. She was a strong girl and not inclined to wallow in self-pity.

More practical than her mother, Kristine usually faced problems square on rather than cower away from them; unless a situation became intolerable, such as with Fiona's irrational behaviour.

"Do you think Dad will come back to us, Nana?" Kristine asked Emily during an after-school visit.

"I don't know. It's early days, yet. Hopefully he'll retain enough interest in his family to come back home. It rather depends how close he and your mother were, I would say. Were they close?"

"When I was little, they were. We did everything as a family. You know yourself the fun we had at Christmas, and when you and Grandpa came away on holidays with us. Over the last few years they argued more, but didn't actually fight – until this business with the overspending. On the other hand, I don't recall them being romantic, either. They were just...there. They are my parents, and do what parents usually do. I can't say I really thought about it all that much. Do you know what I mean?"

"Yes, indeed I do. I suppose we must wait and see what happens. I hope your father contacts you though, Kristine. There's no reason why he should break off with you. His quarrel is with his wife, not his only daughter."

"I hope you're right, Nana: that he does contact me. I don't want to lose him. He'll always be my Dad."

Kristine turned to leave, but then stopped and said, "By the way, Nana. I almost forgot to mention: Auntie Ruth phoned this morning to say Uncle Wilbur's coming home today. He's been discharged from the hospital."

"Oh, that's brilliant! It must have been only a mild attack after all. ...But I wonder why she didn't ring me."

"Auntie Ruth said she did try to ring you first thing this morning, but couldn't get through. She asked us to pass on the message. Perhaps we should get you a mobile phone to keep in your handbag."

"Oh, I don't know about that. I'm not very good with the idea of new-fangled contraptions. I might lose it..."

After Kristine left the house, Emily found herself plagued with curiosity about Ruth's inability to get through to her on the phone.

Did she mean the line was engaged? In which case, she must have dialled a wrong number, because Emily had not used the telephone during the morning. Or did she mean the phone was out of order?

To find out if it was the latter, Emily went into the kitchen and picked up the phone. There had been no wrong dialling; the phone was indeed out of order. In fact, from the total absence of any sound whatsoever, Emily deduced that the line was actually dead.

How strange, she thought; perhaps the linemen have tampered with my connection. Emily remembered, from earlier in the afternoon, that Telecom personnel were at work just up the street.

On looking out of the front door, she could see that they were still there. As their van seemed to be even further along the street, then it was conceivable, she guessed, that her own line may have been affected by their work, too. She decided to find out. ...And maybe persuade the men to fix the problem before they finished for the day.

Snubbing back the lock, Emily pulled the door to and started off down the road.

Within a few short minutes she reached the 'linemen at work' sign. Then, seeing nobody actually working, she called out, "Is anybody there?"

Immediately, a head looked out from the back of the van, and a workman jumped down, a half-eaten sandwich in his hand.

Still chewing, he asked, "Do you want something, lady?"

"Yes. My phone isn't working. I was wondering whether you people have cut me off by mistake."

Emily shifted uneasily. The thickset man did not seem to be the obliging type.

"What's your number? We may have been working on it as well. I'll check my list."

He reached into the back of the van and took out a clipboard; then thumbed down his computer-generated list as Emily recited her number.

Shaking his head, he said, "No. We haven't worked on yours. You'll have to ring Faults."

"Do I have to? I thought that as you people are already working in the street you might be able to take a look at it before you finish for the day."

"Sorry, we don't do private work. We're only booked to do this job, and it's taking all day as it is. You'll have to phone for someone to come out specially."

"How can I? My phone is out of order."

"You've got neighbours, haven't you?" he said, more as a statement than a question.

The workman was becoming impatient now. Emily had already used up one whole minute of his break time and he was anxious to be rid of her; but then he relented.

"...Oh come on then," he said, beckoning her to follow him round to the cab. He picked up a handset from the passenger seat and waved it at her. "I'll phone through on this one."

"Thank you. I'd appreciate that."

"Silly old cow!" he muttered under his breath when Emily started back along the road. Then he struck a match to light his cigarette.

It was not until the following morning that the repairman turned up.

"We've tested the line in, and that's alright," he told Emily. "I'll have a look at your phone."

Yet when he checked and found nothing wrong there either, he stood back and scratched his head; puzzled.

"I can't understand it. Everything's fine; but there is still no connection. Have you had trouble with it before?"

"Not that I'm aware of."

Up until now, Emily had not been too bothered by the fact that her phone was out of order. As far as she was concerned, it was simply a matter of getting it fixed. But now, when she saw his perplexed expression, she began to feel uneasy.

"What do you suppose is the problem?" she asked.

"I don't know. I haven't come across this before, where there's no indication of what's gone wrong – except just once, now I come to think of it. ...But that was where wires had been severed. This has got me stumped, though. Even so, I'd better check along the length of your cable."

The telephone wires in Emily's house ran from the unit in her kitchen, beneath the house, and out to the junction box in the driveway, where the cables then disappeared into their conduit underground.

The repairman had checked the external connections as part of his service call, but was yet to examine the wiring underneath the house.

Access to the crawl space could be gained externally through a tiny door, or by way of a small trapdoor situated in the hall floor.

On his enquiry about the trapdoor, Emily rolled back the hallway carpet to reveal the internal access. Then the serviceman raised the trapdoor and slipped with ease into a square-shaped opening.

"It must be years since anyone has been down there," said Emily to the man whose head was now disappearing into the blackness.

The space between the ground and the floorboards was deep enough only for the man to crawl on his elbows. As he adjusted his position and switched on a powerful torch, Emily reminisced briefly on the few occasions when Arthur had needed to go down there. But no sooner had she begun to cast her mind back in time than a muffled cry caught her wandering attention.

She squatted by the trapdoor opening and called down, "Is everything alright?"

"Yes...and I've discovered what's wrong!" Moments later he reappeared to inform her, "It looks like your phone wire has been cut!"

"Cut? Do you mean, deliberately cut?"

"...Sure thing!"

"But how can you tell?"

"Madam, I know a cut wire when I see one, and this one has been snipped with wire cutters."

He hauled himself out of the hole, covered in cobwebs and dirt.

Emily squirmed to see the state he was in.

Fearing for the cleanliness of her home, she opened the front door so he could brush himself down outside, while she stood on the doorstep to make sure he did.

Flicking at his clothing, he said, "Look, I'll show you. We can probably see it better through the access door outside. Whoever did it must have gone in that way."

He led Emily round to the side of the house and knelt to draw back the bolt that secured the crawlspace door.

Arthur usually used the trapdoor whenever he had to go down there because, as he once told Emily, whoever built the house must have been a midget to put in a door so small only a child could get in.

However, the tall repairman merely reached inside to pull out the wire.

Emily gasped at the sight of the shiny ends of a cable which had indeed been cleanly cut through.

"Do you mean to tell me that somebody intentionally cut through my telephone wire?"

"...It looks like it."

He closed the door and pulled himself to his feet.

"But who would want to do a thing like that?" asked Emily, her disbelief turning into anxiety.

"I'm afraid I don't know. That's something you'll have to find out for yourself. I can repair it so you can use your phone, though."

"You can do that now?"

"Oh yes. It's easy enough to renew the connection; but I'll have to go back to the depot to get the part I need and won't be back till this afternoon. I've still got two more calls to make before my break." And then he added when he saw the look of concern on Emily's face, "...But don't worry; I'll come as soon as I can."

While the repairman ran to his van and drove off, Emily wandered up to the front door again; her mind in a whirl. The realisation that somebody had recently reached under her house, taken hold of her phone wire and vindictively cut it in two, made her feel nauseous and more than a little frightened.

She knew of nobody who wished her harm, or who was foolish enough to execute such an unkind prank, and yet the evidence before her confirmed that it had been done.

Emily was fearful now of being alone in the house.

She wanted to speak to James – to speak to anyone! But who could she trust? Even her close neighbours might be under suspicion. She couldn't ring James from home for her phone was still dead.

She shuddered remembering why.

To ring him she would have to go to the corner and use the public phone box. Oh, why did she so glibly reject Kristine's idea of a mobile phone!

Quickly she threw on her coat, took out some change from her purse, and left the house.

James listened to her story, amazed.

"I'll come over right away," he said, taking charge.

The urgency in Emily's voice dictated only one course of action, and he was out of the house and driving off almost before she had stepped back out of the phone box. By the time Emily reached her gate, James was already pulling up at the kerb. He jumped out spritely and bounded up to her, the policeman in him reawakened.

"Come round here," she said after a brief greeting.

She showed him the little door at the side of the house and bent to open it. But James gently raised Emily to her feet and instead squatted down himself.

"Here, let me do that," he insisted, quickly wrenching back the bolt that Emily would have struggled to manage.

With no torch immediately at hand to aid him, he found the wire only by groping.

"This is incredible!" he cried out. "It's been deliberately cut, alright. But who would want to do it?"

"That's what I wondered. I don't know anyone who is capable of doing something like that; certainly not to me!"

"Well, it must be somebody familiar with the cable setup under here."

Emily shuddered violently. "Oh, please don't say things like that, James. You're scaring me."

"I'm sorry, Emily – that was thoughtless of me. Look, you're trembling. Let's go inside to warm up."

Despite the sunny day, Emily was indeed shivering. The shock of such a worrying discovery was taking its toll, and she reacted now in the same way she did when Wilbur was rushed to hospital.

James put his arm around her for support; then he led her indoors.

"Do you want me to bring in the force?" James asked over the warming cup of coffee he quickly prepared for them both.

"What do you mean by 'the force'?" asked Emily; still in a state of shock.

"I mean the police, of course. Shall I contact the local police station? I still carry some weight there even though I've long since retired from it."

"Do you think it's necessary?"

"They could finger-print the door and wire; although if other people have been touching them as well, the prints probably won't be very clear by now."

Emily groaned under the pressure of decision.

"I don't know, James," she said gloomily. "I'm still very confused about all of this...and disbelieving, as well. This is something that happens to people on television, not to old ladies in real life. It's hard for me to get my head around it just now. What do you suggest?"

"Personally, I don't think we've enough to go on. It may be just an isolated incident – the work of some crackpot out for kicks. Or – and I hesitate to say this; if there really is somebody out there with a grudge against you, we will have to wait until he strikes again."

Emily almost choked on her coffee.

"...Strikes again! No, James! Surely not! Please don't say things like that! I couldn't live fearing someone might be lurking in the shadows. ...And, who would want to hurt an old lady like me?"

Thinking hard, James leant forward on the couch with his elbows resting on his knees.

"I must say, I don't like the idea of you being alone in this house under the circumstances. Is there anyone you could stay with?"

"I have my daughters; but Fiona wouldn't have me near the place at the moment, and Ruth is nursing her husband who came out of hospital just yesterday."

"You can always stay with me!"

James looked sheepishly at Emily while he made the suggestion, but then retracted it smartly when a look of disapproval crossed her features.

"Sorry," he said. "It was a silly thing to suggest. I don't know why I said it. But..." he added quickly, "...If all else fails, the offer is still open. ...And neighbours be-damned!"

Emily laughed. James was so protective of her, even to the point of throwing convention to the wind.

But what would it matter anyway? A few decades ago it might have caused an outcry for a widowed man to invite someone like her into his home. The neighbours would have been peeping through their curtains in animated disapproval; but nowadays... Maybe it wouldn't matter quite so much. Perhaps she had been too hasty in reacting against his offer. She would certainly feel safer in his company. ...And he would doubtless treat her with utmost respect. But even so, there were the twins and Kristine she would need to consider.

She didn't want to make any more waves with them if she could help it..."

"I'll ring Ruth and see if she can put me up," she told him. "I can probably be of some use to her. And if not... Well... We'll see."

She smiled into his eager eyes.

Secretly, James Forsythe was looking forward to the prospect of inviting Emily into his home. He could easily picture her blending into the background of his life; a move he hoped fervently she would one day consider. …But not just yet, and certainly not right now. It wasn't the time or the place to entertain any hopes for the future.

He groped in a pocket for his mobile phone.

"We can ring your daughter on this," he said, holding it out. "…And if it's alright with Ruth, I'll run you over there. She lives across town, doesn't she?"

"Yes. But James, I couldn't put you to the trouble…"

"Emily… Oh, Emily!" he said, placing his hand over hers. "Nothing I can do for you will ever be any trouble. In fact, it would be a pleasure."

"Ruth, I'm inviting myself over for a few days," Emily said when she managed to speak to her. A brief apology for not returning Ruth's call, together with a simple explanation as to why, was accepted without question; a fact which relieved Emily somewhat.

"I guessed you would be too polite to ask me for help while Wilbur is convalescing, so I'm taking it upon myself to do the offering," she went on. "Would it be alright if I come over this afternoon?"

"Of course; it's nice of you to volunteer, Mum…but I've nothing ready for you."

"That doesn't matter. I'm coming over as a helper, not as a guest. I'll see to all that when I get there."

Emily breathed a sigh of relief that she did not need to admit the real reason for her visit to Ruth.

For now, James was the only person who knew about the wires, and she trusted he would keep the information to himself.

Her family would be sure to react badly if they found out, and either worry unduly or insist she was imagining things. It would be better to keep her motives under wraps for the time being.

...Let them think she was just trying to be helpful in a time of need, she decided.

After a quick lunch with James, Emily gathered together some essentials in her overnight case and prepared to go. Then she pinned a scribbled note where the telephone service man could find it, locked the front door securely, and left the house.

The journey through town was pleasant and relaxing.

Emily was happy to sit back; her neck supported by the headrest, and let James shoulder some of the burden, if only for a while.

One thing she was getting tired of lately was being solely responsible for all her actions and decisions, with nobody on hand to share them or offer her moral support.

Arthur had been a great shoulder to lean on, and she now looked across at James; thankful to once again have a tower of strength at her side. Men are so much better at coping with this sort of thing, she thought, reflecting on the situation from which she was escaping; for if it had been his phone that had been tampered with, James would probably have taken steps to identify the culprit himself, and stopped at nothing to locate him. A woman's instinct is to steer clear of such awful trouble; presumably, she guessed, because of feminine vulnerability, or maybe an inbred need to protect home and family...

"Where now?" asked James, breaking into her musing. He was already driving along the wide highway that led to the suburb where Ruth lived.

Emily sat up and took notice of her surroundings. Not accustomed to navigating when en route to Ruth's home, she was suddenly confused about where to turn off. But then a familiar landmark, a line of shops up ahead, jogged her memory.

"Go down there," she said, and pointed to a side-road just beyond the shops.

"I won't come in," James insisted when he pulled up at the kerb outside the house. "She wouldn't appreciate an unexpected and unknown visitor. There will be plenty of time for introductions in the future."

Emily had to agree about the introductions, but still had some reservations about James not staying.

"I can't let you go straight back without having a break! It's quite a long way. Won't you come in?"

"Thanks, but not this time. ...Maybe when her husband has recovered. We could have them over for dinner."

Emily missed the inference in his invitation: that they were already a couple. She was too concerned her visit should not create an extra workload for her daughter – or do anything that might take Ruth's mind off the task at hand: that of nursing Wilbur back to health.

Perhaps James was right. It would be better to wait until another time.

Reluctantly Emily conceded his point.

"Alright," she said. "We'll leave it for now. And thank you for bringing me over. You can't know how much I appreciate having you to help me."

James laughed. "Oh, I think I have a pretty good idea.

He leant over and kissed her on the cheek before she opened the door to get out.

"Ring me when you want to go home, and I'll come and fetch you."

Emily stayed with Ruth for a week. During that time she made herself inconspicuous where her own needs and wishes were concerned, but always available to assist Ruth and the slowly recovering Wilbur. Never once was she tempted to mention the real reason why she had come over, but rather kept herself busy with other things to take her mind off it.

And she succeeded to such an extent that by the end of the week the episode with the cut telephone wires was just a blur in her mind.

Meanwhile, James did some snooping.

He made enquires of Emily's neighbours as to whether any had seen activity around the house on the day of the discovery, but most stated they worked during the day and would not have noticed anything after dark.

Disappointed, he took up the surveillance on his own; observing any comings and goings near the house from a distance. Yet, apart from the postman and the gardener, nobody else visited Emily's address.

James decided not to mention his fruitless vigils to Emily when he collected her from Ruth's, in case it stirred up old memories.

However, Emily was feeling braver now, for the initial fearfulness had mostly worn off. Apart from a slight pang of apprehension when the car drew up at the house, she was confident that staying there by herself again would not be too much of an ordeal.

"I'll just have to make sure everything is secure at all times," she said to reassure him.

"I've been thinking," he said, discreetly picking up the phone to make sure it was still working. "Maybe we should install security to the place, just to be certain nobody will get in either under the house or up here."

"If you think that would be best," she replied with only partial interest.

The following day, after a night that saw Emily only mildly nervous about sleeping in the house on her own, she and

101

James visited the hardware shop in the village with a list of their requirements.

"Have you thought about putting in an alarm system?" the assistant asked Emily. "Many elderly people living alone have them installed just for some peace of mind. We have a large range; most of which are simple to..."

"...No, I don't think I need to go to such drastic lengths," replied Emily confidently. "Besides, I'm assuming it was an isolated incident."

"Oh? Did something happen to you?"

"Yes. Somebody cut..." she began, but James nudged her violently from behind.

"...Somebody unwelcome trespassed on the property," James substituted; a correction unnoticed by the assistant while he focused on their list.

Emily turned and glanced at James apologetically.

"Just be careful who you tell about the wires," James asserted on the way home. "You know what the grapevine is like around here. If you feel the need to talk about it, then be selective in your choice of confidante. Remember; we still don't know who did it."

As the days passed without a further incident, the memory of it slowly faded and Emily gradually slipped back into her normal daily routine without undue concern for her safety.

"It must have been the work of a crank: someone who happened to pick on this house," she told herself assuredly one afternoon, when the peace of sunshine and solitude blissfully enveloped her.

She sat contentedly reading a novel in the back garden, her house secure, her work done; with the welcome glow of satisfaction in knowing that the luxury of taking time out for yourself has been well earned.

Laying the book on her lap, she smiled out at the world.

"How lovely everything looks in the warm sunshine," she reflected happily. "Its brightness seems to dispel all of our negative thoughts; which allows us to regain our focus and start again."

With a smile she looked benevolently at her garden; the roses – Arthur's roses – in full bloom, their various colours enhanced by the sunlight.

The whiskey rose stood head and shoulders above the rest as if reaching out to the heavens. Although Michael wasn't as conscientious now as when he first started, the results of his efforts were still pleasing to the eye.

As Emily took in the tranquil scene she noticed the movement of a dark shadow coming down the driveway at the side of her house.

Abruptly, her heart skipped a beat, while the memory of the phone wires flashed across her mind again. Yet, there was no cause for any concern, for as the shadow approached, the familiar and welcome figure of Kristine came into view.

"Hello, love," said Emily with relief. "...How nice to see you. Come and sit by me."

"I wasn't sure you were in, Nana."

Kristine walked over the manicured lawn, dropped her bicycle onto it, and sat next to her grandmother.

"It's like Fort Knox up there – the house is all locked up. You haven't even got a window open. It was only as an afterthought that I decided to look round the back here. ...What a wonderful show of roses! I love that yellow one in the middle!"

"That's our whiskey rose; named because it was grown in a whiskey barrel; it's Arthur's favourite. ...And I'm so glad you thought to come round the back here. I wouldn't want to miss a visit from you. Now, Kristine; tell me...how are things at home?"

Kristine sighed and twisted uncomfortably on the seat; Emily's question reminding her of the mood at home she came here to escape.

"Oh, alright, I suppose," she said casually.

But Emily saw the downcast look on her face; Kristine's cover-up of the truth not escaping her. She could read her granddaughter like a book.

"Hasn't there been any improvement?"

"Not really."

Kristine screwed up her nose. She didn't want to talk about her home life just now.

The situation had got on her nerves, to the point where any discussion on the subject was tedious. For Kristine, Emily's company was a source of light relief; a welcome interlude in life that she prized highly, and she was reluctant to forfeit even a moment of it.

"Oh, dear," said Emily, disappointed. "I was hoping you'd be able to tell me conditions had settled down."

It was obvious to Emily, now, that Kristine was reluctant to get into it. But ever since Fiona rejected her, Emily had no means of communicating with the family, except by way of Kristine. There were questions she wanted to ask; things she needed to know for her own satisfaction. Fiona might be a madam at times, but she was still her daughter and Emily still cared about her.

"Kristine, I know you are fed up with the whole scene at home, but as you must surely realise, I'm very concerned about you all. I do need to be kept informed of goings on over there. If you could update me on a few things I would very much appreciate it."

Kristine smiled half-heartedly.

"Alright," she said. "I'll tell you what I can."

"Thank you," said Emily with a relieved sigh. "Now... Firstly: have you heard from your father?"

"As a matter of fact, I have. I had a phone call from him last week. It was most peculiar…"

"…Peculiar?" asked Emily in alarm.

"Yes. A few days ago, Mum said that every so often the phone would ring, and when she answered it nobody was there. Then, when I took a call, Dad was on the other end. I asked if he had been ringing, and he said yes, but that he refused to speak to Mum until he had first been in touch with me."

"Have you told her?"

"Oh no; Dad said not to."

"How is he, Kristine?"

"Okay, I think. He's got a little place in town…gave me his new address and phone number."

"…And did he by any chance ask after your mother?"

"Yes…sort of. He just asked me if she had come to her senses. I didn't answer him, though, because Mum was in the house, and I didn't want her to overhear our private chat – she's still very tetchy about it. I was afraid how she would react if she knew Dad had been on the phone to me and not her. …Nana, if you don't mind, I don't want to talk about it anymore. There's nothing more to tell, anyway."

"That's alright. I'm sorry I plied you with questions. But I did need to…"

"…I know. I don't really mind. It's just that… Well… As you know I use you as a sort of refuge, like a port in the storm to get away from my family's problems. It's always so peaceful round here. …But you didn't tell me. Why have you locked the house up? You've never done that before, just to come out into the garden."

Now it was Emily's turn to show reluctance to talk. She hesitated for a moment; unsure whether or not she should tell Kristine about her trouble.

She decided not to.

"I had a little problem a couple of weeks ago, which taught me to be more cautious, that's all."

"...A problem? What sort of a problem?"

"...Nothing terrible. You've no need to worry, Kristine. It's all in the past now."

"Are you sure, Nana?"

For a moment Kristine's own woes were forgotten.

"Yes, I'm positive. Please don't give it another thought."

Emily's tone of voice clearly indicated an end to that topic of conversation. To change the subject completely in case Kristine felt inclined to question her further, Emily stood up and tucked her book under her arm.

"Now, Kristine," she said. "I think it's time I went inside. The air is turning a little too cool for my old bones. Come on in, and I'll put the kettle on."

It was unusual for Emily and Kristine not to share in each other's confidences. The close relationship between them had always paved the way for mutual understanding, and a willingness to talk out their problems, whatever they were. But this was different.

Yet, there comes a time when the pressures of life weigh so heavily that to openly air them only adds to their weight, and this, so it seemed, was such a time; for both Kristine and Emily.

Each sat at the kitchen table virtually in silence, sipping their tea with little more than superficial conversation passing between them.

Later, when Kristine had gone home, Emily was filled with remorse that the visit had been so unsatisfactory.

Why hadn't she been able to cheer Kristine up this time? After all, that was why the girl visited her so often: as an intermission in her home-life's unpredictable drama. She usually left feeling revitalised, looking forward to the next visit. Yet, on this occasion Emily sensed that a slight rift had developed between them; for Kristine looked thoroughly dejected when she left.

"Heaven knows what must have been going through her lovely head," she told James the next time she saw him.

He listened intently while she recounted as best her memory would allow the details of Kristine's visit.

Emily and James had arranged to meet for a stroll in the public gardens. As the day was grey and chilly, they had it almost to themselves. Ever the gentleman, he sympathised with her, offering words of consolation and advice where they were needed.

"It's probably because you are still feeling uneasy in yourself, and don't want to infect Kristine with it. ...A fine, unselfish move in some ways, but not in others. Maybe you should have told her about the wire; considering the closeness of your relationship with her."

"But then she would have worried about me, as well as her parents!" Emily exclaimed in frustration.

She stopped in her tracks; then strode off towards the lagoon: a man-made lake around which the gardens were landscaped. There, she stood forlornly as though to shut out both James and the whole world.

"Emily, please don't do this," James called out. "Please don't cut yourself off from the people who love you. This is only a temporary setback. It will pass. ...You'll see."

Emily turned around to face him, her mind numb from caring too much.

She let out a long, perplexed breath and walked back across the grass. Although unmoved by his plaintive cry, she could not dispute his rationale.

When she came close to him again she said, "I'm sorry, James. I guess I wasn't thinking."

"Then let me see that gracious smile, and convince me you're not going to allow all this to get you down."

So Emily, realising at last the folly of self-pity, smiled meaningfully at James.

She looked with gratitude into his benevolent eyes and, on seeing instead the love of her late husband, slipped her arms round his waist and hugged him.

"Dear James," she said with a lump forming in her throat. "Whatever would I do without you?"

Responding with unexpected fervour, James held her as he had held no one since the death of his beloved wife; and as he never imagined he could hold anyone again.

"Emily, my love," he said softly. "Don't you think it's time we did something about this impossible situation?"

"What do you mean?"

Emily gently pulled back to arm's length and looked at him questioningly.

He took hold of her hand; then escorted her to a nearby bench and motioned her to sit down.

"What I mean is," he continued when they were both seated; "you and I have what appears to be a deep-seated affection for one another. We are both alone, and to some extent, lonely. You are struggling to cope with aspects of your life by yourself, and I can't say I'm too happy, either. What I'm trying to say is: Emily, why don't we stop all this foolishness, and get married?"

After a moment held in suspension, Emily found herself blushing. Had James Forsythe just proposed to her?

"Oh, I don't know..." she said awkwardly, giving herself a little more time for his words to sink in.

A proposal at any time is a shock to the system; certainly it was for Emily, when Arthur went down on his knee all those years ago and produced a lovely diamond ring.

Yet, James Forsythe's proposal, coming out of the blue in the midst of her turmoil, caused her embarrassment.

Thus, rather than feel touched by his obvious sincerity, she turned her head away with apprehension; completely at a loss for words.

James gently raised Emily's chin and drew her round to face him again.

"Emily," he said quietly, "I need you, and I truly believe you need me, too. I care about you a great deal, and would very much like to spend the remaining years of my life with you as my companion. What do you say?"

At last Emily rallied, her embarrassment overcome. She realised that she could not refrain from answering him for much longer.

"I really should give it some thought, James," she said. "You have rather taken me by surprise. It's not as though we are young lovers starting out in life – we're both in our seventies. We've lived our lives! It seems strange to me that either of us might consider starting again at our age."

"...But it's not unheard of!"

James was beginning to feel deflated by Emily's lack of enthusiasm. Maybe he had broached the subject too soon; yet he could not backtrack now.

"Lots of old fogies like us get married these days," he went on. "We're no longer living in the dark ages, where an association like this would have been frowned on."

"Don't get me wrong, James," Emily asserted. "I know I'm a bit old fashioned, and I've got nothing against 'old fogies', as you called us, getting married again. I think it is marvellous when two people find love and companionship late in life. I'm just not sure whether it's something I want! I feel I would be somehow betraying Arthur. After all, it's not all that long since our respective spouses passed on..."

"...Emily, how can you betray him? He's dead!"

Emily looked up sharply; annoyed by his bluntness. How could James make such a heartless comment?

'He's not dead,' she wanted to say, but refrained from doing so. As yet she had not mentioned Arthur's visits to James, and now certainly was not the time to bring it up.

James took note of her annoyance, and apologised for his thoughtless blunder.

"I just wanted to make the point," he went on; "that it is futile maintaining devotion to a deceased partner when you've so much to offer to someone who's still alive!"

"I understand what you are saying, James, and I agree. But please...don't rush me. There are certain things I need to consider before I can give you an answer."

The 'certain things to consider' related to Arthur's opinion of a possible marriage to James.

The family's opinion was not a consideration for Emily; especially at her stage in life. They would just have to accept her plans, like it or not. But Arthur was different. He was her soul-mate. Would he be offended if she were to marry another man so soon, especially if it necessitated the need for her to exclude him from her thoughts from that time on?

Anxiously Emily took her quandary with her into the night. Yet, in her hurry to fall asleep, instead of opening up to the receptive state of consciousness, she tossed and turned; denying herself even an hour of restful sleep.

When she awoke in the morning, she realised Arthur had not appeared before her at all, and neither had he spoken within her thoughts.

With distressed spirits she had to report to James later on that she had no decision for him.

110

Emily wanted to marry James, of that she was now sure. He was right when he said she needed him. However, Arthur's approval was of paramount importance to her.

With it, she was certain the remaining years of her life would be filled with contentment. Without it, she would be miserable and might run the risk of losing Arthur, even in the after-life. It was essential she make contact with him before she gave James an answer; yet the more she worried about it, the harder it became for her to succeed.

After a succession of sleepless nights and weary days, one afternoon she fell asleep; mentally exhausted. Yet in that yielding state, Arthur finally came to her.

"Do you think I would deny you the right to happiness in your twilight years?" he said with compassion.

"I was afraid you might think I no longer loved you," her unconscious thoughts replied.

"My love, in the afterlife it is unnecessary to have vows of love re-affirmed. During our earthly existence, passions like envy, jealousy and hurtfulness may spring up when those affirmations remain unsaid. That does not apply here. You don't need to convince me of the timelessness of our love. Your union with this man is merely a stopgap until you and I can be together again. The remarriage of a partner yet living causes no ripples of disquiet within the realms of heaven. Rather it is a cause for rejoicing that our loved-ones have found contentment in their loneliness. I believe James is the right one for you, and so I say, Emily: go to him if it is your wish, and become his wife in every sense of the word with my blessing."

Emily sobbed; responding with a deep stirring in her soul to every word he uttered. Soon she would awaken, wondering why her hair had been moistened with tears; but just now the sleep in which she found herself suspended still held her full attention.

111

"There is one thing more though," Arthur went on. "It is only right and proper that on your marriage I withdraw from your life experience. There are no peeping toms in this realm. Your need of me for the time being is obsolete, and so I will relinquish my vigil towards you until such time as separation may once again re-kindle the need of it. But do not fear. I release you with love, as though sending you on a journey; to wait patiently for your return. Be blessed and happy, my love..."

And then he was gone.

Emily slept on for a while; waking with a headache and little recollection of the emotional tussle that had pervaded her afternoon nap. But when she slowly arose from the bed, opened the window for some fresh air and then breathed it in, her mind opened up.

Every word exchanged between the two of them came back clear and fresh, and she held on as long as she could to their reverberating echo.

Arthur had given her his blessing to marry James!

Suddenly it hit home. With a little leap for joy she left the window and headed for the phone to ring James. But she had moved too quickly. The queasiness returned and before reaching the stairs she needed to make a detour to the bathroom in case she was going to be sick.

After a few minutes the feeling passed.

Stoically she regained her composure and made her way down the stairs. Nothing would stop her from making that phone call now!

James was overjoyed when she told him the good news and declared, "I'll be round straight away." A short time later he pulled up outside Emily's house.

Instead of putting on the kettle for a cup of tea, Emily took out her precious bottle of imported cream sherry, a luxury she allowed herself only in special instances. Then, having realised she still wore her morning's work clothes, she hastily changed her frock for something more suitable for the occasion.

By the time James arrived she looked elegant, if not a little flushed.

No sooner had he walked in the door than he lifted Emily off her feet and danced round with her into the lounge.

She laughed merrily with him; free at last to do so. A great weight had lifted from her with Arthur's consent to their marriage.

Emily, for the first time since his passing, felt carefree and happy; uninhibited and just a little bit reckless.

But she was still very much Emily Thompson, and soon she had had enough frivolity. Laughing, she insisted that James put her down.

"Spoil-sport!" he said with feigned resentment.

She was so light he could have carried her indefinitely, but he did as she asked, setting her carefully onto her feet.

Still laughing, Emily brushed down his crumpled jacket; then went to tidy her hair in the mirror over the dresser, exclaiming, "I must look a wreck!"

As she pulled open the top drawer of the dresser to take out a comb, James snaked up behind her; then he slipped both arms around her waist, and together they glanced into the dresser mirror.

"Don't we look a happy couple," he said contentedly. "I defy anyone to tell me we're not right for each other."

Emily turned around to look at him. The frivolity gone, a look of serenity now graced her features. She stroked his cheek tenderly.

"I do love you, James," she said softly. "I think we will be very happy together."

"I believe you're right there," he responded, and kissed her on the forehead. "Now...how about a celebration?"

"Oh yes. I almost forgot. I've got out my best sherry."

"My goodness; not the best sherry!" he said teasingly.

Still holding onto her, James followed Emily into the dining room where a tray containing two long-stemmed glasses and the legendary bottle of sherry were waiting.

With hands trembling from excitement Emily opened the bottle. She poured two generous glassfuls and handed one of them to James.

"To us," she said, toasting him.

"...To you. ...And to me. ...Together." he emphasized.

Seated at the table, Emily watched her fiancé take a sip. Then she hesitantly touched the rich liquid in her own glass with her lips.

The last time she savoured the contents of this bottle was when Arthur first gave it to her on their Golden Wedding Anniversary two years earlier. The sweet taste brought back the poignant memories, and a lump formed in her throat. She sighed inwardly; quelling it to conceal from James any look other than happiness on her face.

"I haven't been this contented since we...that is, Arthur and I, last raised a glass together," said Emily without a hint of nostalgia in her voice.

"It's funny you should say that. It was on our wedding anniversary last year that Janet and I toasted all the years we spent together."

"How long were you married, James?"

"We actually married later in life than most couples. I was thirty-five and she was thirty-two; I remember that. This year would have been our fortieth anniversary."

All at once James went quiet, the need of recollection having tugged at his emotions, and Emily realised that just as she had spent a moment or two reflecting, so James now was finding himself reminiscing on the marriage he and his wife had enjoyed. She wondered whether the late Mrs Forsythe – Janet – would have given her blessing on this marriage had she known about it, just as Arthur had given his. Emily's mind lifted briefly, as though in an attempt to touch Janet's spirit, but the onrush of a sudden apology from James that he had been daydreaming broke the spell and returned her to normality.

"I've just realised something," said Emily. "You haven't mentioned your late wife to me before. In fact, I didn't even know her name was Janet until now. Would you like to tell me something about her?"

"There's not a lot to tell, really. She was very much like you; not so much in looks as in personality. Physically, Janet was quite tall – easily as tall as I am. She was reasonably well-built, but kept herself as trim as her build would allow; and she always chose clothes that flattered her figure."

"Did she like to follow the fashions then?"

"She did when she was younger. I would say, during her forties and fifties she kept up with the fashions. But as we got older I think it became less important to her to dress fashionably but rather...tastefully. I was always proud of Janet whenever we went out – right up to the end..."

James tailed off, drifting back in thought again.

Emily guessed the sherry had loosened his emotions, as it had hers; allowing the thoughts of them both to stray uninhibited in conversation.

"Don't go on if you'd rather not," she said.

"No! No, it's all right. I just haven't talked about her very much before now. I suppose it would do me good to bring a few things out into the open, especially with you. I have to admit, though: Janet and I were very close; about as close as a man and wife can be. But I don't intend to let that stand in the way of the happiness you and I will share together: that, I promise you that."

"I don't doubt it for a minute!"

Emily smiled at him, her heart brimming over.

"I'm glad you told me about Janet. It puts us both on the same footing, because Arthur and I were also, as you put it, 'about as close as a man and wife can be'. When he died it was like a part of me died as well..."

James nodded in agreement while Emily spoke.

"...And it took me a long time to adjust, too. But then..." Emily hesitated.

Could she tell him about Arthur? Should she ever tell James about Arthur?

"I know what you mean," James remarked, saving Emily from having to pursue her train of thought. "Of course, it's only natural to take time getting over the death of a loved one; especially someone as close as a spouse."

"What made you decide you wanted to get married again?" asked Emily.

"Do you mean, apart from the fact that I fell in love with you?" he laughed.

Emily grinned. "Yes, I suppose so."

"Loneliness, I would say. I was finding it hard to cope all by myself at home; emotionally, that is, and to a certain extent in a practical way as well. The ladies at the bowling club were very good. They often brought me some baking or a casserole. Last winter one even knitted me a sweater. Actually, I suspected a couple of them were a little bit sweet on me. But they became overpowering; to the extent – and don't you dare tell them this – that I would hide behind the curtain and pretend I wasn't in when they called. They were very different from Janet: much too gushing for my liking. She was quiet; never imposing, but always there for me. That's why I was attracted to you; because you are so like her: utterly dependable."

He lifted Emily's hand to his lips and lightly kissed her slender fingers.

"You are both gracious and precious, and I will always love you for it."

Mesmerised by his sincerity, Emily could do nothing but smile into his eyes, unable to say anything in response; until James broke into her trance.

"And now, my dear," he said in a jovial manner while raising Emily to her feet. "Let us snap out of this nostalgia, and put on our practical hats. We have a wedding to plan!"

CHAPTER FIVE

Emily and James chose a date one month ahead for their wedding. That way, their families and friends would have time to get used to the idea of a marriage between them.

There was also the consideration of their two houses: which would be sold and which they would call home. After all, as James pointed out, they could not keep them both on the go when they were living as man and wife.

But first, Emily insisted, they urgently needed to book a celebrant for their wedding ceremony. The issue of where they will live could wait.

"We could always get married in the local registry office," James quipped.

Emily, however, took his suggestion seriously.

"Oh James, that would be much too impersonal! If you don't mind, I would prefer to have a quiet ceremony somewhere local; conducted by a clergyman, not a Justice of the Peace...and if possible," she added with haste; "somebody known to one or both of us."

James capitulated, realising it would be better not to push the fact that he was joking about the registry office.

"Alright, you win. I assume you don't want too much of a fuss, though; just a few friends and family."

"I don't want any fuss at all! One big wedding is enough for me, and I had that the first time around. No, what seems appropriate this time is to hold it in your house, or mine. Or, if it's sunny we could be married in the garden.

The rose bed here is at its best just now. It should make a wonderful backdrop. I know Arthur would be happy for me to show it off."

"That sounds nice. There's one slight snag, though. Not being a churchgoer, I have had too little contact with the clergy to be able to ask anyone to marry us. It would be a bit of a cheek if I were to phone the minister of Janet's old church and asked him to perform the ceremony, when I haven't set foot in the place since my boy was married years back. ...And, from what I know, you don't go to church, either."

"That's not a problem," said Emily with a satisfied look on her face. "I know somebody who would be perfect, and will no doubt be only too happy to do the honours."

A warm glow ushered in the memory of the Reverend Bill Marriott's declaration of friendship towards her. With great affection she told James about him and, laughing, described the rude woman who shattered their intimate conversation in the coffee shop.

Emily was pleased she could laugh about that now. At the time, when Arthur's ethereal visits were still a source of confusion, to clarify the matter with her confidante had taken on a sense of urgency, and she fretted that the opportunity was snatched from her.

But now, with the passing of time, she felt more at ease about petitioning Reverend Marriott's support once more.

...And that reminded her: she still had not followed up on the topic of Arthur.

Perhaps her enquiry about a convenient date for the wedding would provide an ideal opportunity to bring it up with him.

"Yes," she affirmed with a nod, "I think the Reverend Bill Marriott would be a good choice."

119

As soon as James left the house that day, Emily called the number she had transferred from the Reverend's business card into her 'frequently used numbers'.

On phoning, she made an appointment to meet with him at the Vicarage later in the week. That done, she sat down to contemplate how best to approach the subject of their impending marriage – not only with Bill Marriott, but more directly, with the members of her own family.

Emily chose to tell Ruth first; although the decision was partly made for her when Ruth rang during the evening, both with a progress report on Wilbur and to invite Emily over to see her the following day.

"Our Thursdays seem to have lapsed recently," she said. "I wondered if you would like to come for a visit tomorrow if you're not busy. ...Or is it too short notice?"

"No, it's not short notice; and I'd love to," replied Emily, both relieved and apprehensive now that the moment of truth was almost at hand. Then she added, "...As a matter of fact, I want to talk to you about something, so it would suit me fine to come over tomorrow. Are you sure Wilbur is up to a visitor?"

"...Oh, yes. My amazing husband is making remarkable progress. I almost need to tie him down! He's so eager to get back into the swing of things that I have to remind him he is still only a little way down the road to recovery. But I'm sure he'll be very pleased to see you."

Emily dressed prettily for her long journey across town the next morning.

Her night had been restful, if somewhat sleepless: a mixture of joy and anxiety; with images of perfect wedded bliss alternating with memories of domestic dramas. At one point during the early hours her imaginings took on a negative aspect, and she almost convinced herself that she

120

was just a foolish old woman to think of marrying again; that she didn't know what she was letting herself in for and should call the whole thing off. But by the time dawn broke, after an hour or two of much-needed slumber, she awoke with a renewed feeling of confidence that she had made the right decision.

The sun shone warmly through the bus window. Had Emily been able to see her reflection in the glass she would have noticed a radiance about her, which gave her the same youthful glow commented upon by Bill Marriott.

Emily briskly walked the short distance from the bus stop to Ruth's home.

Feeling stiff after the double bus ride, she both benefited from the exercise and took the opportunity to gather her thoughts ready for the revelation.

Ruth embraced her tenderly. She took Emily's coat, hung it up and led Emily through to the lounge.

"Come and see Wilbur," she said. "I think you'll notice a big difference in him."

Wilbur sat reading in his wing-backed leather chair; a gift from Ruth the Christmas before last.

When Emily entered the room, he made to stand but she raised her hand to stop him, saying, "Please don't get up;" at which Wilbur gratefully relaxed back in the chair.

"You're looking really well, Wilbur," Emily told him with sincerity. "Ruth's nursing is paying dividends."

"Thank you Emily – from both of us. And you're looking pretty good yourself. ...Isn't she, Ruth?"

"I'll say! You're like the cat that's got the cream. What's responsible for it, Mum?" Ruth asked her teasingly.

Emily's eyes sparkled. "Well, there is something I would like to tell you. ...But not just yet; maybe later on."

"That sounds intriguing!" laughed Wilbur.

Emily enjoyed her daughter's company that morning.

The atmosphere in the house had changed since she was last with Ruth and Wilbur, during the awful week when her phone wires were cut. At that time, Wilbur was still sick and Ruth under a lot of strain. But now everything seemed to be alright again: Wilbur was recovering, Ruth in remarkably good spirits, and she...

Well, thought Emily; just now I could not feel any better about my life if I tried.

Shortly after lunch, Wilbur began to display early signs of weariness.

"We must have worn you out with all our gossiping," said Emily in fun. "Why don't you go and have a rest?"

"Yes, Wilbur," Ruth put in. "Remember what the doctor said — you still need plenty of rest. A little nap would do you the world of good."

"You women; you're always treating me like an invalid; and in my own home, too!"

Yet, Wilbur's protest was made only on principle. In fact he was glad to escape the female chatter, and agreeably retired to his room for a couple of hours' sleep.

"Now then, Mum," said Ruth after he had gone. "What do you want to tell me?"

Emily's heart skipped a beat; she had almost forgotten the purpose of her visit.

She grinned at Ruth sheepishly, as though she had been asked to make a confession. But she was enjoying herself so much in the happy home of her favourite daughter, she was sure her news about James and their engagement would receive a good response.

"I've met a man," she said without any hesitation. "He's a kindly man, who has been something of a saviour to me over the last few months. He's asked me to marry him..."

"...To marry him?" cried Ruth, at once bemused. "How quaint; what a delightful picture that conjures up: two old people getting married! I can imagine his disappointment when you declined his proposal. ...You did decline it, didn't you, Mum?"

Emily hesitated. Something about Ruth's cagey reaction troubled her.

"I did at first," she said cautiously. "...At least, I thought long and hard about it."

"I should think you did!" said Ruth, with a little more intensity. She eyed her mother curiously. "...And then you said 'no'. Is that right?"

Intimidated, Emily got up from her chair and looked out of the window; less certain of her daughter's support than she was a moment ago.

"You want me to be happy in my old age, don't you?"

"Yes, Mum. Of course I do; but aren't you happy in your circumstances nowadays? You've never given an indication to the contrary."

Emily turned to face her and took a deep breath for strength. Then she warily asked, "Ruth, can you honestly state that you have always been open with me..?"

Ruth looked away; not knowing how to answer.

"...Take Wilbur, for instance. During his illness you gave me the impression you were coping admirably. As a result I assumed you were. But I don't know for sure, because you didn't discuss it with me."

Ruth sprung to her own defence. She didn't like the way the pleasant chat with her mother was developing into something serious.

"I didn't need to, Mum," she said. "Things weren't all that bad, and we're managing alright now. I didn't discuss it with you because I didn't want to burden you with my worries; after all, you were still getting over the loss of

123

your husband. Besides, Wilbur's illness was our problem, not yours. It was up to us to work out how we would handle it. ...Anyway, what does this have to do with your friend's marriage proposal?"

"Nothing...and everything."

Emily sat back down and faced Ruth squarely.

"It has nothing to do with it, because this will be a very happy occasion rather than the melancholy our family has experienced lately. And it has everything, because just as you have not discussed your problems with me so, to a certain extent, have I not been open with you about my..."

"...Oh, Mother! You must tell me if something is wrong! All those times you came here, you seemed to be pleased for the diversion. You never mentioned you were lonely."

"What makes you think I'm lonely?"

"Isn't that the case?"

"No! I haven't been lonely; at least, not recently. Maybe I was at first...after the trauma of your father's passing. It did take me a while to get used to the fact that he wasn't there anymore; that he wouldn't be by my side when I awoke, or waiting with a cup of tea when I returned from town. But the loneliness just disappeared when I realised he isn't really dead..."

Emily broke off suddenly; fearing she had deviated from her topic and revealed more than she should.

"What do you mean, he isn't really dead?" asked Ruth casually, not sensing for a minute that her mother meant the remark literally.

"Don't you believe in life after death?" asked Emily in an attempt to cover up her indiscretion.

"Yes, of course. ...And I assume you mean that Dad is up there waiting for you."

"Well...something like that."

Emily breathed a sigh of relief. Her secret was still safe.

To get back to the subject of James, she added hastily, "It wasn't that I was lonely, but more that I found it hard to cope with everything by myself. Practical things – like all the jobs your father used to take care of. Having James around has been of great help to me."

"That's not a basis for marriage, though; surely!"

"Not on its own. But I'm very fond of him as well. I'd even go so far as to say I love him…"

"…Mother! Whatever are you saying?" exclaimed Ruth. "…And what would Dad think if he heard you talking like that? I can't believe this of you!"

Emily forlornly withdrew into her own thoughts. …If only she could tell her children that Arthur had already given his blessing for her betrothal to James. It would explain so much that Ruth seemed unable to understand.

"Please don't judge me too harshly," she said; a feeling of despair creeping over her. "I chose to accept only after a great deal of deliberation."

"So you've already decided to marry him?"

Emily nodded.

"Does he know?"

"Yes. I told him yesterday. We've planned our wedding ceremony for next month. Oh. Ruth! It would mean so much if you could be happy for us! He's a lovely man; I know you will like him."

"That's not the point. He would be taking Dad's place; probably living in his house and sleeping in his bed. Oh, no! I can't come to terms with that, Mother."

Ruth shuddered at the thought.

"James won't be replacing your father, Ruth. Let's face it; nobody could ever replace your father! There's always been something very special between Arthur and me that will follow me to the grave – and beyond! This man – and I don't want to sound callous in saying it – will be something of a stopgap: a companion in my last years until Dad and I can be together again. Is that so terrible?"

"So you're using him?"

"No!" Emily was getting angry now. "Ruth, you're not even trying to understand! If I can see it from your point of view, why can't you try and see it from mine? James and I are just two widowed people who would like to spend our few remaining years together…for companionship! That's not 'using' somebody! I'm sorry, Ruth, but I'm saddened by your reaction. I expected more from you."

Emily indignantly stood up, intending to leave. The tenor of the visit had deteriorated; it had not gone as hoped. Rather than remain in the company of someone who was obviously against her union in marriage, she now wanted to wash her hands of the whole discussion, and get on home.

Ruth tried to stop her.

"Mother, don't be hasty. Please!"

"I won't stay if you're going to adopt this unsupportive attitude. I really thought you would be happy for me."

Emily retrieved her coat and slipped it on.

"But I am happy for you," insisted Ruth.

"You've got a funny way of showing it."

"Please don't go. …Not like this."

"I'm not staying, Ruth. You obviously disapprove of my marriage to James. I had hoped for your support, but…"

"…I do want you to be happy, Mother…but not at the expense of Dad's memory. Can't you understand that?"

"As I said before, I can see your point of view. I know how you girls might feel about James filling your father's shoes. But remember: I'm not trying to inflict a stepfather on you; that's something I wouldn't do. I am just bringing a new companion into my own life. Heaven's above, girl, you should be pleased! You won't have to be concerned about me anymore!"

"I suppose you're right..."

Ruth conceded the point without conviction.

"...And wait until you meet him! I'm sure once you get to know him you'll be convinced we made the right decision. ...Ruth, be happy for me, please!"

"Alright, Mother...I'll be happy for you," laughed Ruth, realising she was defeated. "I won't be particularly happy for myself, but I will be for you!"

Relieved that the matter was settled, Emily gave her a heartfelt hug.

"Thank you, Ruth," she said. "I really appreciate that. You will like him; I know you will. And now, I think I'll go. Say goodbye to Wilbur for me."

Emily made to leave, prompting Ruth to follow her out.

"Where are you going?"

"...To catch the bus."

"Of course you're not! I'll run you home in the car."

"No dear. Not today. Wilbur will wonder where you've gone when he wakes up. I'll get the bus – it'll give me a chance to do some thinking."

"Are you sure? It's an awful long way."

"Yes, I'm sure. ...And it's not all that far. ...Really!"

"Alright – if you don't mind another double bus ride."

"Think no more of it."

With a sense of relief, Emily settled into her seat on the bus; her mind still reeling from the session with Ruth. Far from leaving her house in the state of contentment she at first envisaged, she had come away feeling drained.

In the city centre Emily changed buses without thinking, and on the way back to her own suburb was oblivious of anything happening along the way. Even a nose-to-tail car

127

accident at the traffic lights failed to arouse her natural concern for those involved; for her thoughts had remained entrenched in her own problems.

When she arrived home she phoned James and told him about Ruth's response.

"Well, I suppose we've got to expect some resistance," he said. "After all, it's not all that long since our spouses passed on. Some might say not enough time has elapsed for families to accept such a liaison. But I don't want you to worry about it. They'll get used to the idea in time."

"Are you going to tell your son?" asked Emily.

"I already have."

"...Really? That was quick. Did you ring him?"

"Yes. Last night. I thought it best to get it over with."

"And what was his reaction?"

"Naturally he was surprised – and a bit concerned that I saw the need to remarry so soon. But he didn't seem to mind. In fact, he wished us the best of luck and asked me to pass on his regards to you. He said he hopes he will be able to meet you one day."

"That's nice. He sounds a decent sort of fellow."

"Yes; I think so, too. At least, he was when I last had anything to do with him and his family; which is five or so years ago now. I don't suppose he's changed all that much since then."

"You're lucky you had no opposition from your side of the family. Mine, I suspect, is going to be a problem."

"Ruth rallied in the end, didn't she?"

"Yes – eventually. But Ruth wasn't my main concern. I had expected support from her and was disappointed that it wasn't spontaneous, but I was never afraid she might try and put a spanner in the works. Fiona's reaction, though, could be another matter entirely."

"Why do you say that?"

Emily hesitated while she decided how best to answer him. Should she tell him everything she previously omitted from their conversations, or just the basics...?

"Fiona's been having a few problems lately," she said at length. "My son-in-law, Royston, left her some weeks ago and Fiona hasn't settled down. I'm uneasy at the prospect of telling her about our marriage, and might put it off for a while yet."

But later on Emily changed her mind. Delay in advising her could result in Fiona learning about it from Ruth. And that, Emily conceded, would be far worse than having to tell her face-to-face.

The next day she was due to see Reverend Marriott with a view to setting a date for the ceremony. Like it or not, Emily realised, she had no choice but to make sure all her family had been informed beforehand. So, shortly after tea, she nervously rang Fiona and arranged to call round the following morning.

After another night of fitful sleep, Emily brushed aside her anxiousness in an attempt to focus on the task ahead.

Rather than take a taxi, which would have whisked her to Fiona's in only a few minutes, she caught a bus to the local shopping centre and walked the extra distance.

Although puffed on the final stretch, the exercise as usual enlivened her. With a clear head, and precisely what she wanted to say well-rehearsed in her thoughts, she confidently approached the house.

Kristine saw her coming. She rushed to the door to let her in, and gave her a hug; almost bowling Emily over.

"...Careful, love. You nearly knocked me off my feet!"

"Sorry Nana. I guess I was just relieved to see you."

Emily took off her coat and asked, "How's Mum today? ...In reasonably good spirits?"

"Not bad – for Mum. She's planning a little holiday, so she's got something to look forward to."

"That's lovely. I hope it helps her to relax."

Kristine shouted out to her mother in the back garden, "Nana's here to see you!"

All at once, Emily felt uneasy; the moment of dread at hand. But her anxiousness subsided slightly when she heard Fiona's cheery reply.

"Okay...won't be a minute," Fiona called, and moments later appeared in the kitchen, briskly rubbing her hands together. "Gee, that wind's cold," she said. "Hello, Mother. Go on into the lounge, and we'll have a coffee."

Well, Fiona sounds quite chirpy, thought Emily. That's a good sign.

"I'm glad you decided to come," said Fiona after filling the kettle. "I've got something to tell you."

"Oh! So have I..." began Emily; but before she could finish off her sentence, Fiona continued.

"...It's really exciting. Kristine, will you make the coffee so I can let Nana in on our little surprise?"

While Kristine half-heartedly obeyed her mother, Fiona sat down opposite Emily.

"Guess what?" she said impishly, not in the least bit interested in finding out why Emily had called in.

Emily began to feel irritated. She had come to impart her own news, not to play guessing games with Fiona.

"I've got no idea. You'll have to tell me," she replied with marked disinterest.

"Kristine and I are going on holiday!"

"Oh! ...Kristine, too?" remarked Emily. "That will make a nice change for you both."

"Yes. A friend of mine from the coast has to go away on a business trip for a couple of weeks, and he has offered his house to us. We leave at the end of next month. Isn't that brilliant? It's been ages since we've seen the sea; paddled in the surf and breathed in all that fresh air. Can't you just smell it already?"

Fiona leaned back in her chair with a satisfied look on her face, hardly aware of Emily's presence, let alone the fact that Emily was there for a reason of her own.

Despite her carefully rehearsed speech, Emily could now see that advising Fiona of her forthcoming marriage would be even more difficult than previously thought.

"What do you think then, Mother? Aren't we the lucky ones? We'll have a whole beach-house to ourselves!"

"Yes dear. I'm sure a holiday by the sea will do you the world of good."

She smiled at Kristine who was placing the coffee mugs on the table.

"Thank you, dear," she said, with little response.

"I've told Nana about our holiday," said Fiona.

"I know. I heard," was the mechanical reply as she sat on the spare chair.

Emily looked at Kristine. She did not seem enthusiastic.

"Are you looking forward to it, Kristine?" she asked to test the girl's reaction.

"I suppose so."

"What do you mean by that?" exclaimed Fiona in good humour. "Of course you're looking forward to a holiday by the sea. ...Who wouldn't?"

Emily's eyes were still riveted on Kristine. Her face held an expression of resignation, revealing to Emily that in going on holiday with her mother she was being forced to do something she didn't really want to do.

As she glanced back at Emily, Kristine raised her eyes skywards and grimaced, confirming Emily's suspicions. But then, in the same glance, Kristine's face suddenly lit up, and she shot her mother a look.

"Mum! Why don't we ask Nana if she would like to go with us?" she asked excitedly.

Fiona squirmed in her seat; as did Emily. Kristine's idea was something neither of them wanted.

Each, in their own way, said, "Oh, I don't know..."

Fiona jumped to her feet and began pacing the floor, as though giving the suggestion some thought.

"...But it's only a two bedroom house," she insisted. "If three of us stayed there we would be very cramped."

Then, to reinforce Fiona's stance, Emily said, "I won't be able to go away; I've got something planned, too."

Fiona missed Emily's remark. She was too busy thinking up more excuses why her mother could not go with them.

However, Kristine, sensitive to her Nana's every word, took note of the comment and asked, "What have you got planned, Nana?"

Emily looked up and said, "That's why I came over here today: to tell you about something rather wonderful..." Then, when she realised she now had the attention of both her granddaughter and her daughter, she quickly added, "Fiona, dear...you'd better sit down for what I'm about to tell you."

"Oh, Mother; don't be melodramatic," said Fiona; still in a light-hearted mood as she perched sideways on her chair. "What's this all about, then?"

Emily braced herself, for the moment of revelation had arrived once again. With a deep breath for composure she began her prepared speech.

"Fiona... Kristine..." she said, looking at each in turn. "What I'm about to tell you will come as a bit of a shock; in fact, it will come as a great big shock. But nevertheless I have to say it."

"Whatever are you talking about?" asked Fiona with impatient curiosity.

"Shush, Mum," chided Kristine, fascinated by Emily's air of mystery. "Go on Nana; we're listening."

"Approximately one month from now..."

Emily paused as the two pairs of eyes bore down on her. Then, with her heart sitting precariously in her mouth, she continued with her dissertation.

"...In a month's time...I will be getting married again."

A lingering silence ensued; although it was actually only a couple of seconds before Kristine broke into it.

"Nana, did I hear right – you're getting married?"

"Yes, Kristine, you heard right."

"You must be under some kind of misconception here, Mother," said Fiona cautiously. "You've been letting your imagination run away with you again. ...Or watching too many soap operas. How can you possibly get married? For one thing, you're too old and for another...you have to have somebody to get married to! Please stop this absurd charade...it's embarrassing."

"I assure you this is no charade. Neither is it an over-active imagination. It's the truth. I repeat: in one month's time I will be getting married – to a wonderful man by the name of James Forsythe; someone I met a while ago and have since taken to my heart. I accepted his proposal only recently. Ruth knows about it, and has given her blessing; as has your fa... Um...James' family."

"...But what about Grandpa? What would he say if he were here?" asked Kristine without thinking.

Emily laughed.

"If Grandpa was still here I wouldn't want to remarry!"

Kristine's cheeks turned red as she realised her blunder. "Oh Nana; you know what I mean!" she said.

"Yes, Kristine; I do know what you mean. And I promise you that if Grandpa were here to tell you in person, he would assure you both that he consents to our marriage. Have no fear of that."

"Personally, I think it's disgusting," said Fiona, pulling a face. "It's positively demeaning, Mum. ...To think that my mother is taking on a new husband at the age of – what are you now; seventy-two?"

"Seventy-one, actually. But I am only an old woman in your eyes, Fiona. Through my eyes and, I believe, through the eyes of Kristine here, I am not old. I am still a person who is very much alive, still in need of companionship, and not too old to fall in love all over again. And, Fiona, I might add that the qualities which attracted me to James are the same ones which made me fall in love with your father all those years ago..."

Throughout the explanation, Fiona listened animatedly; appalled by the plan being laid out before her.

The little bombshell Emily dropped on her and Kristine had burst her own bubble of happiness about the holiday. She resented the incursion into her surprise, and the upset her mother's announcement inflicted on her household; so much so, that when Emily compared James with her own father, Fiona's displeasure erupted.

"...Mother, stop it this minute!" she shouted, cutting Emily off mid- sentence. "I won't hear any more of it. You are letting me down – and Kristine too. Do you realise that? ...And I for one won't be a party to something I don't agree with."

"Well, I think you're being mean!" shrieked Kristine at her mother.

Kristine had sat quietly throughout the discussion; taking in everything that was being said and trying to grasp the reality of this new situation.

134

True, she was not happy that her beloved grandmother was marrying again. So far she, Kristine, had been the principle companion in her Nana's life since Grandpa died; a relationship she had enjoyed enormously. Emily had been her confidante, welcoming her openly into her home and into her comforting arms whenever the need of sanctuary overwhelmed her. If Nana married again, that would all change. She would have nowhere to go; nobody to talk to. And Nana's need of her would change, too.

As the conversation had progressed, these thoughts, which were not so much conscious in their substance but more like undercurrents of feeling, gradually surfaced; and when Kristine opened her mouth in defiance against her mother, they exploded with such a force that she sprang to her feet and turned on Fiona out of sheer frustration.

"Mum, you're only thinking of yourself!" Kristine went on, still not consciously aware that she had been doing exactly the same thing.

"Now, you two... Please don't fight over it," Emily cried out, in a vain attempt to calm them both down. "Be angry with me if you have to, but not with each other. ...Please!"

Kristine's outburst subsided; her emotion spent.

She gazed forlornly out of the window with her back towards the other two.

Emily addressed her.

"Kristine, how do you feel about all of this?"

Slowly Kristine turned around and self-consciously looked at her, as if the elderly person sitting in front of her was no longer Emily but a stranger who had asked a personal question.

"I can't say I'm happy you're getting married again. I mean... I want you to be happy, Nana, and if marrying this man is the answer for you, then I'll have to support you. But I feel... I think...

"I believe I know what you're trying to say."

Emily felt only compassion for the girl who was trying to be magnanimous.

"Are you concerned that it might affect the relationship between you and me?" she asked.

"Well... Yes," Kristine answered awkwardly. "Oh, Nana! That sounds so selfish of me. Now I'm the one who's only thinking of herself!"

"Of course you're not, love," said Emily, struggling to get out of her chair.

She walked up to a girl who was clearly bewildered by conflicting feelings. Between comforting palms she held the worried face now on the verge of tears; then looked with compassion into her eyes: always an indication to Kristine of Emily's sincerity.

"Let me assure you now, Kristine, that when James and I marry, you and your mother, and your aunt will be just as welcome to call on us, or should I say, on me, as you have always been. And if it's a little bit of company you need from your old Nana, you can be sure of a private chat."

Suddenly a thought occurred to Kristine.

"Nana, where will you be living?" she asked.

"I don't know, yet. We haven't got around to deciding on that side of things. If we move into James's house it will be about the same distance from here as my house."

Kristine purposefully shook her head.

"No...that wouldn't be the same as going to your house. I'd feel like a stranger..."

"...Only if you allow yourself to. Anyway, as I said, we haven't yet decided where we are going to live."

"You needn't think you're going to bring him round her," said Fiona who was listening to their conversation with a frown on her face. "I'm not having some strange old man in my home."

Kristine looked furiously at her mother. But before she could comment Emily, immune now to Fiona's rudeness, cut in with her own retort.

"I wouldn't dream of bringing him here – or anywhere else he was not welcome. ...Although, I'm quite sure that everyone he meets, with the apparent exception of you Fiona, will warm to him instantly. He's a very likeable man. That's why I like him. But if you don't want to meet him... Well...it will be up to you, Fiona."

Emily turned and walked to the door.

"And now I'm going," she said. "I've given you enough to think about for one day. Besides, I have an appointment with the vicar to arrange a date for our....

"...The vicar!" interrupted Fiona. She followed Emily into the hallway. "What are you talking about now? Surely you're not thinking of getting married in a church! ...And don't you mean a priest? We are all Catholics, you know; or had you forgotten?"

"The Reverend Bill Marriott is the vicar of St Aiden's Anglican Church, and is a very good friend of mine. I will be asking him to officiate at a ceremony...probably in our own home. Does that answer your question? I'll let you know when it will be. Goodbye, Fiona. ...Bye-bye, Kristine!" she called back into the room. "Come round and see me soon, love. I think we need to talk some more."

Then, without waiting for a response from either, she walked out into the sunshine and closed the door firmly behind her.

CHAPTER SIX

Emily felt elated. For the very first time, she was sure she had the upper hand over Fiona.

At long last, her overbearing daughter's cruel remarks washed right over her; leaving in their wake a calmness bordering on ecstasy.

While she walked the distance to the vicarage, Emily's heart was full of laughter. Why she saw the funny side of it she could only guess. Kristine had been quite put out by her announcement, and the last thing she had wanted to do was upset the girl; yet, still she saw no cause for concern. Emily felt sure that in time Kristine would come round to accepting their marriage. But as for Fiona...

She sighed and then paused in her brisk striding in order to catch her breath.

...As for dear, irrepressible Fiona; it was possible she would never come to terms with the source of her mother's newfound happiness.

But Emily did not care. Fiona's opinion on the matter was unimportant to her. Whether she offered her support or not, whether she went to the wedding or not, were all considerations which would once have haunted Emily and given her no peace until they had been resolved. ...But not now. Let Fiona rant and rave, she quietly declared. Let the older of her twins behave as though she had been born of some other stock, and treat her mother with contempt. Never again would Emily allow herself to be intimidated by her. Fiona had built her own nest; now she could feather it in whatever way she pleased. It was no longer of concern.

With glee, she realised that Fiona and her selfish ways were once and for all out of her system.

A militant sparkle lit her eye as she said hello to the vicar. Many changes had taken place since Emily and Bill last sat down together; changes which she would now be pleased to tell him about...

"How is life treating you nowadays?" asked Reverend Marriott in his usual manner; demonstrating to Emily that, despite the efficiency of the local grapevine, he knew nothing about the goings on in her life.

"Life is treating me very well at the moment," Emily replied as he escorted her into the vicarage.

She looked around. It was a simply adorned house, and the décor of the room into which he led her reflected its purpose: to interview rather than entertain. A plain desk topped with old-fashioned dark green leather was placed centrally in the room. Behind it stood a large swivel chair upholstered in the same dark green leather. And apart from some other items of unimposing furniture, together with a large oil painting with a religious flavour almost filling the wall on which it hung, Reverend Marriott's study contained little to distract his visitor.

The vicar lifted up a straight-backed chair from a row of chairs placed conveniently at the side of the room in case a group of people came to see him.

He stood the chair directly in front of his desk, where he could get a clear view of Emily sitting before him. Then, after motioning her to sit down, he went round the desk to sit in his own chair.

"I must say, Emily," he said earnestly. "The sparkle in your eye really gets to me. Many of my parishioners would give all their worldly goods to possess such radiance. How do you do it?"

"Well, if you will give me half a chance, I'll tell you!" said Emily, laughing.

Just then a thought came to her. She turned her head to check if the door was still open, and was pleased to discover that her confidante had shut it behind him when they came in. Their conversation, then, would be private.

Nobody's going to interrupt me this time, she declared in secret.

In triumph she turned back to him, and settled in her seat ready for meaningful banter, which she hoped would prepare the way for her exciting news.

"I'm sorry I haven't been in touch with you recently," said Bill, oblivious of her thoughts. "At first I just didn't seem to have the opportunity to ring you. Then a couple of times I tried, but got no answer. In the end, I assumed that if you wanted to talk urgently enough you would contact me. Obviously you still do, as here you are!"

"Yes, I do still want to talk to you – but for a different reason. After our chat I wanted to explain about Arthur's visitations. I knew I wasn't imagining his presence – and I knew I could discuss it openly with you. It was important to me back then to hear your opinion. ...After all, not every widow can hold a conversation with her dead husband! ...But it's different, now."

"In what way? Doesn't Arthur visit you anymore?"

"Oh yes! Well...actually, no. Dear me, now I'm confusing you," Emily conceded; feeling flustered.

Bill Marriott laughed. "Maybe I'm just a little confused. Emily, do tell me what you mean."

"Yes; I'm so sorry; I'll start again... For a while Arthur's presence was a source of real inspiration and support. He was the difference between my sinking and swimming, so to speak. Knowing he was there had the same effect on me as you might feel when in the presence of Jesus. It was wonderful. And Arthur was always there when I needed his guidance."

"You say, 'was'. Does that mean he's gone away now?"

"Yes…and no. He's gone away for the time being…but for a very special reason. Not because we've drawn apart, but because…"

Emily hesitated. It was the third time in only a couple of days that she had been faced with this: the prospect of selecting the words to tell of her impending marriage.

"…Because what, Emily?"

In order to explain properly to Bill Marriott about how she met and fell in love with another man, without invoking the same reaction that she received from the family, she would have to go back to the beginning of her relationship with James Forsythe.

Starting from her very first encounter with him, Emily recounted to the Reverend Marriott everything that had happened; both in actual occurrence and in the depths of her heart.

She spoke briefly and to the point; he listened intently, formulating not an opinion of the information she gave him, but an understanding.

As she progressed in her story he began to smile, until when she told him she had actually accepted a proposal of marriage, he broke out in a loud cheer.

"Good for you, Emily!" he cried. "My dear; let me be the first to congratulate you!"

"Well, thank you," Emily replied in good humour, and then a thought occurred to her. "Now I come to think of it, though, you really are the first to offer me congratulations. Everyone else I've told has given me all sorts of reasons why I shouldn't be marrying again. It's nice to feel that I have an ally at last."

"Emily, I do believe this warrants a little celebration, don't you?"

Reverend Marriott stood up, pushed back his chair, and walked over to one of the pieces of unimposing furniture. He pulled out a key from his pocket; then unlocked the cupboard door.

Inside were shelves untidily stacked with books, files and loose papers; except for one shelf that contained an assortment of beverages and drinking glasses. He noticed Emily's astonished expression when she saw them, and laughed at her reaction.

"Don't worry," he assured her. "I'm not one of those closet dipsomaniacs. These bottles are gifts from grateful parishioners, and are mostly unopened; waiting, I suppose, for a special reason to sample their contents. ...And I can't think of a better reason than this, can you?"

He pulled out a couple of bottles: one of sherry, the other of brandy.

"Which do you fancy? Or..." he added, reaching further into the shelf, "...there's some apricot liqueur, half a bottle of Vodka, and even a couple of beers; though I can't imagine who would have given me those!"

He turned to Emily with an impish look on his face.

Emily was laughing uncontrollably by now, thoroughly enjoying herself in his presence. "Bill," she said, "I suspect you may missed your true vocation. You should have been a hotel barman!"

"You're probably right. Barmen are great at listening to people's troubles, too! ...Anyway: sherry or brandy?"

"Um...sherry, I think. Only a drop, though! I feel tiddly enough as it is; just on your company!"

While Bill poured out two glasses of sherry, Emily sat back contentedly in his presence.

It was inconceivable, now, to think that only an hour ago she was in an atmosphere so demoralising that she would once have taken days to recover from it...yet here she was, sharing a toast with Bill Marriott; enthusiastically chinking her glass against his in joyful celebration of her forthcoming marriage, with all thoughts of Fiona and her misgivings forgotten.

Was it thanks to Bill for his friendship, to James for the anticipation of a life no longer alone, or to Arthur for his reassurance? Whichever of the three men in her life had given her the strength to forge ahead, she would probably never know.

"Tell me," asked Bill after his first sip of sherry. "Have you set a date for your wedding?"

"Not yet. ...And that's the main reason I came to see you: to ask if you would do the honour of marrying us in about a month's time."

"Emily, the honour is all mine – and it will be a pleasure, too. Would you like to fix a date now?"

"Yes, please."

He took out a large diary from the side drawer of his desk, opened it at the place marked by a length of narrow braid; then flipped ahead several pages.

"Now, let me see... One month from... Let's say... This Saturday... How does that sound?"

"Yes, a Saturday would be fine. James has given me free rein on choosing the date."

"That makes it the 17th of next month," he said, taking out a pen from the desk drawer.

Then, with the pen poised above the page, he added, "Right...when and where would you like the wedding to take place?"

143

"I thought we might have the ceremony at home rather than in a church – probably my house. ...If that fits in with your schedule?"

"Yes, of course!"

"Then what about mid-day? Would you be available at that time?"

"Yes. It seems I'm free all day, actually."

"Good. Then you'll also stay for our little get-together afterwards?"

Reverend Marriott looked up from writing in his diary. He flashed Emily a beaming smile.

"You bet I'll stay. I wouldn't miss it for the world! Tell me again, what's the name of this chap you're marrying?"

"James...James Forsythe."

"Forsythe... James Forsythe." Bill scratched his head as though thinking hard. "Now, where have I come across that name before?"

"He's a local man...has lived here for years."

"The only Forsythe I recall was in the police force; Chief Constable, or something. ...Many years ago now."

"Yes. That's him!"

"Well, Emily Thompson. He must be pretty special to be accepted in marriage by you."

Reverend Marriott wrote in his diary again, and then sat back, a thought having occurred to him.

"Emily," he said. "You mentioned earlier that Arthur no longer connects with you – at least, you implied it. Now you've told me that you are remarrying, I'm concerned as to why he has backed away. Is it because he disapproves of the marriage?"

"No, quite the reverse!" said Emily, alarmed at the idea. "In fact, Arthur encouraged our friendship. He gave me his blessing to marry James. It was lovely, what he said."

"What was that?"

144

"He said he realised my marriage to James would help me fill in the time until he and I could be together again."

Suddenly Emily chuckled.

"It still seems funny: my talking about Arthur as being alive, but also deceased."

"I see what you mean. Tell me, though. What makes you think he has gone away? After all, he's just given you his blessing, hasn't he?"

"Oh! That was only because, as he put it, he didn't want to be like a 'peeping tom' on our marriage. ...He is still there...and yet at the same time, he's not. Does that make any sense?"

"I think so. I must admit, though, I have never before come across a situation like this; but certainly I accept what you're telling me."

"Bill, you've got no idea what it means to me, hearing you say that. Just lately, I've wondered if I should question my own sanity– talking to a dead husband, getting married again at my stage in life. I seem to be going against the norm in everything I do. It's reassuring to know that I'm not going senile. ...And as far as I am concerned, Bill; if you think I'm still sane, then I believe it to be so."

Reverend Marriott leant across the desk, took her hand in his and said, "If more people were as sane as you, Emily, the world would be a much happier place."

The weeks that followed proved hectic for Emily and her fiancé; nevertheless, Emily now felt free to make her plans without the weight family disapproval.

Just the one person brought a twinge to her heart when she gave it thought: Kristine; and the only way to alleviate that problem, Emily decided, was for her to meet James and hopefully get to like him.

Kristine, though, had other thoughts on the matter.

145

When Emily asked her to have lunch with them one Sunday, Kristine declined outright, stating that she was too busy. But Emily, who knew Kristine better than anybody, instantly saw through the excuse; and far from accepting Kristine's refusal, told her outright to show some courtesy and meet the man her grandmother would be marrying.

"It's funny," said James as he and Emily peered through the curtains, waiting for Kristine to arrive. "I expected to feel nervous about meeting the twins, from what you have told me, but in fact it is the prospect of meeting Kristine that I find daunting. Maybe it's because she's so important to you; or because she regards me as an obstruction to the relationship she has with you."

"Then it's up to me to set both of your minds at rest," said Emily in reply; yet she was unsure how she would be able to achieve it.

When Kristine eventually turned up, it was James who happened to notice her. Having seen a stain on her blouse, Emily had slipped upstairs to change it and knew nothing of her arrival.

At first James was unsure the girl on the bright red ten-speed was Emily's granddaughter. It seemed, to the man watching from the window, that she was cycling straight past; yet at the last minute she swerved into the driveway, only to disappear down the side of the house. ...And that was a few minutes ago.

Assuming the rider must have been Kristine, he called up to Emily that she had arrived.

"...At least, I think it's Kristine," he muttered to himself as the seconds ticked by and Emily, still rummaging in her wardrobe for a suitable blouse, had not reappeared.

Then, when neither of them materialised, James decided to take the initiative, and slipped outside to see what had happened to the girl and her red bike.

He found Kristine sitting on a low stone wall; unaware that her arrival had been witnessed.

As James appeared from the front of the house, Kristine saw him and sprang defensively to her feet.

"You must be Kristine," said James, taken aback by her obvious alarm. "...I saw you from the window."

"Where's Nana?" asked Kristine, and then realised that she must have sounded very rude.

"Your grandmother is upstairs. She won't be a minute. I'm James Forsythe, by the way."

He stepped forward in order to shake her hand.

Instinctively, Kristine volunteered hers in response, but then withdrew it sharply when she heard Emily calling from the house, "James, are you out there?"

"Nana's calling you," said Kristine, and brushed past him. "I'll let her know I'm here."

Oh dear, thought James. That wasn't a very good start.

As the lunch progressed, it became apparent that Kristine was digging her heels in about opening up to James, let alone accepting him.

In fact, she had decided from the moment she found out about Emily's impending marriage that she was not going to accept it; that life would never be the same with Nana living in the same house as a strange man, and that she didn't wish to know somebody called 'James Forsythe'.

She was polite, though; Kristine could never wilfully be impolite to anyone, and she presented the impression of friendship without offering anything of herself.

But Emily knew deep down that it was all an act. By the tone of her voice and her unnatural carriage while seated at the table – the complete opposite of her normal relaxed demeanour – Emily knew Kristine was not even trying to let her guard down.

Afterwards, Emily insisted that she and Kristine wash the dishes together while James watched a football match on television, so that the pent-up fury she was beginning to feel towards her granddaughter could find release in the best way possible under awkward circumstances.

Ever mindful of Emily's influence, Kristine reluctantly complied with the request.

"Nana, you know I didn't want to come here," Kristine said in a hoarse whisper.

"But you didn't have to be so obvious! You were as stiff as a sentinel. Whatever will James have thought of you?"

"To be quite honest, I don't really care what he thinks of me. It's you he's marrying, not me!"

"Kristine! How dare you!"

Emily was almost shouting now, but swiftly checked herself; and while her gloved hands swished the washing up water she spoke more rationally.

"The trouble is, Kristine, I've made myself too available to you in the past. I've always been there when you need me. You've seen me just as an extension of yourself, not as a separate person who is entitled to lead her own life. And now that I've chosen to do something that appears – only appears, mind you – to exclude you and your mother, you come down on me like a ton of bricks; as though I've no right to do it. You really should examine your principles!"

"I'm sorry you see it that way," said Kristine crossly. "But I can't change the way I feel just because you don't like it. As you say, you've always been here for me. Maybe I've been spoilt that way – but it was you who did the spoiling. You can't blame me for that! But you don't need to worry about it, because I'm not staying any longer!"

Kristine angrily tossed the tea towel onto the draining rack and made to go out through the back door; but then turned at the last minute with a final jab.

"You can tell Mr Wots-'is-Name that I hope you'll be very happy. I doubt if he will be seeing me again!"

As Kristine wrenched open the door and fled from the house, Emily could hear the girl was sobbing.

Her first reaction was to follow...

...But what good would it do? she asked herself.

James, who had heard the commotion, peered round the doorpost; to be confronted by a look of utter dejection on Emily's face.

"Never mind," he said. "It's early days yet. She'll come around; you'll see."

Emily was visibly trembling now, so James led her into the lounge and gently lowered her into her favourite chair. Then he returned to the kitchen.

"Here. This will do you good," he said moments later, handing Emily a glass of her special sherry.

She thanked him, and touched the liquid to her lips.

"Do you know, James," she said, savouring the sherry's welcome sweetness. "That was the first time Kristine and I have ever quarrelled."

"Then you should both be very proud of yourselves."

James smiled reassuringly at her concerned face, and squatted on a stool beside her.

Emily looked up at him as he did so.

"Why proud?" she asked.

"...Because the two of you have lasted this long without crossing swords."

"But it's different for Kristine and me. We aren't like ordinary people; ours is a special relationship. And for the very first time I'm beginning to think I've done Kristine a terrible injustice by destroying it."

"Darling, you haven't 'destroyed' anything. You've just altered it slightly. If that girl has half the regard for you that you claim, then sooner or later she'll climb down from

149

her high horse and see things differently. If not, then she's been deluding you all along; and I don't believe that to be the case. ...Just give her time."

"Kristine has never deluded me...she has always been open and honest. I guess she's growing up, that's all. Her teen years are revealing another aspect of her nature; that of wilfulness. It remains to be seen whether she can keep it under control enough to come back to me. If not, then I'm wondering if I have the right to put my own needs before hers; especially when I should be supporting her with all the issues she's facing at home right now."

"What do you mean by that?" asked James, uneasily.

She looked at him soulfully, shrinking from the thoughts arising in her head.

"All I'm saying is, do you think it's fair that we marry so soon? I didn't realise it might cause a rift between Kristine and me. Perhaps we'd better put the ceremony off for a few months till she comes around."

"Emily! I can't believe you're thinking that way. You are doing the one thing you said you'd never do!"

James angrily sprang to his feet, intending to walk out on the deteriorating situation; but then he relented when he saw the look of anguish on Emily's face.

He sat down again and placed his hand on hers.

"I'm sorry," he said. "I didn't mean to be so abrupt. But you are putting too much importance on this one incident. And..." he emphasized, "...you're still allowing the whims of the family to sway you. I thought you were over that!"

"...So did I! When we began making arrangements I was very strong-willed. The family's opinion didn't worry me at all. It's just Kristine... How can I live with myself if I marry you and lose her altogether?"

Emily burst into tears. James looked on, suddenly at a loss to know what to do.

150

He sat quietly by her side while Emily, face now flushed from anguish and the sherry, cried her tears away; then, when she had calmed down, he rose to his feet again, drawing Emily up with him.

"I think it would be for the best if I left," he said solemnly. "I'm not really helping matters by staying here. And you've got some thinking to do."

"Maybe you're right...I'm not very good company."

James kissed her gently on the forehead.

"I'll give you a ring tomorrow," he said, and slipped out, while Emily remained motionless and bewildered by all that had happened.

Later that night, Emily called for Arthur

Desperately, she cried out to him in her sleep; but there came no response.

Arthur, she realised, had honoured his promise to keep out of the way. It looked like she would have to sort this problem out for herself.

But then, as though in answer to her plea, the following day Kristine unexpectedly turned up after school.

Warily, Emily let her in. The girl walked past her without a word of greeting, and only after Emily had closed the door did she speak.

"I wasn't sure you would want to see me again after yesterday," Kristine ventured timidly.

"You don't stop loving somebody just because of a tiff," said Emily in reply. "My door is always open to you, and it always will be."

"Nana, I've come to say how sorry I am for my bad manners. It was unforgivable of me, especially in front of your...your boyfriend."

"Apology accepted – and I, too, am sorry for the things I said. Come through and sit down."

"Not just now, I just came to apologise and to tell you something else."

"To tell me what?" asked Emily cautiously, anticipating unfavourable news.

"You were quite right when you said you are always here for me. The truth of the matter is, I've taken it for granted. I did think of you as an extension of me. But I've learnt my lesson, and from now on I'm going to be more aware of you."

"Thank you, Kristine. I knew you'd be able to make the right judgement..."

"...What's more," Kristine went on; "I don't want you to think I'm against your marriage, because I'm not...not really, anyway. I can't say I'm particularly happy about it, nor am I certain I will ever get to like Mr Forsythe, but I want you to know that I trust you, and I believe you've made what you consider to be the right decision. So I will go along with it..."

"...Bless you, my darling," said Emily, tears welling up in her eyes. She reached forward to give the girl a hug, and was relieved when Kristine responded. "You have no idea how pleased I am to hear you say that. I had the most awful night last night just thinking about it."

"I know...and I feel rotten for putting you through all the worry. I must have been bottling it up ever since you told Mum and me that you were going to get married; and it all had to come out. That's why I blew a fuse...I think that was why, anyway. But I'm over it now."

"Thank the Lord!"

With a relieved mind, Emily continued on her journey of preparation for marriage. Kristine's about-face had made life tolerable once more, sparking off renewed enthusiasm for the tasks ahead.

Pleased for his fiancée's sake that the matter of family acceptance had now been resolved, James contributed eagerly to all the preparations with a vitality befitting a man half his age; much to Emily's amusement.

Despite the fact that the wedding was to be a second-time-around affair for them both, with little fuss and even less flair, they were amazed, as each arrangement neared completion, just how much there remained to do – and to pay for. Before long they found themselves looking at an itemised schedule and related expenses equal to that of a big society wedding.

...At least, that was how it seemed.

Although there would only be a few guests if Emily's family all turned up, it still meant a caterer was needed as Emily was not prepared to tackle it alone. A bride's outfit, though not lavish, had to be chosen; likewise one for her maid of honour – hopefully Kristine.

Then Emily realised with horror that she still had not introduced James to Ruth and Wilbur. It was unthinkable that a meeting like that be left to the day of the wedding! There were flowers to be ordered, church and newspaper notices to be written and sent off; a hundred and one other, smaller items requiring attention...

Almost as an afterthought, Emily asked of James, "Will we be going on a honeymoon?"

"Of course!" was his spontaneous answer; which then brought up the question of which destination. So a visit was made to the travel agent in the village, where they spent a good hour glossing over brochures of resorts.

"Didn't you once tell me you were thinking of visiting your son again?" asked Emily, when they couldn't make up their minds what to choose. "I've never been overseas, and going there on our honeymoon would give David a chance to look over his new step-mother!"

But James was not too keen.

"I think we should settle in a bit first. Perhaps plan a trip for next year; or maybe the year after that. ...When we're accustomed to being Mr and Mrs," he said with a twinkle in his eye; and then he suggested, pointing at a brochure, that the lake resort in the mountains would be more in keeping with the needs of the newly-weds.

During all of this, with some arrangements finalised and others still in the pipeline, the matter of where they would live surfaced again.

Neither Emily nor James, both with property which had been their respective marital homes and therefore filled with precious memories, wanted to entertain the prospect of giving them up. The difficult choice was not made until, only a week before the ceremony, did it register that a decision one way or the other must be reached.

Both were aware that they had been burying their heads in the sand over the subject. One would bring it up, and the other would quickly move the conversation onto something else. Thus, in desperation one evening, James cornered Emily just as she was about to shoo him out for the night, saying, "I'm not going until we get this settled!"

Emily panicked. In alarm she knew the awful moment had arrived, and that as a result she might lose her home, where Arthur had resided in body for so many years and more recently in spirit.

In an instant, James recognised her turmoil and knew what he must do.

With a heavy heart, camouflaged for Emily's sake, he reluctantly conceded, "I think it would be better if we lived here rather than at my place." Then he followed it up with a conciliatory, "Is that alright with you?"

The weight of worry lifted from Emily so abruptly that she almost collapsed with relief, and put out a hand in order to steady herself.

"It's only natural...that I would prefer to stay in...my own home..." she stammered.

"...Then it's settled. I'll arrange to have my belongings brought over here when we return from the honeymoon."

"What will you do with your own house?" asked Emily; feeling sorry for him whilst also appreciating his gesture.

"I don't want to sell it; not yet, anyway. It still means a lot to me...memories and everything. ...Probably rent it out for now. I haven't really thought it through yet..."

His voice petering out with distant memories, James suddenly felt sad; the reality of his decision at last sinking in. But Emily did not notice. All she knew was, they were going to remain in Arthur's house, and for that she would always be grateful to James.

Shortly after tea on the eve of the wedding Kristine, who had agreed to be Emily's bridesmaid, rang her briefly and said she was coming round.

"What...now?" asked Emily; puzzled.

"Yes, Nana. ...Now!"

"...But I'm terribly busy. Can't it wait until tomorrow?"

"No, it can't. I may not be here tomorrow!"

"What do you mean?"

"Can't talk... I'll be round straight away."

In the few minutes it took for Kristine to cycle over to her grandmother's house, all manner of uncertainties invaded Emily's mind. By the time she arrived, Emily was convinced it meant the wedding would have to be called off.

A look of despair covered Kristine's face as she hastily submitted her explanation.

"Mum's holiday has been brought forward. It means that in the morning we're catching the train to the coast."

Emily sat down with a thud, open-mouthed.

"Are you saying she's brought it forward deliberately?"

"I don't know. I saw a letter from Mr Allendale – he's the man who offered Mum his house. It was to confirm his date of departure as the seventeenth; which is the day of your wedding. ...And yet Mum told me it's the following week. So, I'm sorry, Nana, but I can't be your bridesmaid!"

"O Kristine! What on earth are we going to do?"

"I don't know!" Kristine wailed. "I don't even want to go with her – I want to be with you! I can't let you down, right at the last minute!"

All at once, the reality of Kristine's revelation hit home, and Emily's eyes reflected unflinching resentment towards her contrary daughter.

"What is it?" asked Kristine when she saw the strange look on Emily's face. Concerned for her state of mind, she put in, "Nana...you look like you could kill somebody."

Emily's breathing was laboured now. Shaking with rage she slowly said, "Just at the moment I think I could – your mother, Kristine!"

"Do you suppose it was deliberate?"

"Of course it was! Fiona has been against our marriage all along. I knew she was capable of underhand tactics, but didn't think she would stoop this low!"

"If what you say is true, then she must really hate you."

"Yes...and she knows how to hurt me, as well. But it was a bit below-the-belt to bring you down, too."

Emily sat thinking for a moment; then she got up and went out to the phone.

"I'm going to have it out with her," she told Kristine en route. "She's not going to get her own way...not this time."

"Fiona, what are you playing at?" Emily demanded to know as soon as her call was answered.

"I don't know what you're talking about," Fiona replied, taken aback by the angst in her mother's voice.

"Oh, come on, Fiona. Don't play the innocent; you know exactly what I'm talking about. Out of spitefulness you are preventing Kristine from coming to my wedding."

Then, when Fiona's defensive manner changed to one of well-rehearsed control, the tenor of her voice lacking emotion, Emily knew for certain that the mix-up in dates was no coincidence.

"As far as I'm concerned there is no wedding," said Fiona coldly. "In my opinion, this farce of a relationship between you and your boyfriend is nothing more than infatuation. It will never be valid in my eyes. So when you accuse me of preventing Kristine from coming to your wedding, you're talking through your hat."

Emily groaned, wishing fervently that the ongoing feud between them would dissolve into thin air. Weddings aside, the constant bickering was becoming tedious.

"Fiona," she said begrudgingly; "I suppose I must accept that for some reason – which I'm sure has more to do with the ongoing grudge you bear against me than anything else – you have chosen to deny that James and I are to be married. But your acceptance of it apart, the wedding is going ahead tomorrow, and despite your wish to prevent her from doing so, Kristine will stand for me as my maid of honour. She is old enough to make her own decisions, and she has decided she wants to stay here with James and me rather than go on holiday..."

"...Don't you tell me what my child can or cannot do!" barked Fiona, her prepared speech at an end. "Kristine is still a minor, in my charge, and she will do as she is told. Tomorrow she comes with me! Is that understood?"

157

The telephone clicked off decisively in Emily's ear as Fiona hung up.

Despair crept through her; not just because she would be without her maid of honour, but because of the impossible stalemate between herself and Fiona.

Would it never end?

Dreading Kristine's reaction, she returned to report on the ultimatum.

"Well, I suppose that's that, then," said Kristine, and shrugged her shoulders at the hopeless state of affairs. "It looks like I've got no choice but to go with her!"

She leapt to her feet and fled from the house, leaving her bicycle where she had left it propped up in the porch.

"Oh, Kristine," sighed Emily as she followed, hoping to stop her; but Kristine had disappeared up the road.

Then Emily noticed the bike.

With relief, she realised that she would have the chance to speak to Kristine again when she returned for it.

Yet, by the time it got dark, Kristine still had not come back to retrieve her precious bicycle.

Worried, now, for the girl's wellbeing, Emily reluctantly came to the conclusion that she should contact Fiona to see if she had gone home. However, just as she was about to pick up the phone, it rang.

Quickly she answered it.

"Kristine...thank goodness."

"What have you done with my daughter!" barked the voice of Fiona; furious that the girl had not returned home. "I told you she was to come with me. Don't you dare try to harbour her when you know..."

"...Fiona, when you've quite finished!" cut in Emily. "For one thing, would you please not bellow at me down the phone, and for another...Kristine's not here."

"Of course she is! You told me she wanted to stay with you. Where else would she be?"

"Although it's against my better judgement, I wouldn't dream of harbouring Kristine, even though she's better off with me. You don't exactly bring out the best in her just now! In other words – as I have already told you – she is not here. She left in a hurry after our conversation, and hasn't been back; not even to collect her bike."

"…Her bike?"

"Yes. She left it here. I assumed she rushed off to be on her own for a while, with the intention of coming back for it. But she hasn't returned. And quite frankly, I'm worried."

"You and your ridiculous arrangements! If it wasn't for you there would be no problem. Don't you realise we are due to go away tomorrow? I've been looking forward to this holiday for weeks."

"What about Kristine, though? She always has her bike with her; it's her only form of transport. She would not leave it behind intentionally."

"She'll come back when she sees sense. So long as she is here by the time we're due to leave in the morning. I've got a taxi booked for nine-o'clock to take us to the station. If she goes to your place, make sure you send her straight home, do you hear!"

"Don't you care about her? Kristine has disappeared into the night, and all you care about is being on time to catch your damn train! What sort of mother are you?"

Emily's use of harsh words was generally reserved for desperate situations only; none more than this. Yet, with her fear for Kristine's safety mounting and frustration with Fiona's attitude boiling over, the outburst came by way of a safety valve which, once released, restored her to a more normal state of mind.

Immediately, she apologised.

159

"I'm sorry for being irrational, Fiona, but I can't for the life of me understand how you came to be my daughter. You are so different from... Oh...never mind."

Emily didn't even try to finish her sentence; she had had enough. Without bothering to say goodbye she hung up on Fiona, hardly realising she had done so.

She looked around her home.

It was now wearing all the trappings of happiness; the adornments of a wedding transforming an ordinary lounge into a venue for celebration.

Yet, something was glaringly missing. Something vital had been wrenched away from her. The joy she should have been experiencing at that moment had turned into dismay: a foreboding of what was surely to come.

It seemed tomorrow could hold only disappointment.

CHAPTER SEVEN

The next morning, defying convention, James decided to steal a quick word with his bride to be and telephoned her; with no idea of the happenings of the previous night.

"How is my lovely bride this morning?" he enquired in a cheerful voice.

Trying to disguise her sorrow, Emily answered as jovially as she could; but James saw straight through the pretence.

"What's wrong, sweetheart?" he asked; his demeanour now that of concern.

With reluctance, Emily told him about Kristine.

Unaffected emotionally that his bride's maid wouldn't be available now, James declared, "That is a shame; but the wedding can still go ahead, can't it? You shouldn't think of cancelling everything just because of that. It's not as though she's required as a witness."

James felt deeply for Emily, for he knew just how much Kristine's involvement in their wedding meant to her. Yet, the policeman in him had by now surfaced and, concerned more for the girl's safety, he turned his attention to her disappearance.

All the same, he gave no indication of this to Emily, but instead proffered words of reassurance, reminding her that Kristine was a sensible girl, would no doubt have spent the night with friends, and was probably back home safe and sound by now...

"...Hang on a minute," said Emily. "I'll just see if her bike is still outside."

161

On looking, Emily discovered that in fact it had gone from the front porch, and reported this back to James.

"Well then," he retorted; making light of the situation, while also hoping the bike's removal was not because it had been stolen. "It looks like your granddaughter did pick it up and went back home after all."

"Fiona told me the taxi was due at nine o'clock this morning," Emily went on. She glanced at her wristwatch. "It's half-past nine now. If Kristine did go home last night, then they will have left for the station by now. I'll try their number in a minute, and see if anyone's there."

"What time is Ruth and Wilbur coming?" asked James, having now met the other half of Emily's family.

"They should be here at half past ten," Emily replied. "We'll need to dress the tables before the caterers arrive with the food. Wilbur is bringing the drinks."

"You'll be able to manage, then?"

"Oh yes; even without Kristine," Emily said confidently. "Traditionally," she continued, "the bride's maid helps the bride with her wedding gown, but the outfit I have bought isn't a gown as such; just a nice suit – although I shouldn't really be telling the bridegroom that!"

James laughed. "Your secret's safe with me."

Emily instinctively responded in kind; but then sighed, remembering again why she would not be enjoying the assistance of her maid of honour.

She told him sadly, "I'd hoped to have Kristine with me for moral support, but it's not a problem. We should be able to manage just fine. Come along at a quarter to twelve as arranged. Reverend Marriott will probably be here by then."

When she put the phone down, Emily realised her hands were shaking. Having methodically worked through all the preparations during the week, it had not really registered until now that the Big Day was finally upon her. But talking to James had driven it home, and out of nowhere she felt a twinge of nervousness.

Emily put her hands to her face. Chilled fingers touched flushed cheeks: a sure symptom of nerves. With difficulty she brought her focus back onto the preparations that still required attention.

But first, she reminded herself sternly, she should ring Kristine's house.

Uneasily, she dialled the number.

Predictably there was no reply.

"They must have gone," Emily stated out loud, almost with relief.

Again, she felt remorse about the events of the last evening, but then shook it away, determined that nothing else was going to spoil the occasion.

"That's that, then," she thought with resignation.

At ten-thirty exactly, Emily's quiet residence burst into life with the arrival, not only of Ruth and Wilbur, but also the caterer delivering containers laden with everything from pastries to cooked chicken.

The final item the caterer carefully brought in was the two-tiered wedding cake; its centrepiece a tiny white dove within a ring of silver laurel leaves – especially chosen by Emily as a symbol of the peace she hoped her union with James would bring. This he placed in the middle of the crisp white cloth on Emily's main dining table.

Once he had left, Ruth and Emily set about arranging savouries, cakes and other dainties on silver platters around the centrepiece, while Wilbur brought in a crate of beer, a magnum of medium white wine and two bottles of pink champagne.

One by one, he transferred the bottles to a smaller table that already housed an assortment of glasses. When he had finished, he stood back checking the fare, and nodded with satisfaction at its presentation.

He called through to Emily in the kitchen, "I'm not sure there'll be enough room to move around in here...it's pretty cramped now that everything is set up."

She poked her head round the door to investigate.

"I think it will be alright. Without Fiona and Kristine there won't be so many of us, and I doubt if everybody will be in there at the same time."

With all the preparations completed ahead of schedule Emily, Ruth and Wilbur stole a few minutes for relaxation, before Emily was due to prepare for her grand entrance and the guests would begin to arrive.

With a drop of wine for a toast, Ruth and Wilbur, as her only immediate family present, gave their mother a special blessing; wishing her every happiness. And then, with the clock ticking on, it was time to anticipate the arrival of the wedding guests.

The first to arrive, not long after Emily withdrew to her bridal dressing room, was James – In his own car; the need to use a chauffeur-driven vehicle waived in favour of a quick getaway afterwards.

Following on came an elderly couple: old and valued friends of James; the husband of whom had agreed to act as his best man. The McLeods had been neighbours of his for many years, had helped him after his wife died, and supported him in his decision to re-marry. To James, they were the natural choice for his only guests at the wedding.

Shortly before midday, Reverend Marriott arrived; with apologies for not being there sooner. ...Trouble with the car, he explained after introducing himself to James. He went into the lounge, and was surprised to see so few people. Ruth noticed this on his face, and explained that two of the guests would not now be attending.

"I understand," he responded politely; then said to her, "You must be Emily's daughter; but is it Ruth, or Fiona?"

"Ruth, actually," she said, warming to him. "Fiona won't be here...and neither will her daughter, Kristine; which is a shame, because she was to be Mother's maid of honour..."

Reverend Marriott expressed regret.

"...But not to worry," Ruth went on. "I will attend to those duties...starting right now!" she exclaimed when she noticed the time on the wall clock. "If you'll excuse me, I'll go and see how our bride is getting on."

While Ruth assisted Emily with her embellishments, everyone downstairs assembled in the temporary chapel that was Emily's transformed lounge.

The dining chairs were arranged in two rows, with a gap down the middle, in front of the makeshift altar – a coffee table on which stood a floral decoration which Emily had lovingly arranged; comprised of lilies and whiskey roses, interspersed with fern leaves and gypsophila.

On the table, Reverend Marriott had placed his Bible; a white ribbon marking the page from which he would take the reading. The McLeods took their seats to the right of the altar. As yet, the seats to the left: the bride's side, remained empty; for Fiona and Kristine would not be there, Ruth was upstairs with Emily, and Wilbur had seated himself at the piano ready to begin the opening lines of *Lohengrin*; customarily played as a bride enters, which Emily had insisted would make it seem more like a formal ceremony.

James and Reverend Marriott stood at the front, their eyes fixed on the stairs, waiting for Emily to come down.

Just then Ruth appeared, skipping down the last few steps in order to give Wilbur a sign that all was ready.

Distantly he started to play, providing the magical effect Emily had hoped for. ...Then moments later Emily herself appeared, her face radiant with happiness, her cheeks still flushed from nerves.

The bride wore a silver grey suit of finely woven virgin wool; fitted into her tiny waist and complemented with a frilly-necked white silk blouse. On her head, a matching pillbox hat with fine net cascading over her forehead, gave the impression she was wearing a veil. An exquisite white orchid inverted as a corsage, adorned the lapel of the suit. James, who discreetly found out the colour she would be wearing beforehand, had slipped it to Ruth on his arrival. And finally, to complete the outfit, on her dainty feet Emily wore grey satin court shoes.

Emily paused in the lounge doorway, and smiled as she noticed the approving look on the faces of her guests. Then she walked gracefully down the aisle between the rows of chairs, to stand at her bridegroom's side.

James was consumed with love. God has been good to me, he thought, that I should find a woman as wonderful as Emily with whom to share my sunset years.

Reverend Marriott waited quietly for Wilbur to finish the last few strains of music, and then moved forward, Bible in hand, to stand before Emily and James.

The brief service was not the conventional format, but one he used often; created for couples who wished to veer away from the traditional wording.

Emily had left the choice up to him, trusting him to select wording appropriate for her and James; and she was not disappointed.

"Dear friends," he began. "We are gathered here in this lovely home and in the sight of God to witness the uniting of two souls who have agreed to spend the rest of their lives together.

"In as much as marriage is considered sacred, no matter how long or how short its duration; no matter at what stage in life it is entered into; I ask those of you present today, that if you know of any reason why Emily and James should not be joined together, to please speak up now."

A moment of unanticipated concern passed between James and Emily as they glanced at one another, with Emily wondering, if Fiona had been there would she have said something. But as expected, the moment passed without comment, and Reverend Marriott continued.

"James Albert Reginald," he said, turning to James. "Do you take Emily Elizabeth as your wife;" to which James responded tenderly, "I do."

Then he addressed Emily with the same question.

She drew breath sharply with the realisation that this was her moment. It was too late to change her mind.

"Emily Elizabeth, do you take James Albert Reginald as your husband?"

And Emily, gazing first into the eyes of her betrothed and then at Bill Marriott, echoed the response.

Then followed their promises: not the solemnly stated vows of devotion and obedience through good times and bad, but the gentle reinforcement of a loving commitment already made.

After that came the exchange of rings. They had chosen simple bands of gold: nothing ornate; just two endless circles cast from the same mould to cement their union and their love.

The words, 'With this ring do I unite with you,' brought a lump to James's throat, so that by the time he had repeated the vows and placed the ring firmly on Emily's finger, his voice was little more than a choked whisper.

Emily, too, had difficulty with the words. For a split second it was not James but Arthur who stood beside her to receive the ring. But straight away she dispelled the thought with a nervous clearing of her throat, and said with renewed confidence, "With this ring..."

Just then a loud hammering at the front door interrupted the proceedings, making Emily jump with its suddenness.

For a moment, worried heads turned as Wilbur quietly slipped out of the room, closing the door behind him to cause as little distraction as possible to the ceremony taking place. When everybody's attention was once more back on him, Reverend Marriott continued.

"And so, by the power..."

Abruptly the lounge door burst open, cutting him off mid-sentence, and he stopped, gazing with disbelief at what he saw.

A girl, dishevelled and panting from exhaustion, the leg of her jeans stained with dried blood, staggered into the room clutching at the door handle for support.

Alarmed, Emily swung around.

"Kristine!" she exclaimed.

Ruth leapt to her feet and, while Emily stood frozen to the spot, led Kristine to an easy chair pushed to one side.

"I'm alright...please carry on," gasped Kristine; then as an afterthought she stuttered, "I'm sorry to interrupt your ceremony, Nana."

Reverend Marriott touched Emily on the arm. With her attention still on Kristine, she turned around in response; a dazed expression on her face.

"May we conclude the service?" whispered Reverend Marriott to Emily when Kristine was seated. "...It won't take more than a minute."

"Yes, of course," she replied; but Emily's mind was no longer on the ceremony. Curiosity was driving her mad. Whatever had happened to her granddaughter?

Reverend Marriott went on; more slowly than before to try and bring some calm to the agitation that had invaded the sacred occasion.

"...And now, by the power vested in me," he said to finish off; "I pronounce you man and wife. James, you may kiss your bride."

James bent to kiss his wife, knowing only too well that Emily's mind, at that particular moment, was elsewhere. But he understood why; so with a smile he released her.

"Go to her," he whispered in Emily's ear.

She placed a hand on his cheek and mouthed 'thank you' in return; then with dignity and great haste, Emily rushed over to question Kristine.

"I'm sorry I barged in like that, Nana..." the still breathless girl muttered. "...But I wouldn't have missed your wedding for the world."

"What happened? How did you get here...and where is your mother?"

There were so many questions Emily needed to have answered on the spot.

"Don't rush her, Mum," said Ruth gently. "Let Kristine get her breath back first."

"I'm okay now, Auntie Ruth. ...Really." Kristine took a deep breath and then said, "I jumped off the train in the station without Mum seeing. As far as I know she's still on her way to the coast. But I had to do it... I just had to be with you on your wedding day."

"That's alright by me, darling," said Emily. "Now, let me get you something to drink, and then you can tell me all about it."

"I'll do that, Mum...you've got guests to see to," said Ruth, reminding Emily of the occasion Kristine had rushed back to attend.

"Yes, of course. Thank you, Ruth." And then she said to Kristine, "Come and talk to me in a few minutes...when you're feeling a bit better."

Noticing the uneasiness of his guests, James apologised to them for the commotion.

He explained briefly how Emily's granddaughter had been forced by her mother to accompany her on a holiday instead of acting as Emily's bridesmaid, but had apparently seen fit to go against her mother's wishes.

They looked perturbed as the girl disappeared upstairs; to return shortly afterwards cleaner but only slightly more presentable than before.

To neutralise the disturbance, James then introduced Kristine first to Reverend Marriott, who had realised what was going on and taken it all in his conditioned stride, and then to the McLeods. Immediately, they saw through the unsettling impression they were first presented with, to a genuine desire of a girl to be with her grandmother on as special an occasion as this. Reservations dispelled, they warmed to her. Later on, Mrs McLeod admitted to Kristine that she admired her pluck for going to such extremes to support Emily and James.

When courtesy permitted, Emily stole a few moments alone with Kristine.

"I must ask you," she said, looking at her leg. "Whatever happened? Did you have an accident? There's blood on your trousers!"

Kristine glanced down.

Her appearance, though better than before, was still an eyesore. The jagged and bloodstained tear in her jeans

170

showed up starkly against the pristine elegance of Emily's wedding event.

She picked at the torn jeans. "That was when I jumped off the train... But don't worry, Nana," she added hastily when she saw a look of horror cross Emily's face. "It had only just started to move..."

"...You jumped off a moving train...good grief, girl! ...And while we're at it, where did you go last night? We were so worried about you!"

Emily recalled with clarity and upset the events of the previous day, which resulted in Kristine angrily running off into the night.

"I think you had better start at the beginning...and tell me everything," she said sternly.

"Alright, Nana. Can we go somewhere quiet? I wouldn't want to air my dirty laundry in public."

Kristine looked around the room. Although there were not many people in the house, to her it seemed more like a crowd; something she could do without.

After her gruelling escapade, she wanted to talk to Emily only in private.

"I don't think I should leave my guests at the moment," replied Emily, caught between two priorities. "It would be most impolite if the bride disappeared while all her guests were still at the wedding. But why don't you come into the kitchen? You can help me make the coffee; then it won't seem like I'm deserting everyone."

With no choice but to go along with Emily's suggestion, Kristine agreed.

While the wedding guests helped themselves to drinks and food from the buffet table, Emily and Kristine chatted in the kitchen.

"I decided last night that I wasn't going away with her," said Kristine.

She leant against the fridge while Emily spooned coffee into a diffuser.

"I knew if I didn't turn up at home Mum just wouldn't go; which would not help with my attempts to come here. You see, I wanted her to catch the train but she wouldn't unless I was with her. Do you understand my logic?"

"I think I do. So you went back home last night?"

"Yes. When I took off from here I was so upset I didn't know what to do, and I went to the park to get away. Then, after it closed I ran to the coffee bar opposite where a lot of students hang out. My friend Richard was there with his cousin Tim. I told them about my problem, and they came up with the plan of jumping off the train. I think it worked quite well, don't you?"

Emily grunted; in a way which Kristine interpreted as approval, but really she was quite horrified by the whole affair. Deceit or the contemplation of dangerous activities were not normally a part of Kristine's behaviour. To think that irresponsible boys had encouraged the girl to do both in order to attend the wedding shocked Emily, and left her feeling far from happy. Had it really been worth it?

"Anyway," Kristine continued after a brief pause when Ruth came in with empty plates and left with the coffee. "We left the café at around eleven, and Richard gave me a ride back here to pick up my bike. There were no lights on, so I figured you had gone to bed. I'm sorry if I alarmed you by disappearing for so long, by the way."

"Admittedly I was worried, but I assumed you would be mature enough not to let yourself get into any strife."

Kristine smiled appreciatively; then went on, "When I got home, Mum was still up and finishing her packing. I wanted her to think I was going along with the holiday business, but only reluctantly; so I told her I would go but she wasn't to expect me to enjoy myself. That seemed to satisfy her. I don't really think she cared how I felt, just as long as she kept me away from the wedding. This morning we went down to the station and got on the train. Just as the whistle blew, I told Mum I had spotted a school friend in another compartment and wanted to go and see her. In actual fact, I rushed back and jumped off as the train started to move. Only I didn't land properly and stumbled, banging my knee; hence the blood on my jeans. It's alright, though...just a graze which I cleaned up. My plan worked beautifully. Mum never suspected a thing; except I made a silly mistake."

"What was that?"

Another pause while James breezed through to get the cloth for a spilt drink. He kissed Emily on the forehead, and winked at Kristine without saying a word to either.

"I won't be a minute," Emily said fondly as he went back out. "What was your mistake, Kristine?"

"I left my bag on the seat next to Mum. My purse was in it, so I had no money to get me here..."

"...And that's why you arrived only now. You didn't walk, though...did you?"

"I did for part of the way, but managed to hitch a ride on Main Street. It took ages to get anyone to stop. Eventually, two girls in a Subaru took pity on me. They dropped me off near the motorway on-ramp the other side of the shopping centre. They were on their way down south, otherwise I'm sure they would have brought me to the door. I walked, or rather, walked and ran the rest of the way. ...I didn't realise just how far it is!"

"No wonder you look as though you've been through the mill!"

"Yes...sorry about that. I must have given you all a bit of a shock."

Emily put her arms around Kristine and gave her a hug.

"That doesn't matter now. The important thing is...you came to the wedding! I shall never forget this effort you have made for James and me – even if you did make Fiona look silly into the bargain." Then Emily added with a shade of guilt, "I wonder where she is now. I expect she'll phone, but will she come straight back; that's the question. We'll just have to wait and see what happens.'"

"Yes. I suppose the piper must be paid over it. Mum will blow a fuse, that's for certain. But it was worth it. I may not have been your bridesmaid, but I made it in time to see you tie the knot!"

She kissed Emily on the cheek.

"Congratulations by the way; you look lovely. I only wish I could say the same for me!"

"Oh, you'll do under the circumstances. Come on now. Let's go and mingle. I think you owe poor Auntie Ruth an explanation, if you can face saying it all again. I'm sure she will get a chuckle out of it when she hears how you duped her twin sister!"

When they returned to the lounge, James pulled his new wife away from Kristine.

"You've had her long enough," he said to Kristine with a twinkle in his eye. "...Now it's my turn."

"She's all yours," Kristine assured him; then said as an afterthought, "What do I call you now? Officially you're my step-grandfather, but that sounds awful."

"Just call me James, if you like," he replied. "...Or invent a nickname of your own. I don't mind in the least."

Kristine stood thinking for a moment of a suitable name that would slip easily off the tongue: Poppa; Gramps. ...No, they didn't sound right. She decided to stick with 'James'.

Emily and James went through to the dining room where Wilbur was waiting to begin the few formalities they had decided upon. Straight away he tapped a spoon against a wine glass to attract attention.

"Ladies and Gentlemen," he began, and then added as if correcting himself of an error, "Gosh; that sounds like the beginnings of a speech, doesn't it? I'm sorry; there will be no speech from me, just a few words which I think must be said on this very special occasion."

He cleared his throat in preparation for what he was about to say.

"Dear friends...that's better. We have all just witnessed the union of two lovely people: Emily and James; and may I say, they make a grand couple, too!"

A cheer went up, accompanied by "hear, hear," from the Reverend Marriott.

Wilbur went on, "When my father-in-law passed away, the last thing the family envisaged was that Emily would marry again. But now, admittedly after a few moments of trepidation, it is with great joy that we welcome you, James, into our midst; and we hope that the two of you will always be as happy as you are this day. Ladies and Gentleman," he said, raising his glass: "Emily and James."

"Emily and James!" was the resounding reply as glasses were chinked together.

"Do you think I might be allowed to have a drop of wine?" Kristine whispered into her aunt's ear.

"I think we could allow you a little tipple...you deserve one," replied Ruth in a secretive voice, and moved aside to pour Kristine a small glass of champagne.

Emily witnessed the manoeuvre and chuckled.

"Kristine, if your mother could see you now!"

Next up, James came forward in response to Wilbur's much appreciated toast.

After his formal acknowledgement, he added, "I have to tell you, though: for a while it was touch and go that the lady would say 'yes'. I really had to use all my powers of persuasion. I don't know what made her finally accept my marriage proposal, but I am honoured – and extremely proud – that she did!"

All the while he was speaking James had his arm around Emily, she looking up into his face; until the question of what swayed her decision came up. At that point she looked away, and in a distant part of her mind she recalled the main reason why she did finally accept him: Arthur's consent to her marriage.

Dear Arthur, she thought. How is it possible to truly love more than one person? But then the thought passed, and she was again aware of James by her side, while the guests clapped and cheered once more.

The formalities complete, James placed his hand over Emily's, and together they cut the wedding cake. Once each of the guests had been offered a piece, they moved into the lounge; now restored from the temporary sanctuary to its intended place of leisure.

Emily made to clear the refreshments and empty plates away, but Ruth hastily stopped her and instead dragged her back into the lounge, firmly shutting the dining room door behind her.

"The dishes can wait!" she insisted.

And then, after what seemed like only a short time of socialising, it was all over.

James looked at his watch and suggested it was time he and his bride left if they were to get to the lake hotel 'this side of midnight,' as he put it. And Ruth, aware that Wilbur was looking tired, said they needed to get going soon, too.

"Where will you go, Kristine?" asked Emily after bidding goodbye to Reverend Marriott and the other guests. "I'd love to say you can come with us, but..." She cleared her throat self-consciously. "...it will be our honeymoon. I

176

don't think James would appreciate having somebody else along; not even you!"

Kristine laughed out loud.

"Oh, Nana! You are a hoot. I've only just got out of one holiday by the skin of my teeth. I've no wish to get caught up in another one!"

"Kristine, you can stay with us for a while if you like," offered Ruth.

"Thanks, Auntie. But I think I'll just go back home, if you wouldn't mind dropping me off. I know where the spare key is, so I can get in. I'll be okay. ...In fact, I'll quite enjoy a bit of time on my own. It's not very often that I get the house completely to myself."

"Alright...but if you change your mind about staying there alone – or if things get difficult when that sister of mine returns – please give me a ring. ...Promise?"

"I promise. ...She'll probably come home sooner rather than later. I can't imagine Mum staying in her posh beach house all by herself, especially as she will be absolutely furious about the trick I played on her. But she did have it coming to her, didn't she, Nana?"

Emily looked up at the mention of her name.

"Well... Um, yes... I'd better not get into that now, Kristine. Are you sure you don't want me to help with the clearing up, Ruth?"

"Of course! This won't take long. Kristine and I will be done in no time at all. You two get going. James is pacing the floor already. You don't want to begin your married life with an argument!"

After embracing each of her family members, Emily walked up the path arm in arm with her new husband, under a shower of rose-petal confetti plucked from the garden earlier in the day.

However, before she drove off to begin a new life, she let go of his arm, and turned around to look with nostalgia at the life she was leaving.

As she did so, she caught a glimpse of something odd in the lounge window, and it momentarily caught her breath. For standing there in full view was a ghostlike apparition of Arthur; and the expression on his face she would never forget. It reflected not happiness for her, nor sadness that she was with another man; but concern.

A new bride his beloved Emily might be, but her future happiness could not be assured.

Wondering what the vision was all about, Emily turned anxiously back to James. Yet, when she saw her groom waiting to whisk his bride away, she set aside the image and got into the car beside him; to drive away moments later as Mrs James Forsythe.

PART TWO

CHAPTER ONE

The honeymoon had gone well. It was one of those idyllic holidays only dreamt of or read about in books.

True to the forecast, the weather was fine and warm throughout their fortnight away, with just a sprinkle of rain on one of the days; which gave Emily the added bonus of viewing, across the lake from their hotel balcony, the most magnificent rainbow she had ever seen. She and James stood looking at it for quite some time; until at last it faded with the passing of the shower.

James had said, "The pot of gold is missing from the end of this rainbow."

"Why do you say that?" Emily jested.

"Because it is here beside me," came his spontaneous reply, prompting Emily to giggle with delight.

This and many other happy memories filtered through Emily's mind during the long drive home; though not many words were spoken for there was no need for them.

Each basked in their recollections, and in the presence of one another: words enough for the newlyweds.

They were ideally suited: James and Emily. If Arthur and Janet had looked on from above, they would have been pleased that their spouses found someone so compatible with whom to spend their remaining years.

Each seemed to be intuitively aware of the other, and although both Emily and James were set in their individual ways, they found, during the honeymoon at least, that their individual ways were really quite similar.

Only one thing concerned Emily throughout the holiday and caused her to think about home: Fiona's reaction to the trick Kristine played on her.

By the end of their first week away, the worry of this was beginning to get the better of her. For some peace of mind she telephoned Ruth for an update on the situation, only to be told that up until the previous night Fiona had neither returned home nor contacted Kristine. It appeared she had gone to the beach as planned. So Emily had to be content with waiting until they returned from their honeymoon in order to find out for sure. Somehow, she suspected, sparks were going to fly.

The thought of this created a ripple in the tranquillity that otherwise enveloped her. Yet she dismissed it from her mind, refraining until the very last minute from facing it as a definite probability. After all, she reminded herself, she was still on her honeymoon. Her centre of attention should be James, not the family.

They arrived home in the early evening. James dropped off Emily and their luggage, and then drove round to his own house to collect a few more belongings; the rest to be transferred by removal van the following day.

After he left, Emily stood in the hall, surrounded by bags, suitcases...and silence.

It felt inexplicably strange, coming back into this house. The last couple of weeks had taken her into another world: one that was bright and full of sound. The sight of the old homestead looking the same as it had for years made her feel almost alien, as though she no longer belonged there. Had she made a mistake in accepting James's suggestion that they live in her house instead of his?

In the lounge, everything was back in its rightful place after the wedding ceremony. In fact, except for the cards on the mantelpiece, and the wilting flower arrangement still on the coffee table, there was no sign that an out-of-the-ordinary activity had taken place there at all; for Ruth had meticulously cleaned up, and tidied everything away.

Nothing was amiss; except for one rather odd thing: Emily noticed that some kitchen cupboard doors had been left wide open.

How peculiar, thought Emily. Maybe Kristine omitted to close them after they finished the washing up.

Emily chuckled; remembering how she had to chastise her twins for leaving open drawers and cupboards when they were young.

Yes, that's all this is, she declared. It must have been Ruth or Kristine.

Emily pushed the doors shut, returned to the hallway, and carried the lighter cases up to the bedroom.

This time, the strange feeling took on a different aspect: a short-lived but very real sense of guilt.

She raised her hands to her face; shutting her eyes against the realisation that she would now be sharing her bed – hers and Arthur's – with another man.

"Oh, this is going to take some getting used to," she said out loud, looking down at the bed.

But then she remembered: if it was difficult for her to invite her new husband to live in Arthur's house, how hard must it be for James? He was leaving behind the home that had been his and Janet's to live in this one – and to sleep in the bed of someone as beloved to her as Arthur. Would James ever truly feel at home here? The neutral territory of a hotel room was one thing, but this...

Emily resolved there and then to do all she could to make James feel that this was as much his home as hers, and with a flick of her head turned away from the doubts that were consuming her.

"I'll put the kettle on – James will be here soon," she said out loud to break the spell. "...Then I must ring Ruth for a progress report," she added decisively.

Emily was still talking to Ruth when James arrived. She smiled at him when he came in carrying a heavy ornament. Then she blew him a kiss with her spare hand; reluctant to end the call just yet as Ruth was giving her an update on Fiona's return.

According to Kristine, Ruth reported, Fiona must have put the prank behind her, because she was quite friendly.

"I was expecting a right roasting," Kristine had said. Yet Fiona made no reference to her jumping off the train; merely asking if she realised she had left her bag behind, to which Kristine replied, yes.

Kristine had also confessed to Ruth how much she enjoyed her quiet fortnight at home without her mother, and about a party she had thrown for Richard and some of her friends the weekend following the wedding. Kristine even admitted that by the time Fiona eventually got back from her holiday she had just about had enough of being by herself with no word from her mother, and was in some ways relieved to see Fiona's taxi pull up outside...

But if the truth were ever to come out, it would reveal that Fiona, also with a fortnight in which to think things through, had in her fury alienated herself not only from her mother, but now from her daughter, too. In her anger at Kristine's underhand conduct in setting out to make a laughingstock of her, Fiona had created for herself an emotional cocoon in which she planned to reside from now on; isolated from the family she fiercely resented.

Yet, of one thing Fiona was also certain: somehow she would have her revenge.

Emily chatted with Ruth for a few more minutes, and was just about to say her goodbyes when she remembered the open cupboard doors.

"...By the way," she said. "Did any of you go through the kitchen cupboards before you left after the wedding? Some of the doors were open when I came home earlier."

"No, not that I recall," replied Ruth. "...Although Kristine might have. ...But now I come to think of it, she went out to the car before I locked up, and I remember checking all the rooms first; so it couldn't have been either of us."

"...How odd," said Emily, mystified.

"Is anything missing?"

"I don't know. It's hard to tell. From what I can see, nothing seems to be out of place."

"So it's unlikely you've been burgled?"

Emily shuddered at the thought.

"What a horrible thing to contemplate straight after our honeymoon."

"Sorry, Mum. I didn't mean to alarm you."

"I don't see how I can have been burgled, though. My security was upgraded a while ago. Anyway, I've been in all the rooms and tried the back door. Everything is alright. I guess I'll just have to put it down to an Act of God."

Emily chuckled at her last remark, but underneath she felt uneasy.

James' detective ears picked up the word 'burgled', and he approached her with a concerned look on his face.

Emily followed his eyes as he walked towards her.

"What's going on?" he mouthed.

Emily put her hand over the mouthpiece and whispered back, "I'll tell you in a minute." A moment later she said goodbye to Ruth and clicked off the phone.

"I'm sure it's nothing to worry about..."

"...What is, for heaven's sake?"

185

All James had heard from her was something about being burgled.

And so Emily repeated her account of the open doors.

"...Like I said," she reiterated, "it's probably nothing to worry about, but it's left me somewhat puzzled."

James opened up the cupboard doors in question. Their shelves contained only crockery, drinking glasses, and an assortment of plastic containers. Everything looked aright, so he closed them again and went through into the dining room. Again, everything seemed to be in order. Even a silver canteen of cutlery in the dresser was untouched.

He returned to Emily as puzzled as she was.

"I see what you mean," he told her. "It's a real mystery. I can only assume Ruth actually made a mistake in stating that she checked everything; but even so..."

After a moment of consideration, James decided not to pursue the matter. For one thing, there was likely nothing further to pursue, and for another...he and Emily had just returned from a magical honeymoon. It was far too soon to allow his bride to be troubled by a trivial problem. He just would not let it happen. So he dismissed the matter by re-boiling the kettle for their cup of tea.

"Do you want to start the unpacking while I make us a cuppa?" he asked cheerfully. "I don't know about you, but I'm gasping for one."

From then on, the subject of cupboard doors was dropped completely; except that in the back of Emily's mind, every now and then she would recall the incident, each time shuddering slightly at the recollection.

From back even further, the faded memory of severed telephone wires also emerged, and somehow she could not help but link the two incidents. Were they actually related? It seemed this would be one of life's unsolved

186

mysteries; something they will never know for sure. The only person who could have advised her had now gone away from her presence.

Emily often thought distantly about Arthur. Despite her happiness with James, Arthur was still her true love, and in her own way she missed him.

She imagined James missed Janet, too...

Yet, those thoughts sprang to mind only occasionally, such as when she was tired or feeling unwell, and when something reminded her of events now in the past.

On the whole, from the moment the incident with the cupboard doors was deemed to be a fluke, Emily became a happy, vibrant wife, who lived not only for herself but also for a husband whose love was priceless.

Over the ensuing months, Emily's joy became infectious. She and James attracted approving glances whenever they went out together; which they did often.

Once his own house had been dealt with — rented to a business couple on indefinite transfer — James was able to relax and enjoy his life free of additional responsibilities; and this reflected in his demeanour.

Every week the couple visited the bowling club. Anyone who may once have frowned on their union, especially so soon after their respective bereavements, began to think differently once they witnessed the bond between Emily and James.

However, there were some exceptions.

"It's too good to last," said one rather bitter divorcee; an old acquaintance of Janet's, who spitefully condemned her widower's marriage.

But few others thought that way.

Most remembered Emily, whom they had seen, just occasionally during her bereavement period, as a frail little lady who was a shadow of her old self after the death of her husband, Arthur. They knew nothing of the company she had subliminally been keeping with him. And James they remembered as a reserved widower: too shy to come out of his shell and let some of the willing local widows comfort him; something many had tried to do, yet all had failed. ...For once he met Emily there was room in his heart for no-one else.

But now they all saw a happy couple who might have been celebrating their Golden Wedding Anniversary rather than their marriage, they looked so comfortable together.

Kristine visited the house regularly now. On one occasion she brought her father along.

Since Fiona had switched off to her – a welcome release in itself – Kristine spent far more time with Royston, and called frequently to visit him in his cosy one-bedroom flat. Persuading him to meet James was easy; especially as she had promised her father there would be no likelihood of Fiona turning up.

The two men hit it off straight away; to the delight of Emily. She was of the opinion that men get on together so much more readily than females, who tend to scrutinise each other before acceptance. And it was a great relief to James that Royston turned out to be something of an ally. He now felt he had some moral support; surrounded as he was by females.

This, James confided to Emily one Sunday while Kristine and her father were there.

Kristine had laughed at his openness.

As Emily once assured her, she had come to love James as much as she loved her grandfather.

Kristine looked fondly at both him and her father on that day. Maybe she lived with her mother, she realised, but the people with her at that moment were her real family. She hoped they could get together often.

Emily could not have been happier that Royston was once more part of Kristine's life. With Fiona absent from family get-togethers, Kristine could have developed a sense of isolation in that unhappy home; especially in the wake of Emily's marriage. His reappearance in their lives was a real blessing; for it meant that she could spend more time with her father, too.

As it worked out, Royston also provided Kristine with the kind of emotional support she once sought only from her grandmother, which relieved Emily enormously. This in itself left Emily feeling free; unrestricted by Kristine's expectations of her, and allowed Emily's delight in her company to become enhanced, as though nothing of recent events had marred their relationship at all.

With the passage of time, a rapport developed between Emily and her son-in-law.

In the past she had had little to do with Royston, except as Fiona's husband. But now she regarded him more as a son than a son-in-law, and as such found herself able to discuss many of the issues she would never have brought up when Fiona was present. And one issue she wanted very much to bring up with him was whether he had any intention of getting back together with his wife.

During one of the visits, James and Kristine slipped out to buy ice creams from a Mr Whippy van, and in their brief absence Emily plucked up the courage to speak privately to Royston about it.

"Do you think there's a chance you and Fiona might ever reconcile?" she asked casually.

For a moment Royston looked perplexed, having been caught off guard by such a personal question from his mother-in-law. Nevertheless he told her, "I suppose you have a right to know that I regard my life with Fiona as well and truly over. And besides, I wouldn't want to go back to her just at the moment because…"

Royston paused, as though on the verge of divulging a guarded secret.

"Because what, Royston?"

"…Because just recently another woman has come into my life."

"Oh…is that right!"

Now it was Emily's turn to be taken aback. Somehow the idea of Royston having a lady friend had not occurred to her. But, of need, her indignation was short-lived when she remembered that her family had felt exactly the same after she told them about James. …So what right did she have to object here?

"Does Kristine know about your new lady friend?" she asked with concealed indignation.

Then, on seeing James and Kristine about to come in with the ice creams, she looked at him with a sense of urgency; hoping to hear his reply before they came in.

Royston was swift to oblige: "No, she doesn't…and I'd rather you didn't say anything to her about it."

"Of course…"

And then the other two were upon them, leaving Emily unsatisfied with Royston's explanation.

She wanted to know so much more: Did he intend to keep his new love a secret from Kristine? Had he plans to marry this woman, assuming Fiona would release him from their marriage vows?

For now, many questions must remain unanswered. Perhaps it would have been better if she had not brought up the subject in the first place…

190

And yet, somehow the knowledge of Royston's new lady pleased Emily. She had felt sorry for his plight during those trying months when Fiona was being so difficult.

At the time, she was saddened, if not shocked, when Kristine informed her of his departure from the family fold. She later hoped, once reconciliation seemed unlikely, that Royston might find peace in his solitary life with only easy-going Kristine for company. But now that he had found someone else, Emily felt not so much regret as warmth of friendship towards whoever might bring joy into his life. Emily hoped to meet her one day.

"It surprised me to discover..." Emily later confided in James, "...that my attitude towards Royston's lady friend is exactly how I once hoped my family would be towards you. I don't feel as though she's stealing my daughter's husband. In fact, it's rather nice that someone has come into the picture to add a little sparkle to his life. Now, if I can feel that towards a total stranger, why couldn't my own family afford me the same consideration when I told them I was going to marry you?"

"Because, my darling, they are not you!" James replied passionately. "They see things differently."

Emily was getting used to his remarks these days, and did not blush as readily as she used to. Instead, she squeezed his hand contentedly, and realised that on one point he was quite right: her family did see everything in a different light. It made her wonder how they would react if they found out about Arthur's visits.

Come to think of it, she thought to herself. I wonder how James would react! Am I ever going to tell him?

Royston, Emily discovered, enjoyed an occasional game of golf as, coincidentally, did James. It was not until the two men became friends that the coincidence came to light, and when it did, there was no stopping them. As a result, James and Royston agreed to become golfing partners, and almost immediately headed off to the local golf course to register as members.

At first, Emily thought it was wonderful that the two men in her life had found a common interest; one that took them away from the constant company of females. ...That is, until she found out something about the game of golf: Whereas a game of football is completed in a relatively short space of time, a game of golf, if time spent socialising in the clubhouse afterwards is also taken into account, can last for many hours.

On the first Sunday that James and Royston went to the golf club, Emily spent the day alone. Although she did not mind it on that occasion, once the game of golf became a weekly occurrence, the novelty of their time-consuming hobby soon wore off for her.

Emily started to dread Sundays. She knew that unless it was pouring with rain, thus preventing the men from going out, for they were essentially fair-weather golfers only, she would have to occupy her time alone; a habit Emily had long-since left behind.

For several months she endured the weekly period of enforced solitude. Even the occasional visit from Kristine did not provide much relief from her endless hours of boredom. Then, when a drought ensured weeks of good golfing weather, Emily decided that enough was enough. Something had to be done about it.

As chance would have it, Kristine was bemoaning the same fate. With Fiona at home all day on Sundays, Kristine had at first escaped her company by visiting Royston. But once the golfing appetite took hold, and James started to monopolize her father's time, she found herself at a loss to know what to do on a Sunday. Then, when she looked particularly fed up during a visit to her grandmother, Emily felt obliged to ask what was wrong.

"It's that husband of yours!" she told Emily with a hint of exasperation.

"James? What has James done to upset you?"

"He carts Dad off to the golf course every weekend and I don't get to see him like I used to!"

Emily burst out laughing. "I might have known..."

"...Known what?"

"...That you would be suffering from desertion, too!"

Suddenly Kristine realised what Emily was driving at, and likewise started to laugh.

"We sound like squawking old hens," she chuckled.

"Those poor men," Emily put in. "If they could only hear us now... I don't suppose for one minute they would guess that you and I are affected by their absence. In fact, they probably don't give us a second thought, once they're out on the golf course."

"I can't say I blame them," said Kristine. "They probably enjoy their freedom."

"Well, thank you very much!" Emily quipped. She was beginning to feel less tense about her Sunday situation now, knowing Kristine felt the same.

"Oh, Nana, I didn't mean anything against you!"

"I know. I was just teasing. But seriously...what can we do? I get sick and tired of spending my Sundays at home, especially when it's fine. I don't drive, so I'm restricted to walking everywhere; and since James and I married, I've got used to going out with him... I must have been spoilt rotten these last few months that I can't be satisfied with my own company anymore."

"I know what we can do!" exclaimed Kristine suddenly, breaking into Emily's narrative.

"...About what, love?"

"Nana! Have you already forgotten what we were just talking about? ...Our Sundays, of course!"

"Do you have something in mind?"

"Yes! I don't know why we didn't think of it before."

"And are you going to tell me what this oversight is?" asked Emily; intrigued.

"When I was little, Mum and Dad played golf regularly. But they didn't have much money, so shared the bag of golf clubs between them. ...And I used to caddy for them."

"What; they made you carry a heavy golf bag all the way round the course?"

"No, Nana; of course not! I pulled the bag on a trolley. You must have seen them."

"Oh, you mean a golf trundler! Yes, of course. How silly of me. Are you suggesting you caddy for your father now, and leave me all by myself again?"

"Not just me, Nana. You as well! I know they've both got trundlers; I've seen them. It would be no effort to pull them around after James and my Dad. We would be able to talk, and be with them at the same time. It would be fun. What do you say?"

"It certainly sounds like the solution to our problem. ...And it would be good exercise." Emily slapped her hips with both hands. "I could definitely do with some of that! But what about the men? They might not want us there. We would be intruding on their time alone."

"I don't think so, Nana. I'm sure they'd be only too happy to have us along as caddies. It won't hurt to ask."

"I suppose not. I'll mention it to them when your father drops James off."

Kristine returned home, satisfied a solution had been found for their lonely Sundays. However, her certainty proved to be premature; for when Emily broached the subject just as James and Royston were unloading the car, their reaction was not one of enthusiasm.

Emily backed down, suddenly aware that she may have spoken too soon.

"Forget I said anything...it was just an idea," she said with embarrassment.

James caught Royston's eye and winked.

"Why don't we go inside and talk about it," he said.

Carrying his heavy golf bag, he followed Emily up the path to the house.

"Kristine was here earlier," she told them over coffee. "We thought it would be nice if we came round the course with you occasionally." Then, as if to make light of her suggestion, she said, "I expect you two are hungry. Would you like something to eat?"

"No thanks," said James. "We stopped in the clubhouse for a bite and a beer afterwards..."

"...Oh, really!" exclaimed Emily; mostly to herself.

Emily had not considered, during her discussion with Kristine, the possibility of their going into the clubhouse after the game. If James and Royston were to accept their company, Emily could go into the clubhouse, but what of Kristine? The girl was still under the drinking age. Would it make a difference..? Perhaps they had better forget the whole thing.

"Emily, why do you two want to come round with us?" asked Royston. He somehow sensed she and his daughter had already discussed it at length.

"A bit of exercise and fresh air would do us good," replied Emily defensively. To mention that she and Kristine really wanted to combat their sense of abandonment by accompanying the men suddenly seemed foolish; for they probably would not understand, and scoff at the inability of the females to manage without them.

195

Emily wished fervently that she had not brought up the subject; or at least waited until she could sound James out about it first. Right now, confronted by both men at once, she suspected that asking to enter their male domain of a private game of golf would be perceived as over-stepping the mark. In bringing it up she may even have wrecked their chance of ever accompanying them.

Emily sighed with discouragement. However, the seed had been sown; the question asked. She had to see it through to its conclusion, whatever that might be.

If only Kristine had stayed, she wished secretly. The disarming girl would have had both men eating out of her hand in no time at all. She could have used an approach inappropriate for a woman of mature years but expected of a teenager: that of petulance. She would no doubt have begged her father to let them go. But Kristine was not there to support her. Emily was on her own with this one.

Royston was in no way fooled by Emily's reasoning. Slowly a smirk crossed his face as he began to see through her attempted pretence.

"What's the matter, Emily? Can't you cope without your man for a couple of hours?" he teased.

Emily's sense of embarrassment escalated. She blushed fiercely, a trace of anger rising in her throat.

Just as a cornered animal turns on its assailant, Emily all at once became the aggressor, and before she knew what she was saying, she hurled her incensed feelings upon the two startled men.

"How dare you demean me in my own home!" she cried; her angst aimed at Royston but also felt by James.

Royston retorted sheepishly, "...I was only teasing."

"I know you were; but it was in very poor taste. I'll have you know the reason Kristine and I wanted to come round the course with you was because we are sick of you and James disappearing for hours on end, week after week. You take it for granted we don't mind spending our Sundays on our own; probably not even considering our wishes on the matter at all..."

"...It's not for the whole day – only a couple of hours," ventured James, rather embarrassed. He had never seen his bride in full battle cry before, and felt quite intimidated by the onslaught.

"I might have known you two would stick together over this," she snapped back; still furious. "...And it's not just a couple of hours, either. By the time you've eaten the early lunch you expect to have made for you, played eighteen holes of golf, enjoyed your 'bite and a beer' when you've finished, then packed up to come home, it's usually long after teatime. And the infuriating thing is: you don't give us so much as a thought. It's our weekend, too!"

Royston could see he was defeated.

"I suppose it wouldn't hurt if the girls walked round with us once in a while," he conceded, searching the face of his buddy for moral support. "They wouldn't really be in the way..."

"...We wouldn't be in the way?" Emily shrieked. "Of all the unmitigated gall! As if we don't have just as much right to walk the length of a golf course as you. If Kristine and I wanted to go, we would do so with or without your consent. But I tell you: just at the moment, accompanying you male chauvinists while you wack a silly ball around is the last thing I would want to do!"

As she hurled the words of abuse at her demoralised son-in-law, Emily removed her diminutive frame from the room, slamming the door behind her. Then she made for the sanctity of the back garden, and solitude.

For a moment a hush descended on the two stunned men. At length Royston, still conscious of his indiscretion, broke the silence.

"Well; what do you make of that?" he asked hesitantly.

"I don't really know," replied James. The whole episode seemed unreal to him. "I've never seen Emily carry on like this before. I guess she must have been stewing over it for quite some time."

James was right in supposing his wife was stewing over the issue; for while taking in the cooling fresh air, Emily still writhed, aiming silent fury towards the male members of her family.

"How could they be so insensitive?" she fumed. "We wouldn't go with them now if they begged us to!"

Minutes later, an apologetic James slipped out to look for her. She was sitting on her favourite garden seat by the rose bed she and Arthur loved so well.

Emily heard his footsteps, and shot a glance towards the house to ascertain just which of the men had come out to see her...no doubt to try and pacify her, she thought. On discovering it was James, she sullenly turned away.

"I really do think it's the limit!" Emily snapped before he could get a word in.

"Emily, that conversation should not have taken place."

"It's a bit late now."

"I mean, not in the way that it did. You should not have sprung your suggestion onto us when the idea of female company was furthest from our minds."

"I suppose you had been drinking with the boys, then?"

"Well, yes, you could say that; although no more than one because Royston was driving. But when you asked if you and Kristine could tag along with us, we just weren't in the right frame of mind to consider it."

198

"You were tiddly, then?"

"...A little bit," he reluctantly admitted.

James sat down beside Emily and took hold of her hand. "Look," he said, "I really am sorry about what happened, and so is Royston."

"Where is Royston?"

"He left a couple of minutes ago...with his tail between his legs, I would say. He did look a bit shamefaced."

Emily began to soften her stance. Furthermore, the fact that she had given Royston a twinge of conscience for his petty-minded comments made her furtively smile. Maybe, she reflected, the timing of her request really had been a bit off... Perhaps it would be better to let the matter drop, and try again some other time. So, to change the subject, Emily turned her attention to the garden.

Despite her troubled frame of mind, since coming into the garden she had noticed something unsettling about it.

...And so, apparently, had James.

Up until now, Emily and James had continued to utilise the services of their gardener. However, Emily had noticed of late that Michael's work was becoming slip-shod. As James now appeared to be casting a critical eye over the garden as well, it seemed to be the perfect opportunity for Emily to mention this.

"It's a bit of a mess, isn't it?" she said.

"Yes. Hasn't Michael been coming lately?" asked James. "The garden definitely has an unkempt look about it now. Either he hasn't been showing up, or he's becoming slack in his work!"

"I usually see him here on Saturday mornings; not that I take much notice. In fact, I'm so used to him coming each week I forget to check on his work. He mows the lawns once a fortnight, but what else he does, I can't tell."

199

"…Not very much, by the look of it. Perhaps it's time we dispensed with Michael's services."

"Ooh, he wouldn't like that. We've been his only source of income for a year or more. He's just a university student, you know…"

"…Even so, he's obviously lost interest in his work. The garden needs looking after properly. We could do a much better job of it ourselves."

James got up and walked over to the rose bed. It was starting to look untidy again, as in the days before Michael took on the job.

The whiskey rose showed no signs of its normal second blooming. A covering of weeds surrounded the overgrown bush, whose first blooms had long since died off and not been pruned away.

"I really should spend more time in the garden, myself," said James pensively. "Having Michael here has spoilt me for wanting to get involved."

"Come to think of it, so should I show more interest in the maintenance of our garden," remarked Emily.

She got up and stood beside him; then bent down to half-heartedly pull at a weed.

"After all," she continued; "the rose garden is Arthur's pride and joy, so nowadays I have a responsibility to make sure it looks nice."

"Maybe we should spend our Sundays here instead of traipsing round a golf course," said James in fun.

Suddenly the tension between them was released, and they both laughed out loud.

"Does that mean you'll let us come with you?" asked Emily, noticing that he had said, 'we'.

"I suppose so," he conceded; happy again.

"…Starting next week," Emily added cheekily.

That evening, James phoned Michael with the news that his services were no longer required. Emily stood apart from him, listening to his side of what developed into a heated conversation.

When James put down the phone, he was flushed and visibly harassed.

"If that young man had used such language to you, my dear, I would have tanned his hide!" he exclaimed.

"I take it he wasn't very pleased."

"No. I think he has come to regard it as his right to be given paid employment, even if he no longer honours his end of the bargain."

"Perhaps we're best rid of him."

"Yes," stated James firmly. "We can do without the likes of young Michael."

The following Sunday, a slightly subdued Royston arrived to pick up James.

...And with him, he brought Kristine.

Emily was both surprised and delighted to see her at his side; for no further discussion on the subject had taken place since their argument.

...In fact she had assumed when, still without comment, her husband hauled out his clubs in the morning, that this would be another boys-only outing.

Kristine bounded up to Emily, and winked cheekily at her grandmother.

"We got our own way, eh Nana?" she said secretively as the men loaded up the car.

"I'm not too sure," replied Emily. "James hasn't actually invited me yet." Then, when he returned, she cautiously enquired, "Do I presume I'm coming with you?"

"Of course," came his nonchalant reply; his acceptance of Kristine's presence presupposing Emily's inclusion, too.

"…Not in these glad-rags, though," Emily added, looking down at her slim-fitting skirt and slip-on sandals. "I'll just pop upstairs and change."

A few minutes later they were all seated in the car, the men in the front; the women excitedly talking in the back.

"Anybody would think you were going away on holiday instead of trudging after us," said Royston, glancing at the chatty women through the car's rear-view mirror.

"Not after you," corrected Kristine. "…With you."

"Well, I'm very sorry!" said her father in a tone which could have been interpreted as sarcastic, but which really reflected his quiet enjoyment of his daughter's company. She was right, though. It was good to have her 'with' him.

"Nana, talking of going away on holiday," said Kristine, speaking into Emily's ear so that she could hear over the noise of the engine. "Did you and James think any more about that overseas trip you were once hoping to make?"

"What overseas trip?"

"…To see his son."

"Oh! …Yes, we did talk about it once, didn't we?"

"And have you discussed it anymore?"

"No, I can't say we have. Why do you ask?"

"I just wondered," replied Kristine, as the idea of house-sitting in their absence crossed her mind.

Their short journey soon brought them to the Greenwood Country Club.

As the morning had turned out to be cool and windy Emily was pleased to be wearing the warm slacks she put on before they left home.

"What a snobbish name for a golf course," said Kristine as she read the placard above the main entrance.

"It's more sophisticated," Royston argued.

"…And an excuse to increase the fees!" added James.

Greenwood Country Club was a long-established golf course, with rows of tall conifer trees separating lengthy fairways that zigzagged across its undulating contours. The trees provided only minimal protection from the wind, but after a few minutes of walking; pulling the lightweight caddy on which James had fastened his golf bag, Emily began to warm up, and to feel invigorated as much by the fresh air as by the exercise.

"I knew it was a good idea to come round with them," she called to Kristine, who stood not far from Royston as he prepared for a tricky shot round a stand of trees.

"Quiet, please!" he shouted good-humouredly at Emily. "I need to concentrate for this one."

While the golfers walked on, their two companions came up with a system whereby they could caddy for their partners and chat at the same time; for in-between strokes, when the players walked up the fairway, they strolled along the middle in order to gossip.

"Don't you two women ever stop talking?" commented Royston jovially.

Back at the clubhouse, Royston spotted a couple of the regular Sunday players who had on occasions made up a foursome. He dragged Kristine over to their table and introduced her to them.

Self-consciously, she acknowledged their comments about father-daughter resemblance, and was eventually pleased to return to the neutrality of Emily's side.

With a glass of lemonade in her hand Kristine then threaded her way between tightly packed tables in the crowded lounge, and sat sideways in a window seat which overlooked the eighteenth hole.

From there, happily sipping at her cold drink, she gazed out at the wide expanses over which she had just ambled, while the other three socialised: the two men exchanging hyped-up remarks about their game; Emily chatting with a couple at the next table.

Later, when they were back at home, Emily asked James if he thought the experiment had been successful.

"I think so," he replied nonchalantly. "You two seemed to be enjoying yourselves."

"I hope we didn't put Royston off with our chatting."

"Don't mind him. Royston's usually like that. He seems to get very nervous when he's about to play a shot. He'll get used to having you both there."

After tea, as the two lazily sat watching television, Emily found her thoughts drifting back to the question Kristine asked her in the car.

The idea of an adventure overseas; which this would be for Emily who had never before been out of the country, appealed to her enormously. But the anticipation was also accompanied by a twinge of concern as to the reception she might receive from her overseas stepson, despite his good wishes for their marriage.

Still lost in thought, she stared blankly at the television screen; until James questioned her about the programme they were watching.

"What do you think, then?" he said, assuming she had heard him. And then, when there was still no response from her, he realised that Emily's mind was elsewhere.

"A penny for them," he said.

"...A penny for what?" asked Emily naively; returning slowly to the present. Then it dawned on her that James had actually been speaking to her.

"Come on, love. I asked you a question! You were miles away. All that fresh air must have got to you."

"My apologies...I must have been daydreaming. What did you want to know?"

"It doesn't matter now. Was it a pleasant daydream?"

"I suppose so. I was thinking about something Kristine asked me in the car. You and I discussed it a while back."

"What was that?"

"...The prospect of visiting your son."

Emily looked across at him to test his reaction.

"Oh!" he said in surprise. "I haven't thought about that since we married. What made you bring it up now?"

"I told you. Kristine mentioned our trip in the car. She asked quite out of the blue if we had made any plans to go over there yet."

"So what did you tell her?"

"...That we haven't discussed it recently. But for some reason, it has set me thinking."

"About going?"

"Yes."

"Do you want to go?"

"I think so...it would be rather exciting. I have travelled very little in my life."

"Alright then. If you'd like to, we'll go!"

"...Just like that?"

"Well, maybe not quite 'just like that'. For one thing, my passport expired last year..."

"...I've never even had one!"

"There you are, then. Our passports are the first things we need to organise!"

"Are you sure about this?" asked Emily, a seed of doubt entering her mind. A minute ago it had only been a whim on her part. Now they were as good as on their way. "Don't you think we should discuss it further?"

"What's to discuss?" asked James. "As you said, a while back it was something I had planned to do...until a certain lovely lady turned my head, and gave me something else to think about!"

He grinned at Emily; his eyes sparkling.

"We would merely be carrying on from where I left off. I'll write to David and ask if we can visit next spring."

James got up and turned off the television.

He sat at the dresser where he extricated a writing pad from the top drawer, and then rummaged for a pen. As he wrote, he narrated each sentence for Emily to hear. Two pages of writing later, he scrawled: 'Love to the family, Dad', slashed a line beneath it, and settled back; satisfied with his missive.

"Right..." he said. "I'll get this off tomorrow. We should hear back fairly soon."

That night Emily's mind, stimulated into activity by talk of their exciting adventure, prevented the rest that precedes sleep, and she lay awake; trying not to disturb James.

Yet, even though Emily succeeded in her resolve, James was still aware of her.

In the middle of the night he whispered across to her, "Are you awake?"

"Yes," she replied, a little more loudly than his whisper. "I haven't been able to sleep at all."

James turned over to face her.

"Why?" he asked. "What's wrong?"

"I can't get that trip off my mind."

"Don't you want to go?"

"Oh, yes. ...At least, I think I still do. I've had such a rotten night I'm beginning to wish I never dreamt up a scheme like that in the first place! I hope it's not going to keep me awake every night."

"It's a new idea, that's all. It did come as a surprise..."

"...Well, maybe I'm getting a bit too old for surprises!"

James thought for a moment; then he said, "Would you like a cup of tea?"

Emily laughed. "Yes, please; that would be nice. I don't suppose either of us will be able to sleep anymore."

By ten o'clock the next morning the sleep that had eluded Emily all night finally caught up with her, and she excused herself to James, slipping up to the bedroom to catnap away the worst of her tiredness.

While she was lost to oblivion, the phone rang.

It was Ruth, wanting to talk to Emily.

"She's asleep at the moment," James told her.

"Asleep...at this hour? Is she alright?"

"Yes, she's fine. She just had a bad night: a few things on her mind. But it will pass. Shall I get her to phone you when she wakes up?"

"...If you don't mind. I'll be here until just after lunch."

Later on, only slightly refreshed, Emily rang her back.

"I wanted to let you know of a decision Wilbur and I have made," said Ruth.

"Oh, what's that?"

"Wilbur is officially retiring from school."

"My goodness," said Emily in surprise. "That's sudden, isn't it? He hasn't been taken ill again, has he?"

"No, nothing like that, thank goodness. That's why he's making the break now – before he has any more problems. As long as he takes it easy, he's alright. It's being at work that wears him out."

The following week, Ruth phoned again with some more information for Emily.

The official retirement date was in three weeks' time, and Ruth had secretively arranged with school staff that a surprise party be planned for Wilbur in their home; after the staid affair the members of the Board were holding for him on school premises.

Ruth told her that although only staff and department personnel were invited to the official function, Emily and James would be welcome to attend the party at the house.

"...In fact," Ruth insisted, "I want you to come."

Readily, Emily accepted and made a mental note of the date and time.

With two things to look forward to – a reply from David regarding the trip, and Wilbur's party – Emily brushed off the last of her misgivings.

A change in her pace of life succeeded in breaking the monotony of retirement, and the stimulus of anticipation gave her something to look forward to.

"It's nice to see you happy again," James remarked one day. "I was beginning to worry you weren't finding any joy in life, especially since that argument over golf. ...And I'm no help: it must be pretty dull, living with me," he added with a feigned expression of shame.

Emily nudged him playfully and slipped her arm around his waist.

"Oh, don't be silly, James. How could my life be boring with you? ...Quiet contentment; that's what I would call it. Please don't ever think you are dull!"

The reply from David, although expected, arrived at a time when Emily's thoughts were elsewhere, and it caught her off-guard.

Her heart skipped a beat when she watched James slit open the colourful airmail envelope and glanced down the typewritten page.

At long last he spoke.

"David says the timing of our visit suits them perfectly," James read out, grinning broadly. "...And they would love to have us."

Emily excitedly cupped her hands to her mouth; then took the letter off James to read it for herself.

Afterwards, with knees feeling decidedly shaky, she suggested they seal their decision to go overseas with a toast, and pulled out the bottle of sherry: Arthur's sherry, as she had come to regard it. And while Emily and her husband once more chinked glasses together, with 'a Happy Holiday when it comes', she added a silent and very private toast of her own.

"...To you, Arthur; wherever you are."

CHAPTER TWO

Outside Ruth and Wilbur's house, Emily fingered the spare key her daughter had left for them.

She waited for James to lock up the car; then made the covert entry deemed necessary to begin preparations for Wilbur's surprise party later in the day.

"I don't know where these last couple of weeks have got to," she said to James as they slipped inside.

"I know what you mean. It barely seems five minutes since Ruth told us about Wilbur's retirement."

James placed grocery bags full of party items onto the kitchen bench.

"Mind you," he went on, while straightening a bag that had fallen over. "We have been very busy just lately, and that does make the time seem to go by more quickly, don't you think?"

It surprised Emily that the house was devoid of all signs of the coming festivities; although, when she thought about it, she realised that Ruth would have planned it that way. As Ruth left for work at the same time as Wilbur, she could not have even begun to prepare for something like that without Wilbur wondering what was going on. So to Emily's way of thinking, out of necessity the house had to be left in its usual state...for the time being, anyway.

Emily drew breath to help her focus on the mammoth task ahead: that of transforming the house into a venue, and could not help but be reminded of how she lovingly changed her own home into a temporary wedding chapel.

She smiled, remembering how her sorrow that Kristine had been denied a part in the ceremony turned into joy when the bedraggled girl appeared half way through it.

Stimulated by her thoughts, Emily pressured James into useful action, and before long the living area had taken on a whole new appearance.

The arrangement made secretively by Ruth and members of the school staff, was that items required for catering were to be left at the school kitchen under lock and key against misappropriation by hungry youngsters. Then, later on they could be brought round to Ruth's house by helpers and teachers who were not actually on duty. When the official proceedings had finished, Wilbur was to be detained at the school for a few minutes, giving the rest of the staff time to race round to the house ahead of him.

There was but one fly in the ointment of the otherwise perfect scheme: Wilbur, as always, would want to walk the short distance home.

"He'll see all the cars parked outside," Ruth complained when the arrangements were being made; so permission was sought from the pastor of a local church for guests to utilise the car park.

Yet, all of this still lay some time ahead; although, by the time the transformation of the house had been completed Emily realised that the moment was much closer than thought. So she and James snatched a quick coffee before the people started to arrive with their contributions.

"Have the staff bought Wilbur a present?" James asked while they enjoyed their moment of rest.

"I expect so," Emily replied. "...And after all his years as school principal, I imagine it will be something special."

"I wonder what it is."

"Well, you won't have to wait long to find out," Emily said, glancing at the kitchen clock. "They'll be making the presentation to Wilbur right about now."

James also looked at the time, but from a vastly different perspective.

"Goodness!" he exclaimed. "Is it really that late? They'll all be coming round soon!"

"Relax, James," Emily insisted. "We've a few minutes in hand yet. Once those people come hurtling through the front door, our work will be done."

Emily and James were ready and waiting when the guests started to arrive.

Ruth was the first to appear, travelling home with three other ladies, who busily removed containers, plates and other items of food and beverage from the back of their car; now hidden from sight in the garage.

"Hello, Mum, is everything ready?" Ruth asked furtively as Emily let her in through the back door. After pecking her mother on the cheek, she rushed straight into the kitchen and turned on her oven for the savouries, then hurried back out to the car, saying as she passed, "You couldn't give us a hand to bring some of this stuff in, could you Mum? Time is of the essence now."

Emily followed her out to the garage, smiling a 'hello' to a couple of the ladies who were on their way into the house with more containers of food.

Soon another car pulled up outside the house. Two men jumped out and quickly opened up the boot to reveal crates of beer and a couple of wine casks.

Ruth slipped out to meet them.

"We'll have to be quick," one of the men called to her. "Wilbur's getting a lift home with the monstrosity. They'll be leaving very soon."

"Monstrosity?" said Ruth quizzically. "Do you mean his retirement gift?"

"Yes. I think it's awful. I wouldn't like to have it sitting in my house!"

"Perhaps it's as well it wasn't presented to you then," joked Ruth on her way back inside.

As soon as the last of the crates had been removed, the car at the kerbside sped away.

At the same time, what seemed like an army of people, some running, some half jogging, came hurrying along the footpath from the direction of the church car park.

The first to arrive at the house breathlessly shouted, "Quick, everyone. He'll be here any minute!"

Within seconds of the last person hurrying through the door, another car pulled up: this one carrying Wilbur and the deputy principal.

All the guests bundled themselves into the kitchen as planned, and were instructed not to make any noise.

Ruth casually went out to meet Wilbur and his colleague, hoping they would not be able to hear the stifled giggling and half-hearted attempts to keep quiet filtering out from the kitchen.

Wilbur smiled an acknowledgement at Ruth; then the men lifted something heavy from the back seat of the car: a large object that had been roughly re-wrapped in its ornate gift paper for protection during transit.

Carefully, they carried the object up the front steps. The instant they set foot in the house the kitchen fell silent. Ruth breathed a sigh of relief, and held open the lounge door for the men to carry in the expensive gift, which they set down on the floor against the far wall.

Wilbur groaned, and rubbed his back as he stood up.

"Gee, that thing is heavy. I am absolutely bushed!" he moaned to Ruth, and slumped into an easy chair. "Thank goodness it's all over. I don't think I could have gone on a moment longer!"

Ruth looked at the deputy principal in alarm. She had not reckoned on this: that Wilbur might be too weary to cope with something like a party.

What can we do, her eyes beseeched him.

The man saw her concern, and thinking quickly said to Wilbur, "You'll be fine after a rest."

"Yes, you're right," responded Wilbur. "I just needed to sit down. Standing for all those speeches was a bit much."

Suddenly a clatter from somewhere within the house arrested Wilbur's attention.

Another alarmed glance passed between Ruth and the deputy principal.

"What was that?" asked Wilbur, sitting up abruptly. "It sounded like it came from the kitchen. I hope next door's tom-cat hasn't got in through the window again; it leaves a terrible smell." And before Ruth could stop him, Wilbur sprang to his feet and rushed out of the room.

"Wilbur!" cried Ruth in a vain attempt to stop him, but it was too late.

Wilbur wrenched open the kitchen door, expecting to be confronted only by an errant cat.

"Oh, my God!" he shrieked, and clutched frantically at the door for support as the shock of seeing his kitchen full of people hit home.

"Surprise!" they all cried.

Once the party-goers saw Wilbur's shocked reaction, they fell silent.

The guest nearest to him reached out a helping hand and asked, "Wilbur, are you alright?"

Ruth rushed up to him, suddenly afraid that the shock of surprise may have adversely affected her husband's heart condition.

How could I have been so stupid, she told herself, to be persuaded that a surprise party would be a good idea?

She escorted Wilbur, now shaking, into the lounge and eased him onto the couch; then she sat down beside him, watching his every move.

One by one the guests sheepishly made their way out of the kitchen and through the hall; aware of the fright they had inflicted on their treasured colleague; each also afraid for his wellbeing.

Wilbur's face was now ashen and he appeared to be short of breath, causing great concern for Ruth.

By now Emily had squeezed through the mass of people and was by her daughter's side.

"Do you want me to call for an ambulance?" she asked.

"No, not just yet, Mum. Let's give him a few minutes to recover. A shock like that would turn anybody this colour."

Wilbur rebuked her. "I'll be alright soon. ...Really."

"Perhaps we'd better go," suggested one of the guests.

"No.... No, I won't hear of it," insisted Wilbur, perking up slightly. "You have all gone to so much trouble just for me; I don't intend to send you away." And then, waving a hand towards them he said, "Please, pour yourselves a drink, or whatever you've got tucked away through there. I'll just sit here and watch for the time being."

At first, nobody moved. Each guest had become acutely aware of their folly in organising a party under present circumstances.

A teacher standing close to the refreshments nudged his neighbour.

"Come on," he said; "let's get this party underway," and handed him a glass.

Then others followed suit. Within a few minutes a hum of quiet conversation was established; nobody as yet willing to speak in normal tones for fear of upsetting their treasured colleague.

All this time, Ruth sat beside her husband; keeping an eye on him for signs of improvement or deterioration.

After a period of gentle respite, observing the goings on and nodding occasionally to people with whom he worked, he started to feel better.

To Ruth, Wilbur's breathing seemed more relaxed than before, and a rosy hue came back to his cheeks. It looked like the crisis was over.

Gradually she began to feel the weight of worry lifting from her shoulders.

Ruth looked up at Emily who had remained close by; ready to be of assistance to her daughter and son-in-law if the need arose.

Emily smiled at them both, and gently squeezed Ruth's shoulder for reassurance.

"I'll get you a drink," she informed her daughter. "You look as though you could use one. ...Just an orange juice for you, Wilbur?"

Wilbur lifted his drawn features to her. "Yes, that would be great... Thank you." He leaned over to speak to his wife. "Ruth, love, do you think we could have a window or two opened? It's very stuffy in here."

"Yes, of course," she replied, getting up.

She crossed over to the wide ranch slider window and, snapping back the lock, pulled it right back to let in some fresh air.

Then she went round each of the windows in turn, opening them all slightly to create a gentle movement of air within the stuffy room.

216

A few minutes later one of the guests started some music playing, keeping the volume control turned down in deference to Wilbur's delicate state.

Ruth glanced at Wilbur. Would the music on top of their conversation prove too much for him?

But Wilbur looked more at ease now, quietly sipping the drink Emily had handed to him, so Ruth let the music play on; reminding herself of the necessity to watch out for an increase in volume as alcohol drove the guests to become less inhibited.

However, they remained subdued during the course of the evening, much to her relief. Each of the guests had, in their own way, received almost as bad a shock as Wilbur, and all were mindful of the need not to upset him further. By the time the food had been eaten and the moderate amount of drink consumed, the party had still managed to retain a degree of discipline. And each person eventually left, content in the knowledge that Wilbur was alright.

Ruth thanked them individually for coming and for their patience, kissing on the cheek her special friends; wishing them all well, as they did to her in return. At last she closed the door behind them. She desperately wanted to cry from exhaustion, but was too tired.

Soon a welcome peace descended over the house. Back in the lounge Wilbur, James and Emily were seated in easy chairs, talking amongst themselves.

Ruth stood in the doorway for a moment, taking in the tranquil scene.

She was encouraged that nothing had come of the unfortunate incident, and deeply thankful that Wilbur's improving condition had not been jeopardised, as much for her own sake as for Wilbur's. For had he been rushed to hospital, had he suffered a second heart-attack as a result of their stupidity; had she lost him...she would never have forgiven herself.

"Ruth, come and take the weight off your feet; you look worn out," said Emily, offering the chair she was sitting on. "I'll sit with Wilbur for a while."

She pulled Ruth over to the vacated chair with minimal protest in reply.

For once, Ruth was glad to be relieved of responsibility. It had been quite a day, all in all, and now that it was over she realised just how weary she was.

She closed her tired eyes to rest them, and a moment later had unintentionally slipped into a shallow doze.

Emily busied herself clearing up in the kitchen. Most of the work had already been done.

She was touched that everyone had gone to the trouble of leaving as little mess from the impromptu party as possible. Leftover food had been neatly stowed away in the fridge, and most of the empty bottles crated and taken out to one of the cars.

Within only a few minutes she found herself free to re-join the others in the lounge. But just as she was in the process of replacing the tea towel ready to do so, James appeared in the kitchen.

"Oh," said Emily. "I was just coming back in."

"Ruth and Wilbur have nodded off," said James in a lowered voice. "I thought we might slip away."

Emily paused in her bid to hang her tea towel over the oven door handle.

"I don't think we should go just yet. It would seem a bit rude to just disappear; leaving them asleep. They'll only be dozing. I'm sure it wouldn't take much to rouse them, and I'd hate for them to wake up and see us creeping out. How about we sit outside instead? I could use some fresh air."

A few minutes later, Ruth joined Emily and James in her modest back garden – a plot much smaller than Emily's but nevertheless well-manicured, with dahlias abounding.

"Wilbur's still snoozing," she told them. "I put his feet up on the stool and covered him with a rug. He should sleep for a while yet. It will do him good."

"We were tempted to leave while you were resting," James admitted sheepishly.

"I'm sorry I dropped off, but I couldn't keep my eyes open. I'm glad you didn't go, though."

"Come and sit with us," urged Emily. "We're admiring Wilbur's dahlias."

Ruth sat down obediently.

"Yes, Wilbur still loves his dahlias. If he can't spend time in his garden every day he seems to stagnate. Gardening helps him to maintain a balance. It may sound strange, but I'm relieved it was a heart attack he had, and not a stroke. I think he would vegetate if he ever lost the ability to work in the garden...and I don't how I would cope if he ever had a stroke. The idea of looking after someone like that sends shivers down my spine..."

"He's going to find it quiet round here while you are at work," ventured James.

"Oh, didn't you know – I've given up work, too!"

"No, I didn't realise this was your retirement as well as Wilbur's. Nothing was said..."

Embarrassed by his mistake, James looked critically at Emily for an explanation.

"I'm afraid it slipped my mind," admitted Emily, feeling guilty now that this important factor had been overlooked. "We planned everything for Wilbur when really the party should have been to honour you both."

"Don't worry about it. The school board made a fuss of me as well as Wilbur; so I wasn't forgotten."

"How long did you work at the school?" asked Emily; searching her mind for the answer. "My concept of timing has gone hay-wire over the years."

"I took on the role of school secretary a few months after Wilbur joined the staff; which makes it about twenty years. That's how we met...don't you remember?"

"Oh yes, of course. ...How forgetful of me," said Emily, all at once feeling foolish.

"What did they give you, Ruth?" asked James, leaning round Emily to address her. "Oh, I know...the monstrosity. ...And that reminds me. We still haven't seen it."

"The monstrosity? Is that how they described it?" Ruth laughed, realising what James was referring to. Then she added, "It's actually a beautiful baby grandfather clock."

Emily chuckled.

"A baby grandfather. That's a contradiction in terms if ever I heard one."

"I know it sounds silly, but that's what I call it, because that is what it looks like; I'm not sure of the correct name. Come back inside, and see for yourselves. I should check on my poor husband, anyway."

Wilbur was still asleep when they tiptoed into the lounge. Emily and James stood just inside the doorway while Ruth crept over the carpet to where their gift stood.

Squatting down in front of it, she delicately fingered its stiff, colourful wrapping paper. The Sellotape had been re-sealed to aid transportation, causing the paper on which it was fixed to crackle as Ruth tried to ease it off.

She stopped what she was doing and glanced towards Wilbur to see if he had been awakened by the noise; but apparently not.

Looking up, she grinned at the pair of observers; then carried on with her mission.

220

Emily was concerned now that the rustling of the paper, though almost imperceptible, might still waken the sleeping invalid and cause an adverse reaction.

She mouthed with only a trace of a whisper, "Ruth, don't bother...we can see it some other time."

"I'm nearly finished," Ruth mouthed back.

With another gentle tug, the paper fell away revealing, as Ruth had described it, a baby grandfather clock; standing no more than three feet in height.

Though modern in design, the clock also retained many classic features; its brass pendulum glinting against a dark mahogany surround.

Emily let out a little gasp of admiration.

"It's beautiful," she mouthed expressively. "Why would anyone say it's a monstrosity?"

"You should just hear the chime," whispered Ruth with excitement, now that the clock was finally in their home.

She ushered them back into the hall so that they could speak normally.

"It's electronic," she said. "There are two settings, and both are lovely and melodic; not harsh or clanking at all. I can see myself waiting for the top of each hour, so that I can hear the pretty chime. Maybe when Wilbur's woken up I'll set it going..."

"...I'm already awake," came Wilbur's voice through the half-open doorway.

Ruth grimaced and peered round the door. "Sorry love. We didn't mean to wake you."

"That's alright. I didn't want to doze too long anyway, or I won't be able to sleep tonight."

Wilbur swung his legs off the stool and pushed the knee rug aside. He started to get up; then slumped back as his legs failed to produce enough strength.

Ruth helped him to his feet.

221

"It's time we were going," said Emily.

"Thank you so much for all your help, both of you," said Ruth, appreciatively.

"It was our pleasure. I'm so glad everything turned out alright in the end."

Some weeks later – during the in between stage, as Emily regarded it, when the early plans for their trip had been made but not yet implemented – she and James waited for Royston to pick them up for what was now their regular Sunday outing.

However, this time Kristine would not be accompanying them around the golf course. She had phoned her father the night before, excusing herself because of other plans, and he had then informed Emily in case it altered her wish to go with them.

Yet Emily always enjoyed the outing, with or without the company of her granddaughter. It provided her with fresh air and exercise, a chance to socialise afterwards with an amiable group of people, some of whom she had come to know quite well, and it was also an opportunity to keep in touch with Royston, who was now more of a son to her than Fiona had ever been a daughter.

So, with her usual enthusiasm for their day's activities, she sat by the window; eagerly watching out for the familiar shape of Royston's car. And when at last she saw it turn the corner and cruise slowly up the narrow road, she yelped with delight to see that somebody was sitting in the front seat next to him.

"Here he is!" she called out to James. "And it looks like he's got Kristine with him. She must have changed her plans and decided to come after all!"

However, when the car drew up, and she waited for its two occupants to emerge, Emily realised the female figure accompanying Royston could not be Kristine. This person had blonde hair, not dark; and rather than the shapeless form of a girl, this person seemed to be a mature woman.

"Oh, help!" cried Emily and moved from the window; to conceal herself from the interloper she now guessed to be Royston's lady friend.

She rushed into the kitchen where James was taking a sip of water.

"It's not Kristine! It's a woman!" she shrieked at him in little more than a hoarse whisper.

James put his glass in the sink and, swallowing quickly in order to respond, turned around.

"Not Fiona; surely!"

"No. This one's a stranger. I think she must be Royston's girlfriend. He confided in me not long ago that he had met somebody; but fancy bringing her here, today of all days!"

"Lower your voice, Emily. They're coming inside..."

"...Anybody home?"

Royston walked straight in; pulling his lady behind him, while James and Emily emerged from the kitchen.

"Ah! There you are! I've brought a friend...she's going to caddy for me. Emily, this is Sylvia."

Royston stood back slightly so the two startled figures could see the woman more clearly. Then he said, "Darling, I'd like you to meet Emily and James."

Sylvia stepped out further into the hallway, smiled and bobbed her head as she affectedly said, "Pleased to meet you, I'm quite sure."

Emily returned the acknowledgement and, still looking at Sylvia, directed a comment at Royston.

"You didn't tell us you were bringing a friend, Royston."

Instantly, James picked up a hint of criticism in her voice. To disguise it he said, "Shall we get going before the course becomes too crowded?"

223

Royston also noted Emily's tone.

He responded quickly with, "Yes...good idea;" then he ushered Sylvia out again.

Emily held back for a moment; watching as the woman sashayed along the path.

Sylvia's sandal-clad feet looked too dainty to survive the arduous trek around eighteen holes of golf course, as did the rest of her voluptuous form bedecked in a frilly blouse and tight-fitting pants: attire more suitable for a barbeque party than a game of golf.

James came up behind her, clutching his unwieldy bag of clubs.

"Well what do you make of that?" Emily asked him; still taken aback by the realisation that a stranger would be accompanying them.

"What is there to make of it, love?" James responded. "Royston has brought his new girlfriend with him. We can do nothing but accept it – just like your family once had no choice but to accept me!"

"Yes, I suppose you're right," conceded Emily without much sincerity.

As they drove to the golf course, she and James in the back seat while Sylvia sat cosily beside Royston at the front, Emily made an analysis of her.

She searched for flaws in every giggle, every shake of the luscious blonde hair, any remark directed at Royston which might give Emily cause for disapproval. Yet to her dismay she found none. The woman seemed to be a reasonable individual after all – except for her overstated appearance and familiar behaviour towards Royston.

Emily wished fervently she would leave him alone for a moment. Why did she have to snuggle up to him like that when they were all in the car? It was embarrassing.

Throughout the game, Emily remained close to James. Rather than chat in between shots, as she normally did with Kristine, she strolled along by herself, preferring to caddy like a dutiful servant; often weaving from one side of the fairway to the other when his shots strayed, rather than risk meeting up with Sylvia in the middle. Only when the party of four arrived at each putting green did Emily afford her any courtesy.

On the other hand, Royston's new lady friend spent very little time at her golfing partner's side; much to his developing annoyance.

Sylvia had never been on a golf course before. As such, the vast expanse of manicured landscape over which they crisscrossed intrigued her. Now and then she disappeared into wooded areas to see what lay within them; emerging once or twice with a golf ball she had found. For this, Royston forgave her. The prizes with which she presented him made up for her absence when he needed her.

"You're doing well; finding all those golf balls," Emily remarked while they halted for the men to drive off on the final hole.

It irked her that Sylvia found more on her own than she and Kristine had ever produced between them.

"Think of it as beginner's luck," Sylvia retorted; secretly proud of her accomplishment.

All in all Sylvia was enjoying herself; although she would have preferred it if the other half of the foursome had been a bit younger. The woman, she quickly noticed, seemed to deliberately keep away from her; which made socialising difficult. ...But then, she had no great wish to make friends with the ex-in-laws of her new boyfriend, either. As far as she was concerned, she was out with Royston, not a couple of old fuddy-duddies.

225

The game completed, Royston suggested a drink in the clubhouse would be nice.

Yet, before James or Sylvia could get a word in, Emily reacted in obvious haste..

"No, Royston. Not today, if you don't mind. I would like to go home, please."

The thought of having to introduce Sylvia to the friends she had made at the golf club was too much.

To cover her obvious unwillingness to spend more time in the woman's company, Emily feebly added, "I... I've got a bit of headache. The atmosphere inside will make it far worse than it is already."

"We could bring our drinks outside!" suggested Sylvia. "Oh, please Royston. Let's stay. I just love it here."

"Well...I don't know."

Royston wanted desperately to accommodate his lady friend, but Emily had seemed adamant.

Then, as if to come to the rescue of his troubled wife, James made the final decision on the matter.

"Sorry, Royston, but I agree with Emily; we really should get going. It won't hurt us if we miss out on our after-golf drinks for once."

On the way home, Sylvia sulked petulantly.

She barely acknowledged either Emily or James when they got out of the car to remove the golfing equipment. Even Emily's half-hearted, "Good-bye...see you next time," was ignored.

"I knew I had good reason to dislike that woman," Emily told James back in the house. "I don't know what Royston sees in her."

"Oh, I do!" kidded James. "It's quite obvious...to a man, anyway. Feminine charm fair oozes out of that one! Poor Royston is hooked, I'm afraid. It will be a while before young Sylvia lets go of him!"

"You don't suppose he'll want to marry her, do you?" asked Emily in horror.

"I hope not," James retorted.

"What an awful state of affairs!" moaned Emily. "I feel so sorry for Kristine."

"...Why Kristine?"

"Because she won't be happy visiting her father if Sylvia is there; I'm sure of that." And then a thought occurred to her. "I wonder if she even knows about Sylvia."

"You can ask her yourself if you like...here she comes now!" said James, pointing through the window as Kristine pushed her bike across the road towards them.

"Oh dear!" exclaimed Emily; "...Maybe she does."

Emily moved closer to the window.

Discreetly she watched her granddaughter park the bicycle in its usual place; then she discreetly whispered as the girl came up the front steps, "She looks happy enough, so there can't be a problem."

"Hi, Nana! Hello...James," Kristine said, walking straight in. To call the husband of her grandmother by his first name still did not readily slip off the tongue.

"It's nice to see you..." remarked Emily; "...considering I didn't think we would have the pleasure of your company at all today."

"Sorry about that. It couldn't be helped, I'm afraid. My friend Richard needed me to help with a school project for tomorrow. I should have phoned you, but Dad said he'd explain. I hope you didn't mind walking round by yourself."

"I wasn't by myself..." Emily began to say, but stopped; realising she should not mention Sylvia.

"What do you mean by that?" asked Kristine, and then, chuckling, answered her own question. "Oh, of course; you were with Dad and James. You wouldn't have been on your own, would you?"

227

Emily felt alarm bells ring in her head. Royston can't have told Kristine that Sylvia was going with him, she thought. How can I find out if she even knows about her without letting the cat out of the bag?

"Will you stay for a while?" Emily ventured. "We've not long been home ourselves. I was just going to put the kettle on for a cuppa."

"I won't stay now, if you don't mind. I only called in to apologise for ducking out on you this morning." Then she added as an afterthought, "I also wanted to tell you about something interesting..."

Perhaps she's going to tell us about Sylvia now, Emily thought hopefully.

"...It's about Mum."

"Fiona? What's the problem?"

"Oh, there's no problem...for once. I just thought you'd like to know she's got a job."

"How incredible! I didn't think your mother had it in her to go out and look for a job!"

"She didn't. She was offered it."

Emily laughed. "I might have known. What sort of job has she got? Is it in the city or somewhere close to home? And how come she was offered it..?"

"...Wait on; I can't answer all your questions at once!"

"Sorry. It's just great to hear that my wayward daughter has taken the initiative and done something for herself. Are you sure you won't stay and tell me more about it?"

"No, I can't. There's not much more to tell, anyway. An old friend of Mum's has set up a cottage industry with her husband, making hand-knitted angora jerseys, and they need someone to help with the office work. Apparently Mum worked in an office before she had me, so the friend suggested they give her a try. I was there when they asked her. Mum accepted straight away. I couldn't believe that

228

my mother actually agreed to go out to work. The job is in town, so she has to use the bus to begin with. She said something about buying a little car later on – she's been without one since Dad left. It hasn't mattered before now because she never goes out except to the shops, and then she uses a taxi. I suppose buying a little a car for work can't be called excessive!

Kristine laughed, remembering the flashy new car her mother nearly bought.

Afterwards, Emily could not get over Kristine's news.

So Fiona is branching out, she thought; or is it that she is getting tired of her own company? Maybe this job will help her organise a few things in her own life, as well as for her new boss.

A feeling of relief began to enter Emily's mind, that this particular twin was taking hold of her life and bringing some meaning back into it – if only the routine of a regular job. To have something into which she could pour all her energy should benefit her, both socially and financially. ...And, if she remembered correctly, Fiona was very good at her job in her early working days.

In fact, Emily reflected, Fiona would probably have made it to the top in her line of work if, like Ruth, she had remained childless.

How differently everything would have turned out if that had been the case. She would not have stagnated at home; she could have afforded all those luxuries of which, she had claimed, Emily deprived her in her childhood.

As a result, there would not now be the feud between them, but rather a normal friendly relationship.

On the other hand, she thought; if Fiona had remained a career woman like her sister, she would probably not have had Kristine...

Dear Kristine: closer to her heart than any other soul; except for James, of course...and Arthur.

The thought of Arthur again produced a sigh and a quiet longing for times past.

Oh, how things have changed in recent years.

'I'm too old now for changes,' Emily moaned to herself as she prepared the evening meal.

'My autumn years should be progressing smoothly in harmony with my environment, without the upheaval of matrimonial break-ups, family discontent; even remarrying at this time of life.

And now...there's Sylvia!'

James did not notice his wife's quietness during the evening. They were both tired from the strain of meeting Royston's girlfriend and after the exertion of their game of golf; so neither made any demands of the other, save to agree that they should both have an early night.

By the time she got up the next morning, Emily had already filed away the anxieties of the previous day, and returned her attention to domestic matters.

Routine, she had long since realised, can sometimes be a good means of escape from life's little worries.

CHAPTER THREE

The bowling club birthday party, to mark the anniversary of its inception, was regarded as the highlight of the club's social calendar. In all the years Emily had been a member of the club she rarely missed the event, and this year she was keenly looking forward to it.

The previous year, the anniversary had been something of a shambles for Emily. On tenterhooks the whole time, parading before the community with a new husband, she had been sensitive to the stares of the ladies, and suspected the pair must have been the butt of many male jokes. After all, she later reflected, back then they looked on James as a usurper who swept Emily off her feet in the wake of her sad loss; an action she seemed not to resist, and one which they regarded disapprovingly.

The reverberation from their unkind attitude was felt through the whole club, and therefore within Emily's heart, for many months after that occasion.

But this year it was different. Everything had settled down. Now she and James were accepted in the same spirit as she and Arthur had once been accepted.

Happily, Emily felt sure that the months of trial were at last behind them, and they could move ahead with dignity within the club, as an established married couple.

In fact, the celebration turned out to be everything Emily hoped for: a thoroughly enjoyable night out with friends; at which she and James stayed until its conclusion, savouring the last of the convivial atmosphere.

It was not particularly late when they made their way home; but late enough for the older couple whose stamina was not quite the same as it was in their younger days.

In the car with them was another couple to whom James had offered a lift home. As they lived in the same direction, Emily had asked to be dropped off first while James drove his passengers the rest of their way.

The house was in darkness when she entered, and silent as a mausoleum. Before switching on the light, she basked in the tranquillity which contrasted markedly with the noisy environment earlier in the evening.

Suddenly she heard a sound within the house, and it alarmed her. Holding her breath she listened intently.

There it was again.

Emily's attention was drawn upstairs. Maybe it was the neighbour's cat. ...Or maybe not.

"Is anybody there?" she timidly called out.

Frantically her fingers searched the wall for the light switch. The hallway mercifully burst into light; then, with a pop the light bulb blew out, plunging her into darkness again. No matter, she thought, there's a switch at the top of the stairs, too.

Suspicious now that her misgivings were not without foundation, Emily cautiously climbed the stairs; her heart pounding. One hand slid up the wall for support while the other firmly grasped her handbag. She was more than ready to use it as a weapon against the cat, if need be.

At the top step she hesitated; holding her breath both out of fear and out of a desperate desire to hear nothing more than a deep silence, which would reassure her that she was alone.

But somebody really was there...and it could not have been the cat.

Almost indiscernibly she could hear guarded breathing close by; very close by. ...Only inches, in fact, from where she was standing.

Panicking, she screamed and lunged at the light switch she knew to be on the opposite wall. At the same time a shadowy figure jumped out at her, shoving her hard against the doorpost.

Emily dropped to the floor with a shriek of pain.

In an instant, a man leapt down the flight of stairs two at a time; then, banging the front door against the wall as he wrenched it open, disappeared into the night.

The house suddenly fell silent again. Not a sound could be heard from Emily, not even a groan; for the impact of flesh and bone against the unyielding doorpost had jolted all sensibility out of her frail form, and she fell down unconscious; unaware of anything but oblivion.

When James arrived home some fifteen minutes later, the house was still in darkness.

Puzzled as to why, he called Emily's name and reached for the hall light. With no response from either, concern swept through him and he groped for another light switch.

He found Emily lying in a heap at the top of the stairs.

Flicking on the light that Emily had tried in vain to locate, he knelt beside her.

For a panic-stricken moment he thought she was dead. But then the policeman in him took over. Before emotion blurred his senses he checked her pulse and her breathing, and found them to be rhythmic. With a token sigh of relief, he relinquished his initial fears.

But James was still ignorant of what had caused her fall. His first thought was that Emily might have blacked out coming up the stairs.

As yet he had no inkling of what had just taken place.

As yet Emily, herself, was unable to give him any clues as to how she fell.

However, of one fact James was absolutely certain. Emily needed help.

Instinctively, he knew what he should do.

Gently sliding a pillow under her head, he hurried down to the phone and called an ambulance. When he came back up the stairs, Emily was showing the first signs of recovering consciousness.

With eyes now open she looked at his face as if reading his features; giving James the impression she was actually trying to remember who he was.

"Oh, Emily!" he cried plaintively, and knelt down beside her again.

But Emily was now in shock after what had happened and too frightened to move; reluctant even to disturb her present position in case movement might reveal injuries she would rather not contemplate.

James slid his arm around the back of her shoulder to help her to a sitting position.

In doing, so he brought her out of the reverie that had numbed her normal functioning, and she groaned as a searing pain shot through the hip onto which she had fallen heavily.

"Don't move me... Please!" she mouthed, with scarcely more than a whisper escaping her lips.

"Alright, I won't touch you again," promised James, and he moved back fractionally to affirm his intention. "The ambulance is on its way," he said. "Is there anything I can do to make you more comfortable?"

Emily raised her hand to his knee and feebly patted it.

"No, I'll be alright for a few minutes... Just too scared to move... It feels like I've broken my back."

"What happened? Did you trip on the stairs?"

234

"No… I was pushed."

"Pushed? What do you mean?"

James stared at her in disbelief.

Surely she was mistaken.

Emily's breathing was becoming laboured now. Talking had wearied her. She knew there was little probability of James tracing the intruder after all this time, and the effort of telling him about it was just too much at the moment. So before a new wave of unconsciousness swept over her, she quickly said, "I'll tell you what happened later."

The ambulance arrived within a few minutes.

Initially, James heard it go straight past, and he rushed outside in the hope of catching it.

In the poorly lit street the ambulance driver, unable to make out the street numbers, and had shot past the house, only to discover his error seconds later.

By the time James reached the gate the ambulance was backing up, its white reversing lights illuminating the way.

Peering into his wing mirror, the driver saw the darkened figure of James waving his arms, and knew now that he had the right address.

"It's my wife," James told the driver and his partner through the open ambulance window. "She's had a fall. I think she must have tripped on the stairs."

For the time being, he decided, Emily's claim that she was pushed must be kept under wraps. He still maintained she was mistaken about what really happened.

The two attendants jumped down from the vehicle, and on opposite sides ran round the back to open up the double doors. Deftly, one of them pulled out a collapsible stretcher, while the other fetched a large bag containing, James guessed, all manner of life-saving gadgets.

Directing them to be careful of the step as they entered the house, he followed them in.

Once inside, the ambulance men set about their work. Space at the top of the stairs where Emily had fallen was restricted, especially when it came to manoeuvring such a bulky object as a stretcher. Yet, somehow they managed to slide it alongside her. Then, while one checked Emily's vital signs, the other opened up the straps and blankets on the stretcher ready to receive her.

James stood back admiring their work, but gasped with anxiety when the still unconscious Emily was turned onto her back ready for transfer onto the stretcher. However, it reassured him to know that her comatose state prevented her from feeling any pain the tricky move would otherwise have caused her.

On their way to the hospital Emily, now receiving oxygen, regained consciousness.

The sight of flashing lights around her, the oxygen mask over her face, and the movement of an unfamiliar vehicle at first alarmed her.

Then she realised she where she was.

She moved her head stiffly to look for James.

On the seat opposite and almost out of her view, he was peering through the windscreen; urging the ambulance on as it wound through the late night traffic. So intently was he concentrating that he failed to notice Emily's face upturned towards him; until he heard, despite the noise around him, his name being softly called out.

Abruptly he turned to look at her.

Seeing her awake and responsive, he slid back along the seat so she could see him properly.

"Hello, love," he said, reaching for the hand she held out to him. "How are you feeling?"

"Not too bad," came her muffled reply from behind the mask. "My hip is very sore, though."

James twisted round to speak to the attendant again.

"My wife is conscious again, and seems to be okay apart from some discomfort," he informed them briefly.

Then he leant back on the bench and breathed deeply with a welcome sense of relief.

Emily was out of danger and in good hands.

Inside the hospital, Emily was taken to the accident and emergency department, where she was transferred onto a trolley in a curtained cubicle to await examination.

The orderlies who assisted her clicked the trolley's sides into place; then a few minutes later a nurse entered to take a blood sample, and more vital signs. After the nurse had left, James pulled up a chair to be near her and for privacy; for the department, even late at night, was both busy and extremely noisy.

After a while Emily began to feel uncomfortable on the narrow cot. She longed to be able to get off it and walk around; to go to the toilet – to go home and get some much-needed sleep.

But she also dreaded the thought of going home. Her most recent experience of being at home was one of shock, horror and pain. How could she ever get James to believe that she had not fallen as such, but had indeed been pushed by a burglar? The whole situation was just too bizarre and frightening for her to contemplate; for in one minute she and her husband had been out enjoying themselves, and in the next...

"...What's wrong, Emily?" asked James.

For a while he had been sitting back; his eyes closed, trying to stop himself from nodding off to sleep, when it came to his attention that Emily was restless. It seemed to

James that many hours had passed since they first arrived at the emergency department, and so far nobody except the nurse had been in to check on them.

"I'm alright," replied Emily gallantly; the twinge in her hip giving her more pain than she had suffered since the birth of the twins.

The last thing she wanted right now was to be a bother to her husband. Hadn't she caused him enough trouble this evening by stupidly falling over?

...Maybe she was mistaken about being pushed; maybe she just wasn't watching where she was going and...

All of a sudden, the curtain surrounding Emily's cubicle was wrenched back, and a man entered.

James assumed from the stethoscope hanging from his neck that he must be a doctor, although the lack of a white coat caused a moment of uncertainty in his mind. But then, when he introduced himself as the ward's night-duty doctor, James relaxed; happy at last that Emily would now be attended to.

"Of course, we'll have to take an X-ray, Mrs Forsythe," he said after examining her. "From the amount of pain you are in, it rather looks like you have broken your right hip."

"Oh, no," groaned Emily. "What does that mean?"

"Depending on the result of the X-ray, it probably means a small operation to insert a metal pin into your hip joint. But don't worry; lots of women from your age-group have operations like this. They usually make a speedy recovery and go on to lead normal lives afterwards. It's really no worse than having your tonsils out!"

The doctor laughed with his last remark to set Emily's mind at ease.

Yet for Emily, the realisation of what had taken place: that she had been assaulted, injured and now brought to hospital, possibly for an operation, was starting to sink in.

As she was wheeled to the surgical ward with James at her side, tears began to well up in her eyes.

"How could this have happened to me, tonight of all nights?" she moaned quietly to him.

Yet, James did not hear her. He was too focused on helping the orderly to guide the trolley with its precious cargo through a service lift door.

Emily was taken to a ward that contained four beds, two of which were empty.

The orderly pushed the trolley alongside one of the empty beds and pulled a set of curtains around it. Then he left James and Emily alone.

Moments later two more orderlies entered.

Without a word they released the clasps on the trolley's cot-sides, and pushed them down. One of the orderlies went around to the bottom end of the hospital bed, slid his foot underneath it and pumped up the bed to match the height of the trolley.

Together they eased their patient from the trolley onto the bed; leaving Emily with an unexpected feeling of relief and freedom.

After they had gone a nurse came in, introduced herself as Emily's care worker for the night and, excusing herself to James, helped Emily to change into a hospital gown.

Meanwhile James looked around the ward, taking in the sights and sounds of an environment that was unusual for him, and which he had experienced only once in recent years when his first wife, Janet was taken ill and brought to this very hospital.

"She's all yours," said the caregiver, drawing back the cubicle curtain.

"Thank you," said James and turned his attention to the ward's newest patient.

239

Pulling up a bedside chair, he sat down and took hold of Emily's hand; grinning, he gave it a squeeze.

Then he noticed her hospital gown of white winceyette with drawstrings that fastened at the back of the neck.

Suddenly he burst out laughing.

"What's so funny?" she snapped. Emily was too tired to appreciate humour just now.

"Have you seen yourself in that?" he asked, pointing at the nightgown.

"It's not exactly the height of fashion, is it?" she said, looking down at her new attire.

"How's the bed, by the way? Is it comfortable?"

"It's like a feather mattress after that other one. I didn't want to worry you, but I was really in quite a lot of pain lying on the trolley."

"And what about now? Has the pain eased? Would you like me to ask the nurse for some painkillers?"

"It's not as bad. I would just like to rest now. Maybe I'll ask them to give me something in the morning."

Emily lay back and closed her eyes.

James could see that sleep wasn't too far away from her...and he, too, needed to have a rest.

He, too, felt the effect of all that had happened over the past few hours. His part in the emergency had been played; and with the weight of care and responsibility at last lifting from him he felt alarmingly weak.

Yet, being the archetypal helper, he strove to conceal it and told Emily, "Yes, my love; rest now; you need it. This whole business has been quite a shock for you. But you're in the best of care, and I will stay with you."

Emily smiled up into his eyes. "James, wherever would I be without you?"

"That's what marriage is all about, isn't it...being there for each other? But I have let you down in one way."

"What's that?" asked Emily.

She could not, in her present situation, imagine any way in which he might have done such a thing.

"In our haste I didn't even think of a bag for you."

"A bag?"

"An overnight bag with a nightie and some toiletries; at very least, a toothbrush."

Emily laughed at his concern, pleasing James that her distress had lessened.

"I'm sure I'll manage. Anyway, they don't yet know that my hip is broken. It may just be bruised. If the X-ray is clear then there will only be the one night involved. I'm sure I can survive it in this beautiful ensemble," she jested, pretending to model her hospital gown on the bed. "And I doubt if my dentures will rot in my head if they are not cleaned properly just once!"

James shared in her hilarity; feeling better now about the whole episode. But then he recalled a comment she made back at the house.

Suddenly he became serious, wondering whether it was too soon to question her over it.

Emily noticed the change in his demeanour.

"You've gone quiet, James. Is anything bothering you?"

"No...not really. It was just something you said before they brought you here...when I came home and discovered you had fallen."

"I don't remember. What did I say?"

"...That you didn't fall, but were pushed. Do you recall saying that?"

Emily searched her mind. In all honesty, she could not remember telling James what happened.

However, amnesia she did not have. Every detail of the brief encounter with the heavy-handed assailant was still

241

clear in her mind. A shiver ran through her as she thought about it again.

She wondered, now, who the intruder had been and why he was there in her home. Was he a common burglar? ...And what of his intent? Had an offence already been committed that as yet they knew nothing about? What kind of disarray would James come across on his return to the house...?

There were so many unknowns. Yet of one thing Emily was absolutely certain. The intruder was male.

At the time, everything happened too quickly for her to give it rational thought. But now, on reflection, something came back to her which she had previously overlooked. It was his aroma.

She remembered that while she stood listening at the top of the stairs – when she first sensed the presence of another person – her perception of it was heightened by a repugnant smell, such as the one given off by a cigarette-smoking, beer-drinking male. His aroma was not strong; just repulsive, and as such: memorable. Yes...her assailant was definitely a man. But when did she mention this to James? That, she could not remember. Nonetheless, he apparently knew about it.

If this was the case, then did he take her revelation seriously? Had he already spoken to his colleagues in the police force about it, prompting a manhunt in the night? These were questions she longed to ask her husband...but they would have to wait.

Emily looked at James. His face had the appearance of one patiently awaiting an explanation. Then she remembered he had asked her a question.

"Sorry, love. I was day-dreaming for a minute. What did you ask me?"

"Don't worry...you were resting. I shouldn't bother you with it now? It can wait until tomorrow."

"No...I was rude to drift away like that. Please tell me, or I will worry about it for the rest of the night..."

"...I just wondered what made you think somebody had pushed you when you fell."

"Oh, yes; that's right. I did say I had been pushed."

"But why did you say it?"

"Because that's what really happened," she said with absolute conviction.

"Do you mean to tell me that somebody was upstairs in our house, and attacked you?"

"Yes. That's precisely what I mean."

James could not believe his ears. This was his first serious consideration that Emily's fall was not an accident. He had assumed all along that she was mistaken. In truth, it never occurred to him before now that his wife knew exactly what she was talking about.

He looked at his watch. It was close to five o'clock in the morning, and far too late to get into conversation about something so grave.

They had both been under considerable strain since the bowling club party, and each needed to rest rather than rehash something that may yet turn out to be a storm in a teacup. But his policeman's mind had been aroused; which meant he was obliged to question her further.

"Do you feel like talking about it?" he asked in a hushed voice, having suddenly remembered other patients in the ward who were still asleep.

"There's not much I can say. He pushed me and I fell."

"How do you know it was a man? Did you see him?"

"No. I could hear his breathing...and I could smell him."

"Smell? Do you mean: aftershave or something?"

243

His policeman's experience told him that if Emily could one day identify the cologne the man was wearing, it would narrow down any search the police might want to initiate in the next few days.

"Oh no James, nothing like that," she said, unaware of his investigative approach. "It was a revolting smell; like the smell we sometimes find in the clubhouse after a game of golf: a pub sort of smell – revolting!"

Emily squirmed as if nauseated by the thought.

"Oh, my darling," he said stroking her hand. "When you said you'd been pushed I thought you were hallucinating. But now it's quite obvious to me that you weren't!"

A feeling of horror took hold of James. Emily's explanation, proof enough that she had not imagined the events earlier in the night, put a new slant on the situation. All at once he knew what he had to do.

He should get back to the house quickly.

So far, he knew nothing specific, except what Emily had told him. Certainly there was no indication of an intrusion when he found Emily; he had not even noticed the smell, only that of Emily's own delicate perfume as he bent over her. But then, a woman's sense of smell might be more finely tuned to something unpleasant than a man's.

And yet, he was now confident that Emily had been sure of her facts. She would not have imagined something as distinct as a man's unpleasant aroma, even under the traumatic circumstances of that occasion.

James jumped to his feet, startling Emily. Then he lifted his chair and moved it out of the way of anyone wishing to attend to the patient.

"Where are you going?" Emily asked.

"I thought I might go home for a while and get some sleep," he said with only partial honesty.

"Didn't you say you were staying here?"

"Yes, I did. But now I'm convinced of two things. One is that you are alright in yourself and can be left in the care of the nurses for the time being. The other concerns what you told me. The fact that an intruder attacked you means that I should get back to the house. We don't yet know what has been disturbed, so I really need to have a look round. ...And besides, although you said you don't want anything from home, I think I will bring back a few essentials later on, just in case you change your mind. You never know what you might need."

Emily was touched at his thoughtfulness, but also a little unnerved. As yet nobody had set foot inside the house since they left in a hurry last night. In the back of her mind, Emily was concerned the intruder might come back. After all, if he could get into the place once he could do it again.

She shuddered at the thought.

"Be careful, James. You don't know what you'll find."

"I will," he said, empathising with her reasoning, but firm in his determination to take the issue a step further.

At this stage it did not really matter if the house had been ransacked, or just burgled. What did matter was the fact that the man – whoever he was – might have left some tell-tale signs of his being there; evidence that only an ex-detective would be able to recognise.

Displaying an air of, 'leave it to me,' he tenderly kissed Emily on the forehead, and left the ward just as a nurse came in with a bedpan.

"I'll be back later in the morning," he told them both.

Downstairs in the hospital foyer, James phoned for a taxi which arrived soon afterwards.

It was still dark when he got home.

He paid the driver and thanked him; then as the taxi drove off, leaving the street once more in its dark silence, he walked carefully up the path. To outward appearances the house showed no sign of the drama that had recently taken place within its walls. Peering into the gloom of the porch he located the keyhole, and after briefly fumbling with the key, he entered the house.

The same stillness greeted him as had greeted Emily on her return from the bowling club party. But this time there was no sound to catch his attention.

Reaching into his top pocket for a handkerchief, as a working detective might in order to preserve fingerprints, he flicked on the hall light. Then, remembering that it was not working, he reached round the lounge doorpost and turned on the light in there. Upstairs he switched on each light in turn.

Systematically his trained detective eye glossed over every room, before turning out the lights again.

There was no sign of disturbance or interference with their possessions, and certainly no indication of theft. The house wore only its usual appearance – that of organised tranquillity, such as James had come to associate with anything involving Emily. Again a seed of doubt began to grow in his mind about Emily's allegation. But then he brushed it off. He had already accepted that she did not imagine the attack, so there was no disputing it. The fault, he determined, must lie with him. He must have carelessly overlooked something.

"Maybe I should leave the detective work until I've had a bit of a sleep," he told himself.

But there was one more room he wanted to look over before he headed for bed: the kitchen.

That, too, looked the same as usual; nothing seemed to be out of place. James switched on the outside light and opened the back door. The patch of garden illuminated by the light revealed nothing unusual, and beyond that it was still too dark to see anything properly. So he went back inside and pushed the door to with a click.

It was only then that he realised something was amiss.

After he had closed the door he went to turn the key to lock it, but to his surprise he discovered that the key – an old fashioned type – was not there. It then registered with him that he had not actually unlocked the door just now, but merely turned the knob; which meant, he assumed, the back door must have been unlocked all the time.

James stood back, frowning. Normally, after locking the door at night, Emily would remove the key and hang it on a hook. As he had checked that it was in place before they left for the birthday party, he knew that this had been done. Furthermore, the key was still there. Emily in her usual meticulous manner had done what was required, and yet the door wasn't locked. Could someone have used the key to gain entry? Or was it just an oversight he and Emily had coincidentally made on the same night that she claimed to have been assaulted?

He scratched his head, worried and perplexed. He could not imagine either himself or Emily hanging the key on its hook without first checking the door was locked.

With a fresh wavering of his conviction that Emily really had encountered an intruder, James lifted the key down with his handkerchief. Holding it with care he attentively looked around the room. Surely, he thought to himself, the evidence speaks for itself: nobody has been in here. Apart from the door being unlocked, nothing is amiss. Emily must have imagined it after all. Perhaps she lost her balance in the dark at the top of the stairs, missed her footing and banged herself sharply, mistaking the bump for a push...

Bit by bit James put together a viable scenario in an attempt to justify his theory.

"But what of the aroma?" he said loudly in frustration, feeling instead that he was going round in circles rather than drawing a conclusion. "Did Emily imagine that, too?"

Distraught, he rammed the key into the lock. But the key, he discovered, would not fit the keyhole.

He took it out and tried again. Yet, still it would not sit properly in the lock. Pulling it out he squatted down to look into the keyhole itself. From the inside he could see an object blocking the hole.

"For goodness' sake," he exclaimed, standing up again. "Something has been pushed into the keyhole on the other side of the door!"

James snatched open the door, and to his amazement saw another key sticking out.

"How very strange," he mumbled. "What is Emily doing, using a spare key, when the main one is here?"

And then it dawned.

"Good grief!! It wasn't Emily who used the key. It must have been the intruder!"

Armed now with validation of Emily's testimony, James backed away from the door and its incriminating evidence; as though his proximity to it might somehow disturb the intruder's fingerprints which he felt sure must cover it.

He slipped back into the kitchen and pulled out a tissue from the box on the sink bench. With the tips of his fingers wrapped in the tissue he delicately removed the key from the outside of the door.

Without touching his prize, he folded the tissue around it and carefully placed the parcel deep in his pocket.

"Now," he said, talking to the appropriated key. "Who the devil used you? Perhaps we'll soon find out!"

Locked once again inside the house, James made himself a cup of tea and sat mulling over the night's revelations.

"The bastard must have discovered the spare key," he declared. "How else could he have got in?"

There were two keys to the back door. One was kept on the hook in the kitchen, with the spare hidden under an old flower pot by the shed; a place so obscure only a seasoned burglar might think to look there.

"At last," James declared, "The pieces of this puzzle are starting to fit together. Our burglar suspect knew where a spare key might be hidden..."

...But on the other hand, he surmised, it may not have been a burglar who used the key, but Emily. If, at any time, she has inadvertently locked herself out of the house, she may have used the spare to get in and failed to return it to its usual place.

James swore out loud. This fresh hypothesis brought him right back to Square One.

The alleged assault on Emily may not have taken place after all, but only in her imagination.

Regrettably, James realised that irresistible doubts were beginning to creep back in.

To silence the fickle demon that kept invading his mind, he avowed on the spot that come Monday morning he would slip into Forensic with the key. His old colleague Alan Galbraith would be able to help him, for sure. ...At very least, he would be able to tell if the last person to use the key was a man or a woman.

It was about time this irritating ghost of uncertainty was laid to rest for good.

After an unsuccessful attempt to get the sleep he had promised himself when he came home, James got up and telephoned the hospital to enquire how Emily was faring.

The duty nurse advised him she was as well as could be expected – the standard response, James assumed. Then, once he had showered and swallowed a bite of breakfast, he gathered up the personal items he thought Emily would need, and bundled them into a case.

Satisfied he'd done everything he possibly could, James headed out to the car.

He was about to drive off when he remembered what day it was.

"Sunday! It's Sunday. Damn it; I forgot about our game of golf. I'd better phone Royston and cancel it."

He looked sternly at his image in the rear view mirror; annoyed that he now needed to delay his departure for the hospital. The staff would have already told Emily he had phoned to say he was on his way, and she would even now be waiting for him to turn up.

But the image in the mirror also reflected feelings born of worry and a sleepless night.

A lump formed in his throat when he realised that the other two from their foursome could not possibly have foreseen that this weekend's jaunt around the golf course would need to be cancelled, or why; and they would indeed want to know about Emily's misfortune. He had no choice but to inform them.

After a moment or two trying to come to terms with everything he had to deal with, James took a deep breath, clicked his seat belt free and got out of the car to go back into the house.

He decided to keep his investigations to himself.

Royston was horrified when he learnt of Emily's accident, and that she had possibly broken her hip.

"Let me know the outcome of the X-ray, won't you," the younger man insisted. "...And give her our love."

Duty done, James returned to the car and his intended course of action.

He found Emily looking cheerful if not a little weary. Redness around her eyes gave away the fact that despite what the nurse had said Emily did not sleep very well, for the relentless pain in her hip had kept her awake.

"I'll be glad when they start doing something about it," she told James. "They said I should go for the X-ray some time after lunch."

While James put away her clothing, Emily looked to see what he had brought.

In the process, she noticed something different about him, and it troubled her: he was not his usual bubbly self, but seemed distracted.

"Is anything the matter, dear? You are very quiet."

James pulled his head out of the narrow wardrobe next to her bed and forced himself to smile.

He chose not to mention his lack of sleep, but instead told her, "I phoned Royston this morning – that's why I'm a bit late getting here..."

"...Oh, James. I wish you hadn't. I don't want the family worrying about me."

"They do have the right to know about your accident!"

"Yes, but why did you phone Royston and not Ruth?"

"...Because we don't play golf with Ruth!"

"Of course! It's Sunday. Well, I'll be..."

Emily tailed off as she, too, realised just how much their lives had changed in the last few hours.

"As you can imagine," James went on; "he was shocked to learn about your accident. I think you may expect a visit from him or Kristine sometime soon."

"I'd better use some of those toiletries you brought and tidy myself up," said Emily, veering away from the morose feelings that threatened to override her cheerful mood.

"By the way..." she said as a thought popped into her head. "What happened when you got home last night?"

"...This morning. It was this morning, not last night, if you recall."

"Oh, yes; that's right. What a dreadful night that was... Anyway, how did you get on?"

James looked at her, wondering just what to say. In a way there was nothing he could tell her. Nothing in the house had been disturbed, and the matter of the spare key may have been purely coincidental...

But Emily was curious to know if anything had been disturbed, and straight away she pushed for an answer.

"You were going to check the house over. What did you find when you got home?"

"Nothing, really..."

"What do you mean?"

"I found nothing out of the ordinary at all. ...Except for one thing."

"What was that?"

"The back door key. It was hanging on its hook in the kitchen as usual, and the spare key from the old plant pot was in the lock – on the outside of the door."

"How strange. Nobody could know about that key..."

"...Emily, I need to ask you, have you needed to use the spare recently?"

"Well, yes, as a matter of fact... Now I come to think of it, I had to use it yesterday morning. You went up to the village, if you remember. I was out talking to the postman and the wind blew the front door shut. So I used the shed key in the back door. But I'm positive I put it back under the plant pot."

"Do you actually remember taking it back?"

"Not specifically. But you know how it is; some things you do so automatically you don't always remember doing them. And I did work in the garden later in the morning, so I could well have returned the key without thinking."

"Would you say it's possible you may have overlooked returning it as well?"

"I suppose so... You sound like you are interrogating me. Why would you want to do that?"

"Sorry. I don't mean to."

"Do you think that's how the burglar got in the house?"

"It could be. There was no other sign of a disturbance."

James chose to keep his own thoughts on the matter to himself. In the deepest recesses of his detective's mind there still remained an element of doubt as to the reality of Emily's allegation.

Despite his earlier affirmation that he believed her, he was leaning more and more towards the probability that she had merely fallen; that somehow all else had become distorted by the circumstances surrounding the incident: the darkness, the shock, the pain...

Yet still, there was no disputing the presence of the key in his pocket. James definitely had some suspicions about it when he removed it from the lock, or he would not have taken it out. It was all too confusing.

He gently touched the little white package in his pocket. It seemed pointless to keep it there now. Surely there was no reason to bother with fingerprinting, when he felt sure his so called evidence would show up only Emily's prints?

Later in the afternoon, when Emily's X-rays had been completed and she was settled back in bed, she looked up to see Kristine entering the room.

"Dad told me you were here," she said as Emily's face lit up. "I came as soon as I could. How are you, Nana?"

James offered Kristine his chair.

253

She smiled at him in thanks and sat down next to Emily.

"I'm alright, thanks love. They haven't done anything to me yet, except take X-rays. We should know soon whether I need an operation."

Kristine looked concerned. It was upsetting for her to see her grandmother stuck in a hospital bed. As best she could remember, Emily had not been hospitalised before. It was unsettling, too, because the last time she visited a ward like this was when the family kept vigil around her grandfather's bed, shortly before he died...

"...Do you really think an operation will be necessary?" she blurted out to mask the painful memory.

"If my hip is broken, it will. If not... Well... I'll just have to take it easy for a while, I suppose. They said something about putting a pin into the hip joint, if need be."

Kristine grimaced. She tended to be squeamish about such things, and had long since decided that when it came to a career choice, she would never make a good nurse.

"Ouch...that sounds awful, Nana," she said, trying to at least sound sympathetic.

"It's not too bad, so I'm told," said Emily. "The doctor assured me it's no worse than having your tonsils out."

She laughed when Kristine clutched at her throat with a pained expression on her face.

The two women talked for a while, and James thankfully left them to it.

He knew of old what they were like when they got together. ...Besides, he thought in justification for walking out on them, it was good to stretch his legs a bit.

He wandered into the corridor and looked out of the window. Emily's ward was on the sixth floor of the eight-storey hospital building. From where James stood he was able to take in an extensive panorama of their town.

He had never seen the view from this aspect before, and took pleasure in identifying familiar landmarks, both in the immediate vicinity and some distance away.

A splash of green over to the left caught his eye, and he supposed it to be the golf course where they all should have been at that moment. He looked at his watch. Yes, they would have been back in the clubrooms by now, socialising and enjoying a well-earned drink.

He sighed, wondering if those days were over.

It didn't seem possible at the moment that Emily would ever be able to manage the trek around the course again. But, as the doctor stated: some patients make a complete recovery from a hip operation...

Here's hoping, he said to the world at large.

Later, after Kristine had left, the doctor came to see Emily with some news.

"I'm sorry, but we won't have the results of the X-ray today," he told her. "The laboratory is short-staffed, so only the urgent cases will have them processed today..."

"...And my wife is not considered urgent?" interrupted James tersely.

The doctor caught his tone and replied, in a manner which James perceived as a little too aloof, "Naturally, to you Mrs Forsythe's case is urgent, but compared with other patients – accident victims and serious sporting injuries from yesterday afternoon – her injury is only minor. It won't hurt to wait another day."

James exchanged questioning glances with Emily.

Since their marriage they had been apart very little; certainly no more than a few hours at a time. Would this enforced separation cause distress?

"Will you be able to manage by yourself?" Emily asked him; more concerned for her husband than for herself.

With a look of feigned outrage he replied, "Emily, I lived by myself for over a year and I am quite capable of cooking up a few meals. I'll even put the vacuum over the floors in the morning, if you're really good."

Emily chuckled at the pretence of umbrage, and watched him walk the doctor to the door. But she was also quietly relieved that he had insisted he could hold his own.

It seemed, now, that they had been together forever. And although they were not exactly newlyweds anymore, their marriage was still in its early stages.

Emily remembered only too well the many months each of them spent in isolation and loneliness, alleviated only by their eventual union.

She remembered also her contentment with the spirit of Arthur at her side...

How could she forget?

"The doctor said we should know what's going on before lunchtime tomorrow," James told her when he came back to her bedside.

"So, this time tomorrow I'll either be preparing for an operation or packing my bags to return home," said Emily hopefully; yet her cheerfulness was more to keep her own spirits up, than to comfort James.

In truth, it upset her to send him off to an empty house for another night alone.

"Let's keep our fingers crossed as to which it will be," she said silently as he got up to leave.

CHAPTER FOUR

The result of the X-ray confirmed the doctor's suspicion of injury, yet not in the way he expected.

After thoroughly examining the X-ray himself, and then seeking a second opinion from a colleague, he was forced to come to the conclusion that Emily's hip was not in any way broken, but merely badly bruised.

This baffled the senior doctors. Something was causing Emily severe pain in her hip. If it was not the hip itself, then what was it?

Then one of the student doctors accompanying them on their round noticed something odd.

The X-rays of Emily's pelvic region had been taken both from the side and from the front. While the higher-ranking medics were scrutinising the side-on plates, the student remarked to one of his associates that on the other plate Emily's lower spine seemed to be slightly out of alignment. On peering more closely, he could see that a disc between two of the vertebrae was bulging out to one side.

"I think she's got a compressed disc," he covertly said to his peer.

On hearing the words 'compressed disc' the doctors halted their scrutinies and looked up questioningly.

"What did you just say?" asked the most senior of the doctors, switching his attention to the second X-ray.

"I just happened to notice this," the young man replied, pointing to the affected vertebrae.

Then, aware that he, a mere student, should not give the impression he was trying to outsmart his supervisor, he added with an element of humility, "Is it possible this patient has a slipped disc?"

The student stood back, allowing his superiors to take a closer look.

"Well, young man," the supervisor said. "You may be on to something there. Congratulations on your observation."

The young student's team members applauded briefly, causing him slight embarrassment together with a burst of pride. But then his moment in the spotlight was curtailed by the doctor asking him, "...So how do we ascertain the accuracy of your diagnosis?"

The student went quiet, his mind drawing a blank; until someone standing behind him whispered, "MRI."

"Oh, yes," he said quickly. "The patient should have an MRI scan."

"Correct. Now, shall we tell our patient the good news? I'm sure Mrs Forsythe will be very relieved to know her hip is not broken."

Emily took the news well, having kept an open mind as to the outcome of the X-rays and her further prognosis.

In fact, throughout the night she had decided that an attitude of resignation would probably be the best way to go, and resolutely accepted the possibility of either good news or bad.

The doctor told his patient. "Mrs Forsythe, for someone of your age, you must have remarkable bone density; that you were spared what, for many women, would have been an inevitable conclusion."

James was delighted that Emily would not need to have an operation. He had no idea what a slipped disc meant but, to him, it sounded not nearly as bad as a broken hip.

"How long do you think I'll need to stay in hospital?" Emily asked the doctor.

She was thinking of James now. All too soon the reality of her situation would set in and he would be required to look after her disability.

It was obvious to her that, despite reassurance from the doctor her hip was alright, something serious was causing the pain. And from what he was saying, it appeared to be a pinched nerve as a result of the slipped disc in her back.

"We've scheduled the MRI scan for this afternoon," he told her. "The sooner we know what we are dealing with, the sooner we can treat it..."

"...So Emily could still end up by having an operation?" asked James, his euphoria moderating.

"It's not likely. Slipped discs are iffy things to deal with in surgery. Physiotherapy and anti-inflammatory drugs are the norm. Surgery would only be tackled if Emily's pain level did not reduce even with the non-invasive treatment she will be prescribed."

"When do you think I will be able to go home, then?" asked Emily.

All the talk of the treatment was getting to her. She was beginning to feel that she had had enough of it already.

The doctor paused to think, and then said, "Probably tomorrow. We will need to initiate a physiotherapy regime for you before we can discharge you from the hospital."

"Tomorrow! ...So soon?" exclaimed James. This was all happening a little too quickly for his liking.

"Oh, yes," responded the doctor sternly.

He was wary of James by now, interpreting his concern as criticism.

"Your wife needs to get moving again. Sitting around, especially reclining in bed like this, is the worst thing for a compressed disc. Once we know what we are up against and have organised the treatment, Mrs Forsythe should be free to go home – so long as she behaves herself."

He winked at Emily whom he had grown to like, and she grinned back at him.

"I'll try," she laughed, and then looked at James.

His eyes said it all. To Emily he seemed to be confused by conflicting feelings.

Whilst James did not want Emily away from home any longer than necessary, he was concerned she might be discharged and sent home too early. Her gallantry, he had begun to suspect, disguised the fact that she was in more pain than she was admitting to.

Instinctively, Emily knew what he was thinking.

"Don't worry," she said in an attempt to reassure him. "Everything will be alright."

At home again, James threw himself into domestic chores; both to take his mind off Emily's situation and to get all the work up to date.

On his way back to the house he had already decided that his part in Emily's recuperation would be to keep the home fires burning; or at least, to keep everything tidy.

He determined that when Emily came home, he would have the house and garden looking immaculate.

Thus, while Emily's scan was taking place, James was up to his elbows in weeds and garden paraphernalia. Then, keeping a close eye on the clock, he ended his session in the garden in time to shower and change into tidy clothes, drive back to the hospital, and be waiting at her bedside when she returned to her bed.

Yet, Emily's return to the ward was not quite as James anticipated. Much to his surprise, the patient who had only been taken for a simple scan appeared to be under some form of sedation.

In effect, she was sound asleep.

Worried now that something was wrong, James rang the call bell for assistance, and after questioning a young nurse who responded, was politely informed that Emily had needed a sedative for the duration of her scan.

"But why?" he asked in alarm. "What's so awful about an MRI scan that she needed to be sedated?"

"I take it you have never had an MRI scan?" remarked the nurse, whose uniform, James noted, was far too short for one in such a reputable profession.

"No I haven't...not that I know of, anyway. In fact, I have never even heard of MRI until now."

"Well, you would definitely remember if you'd ever had to endure one," the nurse grinned slyly. "They are not for the faint-hearted, and a nightmare for anyone who suffers from claustrophobia."

"Why do you say that?"

"...Because they shove you in a tube."

"A tube?" said James, mystified. The girl was confusing him now. "I'm sorry, but I really don't understand what you're saying."

"An MRI scanning machine is the shape of a tube. You go in head first and have to lie still for about half an hour while the machine does its work."

"Good grief. Is that what they did to Emily?"

"I would think so."

"But why was she sedated so heavily?" James glanced across at the still sleeping patient, who presently seemed to be at peace with the world.

"She needed it because she became restless during the scan, and they had to start all over again a couple of times. Sedation enabled the technician to do the job, and it meant your wife was not aware of what was going on."

With a look of despair, James said, "Oh, I see."

261

After the nurse left, James felt a rising tide of panic.

Whatever next! he screamed inwardly, taking hold of Emily's limp hand.

His poor dear wife, who only days ago was just fine, had since been subjected to an attack – if indeed that was the case; to severe pain, and now she had to suffer the effects of claustrophobia.

A lump formed in his throat as he looked helplessly over Emily's comatose form; her features lifeless. But for the gentle raising and lowering of her chest in breathing she could have been mistaken for dead.

Yet, then something happened which gave the unhappy James encouragement. The hand he gently held twitched beneath his touch. It was followed by the slight flutter of an eyelid, and a minute later, Emily opened her eyes and slowly regarded the nearest face.

As wakefulness returned, Emily smiled with the instant recognition of her husband's face.

"Well, hello there," he said lovingly into her eyes. "How are you, my darling?"

Emily tried to respond, but found herself unable to do so. Then she tried to acknowledge his words by touching his hand; again without success. The patient was still too sleepy to make her muscles respond to command.

But James interpreted the lack of response as failure on her part to hear him, and he leant closer to her face.

Emily's eyes followed his as he did so.

"Emily, can you hear me?" he asked softly.

Still she did no more than gaze into his eyes. Unable to move her mouth in speech, she communicated with him in the only way she could. Slowly Emily's lips creased into a weak smile.

James squeezed her hand affectionately, pleased that a degree of communication had been established.

Just then, the nurse walked back into the ward to attend to another patient.

James sprang up and waylaid her.

"My wife has come round," he said.

"That's good," she remarked; "I'll get the doctor..."

"...But I'm concerned that she seems unable to speak. What has happened? Will she be alright?"

The nurse raised a hand to halt his questioning. "Don't worry, Mr Forsythe. The doctor will examine her." Then she left the ward, still carrying a treatment tray for use on the other patient.

A minute later she returned with the doctor; a different one from before.

This man addressed James more courteously than his off-hand predecessor.

"Hello," he said jovially, "I'm Doctor Chapman, and will be Mrs Forsythe's doctor for the remainder of the day. I understand you have some concerns about her condition."

"Yes. My wife doesn't seem able to speak."

The doctor bent over Emily and pulled back her eyelids.

"Hmm... Yes...her pupils are still dilated, which means she has not yet returned to full consciousness after her sedative. Unfortunately, during the MRI scan we needed to administer a fairly strong sedative as she was showing signs of agitation..."

"...I know. The nurse told me."

The doctor looked at James, and nodded in recognition of his apparent prior knowledge.

"You will find she's unable to induce much movement in her limbs while her brain is still too sleepy to get the message through to them," he said.

Then he addressed Emily directly.

In response, she looked enquiringly at his face.

"Can you move your hands yet, Mrs Forsythe?"

Emily struggled with another feeble nod, but the effort was too much. Her eyelids drooped, and she once more slid into a blissful slumber.

"She's gone back to sleep," said the doctor, turning to James. "It might be less of a worry to you if you leave her for half an hour or so to sleep it off. I suggest you go for a stroll, or have a bite to eat at the cafeteria; something to take your mind of it. I doubt if your wife will be back with us for a while."

He placed his hand reassuringly on James's shoulder.

"Don't worry, though," he added. "Mrs Forsythe will be just fine when she wakes up."

James sighed. There was nothing else he could do, except leave Emily to rest until the sedative was completely out of her system.

She had been so close to him for a fleeting moment, but had slipped away. And once again he would have to wait; to exercise the patience his loving heart found more difficult to maintain with each passing hour.

Yet, frustrations aside, he did as the doctor suggested and, after kissing Emily on the forehead, he left the ward to look for the cafeteria.

The smell of hot food wafting down the corridor both told him he was heading in the right direction, and also reminded him he was actually quite hungry; not having eaten since breakfast. He chose a meal of burger and fries followed by a large juicy apple, and washed them down with two cups of tea. Then, checking the cafeteria clock against his watch, decided there was enough time to take in a quick stroll in the hospital grounds before his time of waiting was over.

When he returned to the ward he found Emily's corner of the room swathed in curtains. A slight uneasiness crept through him. Why had they pulled the screens around the bed? …Was something wrong?

He crept forward and stopped on the outside of the curtain, listening to the lowered voices of what sounded like the doctor and a nurse.

"Is everything alright in there?" he ventured to ask.

Immediately, Doctor Chapman's head popped through a gap in the curtains.

"Yes, Mr Forsythe. Everything is fine," he cheerfully replied, and pulled back the curtains to reveal Emily, now fully awake, peeping out over freshly straightened covers.

She beamed happily at her husband, who brushed past the doctor as though he wasn't there, and squatted at the side of the bed.

The nurse pulled up a chair, which he promptly sat on.

"Hello, my love," he said, grasping Emily's outstretched hand. "How do you feel?"

"A bit groggy," Emily conceded. "But I think I'm alright. Did you know they put me to sleep to go in that machine?"

"We've checked the scan image," the doctor informed the two of them. "It shows pressure on the sciatic nerve on her right side, hence the discomfort in her hip. But with pain relief and regular physiotherapy your wife should be up and about in no time. We'll get her started on an exercise regime first thing in the morning. That will allow her new anti-inflammatory medication time to kick in. You should be able to take her home in a couple of days."

"That's wonderful," James said cheerily, while secretly dreading the thought of any more days alone. How much longer could he bear to be without Emily at his side?

The doctor continued.

"Together with weekly visits from the district nurse, her exercise regime and plenty of rest will help her get back to normal…relatively quickly."

He looked down at Emily's eager face, and was touched by the love that obviously flowed between this woman and her husband. They must have had a long and blissfully happy marriage, the doctor mistakenly thought to himself as he bid them goodnight.

Time passed unbearably slowly for Emily and her husband during the next two days.

The toil of enforced bachelorhood fell hard upon the shoulders of the man who had renewed his marital status so recently, and he found it hard to adjust. And Emily, for her part, lay patiently in her hospital bed, filling her days with old magazines and moments to look forward to, and enforced distractions to break the monotony of inactivity for an otherwise healthy woman.

Visits from Kristine, Ruth and James, together with the physiotherapy appointments, mealtimes and her twice-daily shower, helped to fill in the hours.

Meanwhile, James called into Forensic to see his one-time colleague, Alan Galbraith, and to submit the suspect key for testing.

He still assumed nothing would come of fingerprint-testing the key, but decided to take it in, all the same. If he had been honest with himself, he would have admitted that he used the trip into town more as an excuse for an outing than to achieve an objective. It gave him something to do; something that took his mind off his loneliness. And it gave him a break from his housekeeping chores. So it was with a feeling of slight embarrassment that he handed the key over to his colleague.

However, late on the day before Emily's discharge from hospital, a phone call from Galbraith took him completely by surprise.

"I can see you haven't lost your touch," he told James. "You may be onto something here. The most recent prints on this key are those of an adult male. They belong to someone who's used to manual labour, because they are imperfect. I thought you would like to know."

"Yes, indeed," replied James, stunned by the findings. "You are absolutely sure about this, aren't you; that the prints are from the last person to handle the key?"

James was having difficulty absorbing this unexpected piece of information.

"There's no question or doubt in my mind. If you would like to call in again, I'll show you."

"No, I'll take your word for it. I've no time to come into town today. My wife is due home from hospital tomorrow and I have a lot to do to prepare for it. ...But thanks for the offer, all the same."

"I understand. What do you want me to do with the evidence, then?"

"Evidence? Oh, the key! I suppose it could be classed as evidence now. I hadn't seriously considered it as such before. Well, if you've time, perhaps a cross match with the prints you have on file might be useful. If not, then I'll wait until I have time to do it myself."

"Don't trouble yourself, old man. It will be my pleasure. Have you anyone under suspicion?"

"No. This has come like a bolt from the blue. As I told you the other day, I had come to the conclusion it was Emily who left the key in the back door and that her fall was merely carelessness on her part. But this puts a new complexion on things. I haven't yet considered what to do next. Anyway, it would be too late to look for other clues. I've worked in the house and in the garden since Emily's accident and obliterated further clues. We'll just have to hope the prints belong to someone you have on file."

"Will you tell your wife about this?"

"Good heavens, no! She will have enough on her plate recuperating, without my creating extra worry for her. This must remain between you and me for the time being."

Thus, James chose to keep quiet about the discovery. His final visits to Emily at the hospital would disclose nothing except his efforts at home.

To save her having to climb the stairs too often, James transformed the dining room into a bedroom where Emily could sleep if she wished. This meant squashing the dining table into the lounge, thereby reducing its useable size. But that, he maintained, didn't really matter. It was more important Emily not be disadvantaged on her return home from hospital.

The following day, the ambulance bearing a nervous Emily complete with wheelchair, pulled up outside her home to unload its fragile cargo.

James, who had driven along behind, leapt out of his car while the ambulance driver opened the vehicle's back door, and readied himself to accompany Emily inside. Then the driver carefully pushed the wheelchair along the narrow front path and, with his partner's help, lifted it up the steps and into the house.

Once inside, they raised Emily to her feet.

Leaning on crutches, she hesitantly took her first step without the guidance of a physiotherapist.

It was an anxious moment for Emily; cast adrift for the first time from the security of a hospital environment. All of a sudden her confidence wavered.

"I don't know if I can do this," she said in alarm.

"Just take it quietly," advised the ambulance driver. "You are bound to be a bit shaky at first."

Tentatively, she took another painful step.

In that step Emily's two worlds crashed together: the incapacity which beleaguered the patient converged with her normal domestic life.

With a gasp from sheer uncertainty about her future, Emily knew in an instant that she and James were in for a long period of adjustment.

James, too, worried his preparations were not enough.

As she stepped slowly into the lounge he could see immediately that the easy chair would not be suitable for her delicate condition. It would be too low.

Quickly he reached out to transfer one of the cushions off the settee onto the easy chair, so that she would not have to lower herself too far. It was therefore a relief to both of them when she was finally settled. The few steps it took to get her there had been more than a little worrying.

James thanked the ambulance men and saw them off the premises; then he returned to Emily.

He sat down opposite her chair and scrutinised the thin, weary face.

How different she seems from the last time she was in here, he thought to himself. Her sparkle is missing; though understandable after everything she has been through.

Emily gazed into his eyes.

"You look tired," she said to him, observing in him the same strain that James had seen in her.

"That's funny," he retorted. "I was thinking the same."

"We must look like a couple of old crocks. What about a cuppa to cheer ourselves up?"

"Good idea," said James, getting up again.

Emily groaned apologetically.

"I'd like to say, sit there while I put the kettle on, but I can't even get up to fill it let alone make a cuppa!"

"Of course you can't. And you're not going to; not until the doctor says you're fit enough to lead a normal life again. Now, before I disappear into the kitchen, is there something I can get for you? ...Your bag, a rug for your knees; anything at all? Please don't be afraid to ask. I'm here to do your bidding."

Emily laughed at his last remark which was backed up with a comical gesture.

James, for his part, warmed to see her sparkle break through the weariness, and instantly recognised where his emphasis should lie from now on.

Humour is always good medicine, he thought. I must make sure I remember that.

It had been a long day for James; what with the upheaval of getting rooms ready for Emily's return, and then bringing her back home.

He had envisaged in her return an ending to the trying saga, but in essence it was just the beginning of another. Pleased though he was to have his wife home again; safe and well in the comfort of her own home environment, he did not fully realise just how different their lives would be from now on.

He could not have comprehended how dependant on him Emily would need to be for her every requirement; at least to begin with.

By the end of the first day, after making her the cup of tea, unpacking her bags, preparing their meal and washing up afterwards; then escorting her with the aid of her crutches to the downstairs toilet, and eventually helping her to wash and change ready for bed, he was exhausted and more than a little demoralized. He had not expected the homecoming to be quite as demanding as this.

Although James bore no resentment towards Emily for her disability, there was just a twinge of regret, as he slid between cold sheets on the lonely double bed upstairs, that the situation had not been more in his favour.

The role of nursemaid, on top of everything else, was a brand new experience in which he had quickly recognised his ineptitude.

Yet, after a solid night's sleep, James felt differently.

His first feeling, on waking up, was one of elation that Emily was home again.

His exhaustive effort the previous evening seemed to have dissolved in his memory after restful sleep, and he rose early; anxious to find out how Emily had managed in her makeshift bedroom.

He peeped discreetly round the dining room door to see if she was awake.

She saw him immediately and awkwardly pulled herself up into a sitting position.

"Hello, my sweet lady. How did you sleep?"

James pushed the door open and walked up to her bed. Then he bent over to kiss her on the cheek.

"Actually," she replied, "I slept very well, considering I'm in my dining room! My hip was a bit sore at times, but that's to be expected. ...How about you?"

"I slept quite well, too..."

"...My poor darling," Emily cut in, filled with tenderness towards him. "You must have been exhausted. Today will be much easier for you – I promise"

"Oh, Emily; don't worry about that! You deserve my best attention...and you're going to get it!"

"Even so, I don't want you to wear yourself out babying me. Two invalids in the family won't do at all."

Later on, after breakfasting from a tray and when James had helped Emily with her ablutions, there came a knock on the front door, and a woman by the name of Joyce Brown introduced herself as the district nurse.

She commented on the fact that Emily was already up.

"I will see to Mrs Forsythe's bathing every second day until a home helper can be arranged," Mrs Brown advised James, as though telling him off for doing it himself. "The rest of the time, just a bowl of warm water, soap and a towel, by her bedside at nine o'clock, will be sufficient."

Having someone come in regularly was a great help to James, and a load off Emily's mind; especially when the home-help provided by the hospital board said she was there to do housework as well as showering.

James had begun to wonder whether the chores he so lovingly accomplished before Emily came home might now be neglected because he was too busy attending to her. It reminded him how he and Janet struggled to keep on top of domestic work when their son was but a baby.

Then one day, when both district nurse and home-help happened to be there at the same time, he told them in jest, "Soon I'll have nothing to do around here!"

With the load shared, James and Emily's spirits lifted. She, because she was relieved her husband did not have to work so hard and he, because he really only wanted to sit with Emily, walk with Emily, catch up on gossip with Emily, and not have to disappear every few minutes to attend to the various chores.

The only household task he insisted on carrying out was to prepare something appetising for his wife to eat, and then presenting it to her on a tray with all the trimmings, including a small bunch of roses from her garden; picked fresh each day, for he knew how much she loved the yellow ones.

Emily enjoyed it when he did that.

Her increasing good humour showed on her face; a face that was beginning to beam, giving him a glimpse of the normal life she would soon enjoy again.

Throughout the month that followed, Emily received lots of visits from her family.

Kristine came often to do her nails or set her hair. Ruth and Wilbur also called in when they could manage to get across town.

Occasionally Wilbur would mow the lawns, while Ruth worked alongside him to weed the flower borders.

Only Fiona kept away. Still living her life of isolation from the family, she doggedly refused to connect with her mother even after the accident. But Emily was not hurt by her neglect. She had long since got over any upset caused by Fiona's pettiness.

At the moment, with walking still requiring her absolute concentration, she had other things to think about than her self-serving daughter.

A week or so later a large, cumbersome package arrived by courier. James read the address label out to Emily.

"It's from the hospital's physiotherapy department," he read. "I wonder what it could be."

The box containing mostly metal pipes of different sizes intrigued Emily and James.

They sat in the lounge, with James trying to work out from the instructions how everything fitted together; and when eventually it registered in his mind what the kitset contraption was, he let out a loud guffaw.

"Of course!" he cried. "It's a walking frame!"

Once the frame was assembled, James stood grinning while Emily demonstrated her willingness to use it. Of lightweight construction with a pair of wheels on the front legs and a shelf-seat in between, she quickly proved to him that she could walk with it unassisted.

When the district nurse called in, Emily also gave her a demonstration of ability. Yet, the nurse, though pleased to see her enthusiasm – something she did not always find with her patients – nevertheless urged Emily to curb her excitement and continue to take things easy.

"...But you can't keep a good man down," jested James.

However, Emily heeded the nurse's advice and resumed the role of invalid; if only for the sake of appearance.

"Do you know what I would really like to do, James?" she commented after the nurse had left. "I would love to be able to walk around the shopping centre again. It seems like ages since I indulged in that little luxury, and I miss it."

"Don't you think it might be a bit soon for that?" James responded. "You've only just got the walking frame, and already you're contemplating a ten-mile hike. And that's what it would be like; knowing you and your love of browsing when you shop. I tell you what: give yourself a few more days of short walks, and then I'll consider letting you loose on the shops!"

"Alright...you win!"

Within the week Emily was like a young colt chafing at the bit: impatient to be given full rein.

Bound by his promise, James reluctantly agreed to take her; although he was not yet confident in her ability to walk any distance without tiring. Walks around the back garden, and later on up and down the footpath along the road, were not enough to convince him of her readiness for the outside world. Back to full strength she may be, but

274

she was yet to demonstrate to him that she had regained sufficient ability to walk unaided in safety; for the slipped disc in her back did not just give her pain, it adversely affected the sciatic nerve and therefore her balance.

Emily, though, had other ideas. And it was at the shops that she proved his reservations to be groundless.

James pulled up at the entrance of the shopping centre and helped Emily out of the car with her walking frame. Then he drove off to look for a parking space.

As this was his first time out with Emily, he felt he could not in all good conscience park in a 'disabled drivers' space, for he had no permit.

"That is something I must see to as soon as possible," he told himself while he walked back to the shops.

In the meantime, Emily had casually ambled over to the nearest shop: a chemist. She gasped at all the colourful displays in the window.

Oh, how she had missed her shopping!

With joy, she accosted James as he approached.

"You can't imagine how lovely it is to get out again," she told him. "...To feel like a normal person and derive pleasure from the simple things I've always taken for granted. Do you know what I mean?"

James politely nodded in acknowledgement of what she was saying; although as a man he did not share in her views about shopping.

Unaware of his stance, and absorbed in the ambience of the moment, Emily sensed how people returning from the brink of death better appreciate the ordinary things in life.

While James walked alongside her, Emily inspected her favourite shops. She revelled in all the sights, sounds and colours she had started to believe she would never be able to experience again.

Piped music played in the background; a source of irritation to some, but refreshing to Emily's starved senses. She drank it in hungrily, while James looked around; not for shops that Emily might like to explore, but for obstacles that would get in her way, and seating she could utilise when the ramble became too much; which he knew it would, sooner or later.

Slowly they inched their way along, stopping to look in windows, venturing inside to browse, and in some, to buy; James always at her side, ready to support her arm or her waist, should she forget the need to focus on her walking frame, and falter. But the need of his arm did not arise. Emily coped without it.

In fact, she shunned his attempts to slow her down, and brushed aside his requests that she rest periodically. Not only did she walk all over the shopping centre, but she chatted incessantly while she did so.

Emily talked non-stop to James, frequently to the shop assistants or passers-by, and once or twice to people she knew, who stopped her and with concern enquired as to the reason for her need of a walking frame. Eventually, tired but exhilarated, she conceded that she had just about had enough, and made her way back to the chemist shop with its wide footpath; there to wait while James strolled over to fetch the car for her.

"I'm very proud of you," he told her when she was back home, and safely seated in her chair. "If I ever had any doubts about your recovery, I sure don't have them now."

So Emily quietly resumed her normal lifestyle, relishing each of her familiar and long-missed activities as she was once more able to engage in them.

The objective to which she had aimed as a triumph of recovery was to be able to walk up and down the stairs by herself; unaided by human or mechanical means. The day she achieved this feat, James took her out for a meal to celebrate, along with Kristine and her father.

It was a wonderful evening out for Emily and the family; their first for a very long time.

Emily fussed indulgently over her personal preparations for it, and then insisted they have a pre-meal drink in the lounge bar before sitting at their table.

This was to be her special night and Emily was going to make the most of it.

Only one factor marred the success of the evening; something that would cause considerable upheaval in all of their lives: Royston, on whom alcohol had the effect of loosening his tongue, let slip the fact that he now had a lady-friend; a detail he had unintentionally kept secret from his daughter.

But now, the secret was out, and it was too late for Royston to cover up his mistake.

The look of horror on Kristine's face sent shivers down Emily's spine. She tried to diffuse the situation with a kindly word, but even she could not have envisaged the effect on Kristine that Royston's faux pas would have; for Kristine viewed the revelation in a different light.

She had been shocked; not only that her father was having an affair while still married to her mother, but also because Emily appeared to be aware of it.

"Nana, do you mean to say you know about her, too?" she asked guardedly.

Emily stalled; wishing she had stayed out of it.

She hastily looked at James for support, but received nothing from her husband but a surprised stare.

"How come I'm always the last one to be told anything round here?" Kristine grumbled. "I'm not a child any more, you know. I'll be seventeen years old next week!"

Kristine felt bitterly let down by the two people who were closest to her, and was sure they had been deliberately keeping something from her.

Did they still think she was so immature that she should be sheltered from the truth: that her father had a lover? This in itself hurt her deeply, for she had always thought of herself as his favourite girl. But it was the apparent cover-up that stuck in her throat and turned a celebration into a long drawn-out ordeal.

However, for the sake of the occasion, Kristine kept her feelings to herself and made no further reference to the evening's bombshell.

The following Sunday, Royston telephoned to see if James and Emily would like to resume their golfing regime now that she was completely mobile again.

"What do you think, Emily? Are you up to coming with us?" James asked while Royston was still on the phone.

"Will Kristine be going?" she asked.

"I don't know. Just a minute, I'll find out."

The question asked, James waited for the reply.

His sorry look told Emily what she suspected, and with his confirmation of it she gave her decision.

"Oh Emily, you can still come with us!"

"...Without Kristine?"

Emily sighed, knowing full well that whatever excuses Kristine had given for not accompanying them this time, the truth lay elsewhere.

"I don't think so, James. It might be pushing it where my back is concerned. Do you mind?"

"No not really. I'd probably worry about you, too..."

"...But there's nothing to stop you and Royston going by yourselves," Emily suddenly chipped in.

James thought for a moment. "Are you sure? It doesn't seem right for me to desert you."

"I'm not an invalid any more. I can cope just pottering around the house without needing you to prop me up. Go with my blessing. In fact, I insist you both go; and have a jolly good boys' day out. You deserve it after everything you've done for me over the last few weeks."

Throughout the day, when her enthusiasm for seeing James resume his usual Sunday activity began to fade, Emily found herself missing him.

This was the first time she had been by herself in the house since the accident, and a slight twinge of alarm arose whenever she remembered what had caused it.

However, she rapidly quelled any apprehension. That incident was in the past. She had no reason to fear another intrusion now; of that she was sure.

But it was Kristine who mostly occupied her mind. What made her tell Royston she couldn't go? Was she still so upset with her father's deceit that she could no longer bear to be with him?

It did not occur to Emily at the time that Kristine was also upset with her.

As there had been no communication between Emily and Kristine since the night of the awkward dinner, Emily could only guess how she felt about Royston's romance.

She wanted desperately to speak with her: to give her honest opinion of Sylvia, and to empathise with Kristine's reservations about the situation. It was vital to her that Kristine not be allowed to dwell on her reservations, but rather talk them out with the one person she had always trusted. By mid-afternoon the tension became unbearable for Emily. She knew the only way to relieve the pressure was to phone Kristine; that is, if she was home.

It was possible, she admitted, that Kristine might have had a valid reason for not going with Royston; after all, the golfing foursome had not been together for a few weeks! Was the teenager expected to sit at home waiting for the summons to join the others on the golf course?

...Not if she had any common sense, Emily reckoned; and good sense was something Kristine had plenty of!

Emily dialled her number; hoping Kristine might still be at home and take the call. If not, then the person to answer it would be Fiona, and Emily did not feel like getting into a discussion with her estranged daughter just now.

As the phone rang at the other end, Emily's hand was poised to click it off if the voice she heard was Fiona's and not Kristine's. And such was the case.

Yet, Emily's desire to speak with the girl was so great that when Fiona answered, instead of hanging up without saying a word, Emily pulled her finger away from the off-button, and spoke.

With a rush she said, "Hello Fiona; I would like to speak to Kristine, please."

Fiona was surprised to hear her mother's voice again; and none too pleased, for there had been no contact between them since before her marriage to James.

"Mother, this is a surprise," she said as sarcastically as she could. "Fancy my hearing from you after all this time. They tell me you've recovered after your accident."

Emily was wise to her sarcasm. Not wanting to prolong the conversation any more than necessary, she answered,

"Yes, I am alright again now, thank you. Please may I speak to my granddaughter?"

"Well, you can't"

"Oh...and why not?"

"...Because she isn't here."

"Is she away for the day?"

"No. She went out about an hour ago. Why do you want to know that?"

Emily ignored her and continued with her enquiry.

"Tell me, Fiona. Did she plan to go out, or was it a spur of the moment decision."

"Spur of the moment, I think. A boy came and picked her up on his bike."

"A boy...on a bike? You mean, they went off together on their bicycles?"

"No. It was a motorbike. She just rushed out with hardly a word to me. What's it got to do with you, anyway?"

Again, Emily ignored her.

"...But she was expecting him...was she?"

"I don't know! Why all the questions? There's nothing wrong with her, if that's your worry. She had been moping around, and at the sight of Richard and his bike..."

"...Richard?"

"Yes. Richard. He's a friend from her school. Anyway, if you'll let me finish... When Kristine heard his bike turn up, she seemed surprised. Then she told me she was going out and didn't know when she'd be home. Next thing I knew, she left on the back of his motorbike. I was annoyed, I can tell you; I hate motorbikes y. I'll be giving her a piece of my mind when she comes back. Now, Mother, will you please tell me why the irritating questions?"

But Emily did not want to give her reasons for wanting to talk to Kristine; certainly not with Fiona.

It was possible, she conceded – indeed probable – that Fiona did not know about Sylvia; and Emily was reluctant to be the one to tell her. That information should come from Kristine, or from Royston himself.

"I just wanted to speak to my granddaughter," she said. "Will you please ask her to phone when she comes in?"

Emily worried for many days about Kristine and her odd behaviour; even more so when she failed to return the phone call.

For a while, it crossed her mind that the girl had affixed herself to the wrong crowd; even become involved with a bikies gang.

But then Emily reminded herself that owning a motor bike did not automatically make its rider a bikie.

Instead, she attributed the change in behaviour to the fact that Kristine was growing up quickly, her seventeenth birthday only a couple of days away; and she was probably developing a natural interest in boys now. But even so...

On the eve of her birthday, Emily rang Royston in near panic to ask if Kristine had been in touch, and was greeted by a female voice, which she took to be that of Sylvia.

Without bothering to ascertain if she was correct, Emily asked, "Could I please speak to Royston?"

"Just a minute," came the response.

Moments later, after a muffled conversation with her hand over the mouthpiece, the woman handed the phone over to Royston.

"Hello?" said Royston warily.

Emily could not help but notice his cautiousness....he had answered the phone almost guardedly.

She was curious to know why.

"Royston...this is Emily. I'm sorry to bother you if you have a guest; but I wanted to talk to you about Kristine."

"What about Kristine?"

Emily was getting annoyed now; for both Fiona and Royston were being decidedly unhelpful.

"For one thing," she said in a less than cordial tone; "it's her birthday tomorrow if you recall; and for another… Have you heard from her lately?"

"No, I haven't. …And, yes, I have remembered my own daughter's birthday…but I have been very busy lately," he said gruffly.

"I understand. I apologise for being pushy…"

"…While you're on the phone," he went on brusquely; "there's something I need to tell you."

What now? thought Emily.

"I won't be able to make golf on Sundays from now on. Could you explain that to James for me, please?"

"Explain what, Royston!" asked Emily; annoyance now showing in her voice.

"…That I won't be available!"

Emily sighed as she toned down her response.

"I'm sure he'll be bitterly disappointed if you cancel out on your arrangement with him. …And he will want to know why. What am I supposed to tell him?"

"Tell him… Tell him I don't have the freedom to come and go as I please anymore."

Emily's curiosity was aroused now, and her instincts told her he was intentionally hiding something.

"What do you mean, Royston?" she asked insistently.

Royston again hesitated for a moment; then he said in a hushed tone, "I suppose you might as well know…Sylvia is living here with me now. I didn't tell you sooner because I wasn't sure how you would react."

Predictably, Emily was taken aback by the abruptness of his news. However, she managed to retain her composure, and politely reassured him.

"What you do is really none of my business, Royston. If you like this woman – Sylvia – enough to have her move in with you, I wish you well. But I am concerned about the effect it may have on Kristine. If you remember, she only found about your lady friend when you blurted it out at dinner last week. I was very surprised you hadn't told her about it sooner because the closeness of your relationship these days. ...You do recall the incident, don't you?"

"I don't know what you're talking about, Emily. I didn't even mention Sylvia at the dinner."

"Oh yes you did. It was after you'd had a few drinks. I'm not sure exactly what you said, but Kristine got the message alright, and she wasn't too thrilled about it, either. That's why I'm phoning you now. ...Because she has been acting very strangely."

"...Strangely? ...In what way?"

"...Out of character. She hasn't been in touch with me, which is most odd. And, according to Fiona, she has taken up with a boy who rides a motorcycle."

"I wouldn't be too concerned, Emily. Kristine is getting older now. She's entitled to live her own life in the way that she wants to."

"Royston! Are you listening to yourself?"

Emily was enraged now by his apparent disinterest in his daughter's welfare. Had that dippy blonde stolen his wits as well as his affections?

"Don't you care about Kristine and what she gets up to these days?"

"I'm quite sure Fiona will keep her in line, if need be."

"You two are as bad as each other!" exclaimed Emily in exasperation. "I guess I'll have to look out for her, myself. You've obviously got your hands full now!"

Emily found herself trembling with rage after she hung up on him, and needed the support of her walking frame for the first time in over a week. Furthermore, she realised with dismay, that she still had not ascertained what either of Kristine's parents had planned for her birthday.

At the rate things were going, she might not have the opportunity to celebrate her granddaughter's seventeenth birthday at all!

"Royston's manner has changed since Sylvia came into his life," Emily complained to James when he came in later on.

As expected, James was dismayed by Royston's reason for cancelling their golfing trips. He voiced his displeasure in no uncertain manner.

"It's like the devil has gotten into him," said James with uncharacteristic hostility.

"...More likely it's that woman. The brainless hussy has scattered his sensibility. In the good-old-days he had all the time in the world for Kristine. He was a real father to her. But now... I don't know what's going to happen. I just hope he comes to his senses soon.

"If Sylvia is the flighty woman you seem to think she is, then Royston will see through her. Underneath it all, he's still a decent bloke," James insisted.

"Yes, and I wouldn't like to see him get hurt. ...But in the meantime, what about Kristine?"

"She has already shown us what a resourceful person she can be. Maybe she's trying to establish independence from her family's older generations."

"Do you mean – from us?" asked Emily in alarm.

"Yes. Why not?"

"But she's only just seventeen. That's still very young."

"Seventeen seems very young to us now, but don't you recall how grown-up you felt at that age?"

Emily paused for thought. "I suppose so," she said. "But it was different in our day. We knew our place. There were still certain standards we had to live by, and only the most rebellious of teenagers broke with them."

"Is Kristine really breaking away from the standards of her own generation, or is she just rejecting all the family morals she can't handle at the moment? I think we should give her credit for the sense of decency we both know she possesses, and wait for her to make the first move."

Emily was at a loss for words. She knew James was right; that probably she was overly concerned. That she should let Kristine grow up naturally and not get involved. Yet, as a grandmother, Emily could not help her feelings. She loved Kristine as her own. After all, tomorrow was a very special birthday in the life of any young girl. But until Kristine deigned to contact her, she could do nothing.

Of one thing Emily was quite sure: she would continue to worry about her until she did.

Mercifully, the day of contact was not too long in coming. James breathed a sigh of relief when, a few days later, he saw Kristine cycling up the road, and knew that Emily's agony would soon be over. He called through to her in the kitchen before disappearing into the back garden to give them some privacy.

Emily hobbled through to open the front door.

Yet, her joy at seeing Kristine again soon became tinged with disappointment.

As Kristine got off her bike and propped it by the front steps, it was obvious to Emily that something about her had changed.

Kristine looked different.

The girl on the bike was definitely Kristine; there had been no mistake about that. And yet, it was not Kristine; that is, not the Kristine Emily was familiar with – the young lady full of potential and promise who had thus far grown up according to Emily's expectations. This girl could have been a cousin of that one; a cousin who had perhaps been brought up in different circumstances, who did not have the same values, the same endearing personality.

And yet it was still Kristine.

The facsimile of Emily's granddaughter walked up the steps. She was wearing a short, denim skirt with matching jacket; knee-length leather boots, and an array of beads that partially obscured a jazzy motif emblazoned across the front of her black tee-shirt.

This was a different image entirely from the simple shorts and tee shirt usually seen on Kristine's trim form. Furthermore, this version of the girl was chewing gum, a habit she had previously refrained from adopting.

Kristine brushed past as she strode into the house.

Suddenly Emily became angry.

"Just a minute young lady!" she exclaimed, and caught Kristine's arm. "Where do you think you're going?"

"Inside, of course," came the terse response as Kristine looked disapprovingly at the hand holding on to her.

"Not looking like that, you don't," Emily insisted. "...And certainly not chewing gum. Kristine, you know I hate that stuff. Go into the kitchen and get rid of it, please."

Kristine sighed petulantly.

The confident demeanour she exhibited when she came up to the door suddenly turned broody and, shrugging off Emily's hand, she disappeared into the kitchen; grumbling as she went.

"Alright...if you insist. I don't know what you're making all the fuss about, though. It's only chewing gum!"

Emily followed her.

"I know it's only chewing gum, but I still won't have it in my house. Why did you start with that stuff, anyway?"

"It's no big deal, Nana. Don't get so het-up about it."

The ball of gum dropped silently into the pedal bin as she spat it out.

"There. Are you happy now?"

"Yes. That's better. Now...have you got a hug for your Nana? We haven't seen or heard from you for ages, and I was worried...especially when we missed your birthday!"

Kristine hugged her briefly.

"You shouldn't have worried. The birthday didn't mean anything to me, anyway, except that I am now a woman of the world;" the remark made with a haughty gesture.

Though irritated by Kristine's response, Emily refrained from commenting, and instead laughed jovially.

"My darling, you've a long way to go before you can think of yourself as a woman of the world!"

"Oh, come on now...get real! We're not in the dark ages any more. Girls mature much younger these days..."

"...And you're being mature...dressed like that?"

"Richard likes it."

"And who, might I ask, is Richard?" Emily asked crossly.

""My fr... Um...my boyfriend."

"Oh, yes. That's right. ...I did hear about Richard."

Emily flinched when she recalled Fiona mentioning the boy and his motorbike.

"Has your mother actually met him yet?" she asked.

"No. Why should she?"

Again, Emily refrained from commenting. There was no point. Kristine would not have heeded her reasoning.

Instead, she said, "...And what about your father? Do you honestly see him approving of a young man who likes his girlfriend to dress like that?"

"I don't care what Dad thinks."

"Kristine!"

"Well, I don't! He doesn't care about me anymore. He's got his hands full with that tart, Sylvia!"

"That will do, my girl! Royston's new lady-friend may not be our choice of companion for him, but there is no excuse for language like that!"

Emily's patience with Kristine was at an end. All the same, she felt for the girl; understanding perfectly why she had adopted her defiant attitude. She was hurt, confused and fighting back. Kristine had already lost her mother's interest; certainly there was little love-loss between them. And now, after several months of companionship, she had apparently lost her father's interest, too.

Poor Kristine, thought Emily, her ire subsiding. You are at the wrong end of a pretty raw deal just at the moment.

Kristine stood at the kitchen window, gazing blankly into space, her mind in a whirl; oblivious of James pruning the roses in the garden.

Emily slipped an arm around her waist. As she did so, she noticed tears on Kristine's eyelashes; perilously close to descending onto reddening cheeks and revealing the vulnerability she was trying hard to override.

I must tread very carefully here, thought Emily; her own emotions on the verge of giving way.

"Please don't misunderstand me," she said quietly. "It was only your language I objected to; not you. Oh, Kristine, I know what you are going through! You feel as though your father has betrayed you, and you're lashing out with this uncharacteristic behaviour. I don't like what he's doing any more than you do – I have met the woman, after all! But I'm not going off the deep end about it."

"It's alright for you, Nana. You're an adult. You haven't been hurt by both of your parents!"

"Don't throw that one at me, Kristine. I've suffered in my life, too! Look how your mother has treated me in recent years! But the fact that you are technically still a child does not excuse you from this kind of self-indulgent attitude over it. Family problems are a sign of the times; you know that! But I do agree that when you are at the very beginning of life's sometimes cruel experiences, it is harder to cope with them. I am only more resilient now because I've learnt not to let things get me down: especially your mother's insults!"

Kristine softened her stance.

"I'm sorry, Nana. I forgot about all that. Mum really hurt you, didn't she?"

"At the time, yes she did. I've got over it, though, just as you will get over this; or rather, you will get used to it. Remember, we don't know how long the liaison between your father and Sylvia is going to last. Maybe, when they've been together for a while, he will realise Sylvia is not the woman for him."

"I hope so."

"In the meantime, I would like you to be happier than you have been."

"I'll try, Nana."

"Darling, it's not a question of trying to be happy. What I mean is, I hope happiness comes your way again because you've learnt how to accept what's going on, and don't feel isolated any more. If you need someone to talk to, you can always come to me. There is nothing we can't talk about on an equal footing, and that includes your feelings about your father and Sylvia."

"I know that. You helped me get used to having James around; I guess it could happen with Sylvia, too."

"Never be afraid that Sylvia's presence in your father's life means that he loves you less. It's only his time you will be sharing with her, not his affections – try to think of it that way. Ring him any time you feel a chat, and if Sylvia answers the phone, ask to speak to him. I can't see how she would object to that!"

"I just don't like the thought of her being there with Dad; sharing his..."

Kristine tailed off; a look of disdain on her face.

"Sharing his bed; is that what you were going to say?"

Kristine shuddered inwardly at the thought.

"He's still married to my mother, even though they are long-since separated!"

"But these days it's quite acceptable for people who are not married to live together..."

"...Not when it's my father who is doing it!"

Emily squeezed Kristine's waist again.

"I know, love. I do understand how you feel. It is always harder to accept something like that when it affects you personally. When it's somebody else, it's not as bad."

Kristine sighed; not in acceptance of the situation but with an ardent wish that the bad dream would end and life would return to normal.

"Why don't we break the ice now and ring him – both of us? I'll back you up."

Emily looked at her watch.

"He should be home by now."

"Oh, I don't know..."

Kristine hesitated.

Her revulsion of her father's new living arrangement was stronger than her desire to reconcile with him.

"Come on love..."

Emily pulled her over to the phone.

"...You will have to contact him some time!"

Kristine resisted, wrenching her arm from Emily's hand.

"Not now!" she snapped. "I know what you're trying to do, but I'm not ready yet. I don't know if I'll ever be ready! The whole thing makes me sick!"

Before Emily could protest, Kristine made for the front door, and escape.

Emily had time only to call after her, "Don't forget, love: I'm always here for you!"

"Do you remember how we thought we'd lost her when you and I were engaged," James reminded Emily on his return from the garden.

Without meaning to, he had overheard the argument, and caught Kristine's exit prior to Emily's entreaty.

He stood by Emily's side as she watched the red bike disappear into the distance; then encouraged her to come back inside.

"Kristine will be alright," he went on. "She now accepts our change in circumstances, and there's no reason why she shouldn't do likewise with her father's..."

"...You are so wrong; there are plenty of reasons!" Emily cut in heatedly. "Kristine's very much like me. She has an old-school sense of decency. In spite of the 'anything-goes' attitude of this current generation, she still regards what Royston is doing as immoral – especially as it's so personal to her."

While Emily vehemently aired her point of view, James nodded thoughtfully; recognising that to contradict her when she was in full flight would be asking for trouble.

"It was different in our case," Emily continued; a little more calmly. "We were both unattached, and we married before we lived together. Royston is living in a very loose relationship with a flighty woman while still married to Kristine's mother. The poor girl is going to need a lot of support from us to get her through this crisis. And I don't expect she'll get any from Fiona. Do you think we should ring Royston and tell him Kristine was here?"

James reflectively screwed up his face. The mood Emily was in, was she likely to bite his head off if he said the wrong thing?

He answered her with caution. "I don't think it would be a very good idea. Kristine might regard it as a betrayal of your trust."

Emily sighed; not content to leave well alone.

"I would like to ring him anyway on some pretext or another – just to see how he is. You can tell, from the sound of someone's voice on the phone, whether or not they are happy. I'm just as concerned for Royston as I am for Kristine. He's family, too."

Then, while James opened his mouth to protest, Emily picked up the phone to dial Royston's number.

James shook his head in defeat and started to walk away, but Emily stopped him.

"His line's engaged," she said, and hung up. "I suppose it's as well. I would probably have been tempted to tell him about Kristine's..."

Just then the phone rang, making her jump. Suspecting it might be Fiona, she answered it guardedly.

It was Royston.

"Well, what a coincidence," she said. "I was trying to ring you and the line was engaged..."

"...That's because I was trying to ring you!"

Emily grinned at James who realised at once what had just happened.

He winked back at Emily and then slipped out to the laundry to clean up after his gardening.

"How are you, Royston?" Emily asked as cheerfully as she could. "James and I haven't heard from you lately. Is everything working out alright?"

"Yes, quite good, thank you. Sylvia and I seem to be settling down now. I had forgotten what it's like to share my home with a woman...I must have become a bit too independent in my ways since the separation. Adapting again wasn't quite as straightforward as I had assumed."

"I expect it will take time – getting used to each other," remarked Emily politely; although she had hoped Royston would quickly become tired of his mistress and send her packing. "What did you ring for, Royston? Have you heard from Kristine?"

"No. I don't think she took too kindly to Sylvia's arrival on the scene, but she'll just have to get used to the idea. That's not why I phoned, though. I actually wanted to speak to James."

"Oh!" said Emily in surprise; she had assumed he rang her. "Alright. I'll get him. He's just out the back clearing up after his gardening session. You'll let me know if you hear from Kristine, won't you?"

"...Of course!"

Emily listened covertly as Royston and James talked on the phone.

She gathered from the part conversation she could hear that Royston wanted him to go for another game of golf, an observation that James later confirmed.

"As you know, Sylvia doesn't want Royston to waste his Sundays on golf because she doesn't like being left on her own," James said with a grin. "...However, it seems she's quite happy for him to have one last game."

Emily grunted.

"Well, that's big of her," she said sarcastically; and then added, "It's a shame, though. Sunday golf was something you always looked forward to. You'll miss it."

"Maybe somebody at the club will team up with me for a game or two in the future. I'll make some enquiries next weekend. ...By the way," he added, a thought coming to him. "I forgot to tell you; I've heard from my son."

"David? Did he ring?"

"No. There was a letter from him this morning. He says they can't wait to see us next month..."

"...My goodness...next month! It sounds so close when you put it that way. Where has the time gone?"

"Well, you have had rather a lot on your plate over the last few weeks, don't forget. It's no wonder the time seems to have flown by."

"I suppose you're right."

Sunday dawned brilliantly, with hardly a breath of wind to stir the clear air.

James checked his golfing equipment and dropped it in the hall ready for Royston's arrival.

Emily handed him his usual sandwich lunch and a flask of hot, sweet tea: easily enough for two, as she was sure Sylvia would not have bothered making up something for Royston's herself.

"I hope I'm not going to cook in these warm duds," said James, looking down at his warm jersey and trousers. "The weather forecast last night did say it would be cool today, but they may have got it wrong."

"Best not change into anything cooler," ventured Emily. "The wind does get up in the afternoon on those fairways. You could always take your jersey off and tie it round your waist in case you need it later on."

Royston arrived on time, exhilarated by the fine weather, and by the fact that he had been granted a few hours' leave from home.

Sylvia's constant attention, he was discovering, could be stifling at times.

Emily kissed James on the cheek, waved them off and waited until Royston's car rounded the bend. Then she went back inside and closed the door.

She sighed forlornly for happy times past when she and Kristine had made up the foursome. But at least James and

Royston were able to get another round of golf together. ...And, she thought, we can always team up with someone else in the future.

"Think positive, Emily," she told herself sternly. "There are other partners out there. A regular Sunday outing is still a possibility."

The golf course was busy when James and Royston waited their turn to tee-off; no doubt due to the fine weather, as one pair remarked to another.

In fact, players were driving off in far quicker succession than usual because of the high proportion of members who had arrived early for their game.

The two deliberately chipped their shots short to buy a little time while the group of four players up ahead slowly moved onto the next hole.

James felt faintly ill at ease, surrounded by the biggest turnout of golfers he had ever seen there on a Sunday morning. Yet, he persevered; determined to make the most of what he knew would be their last game of golf together for quite some time.

Well into the third hole, a bottleneck began to develop when James and Royston caught up with the slower group of four in front; while at the same time a quicker husband and wife behind began to catch up with them.

As the two pairs of players waited for the foursome to move away, they discussed the impossible situation on the course brought about by the fine weather.

The husband, clearly agitated, complained to his wife that he was so frustrated with the constant hold-ups that he wanted to give the game away and go back to the clubhouse for a drink.

But then his wife came up with a solution, which she timidly mentioned to the three men:

"Why don't the four of us finish the round together? ...Then we won't be holding each other up."

"What a brilliant idea!" said Royston.

"Thank you for your suggestion, and we accept," James added to clinch the deal.

From then on their game progressed more smoothly, all four players now pacing themselves, so that a steady flow moved from one hole to the next, with as little hold-up as possible under the circumstances.

James began to settle down and enjoy himself now. In conversation with their new partners he learnt that they lived in the street where he and Janet used to live, and that in fact his wife and Janet had been acquaintances.

"It's a small world," they both agreed.

The four new friends played on, paying little attention to how well they played; nor even bothering to keep score after a while.

Whereas their games of golf were usually treated as a competitive sport, to a certain extent this particular one was not. Present conditions dictated that it be regarded more as a convivial pastime than a sport, as the ability to progress in a sportsmanlike way was still hampered by their continual need to stop and wait for the groups up ahead to move on.

Furthermore, due to the delays the foursome chose to play on through lunchtime. To stop and take time out for a picnic was not now an option; it would cause too much inconvenience both for themselves and for other golfers.

So, with only a cursory comment on the need to press on passing between them, the two pairs of partners continued their round without a break.

Yet still, the weather was agreeable, their outing had been enjoyable, and the company in which they all found themselves had become pleasantly congenial.

"What more could I ask for?" James thought to himself.

But then suddenly it all ended...in a flash, without warning or explanation.

...One of those rare, horrific moments in time when the whole world seems to turn upside-down.

As James, head lowered, positioned himself for his next swing, a stray shot from a neighbouring fairway thudded into his left temple; killing him instantly.

CHAPTER FIVE

James dropped to the ground.

His three companions watched in horror and disbelief; suspended in a moment of incredulity before shock set in, when the reality of what took place had not yet registered in stunned minds.

For what seemed like an eternity, they each remained motionless, transfixed to the spot, as though time itself had stood still.

It was the lady in the foursome who, only a second after the accident, made the first move and with a gasp of shock rushed up to their new colleague who now lay in a crumpled heap on the fairway.

There was no need to check his vital signs. The open, staring eyes confirmed what had just occurred.

She turned to the two men, whose reactions were still frozen in the moment.

Dazed by her discovery, she said, "I can't believe it...he's dead! One minute he was playing normally with us all, and now he's dead!"

Royston, his eyes fixed on the sight of his lifeless friend, moved statically over to where James lay partially on his side. Blood oozed from a visible wound in his skull.

"...But he can't be dead. You...you must be mistaken," he stammered mindlessly, and squatted beside the body. But when he saw the wound and the blank, open eyes the truth hit home. Standing up abruptly he shrieked at the others, "Oh my God!"

Then he rushed off to some nearby bushes where he was violently sick.

By now a commotion had set in, as groups of players who witnessed the incident converged on the scene.

A tall, elderly gentleman with an anxious look on his face, hurried up to the group.

"It's my fault! It's all my fault!" he cried, and stumbled over the last few feet of turf to where James was lying; prompting a man standing close by to catch him before he also fell. But he was a man with a mission; a mission to save his victim's life.

Struggling free from his Good Samaritan, he dropped to his knees beside James to try and save his life.

Just then a woman appeared, clearing her way through the gathering crowd.

"Please let me through," she said with authority. "I'm a registered nurse."

She squatted down next to the distraught gentleman, and instructed him to help her turn James over so that she could attempt resuscitation.

As she performed CPR the crowd hung back, holding their collective breath for signs of life, but none came. Then, after several minutes of concerted effort and the inevitable realisation that it was unsuccessful, the nurse sat back on her haunches and looked around her for someone who might be connected with him.

"I'm very sorry," she said to anyone who would listen. "It appears we are too late."

In the meantime, Royston had recovered from his bout of nausea, and while the CPR was taking place he hesitantly returned to the scene.

Deeply traumatised by the nurse's pronouncement, he informed her, "This man is my father-in-law."

"What happened?" she asked him. "Do you think he may have had a heart attack?" The nurse assumed the wound on his head was caused by the fall.

Royston did not answer. Still too deeply held in a state of shock, he could not answer.

It was the woman from their foursome who answered the nurse's question.

"No. It wasn't a heart attack. He was hit by a stray ball. That's what killed him."

"Yes, and I'm afraid I caused it," the distraught golfer confessed. "I side-swiped a shot. It went astray and struck this poor soul down. How awful. How absolutely dreadful... I just can't believe it!"

The old man, now shaking uncontrollably, was led away from the scene by his playing companion.

"Wait a minute," the nurse called out to them.

She seemed to have taken charge.

"Would you mind staying here for a while? I'm sure the police will need to question you." And then she enquired, "Has anyone called the police, by the way?"

"Yes," someone in the crowd replied. "The police and an ambulance are on their way."

Then, as if confirming his statement, a siren could be heard in the distance.

"What do you suppose will happen to me?" asked the anxious gentleman.

He now had in his hand the cup from a flask: from the flask of tea Emily had given to James. For, recognising his plight, Royston had extracted the flask from the golf bag and poured him a drink.

He stood with him while he sipped the sweet beverage.

The nurse spoke to Royston again.

"You said the victim is your father-in-law. Does he have a wife at home?"

301

"A wife?" he replied, not yet able to think clearly. "Yes, Emily. ...Good God! What am I going to tell Emily?"

Panicking, Royston broke down.

He sunk to his knees, covered his face with his hands and wailed.

"How can I tell Emily...that her new husband is dead?"

He glanced pleadingly into the nurse's face, as though seeking salvation from the anguish he was suffering, and from the unbearable pain he knew he would soon have to inflict on Emily.

The nurse looked compassionately at the pitiful figure and suggested, "If it's of any help, I will come back with you when we leave here. I don't think you should be left to cope alone. It'll be too traumatic for you."

"Thank...you," stammered Royston as the nurse helped him to his feet. "I...I would appreciate that."

When the police and an ambulance arrived, just minutes apart, most of the crowd had already dispersed, leaving only those immediately involved.

By now, the shock and general banter at the time of the incident had diminished to a respectful silence.

Royston and the golfer who caused the accident stood back while the professionals took over.

After extensive questioning of those remaining, the old man and his golfing partner went off with a police officer; but not before the man turned back to Royston.

As though to absolve himself of his profound guilt, he said again, "I'm so sorry. I'm so terribly sorry. Please tell his wife I didn't mean to do it."

Royston nodded his understanding, but said nothing. There was nothing to say. What was done was done. His thoughts had already moved on to Emily, and how he was going to break the news to her.

Royston and the nurse watched the ambulance men lift James onto a stretcher and place him in the ambulance.

Soon only Royston and the nurse remained.

She had already dismissed her own golfing companions in order to leave herself free to accompany Royston.

For a moment neither spoke; until the silence of the now empty section of fairway became too much. Then, taking a deep breath for courage, the nurse said, "Come on; let's get out of here. We've got work to do."

Together, the two figures walked silently back to the clubhouse, each pulling a trundler; for the bag James was using had remained throughout the pandemonium exactly where he left it prior to taking his final shot; as though awaiting its owner's return.

"I'll follow you in my car," she told Royston at the club's car park.

Sometime later, they pulled up outside Emily's house.

Emily had not expected the menfolk to return for several hours yet.

To while away the time, she had pulled out her sewing machine and was in the process of repairing the waistband of a pair of trousers, her foot pumping the electric pedal which operated the noisy appliance. She had frequently complained to Arthur about the noise it made, refusing to use it again until it had been fixed yet never was. Only now had she thought to use it again.

So when the two cars arrived at the kerbside, she did not hear them; nor did she recognise the squeak of the front gate as it was opened, or the footsteps on the path leading up to the porch.

On the other hand, a knock at the front door arrested her attention immediately, and she peeped through the lounge window to see who was there.

Failing to notice that two cars were parked outside, she was instead intrigued by the sight of a woman standing at the bottom of the steps. It was only then that her eyes drifted back to the road; to the fact that one of the vehicles belonged to Royston. At least, it looked like his.

Immediately she knew something was wrong. A well-honed sixth sense told her all was not well, and a feeling of alarm arose within her.

While she hurried to the front door she prayed that she might be wrong; that it was not Royston but an innocuous caller standing there.

Yet it was indeed Royston. ...Royston and the woman.

In an instant Emily weighed up the situation: The ashen look on Royston's face, the serious look on the woman's; the absence of her beloved husband...

Where was he?

Dear God, let my fears be groundless!

"Emily..." stammered Royston; but he could say no more.

The nurse took over.

"Mrs Forsythe, may we come in?"

"Yes. ...Of course.

Emily quickly, urgently, stood back to let them pass.

"Royston, what's going on? Where is James?"

He looked at her, but overcome with emotion he could not find the words to answer her.

"Let's go and sit down, shall we?" said the nurse. "There is something we need to tell you."

Aghast, Emily perched bolt upright on the edge of her chair; ready for an immediate and, hopefully, satisfactory explanation as to what had happened to James.

"Mrs Forsythe," began the nurse. "I'm afraid there was an accident at the golf course today."

"It's James, isn't it?"

Emily drew a shaky breath, expecting the worst.

"Yes. I'm sorry. Your husband was accidentally struck in the head by a golf ball..."

"Oh, no!"

"...He died instantly."

With a gasp of disbelief, Emily looked enquiringly at her son-in-law, as if seeking a second opinion.

"Royston, is this true?"

"Yes Emily. I'm afraid it is true. I was there."

Royston got up from his seat and squatted before her. There were tears in his eyes now.

When Emily saw them, she broke down, too.

She placed her arms around his shoulders and rested her head against his, sharing the bitter sting of grief.

The nurse looked away. This moment was too personal for onlookers.

"Please tell me...how it happened," whimpered Emily; barely audible. She gently pulled away from him and looked into his eyes. "Did you see it?" she asked.

Quietly sobbing, Royston replied, "Yes. I was with him."

Then he explained about the golfer and his stray golf ball; about the crowds, the police, and the ambulance. And lastly Royston told her about the help and support of the nurse who had accompanied him home.

He pointed to the woman in the chair opposite, who had remained silent throughout it all: watching and listening, herself very close to tears.

"For what it's worth, Mrs Forsythe," she said at length. "Your husband would not have felt any pain."

Emily smiled a watery smile. She clutched at Royston's hand while he stood up, as if begging him not to leave.

Then the nurse mouthed to Royston, "I must get going."

"Yes, of course," he replied.

305

Gently extricating himself from the grasp, he walked the nurse out into the hall, leaving Emily desperately trying to gain a perspective on the situation.

"Thank you so much for all you've done, both at the golf course and in coming back with me," he said to the nurse. "I don't think I could have managed without you."

"Please think nothing of it," the nurse replied. "Under the circumstances, I could have done nothing else."

"All the same, I would like to express my appreciation. Perhaps you'll let me take you out for dinner or something at a more appropriate time. By the way...I don't even know your name."

"It's Alicia. Alicia Summerville...and thank you for the offer of dinner; I'd like that. I'm the new district nurse in this area. My phone number is in the book under Social Services if you would like to give me a ring...

Alicia looked across at Emily who now sat motionless; her head bowed.

"...Maybe in a couple of weeks," she added.

Alicia started down the steps; then turned around to face Royston. "I think it would be as well if your mother-in-law had company tonight," she said. "After a shock like this, a night alone might prove to be too much for her."

"Thank you for the advice. I'll arrange something with the family."

By the time Royston returned to Emily, the numbing effect of shock had set in and she suddenly looked very frail.

She stared blankly at him as he walked into the room.

He took hold of her hands, observing them to be cold.

"I think we could both do with a nice hot cup of tea," he suggested as lightly as was appropriate, and went through to the kitchen.

A few minutes later, he came back in.

With chilled hands wrapped around a warm mug of tea, Emily revived slightly; just enough to ask, "Exactly how did it happen, Royston? I still can't believe he's gone."

So Royston explained everything again.

This time, he told her more about the elderly man who caused the accident, and how traumatised he was to have been responsible for it.

"I'd like to go and see him."

"...The old man? I don't think he would be up to a visit from you just yet."

"No, not him! I want to see my husband! Where is he?"

Royston was taken aback by Emily's abruptness.

"They took him away in an ambulance...I'm afraid I was in too much of a state of shock to find out where to. I'll ring the hospital now if you like."

"Yes...please! ...If you don't mind!"

The hospital registrar informed Royston that the body of James Forsythe had been taken to the hospital's mortuary to await a coroner's investigation.

"Would it be possible for his wife...his widow...to come and see him?" he asked.

"Yes, I'm sure it can be arranged. I'll transfer you to that extension now, if you would care to hold."

Moments later Royston reported back to Emily.

"We can see him tonight if we go in straight away."

A mortuary is a depressing place, Royston decided as they pushed through the swing doors.

This one was also inordinately cold; yet he could not tell whether the chill he felt running down his spine was from the room's extreme temperature, or his reaction to the environment.

The attendant consulted a list on his clipboard.

307

"Forsythe, did you say? We had three deceased come in this afternoon... Just need to check which one is yours. Oh yes. Here it is...number twenty-seven."

He led Emily and Royston through another set of doors.

For once, Royston cast etiquette aside, and entered before Emily in case there was anything inside which might disturb her. Yet this room, larger and colder even than the first, contained nothing but a mortuary slab and several rows of drawers set into the walls.

The attendant traced his finger round the numbers on each drawer; pausing when he found the one marked with the correct number.

Then he grasped the handle. But before opening it, he turned to Emily.

"Are you sure you're up to this, madam?" he asked in a blunt fashion.

Emily had remained withdrawn throughout the trip to town and their admission to the mortuary. She hardly noticed the attendant's question, let alone his manner.

"Sorry, what did you say?" she asked when she realised he had been addressing her.

Royston put his arm round her shoulder and said, "Do you want to go ahead with this?"

"Of course!" she replied without emotion. "Isn't that what we're here for?"

The attendant slowly pulled the wide drawer open. It slid easily on well-oiled casters, revealing a form covered with a white sheet. He took hold of the top edge of the sheet and gradually peeled it back, uncovering the face of Emily's now deceased husband.

The sight of him caused Emily to gasp.

She cupped her hands over her mouth as if to stifle a scream, but no sound escaped her.

Royston recoiled inwardly, seeing his old friend lying there: nothing but a greying corpse. But he concealed his revulsion for Emily's sake.

"He looks very peaceful," he said reassuringly.

James lay beneath the sheet's crisp whiteness; his eyes now closed in restful sleep, rather than the blank stare of death Royston witnessed at the golf course.

Only his colour gave away the fact that he was deceased. The pink flush of life had been replaced by the unmistakable pallor of death.

Emily noticed this, too.

"His skin looks pale," she remarked dispassionately. Without thinking, she reached out her hand to touch his face, but Royston stopped her.

"I wouldn't do that, if I were you," he urged. "There is no life left in his body, Emily. To touch him would only upset you. And he won't be able to feel it."

Royston led her away. He could tell by the absence of emotion that it had not yet registered that her husband was actually dead. Such a realisation, when it kicked in, would render her immobile; but right now she was still in control.

...At least, that was how it seemed to the attendant when he escorted them to the outer door.

"She's taking her husband's death very well, isn't she?" he said to Royston as he signed them out on the register.

"It hasn't fully sunk in yet. Either that or she's becoming accustomed to losing a husband. James...Mr Forsythe...was her second," he said quietly.

Royston took Emily straight back to her house...except for one brief stop he had already planned to make. He had decided, the moment Alicia suggested it, that he should

309

not yet leave Emily alone. So he stopped off at his flat to throw a few things into a bag in front of a startled Sylvia. Then, after the briefest of explanations, he rushed back out before she had a chance to object.

Sylvia followed him out to the car. In the gloom that descends when all light has faded for the day, she saw only a small, ghostly face at the passenger window; apparently looking out at her.

Yet Emily, her mind numb, was merely looking in the direction from where Royston had just come. She failed to notice Sylvia's voluptuous form silhouetted against the light from the doorway.

The funeral was held a week later. James was laid to rest in his family's plot at the same cemetery where Arthur was buried. Emily felt an appalling sense of déjà vu when, with Kristine once more at her side for support, they all walked along the path back to the car.

Emily shed no tears.

There were three funeral cars in attendance this time. The first carried Emily, Royston and Kristine, the second Ruth and Wilbur.

The third vehicle, a rental car hired at the last minute, brought to the funeral David: the son-in-law Emily and James had planned to visit within that very month; who had been summoned at short notice from overseas.

The most recent addition to Emily's family, the one she had excitedly been waiting to meet on the other side of the world, now became her guest instead of her host; but Emily, too swamped by everything taking place, could barely manage more than a polite, "I'm happy to meet you," when David was introduced to her.

Later, Emily would reflect on the circumstances under which their meeting came about.

Yet, there was one further vehicle involved with this unassuming motorcade.

Unknown to Emily and her family, after the cars had left the cemetery car park a fourth car also pulled away from the kerb; its driver deliberately keeping out of sight; not wanting to be recognised now any more than she did when, from the seclusion of her driver's seat, she watched the funeral proceedings in the cemetery.

It was Fiona.

Though still harbouring hostility towards Emily, she could not help but feel acutely sorry that her mother had lost a second husband in virtually as many years. It seemed so unfair; even to the woman who gauged everything in life according to how it impacted on her.

Fiona never really knew James, saw him and her mother together only once, and considered them to be a married couple never. But Kristine had spoken about him often, had gone from resenting him to loving him, and as a result Fiona had developed a certain amount of respect for him.

It was her regard for him which prompted her to be present at his funeral, albeit from a distance.

That night Kristine telephoned her father at Emily's where Royston had stayed on having promised to organise the funeral and help Emily afterwards.

If but one glimmer of brightness came from the week's great sorrow, it lay in the fact that Kristine and her father were talking again. ...And Kristine was glad of one other factor, too. With Royston staying at Emily's it meant she did not run the risk of having to go through Sylvia in order to contact him.

Nevertheless, Kristine had reservations about phoning him even at her grandmother's house in case Emily should be the one to answer the phone.

311

On the night after the funeral, even though she had willingly stayed by Emily's side the whole time, she still did not know what she could possibly say that might ease Emily's pain. To the affectionate Kristine, a hug said so much more than mere words, but she could not give her grandmother a hug through the telephone.

Ruth, too, found herself at a loss for words. It seemed that every appropriate comment for such an occasion was said two years previously. Repeating it all over again would render it trite and meaningless.

To Emily's side of the family, the funeral of her second husband was not as intensely personal as was that of her first husband. Arthur had been their immediate kin, and he was special. So, while they pledged their love and support to Emily, none could feel the same grievous sense of loss for James as she did.

Kristine breathed a sigh of relief when it was Royston who answered her call and not Emily.

"Hello Dad," she said brightly, pleased to hear his voice.

"Why, Kristine! Hello to you, too! How are you bearing up, my love?"

"I'm alright! What about you? You're the one who is in the thick of things over there. I feel as sorry for you as I do for Nana. How is she, by the way?"

"She's resting on her bed. I think she was pretty glad to get home. I persuaded her to take one of the sedatives the doctor prescribed for her yesterday. She'll probably sleep on into the night now."

Royston paused, a thought coming to mind.

"Kristine," he said. "I'm glad you rang."

"Oh, why's that?"

"I need you to do something for me."

"Is anything wrong?"

"No...not really," he said with a note of hesitance in his voice. "It's just that..."

"It's just what? ...You're beginning to worry me."

"Sorry. There's nothing to worry about; it's just that..."

"Oh Dad; now you're repeating yourself. What are you getting at?"

Royston paused again. He was starting to feel awkward about the request he needed to make.

"I don't want to inconvenience you, but..."

"...For goodness sake!"

"It's just that I really need to get back to my flat," he said. "I've been staying here ever since James died, and Sylvia is beginning to get a bit tetchy about it. She doesn't like being left on her own."

"So... What are you asking me?"

"Would you be willing to fill in for me here while I go home for a few days?"

Kristine laughed. "Is that all? For a minute I thought you were going to ask me to keep company with Sylvia! Of course I will! I hate trying to talk to Nana on the phone, anyway. There's no school this week because of holidays, so it should work out alright."

"That would be marvellous. When can I expect you?"

"Give me a minute to pack a bag; then I'll come over."

Royston was relieved to be going home. Sylvia had made it quite clear to him that she would not put up with playing second fiddle to an old woman who was not even his blood relative. He was sure, then, that she would be pleased to have him back.

Yet, when he arrived at the flat he received a shock; for as he turned into his driveway he could see that the front door was open and all the lights were on.

Assuming Sylvia was inside the flat and had left the door open unintentionally, Royston walked right in.

Glancing around, he called her name.

The one-bedroom flat had an open plan living area, from which a short hallway led to a bathroom and the bedroom. Both of these doors were closed. Receiving no response to his call, Royston knocked tentatively on the bedroom door; still without response.

She may have gone to bed already and forgotten about the front door; an oversight easily made, he conceded.

Royston went back into his kitchen and switched on the kettle; it felt good to be in his own home again.

Looking after Emily had been a privilege – he owed it to her, having been the one to give her the sad news about James. And as the family were only too happy to accept his offer of staying with her, he had been willing to do so.

Yet, Sylvia's ultimatum the previous day worried him. She had threatened to leave if he did not come back forthwith. So when Kristine agreed to take over from him and come straight round, Royston had breathed a sigh of relief and then gratefully headed for home...

While he savoured a brew of his favourite coffee, Royston surveyed his domain.

It's strange just how much you can miss your own home even after a few days, he thought.

Emily's house was so much bigger than his flat, and she had all the furniture needed to fill its three bedrooms. On the other hand, Royston's little one bedroom home had room only for the barest of essentials.

It was so tiny in fact that even the meagre amount of belongings Sylvia had brought with her made his home seem cramped.

In truth, he admitted to himself, it was rather nice to have had the chance to spread out in the bigger house for a while. Leaving his own roomy house had not suited him either, but he'd had no choice...

314

Royston looked around to see if the flat seemed even smaller after his layover in Emily's, and noticed something very strange:

A nest of tables which Sylvia brought with her when she moved in was not in its usual place.

He got up, his curiosity aroused. ...Maybe she shifted it while he was away. But then he realised something else: several more knickknacks of Sylvia's were now missing.

Suddenly a thought occurred to him.

Oh no, he groaned, and made for the bedroom; this time not bothering to knock.

He flung the door open, and what he saw left him with a feeling of dread. The unmade bed was empty.

"Sylvia!" he called again.

His bathroom was adjacent to their bedroom; she could be in there.

He turned the door handle, hoping it would not yield; indicating that she had locked it while she showered or was taking a bath. But it turned with ease.

The bathroom, too, was empty.

Furthermore, he noticed that the toiletries Sylvia kept on the vanity had gone, as had her bath-robe from behind the door. ...And when in desperation Royston checked the wardrobe, so had all her clothes.

"Damn it!" he cried, and angrily sat down on the bed. "She couldn't wait one more day for me to come home!"

Royston wandered back through to the living room, feeling let down.

What price loyalty? he complained bitterly.

He had spent all that time helping the grieving widow, who was the mother of his ex-wife, not his, and what consideration does he get from his girlfriend for such a magnanimous gesture!

315

"Oh well," he conceded later in the evening when the shock of his discovery had worn off, "Sylvia was getting a bit bossy. I'm probably better off without her."

It's ironic, he thought while he got ready for bed. Only last week Sylvia had told him she didn't want to be involved in his golf trips any more. If she hadn't said that, he would not have felt pressured into asking James for that one last game and James, therefore, would still be alive.

Therefore, as the situation now stood, he had lost both his closest friend and his poor excuse for a girlfriend.

For a time Royston lay awake, bewildered by conflicting thoughts and emotions. It had been a hell of a week, all in all. The only saving grace was Kristine.

He looked at his watch. It was just after ten o'clock. Was it too late to give her a ring?

But then, he pondered, she may have gone to bed already; although, when he gave it further thought, he remembered that the schools were on holiday, so she may still be up...

He decided to give it a try; then put the phone down again before it started to ring. He could be wrong after all, and he didn't want to disturb Emily; she might try to answer it herself and rush down the stairs...

Better to leave ringing her till the morning before he left for work...

...Aaagh, work! he moaned.

During his stay with Emily, he had brought a briefcase full of paperwork home, in order to systematically go through it while keeping her company. But during the week there had been a steady stream of visitors and then preparations for the funeral; leaving him very little time to do anything of his own.

But then something came to mind that caused him to smile. Without Sylvia making demands on his time, he would now have the freedom to bring work home...and do anything else he felt like doing.

He could get up or go to bed when it suited him, eat when he felt like eating or not at all.

...And one day he might even feel like taking on another golfing partner.

By the time he fell asleep, Royston had got over the shock of losing his girlfriend, and was quite content with the prospect of living the life of a bachelor once again.

CHAPTER SIX

Emily was more than a little surprised to see Kristine and not Royston come down to breakfast the next morning.

As was her custom, she had been up for a while and was pottering in the kitchen.

"My dear, how lovely to find you are here," she told the girl as the two embraced, but then asked, "...So where is your father?"

"Dad needed to go back to his flat," she replied, and was grateful that Emily did not question her as to why.

"Poor Royston," Emily remarked. "I do feel sorry for him. He's been so gallant through all of this. I don't know what I would have done here without him. It's very useful to have a man around the house."

Kristine and Emily chatted and generally appreciated each other's company during the remainder of the morning. It did Emily the world of good to have a kindred spirit with her. Yet Kristine saw the situation differently.

She could not understand why her grandmother was being so stoical about everything: talking about James as though he had not died but merely gone away for a while. The man who had so recently become her soul mate was now dead, and Emily was speaking of him as though nothing tragic had happened at all.

It was far too confusing for the girl who knew her Nana so well; who expected to see slightly more than a token

318

gesture of grief that, for the second time, the man she loved had been taken from her.

Furthermore, the fact that Emily was discussing James in the present tense bothered her; to the extent that after lunch she felt she could no longer deal with it alone, and in desperation rang her father.

"Oh, hi Kristine, I'm so glad you phoned," he told her jovially. "I was going to ring you first thing this morning, but I slept through my alarm and then had to go to work."

Kristine noticed his unexpected joviality but refrained from commenting; assuming that his good mood must have something to do with his reconciliation with Sylvia.

That was something she did not want to think about...

"How's your grandmother today?" Royston asked.

"That's what I wanted to talk to you about. She seems to be behaving in a very weird manner."

"What do you mean by weird?"

"She's carrying on as though James has just popped out to the shops or something, and will be back soon. At one time this morning she even spoke about the trip they are making to meet his son, when we both know that David was over here for his father's funeral! I really don't know what to make of it."

"It sounds like she's in denial," said Royston. "Emily has been so strong in herself since her marriage to James. Now that he's gone she may be starting to crumble. She looked frail when we got back from the funeral..."

"...I wouldn't say she's exactly frail now. In fact, she's almost the opposite. As you say, she's probably in denial. Or maybe she's in the early stages of a breakdown. How am I expected to cope if she's about to have a breakdown? I'm going to need some help, Dad!"

"Don't worry about it, love; it's early days yet. Give her time to deal with her loss in her own way. Remember, only a week or so ago she was happy, with everything to live for. She could not have foreseen something like this happening; it must have knocked her for six."

While Royston was talking, Kristine started to feel a lump forming in her throat, and for a moment she went quiet as she tried to control the onset of emotion.

"Kristine, my dear; are you alright?" said a gentle voice behind her.

Kristine came to with a start and sniffed back a tear.

Emily stood in the kitchen doorway with a bunch of the whiskey roses. The sight of her granddaughter so close to tears alarmed her.

While Kristine tried to compose herself, Emily went on, "Look at these gorgeous blooms. The 'whiskies' are your grandfather's favourites. I must show them to James..."

Then she went off in search of a vase.

"...Kristine, are you still there?" said Royston. "I heard Emily's voice. She said something about Grandpa."

"That's what I mean, Dad," said Kristine, feeling trapped between two worlds – that of sanity and another, strange world that Emily seemed to be caught in. "She really is away with the fairies. I don't know how to deal with it, or even how to talk to her."

"Maybe it would be better if you went back home after all. Despite what Alicia said, perhaps Emily needs to have some time to herself."

"You're probably right. By the way...who is Alicia?"

"She's a district nurse who just happened to be at the golf course when the accident occurred. She was a great help to me at a very difficult time. And that reminds me; I owe her dinner."

"She sounds like a nice person – much nicer than..."

Kristine went quiet. She didn't see the need to mention Sylvia's name, and was sure that Royston got her drift.

"You don't need to worry about Sylvia anymore," said Royston, immediately catching on.

"Why?" asked Kristine, quietly chuckling that they were of one accord where the woman was concerned.

"That's why I wanted to phone you today. I thought you would be pleased to learn that Sylvia has gone."

"Gone?"

"Yes. She has moved out... Lock, stock and bleached blond hair!"

"Really! Well, thank God for that!"

"Kristine!"

"Sorry, Dad, but there was no way in the world she would have been right for you. And I could never have thought of her as my step-mother!"

While Kristine and her father finished their conversation, Emily located the vase she had been looking for.

She stood in the kitchen arranging the blooms.

In the background she heard Kristine on the phone, but was neither interested in overhearing her conversation, nor paying attention to the task at hand.

Uppermost in her thoughts, as she placed the last yellow rose in the vase, was something that transpired during the night. It was a dream so clear it could only have come from one source: Arthur.

After the death of James, Emily was frequently troubled by vivid nightmares.

Her dreams were never an issue during their marriage, yet since his death her ability to sleep had diminished and the dreams were becoming quite bizarre.

In a lucid moment Emily would have recognised that the nightmares were no more than her mind's reaction to her recent loss. However, in reality the effect they had was so alarming, that while he stayed with her Royston had the doctor prescribe a mild sedative for her. Thus, after taking the first tablet, Emily began to sleep soundly.

After that, her sleep pattern reverted to normal, which meant she was also able to dream properly; and lingering on the periphery of her subconscious mind, Arthur seized the moment for which he had been waiting.

This time, Arthur did not come alone.

With him was the ephemeral presence of someone not yet ascended into the realms of heaven: James.

Yet, Arthur had a message for her from him; a message which gladdened Emily's heart.

Sensing rather than hearing what Arthur had to impart, she hungrily absorbed its implication. James, it transpired, was not as traumatised by the incidence of his death as all had assumed, and having reconnected with Janet had given his blessing for Arthur to return to Emily.

With joy in her heart, she quietly and lovingly thanked them both, and slipped back into restful sleep.

When she awoke, Emily showered and dressed as was her normal habit. But she hardly gave thought to what she was doing. The euphoria that accompanied the nocturnal encounter remained with her; a morning spent with Kristine doing little to jolt her out of it.

In effect, Emily was perfectly happy, now. She did not want to revisit the agony of life following the death of one so cherished as a husband. As far as she was concerned, there had been no death, but merely a transformation of which she was a part.

Kristine and Royston would just have to get used to it.

Knowing nothing of her vivid dream, Kristine merely saw Emily's strange behaviour, and was worried. She had only seen her like this once before, and that was after her Grandpa died.

Maybe, she thought, it was just a phase everybody goes through when someone close to them passes away, and Emily needed plenty of time to work through it before she could get back to normal and resume the relationship they had always enjoyed.

Kristine shook off these thoughts, chastising herself for being so selfish as to place her own desires over the needs of her bereaved grandmother.

Yet there still remained the problem of how to handle someone who was losing touch with reality. Kristine had no experience of keeping company with elderly people, except for her Nana. And Nana had always been perfectly alright up until recently.

It seemed possible, to the inexperienced teenager, that Emily's reaction to her second grievous loss had somehow affected her mind. She sincerely hoped that rest – and lots of support from her favourite family member – would help her grandmother to recover.

Certainly it was Kristine's aim to accomplish this.

A few days later, Kristine found herself facing a dilemma:

Emily was showing no signs of reverting to the kind of behaviour expected of one still grieving, and there was only one more weekend left of her school holiday. On Sunday she would need to return home in order to get ready for the new school term – the last term of her secondary education and therefore the most important.

She was sure her mother would only allow her to visit Emily after school, and take steps to enforce the ruling...

What, then, should she do about an elderly lady who must not be left alone; not even her own grandmother? So far, the only other member of the family who knew of Emily's behaviour was Royston.

The twins, caught up with their own affairs, had paid only conciliatory attention to their mother's plight once the initial shock of James's death had passed.

Certainly, they had no idea of Emily's flights of fancy.

Fiona had not been in touch with Emily at all, and Ruth, though having plenty of time on her hands now that they were both retired, was so obsessive about Wilbur's health that it did not occur to her the capable Kristine might need support from her as well as from Royston.

Of this latter fact, Kristine became increasingly aware.

During the time she kept company with Emily, Kristine had spoken to her aunt only twice; on one occasion acting as go-between when Ruth wanted to enquire after Fiona. And rather than asking Kristine how she was coping, Ruth merely congratulated her on the level of maturity she was showing as Emily's live-in companion.

"Auntie Ruth just regards me as a fixture here," Kristine complained to Royston part way through the week.

Yet, no matter how impressed the family were with her sense of responsibility, it still did not solve Kristine's urgent problem of what to do about school.

She was airing her dilemma to Royston through the phone wires when she heard hesitant footsteps at the front door, followed by a tentative knock.

"Hold on a minute; somebody's here," she said, and laid the phone down while she responded to the knock.

"Yes, can I help you?" she said to an unfamiliar lady in a nurse's uniform.

"Is this the home of Emily Forsythe?" the nurse asked with seasoned courteously.

"That's right. Why do you ask?"

324

"I'm Alicia Summerville, the new district nurse for this area. My predecessor, Joyce Brown, has retired and I took her place. I'm here for a follow-up call on Mrs Forsythe." Then, when Kristine's mind drew a blank as to what she was talking about, the nurse went on; "I understand Mrs Forsythe was hospitalised after a fall a few months ago, and was receiving visits from Joyce..."

Suddenly it dawned.

"...Oh yes! I'm sorry...I didn't mean to be rude," said Kristine. "I'm her granddaughter, Kristine. Please come in, but you'll have to excuse me for a minute; I'm just in the middle of a phone call."

"Dad, I'll have to go," she told Royston when she got back to him. "The district nurse is here to see Nana..."

"...District nurse, did you say?"

"Yes. Something to do with the fall she had some time ago – when she finished up in hospital."

"Did the lady tell you her name?"

"Yes. Alicia something-or-other..."

"...Was it Summerville?" asked Royston, butting in.

"I think so. Do you know her?"

"I certainly do. She's the nurse I told you about: the one who attended James the day he died."

"Oh, that one!"

"Can I speak to her?"

"She came to see Nana."

"I know. I won't keep her a minute. I'm sure she's busy, but I would like to talk to her."

Kristine peered into the lounge where Alicia was waiting, and held the phone out for her.

"My father would like to talk to you," she said with a curious look on her face.

"By all means...thank you."

325

Alicia took the phone from her.

"This is Alicia Summerville," she said into it. "May I ask who I'm speaking to?"

"Alicia...it's Royston from the golf course: James' son-in-law. Don't you remember?"

Emily Forsythe... Royston...

Alicia quickly put two and two together. No wonder the house looked familiar!

"Of course! How could I forget! My predecessor left me her files, and it didn't click until just now who I was coming to see at this address."

Alicia tried to camouflage the embarrassment she now felt. It was very unprofessional to forget a client's name.

"Well, I never..." she went on. "So the Emily I'm visiting today is the same Emily we had to break the sad news to?"

"Yes...unfortunately. Emily has been through the mill in recent months, what with her accident and everything..."

Royston broke off. Through the phone he heard voices in the background. One of them was Emily's.

"Alicia..." he called into the phone.

He did so want to talk to her before she saw Emily.

"Alicia, are you still there?" he called even louder.

"Yes, I'm here," she said. "Emily's just come downstairs. She looks a lot happier now. Isn't that amazing?"

"...Can I ring you tonight?" Royston quickly asked while he had the chance. "I want to discuss that and something else, if possible."

"Of course. My phone number is in..."

"...In the book. Yes, I remember. You told me last time."

"And did I mention that you'll need to look under 'District Nurse'? I haven't been here long enough to get a private listing in the directory yet."

"Yes. I remember that, too."

Emily had no memory of the woman who accompanied Royston on the day she heard about James.

Although Alicia carefully explained that she had already met Emily, there was neither any recognition on her part nor interest in trying to remember their meeting. Instead, Emily seemed intent on entertaining her; as though Alicia was not just her nurse – a detail firmly established in her mind when she saw the uniform – but also someone over whom she should make a fuss.

"Come and take the weight off your feet, dear," she urged, guiding the mystified woman towards the couch. "I'll put the kettle on, and then we'll have a cup of tea. Kristine, would you like one, too?"

Kristine exchanged a glance with the district nurse; a glance that indicated something was not quite right. Then, while Emily busied herself in the kitchen, she whispered, "Nana is behaving very oddly. I've never seen her like this before; not even when Grandpa died. I think she expects James to walk back in at any minute."

"It sounds like she is in denial," Alicia whispered back.

"Yes, that's what Dad said. When Grandpa died she was terribly upset; at least, she was for a while. But then she seemed to get over it far more quickly than we expected. There is a real similarity here with the way she acted back then. On the surface it looks like she has got over James already. Do you think she may have?"

"To be quite honest, I don't think she could have in this short time. It takes even the strongest of characters a long time to get over a shock like that, and I would say Emily is not a particularly resilient..."

"...Here we are," said Emily, halting their conversation. She brought in a tray full of teacups and a plate of biscuits; then said, "...Won't be a minute, I'll just get the teapot."

Kristine leapt to her feet to help her.

327

"I can manage," Emily insisted. "I'm not senile yet."

Kristine cringed with her grandmother's curt remark. It seemed to her, and now to Alicia, that Emily's words were speaking louder than her actions.

Alicia accepted the cup of tea Emily handed to her with a courteous, "Thank you, Emily; that's lovely."

Taking a sip, she went on, "So how are you keeping in yourself now?"

"As well as can be expected, thank you," said Emily in reply. "James, bless him, set up a bed for me in the dining room so I didn't need to climb the stairs. But once my back was better I stopped using it. And as you're a nurse, I can tell you it was wonderful to be able to snuggle up with my husband again. We do enjoy our cuddles..."

Alicia could see from a grimace on Kristine's face that she was embarrassed by the way her grandmother was speaking to a stranger.

She cut in quickly, trying to draw Emily out of her uncharacteristic reverie.

"...Your back is better now, then?"

Oh, yes! The doctor's tablets and my husband's support have been a godsend. Why, only yesterday, James and I went over our itinerary for when we visit David overseas next month – that's his son, you know."

Suddenly Kristine got angry. The frustration at seeing her precious Nana slipping into some form of dementia started to boil over.

"Nana, will you stop it!" she exploded. "You know very well David came over here for his father's funeral. Don't you remember that? It was only a few days ago?"

Wide-eyed and bewildered, Emily tried to retrieve the information from her memory. Then she said, "Oh yes. I do remember he was here. We must invite him over for dinner some time..."

Kristine leapt up, and with an infuriated bellow ran out into the back garden.

Checking for an adverse reaction in her client and seeing none, Alicia excused herself from Emily, put down her cup and saucer, and quickly followed Kristine.

It was cool and tranquil in the garden. Kristine gulped in the stillness to soothe her troubled soul.

Just then, she had a vision. In her mind's eye Arthur was with her, and for a blessed moment a feeling of peace enveloped her

But then Alicia caught up with her; and the apparition disappeared.

"I'm really sorry you are struggling with this situation," said Alicia, unaware of Kristine's vision. "You are all such lovely people; you don't deserve to suffer in this way."

Kristine stood motionless with a faraway look in her eye; not knowing how to respond.

Alicia noticed it and commented.

"Kristine, are you alright?" she asked. "You look like you have just seen a ghost."

"Yes, I'm fine," Kristine said curtly; the trance broken.

Kristine felt sure the image she saw of her grandfather was real. She could not have imagined it, or even invoked it.

Now it was her turn to be lost in another world. She wanted more than anything to relive what had happened, but could not. She wanted, also, to go back up to the house and tell her grandmother what she had just seen. Somehow she knew that Emily would understand.

...Maybe Arthur had appeared to both of them at the same time. And if he or James had already communicated with Emily, then it would explain why Emily spoke of them both in the present tense...

Alicia tugged at her sleeve.

"Kristine, you've gone quite pale. Please let me take your pulse – I'm concerned about your state of health!"

"I'm fine. You've no need to worry," Kristine reiterated; then added, "...But thank you for caring."

Kristine was anxious now to go back inside and follow up on her supposition.

She turned to Alicia.

"I really need to get back to my grandmother," she said in a serious voice, "I don't wish to be impolite, but if you've finished the check-up, would you mind leaving?"

Although Alicia was taken aback by the request, she readied herself to comply; but not before she thought to ask, "Is there anything you need for your grandmother?"

"No, not that I can think of..." Kristine replied; but then added, "...Unless you can get me a private tutor."

"What do you mean?"

"...A school tutor. The new school term starts up this coming Monday. I haven't yet made any arrangements for looking after Nana."

"Do you think she still needs someone during the day?"

"...More than that. I would say she still needs twenty-four hour supervision. Her back's okay, but she's not with-it at all. The problem is, my mother won't let me stay here during term time, and I don't know what to do about it."

Alicia thought for a minute, and then said, "Leave it to me...I may be able to help you there."

When Kristine was certain Alicia had said her goodbyes to Emily and left the property, she hurried up to the house.

The desire to talk about her vision was overwhelming. To her relief, Emily was still in the lounge. But before she could bring up such a sensitive subject, Kristine realised there was something she first needed to do.

She should apologise for her outburst.

Even though she said nothing about it at the time, Emily harboured resentment over the way her granddaughter had spoken to her; especially in front of a guest. Thus, when Kristine approached her, she looked away; still too hurt to yield to the remorse that was written all over the girl's face.

Seeing this, Kristine's need to apologise became even more urgent. She did not want to risk losing the chance to find out if Arthur had also visited Emily.

"Nana, I'm really sorry for being rude just now," she said quickly to dispel Emily's visible annoyance. And when she received only an exasperated sigh in response, she added, "I haven't been myself over these last couple of weeks. Will you forgive me?"

Emily relented.

"It was so unlike you, Kristine," she said sternly. "But I do understand that we've all been under a lot of strain lately; so I mustn't take your comments to heart. You didn't really mean what you said, did you?"

"No! Definitely not!"

Kristine gave her a hug, then followed it up with, "Nana, come and sit with me. There's something I'd like to discuss with you."

Kristine found a spellbound audience in Emily. The mere mention of Arthur's name ensured her attention.

As Kristine described how he had appeared to her in the rose garden, her story took on a reality Emily could easily identify with; to the extent that she got up straight away and went to the kitchen window as though looking for him. But when Kristine asked the question she had been itching to ask, Emily backed off.

"What do you mean...has he appeared to me?"

Emily's response came as a surprise to Kristine. She had thought it was a reasonable enquiry in light of what they were talking about. Had not Emily just shown a great deal of interest in her revelation?

She hesitated, not knowing how to reply; not knowing what might be going through Emily's mind that she could tap into. At length she said, "Don't worry; I just wondered if Grandpa ever came into your thoughts like he did with me in the garden: that's all."

"Well of course he does, love. Why would you suppose otherwise. I think about dear Arthur all the time. Why, he and James were here a short time ago..."

Kristine looked at her Nana, aghast. It was obvious to her now just what had been going on.

Arthur must have been communicating with Emily, too. But she had interpreted her vision for the real thing. She had been speaking of him – and of James –as though they were actually present.

In a way, Kristine reflected, that was right. Arthur was still around – in spirit.

While Emily continued to sing Arthur's praises, Kristine studied her grandmother's face, seeing not the grief of a widow, but the contentment of a vibrant woman whose greatest love was still a dynamic presence in her life.

Without a shadow of doubt, Kristine had the answer to her question.

She stood beside Emily at the window and looked out at the rose garden with her.

"Grandpa does so love his roses, doesn't he?" she said, and affectionately kissed Emily on the cheek.